Saving All That Remains

Erika Fitzpatrick

Printed in the United States of America

First Printing, 2016

ISBN 978-0-692-78158-6

Fire Feather Press
Keizer, OR 97303
e.fitzpatrick@gmail.com

To the endangered species – May the wild world remain

Table of Contents

New Year

I was pressed against the glass, my nose squished, hands balled into fists.

People and children and strollers were encircled about me, pressing me from every angle.

I was crouched down, stuck against the glass barricades of the tiger exhibit at the zoo. All I could see were two very small, frightened looking tiger cubs huddled beside one another, their bright orange fur strikingly vivid against the black of their stripes and the dullness of their surroundings. Their wide, yellow-and-black eyes swiveled from end to end of the crowd that was hungrily snapping pictures and squealing and pointing.

They were a new attraction at the zoo, freshly added, an exciting scene for the Portland zoo-comers. But I hadn't come to coo and gush over the novel tiger cubs.

I'd come to see if they were really here and to perceive how frightened they were. I had been trying to find them for days. Just a few short weeks earlier, the two tiger cubs had been a source of interest on the local news. Found in downtown Portland, they'd been rushed to the zoo where they could be looked after and properly fed.

I understood. Two tiger cubs loose in the city could have only meant pure destruction of the people. Of course, the public would see them as monsters. It was likely someone would have hunted them down, killed them, skinned them, and made a fortune. Who were the real monsters?

This was why I had returned to Portland—to the United States in general: to try to put a stop the illegal hunting and brutality administered to the endangered tigers. Their species weren't going to last long at the rate I had witnessed during my two years in India.

A lady's hip rammed into my head, and a feral snarl erupted unbidden from my throat. Her eyes suddenly darted to me, her pupils dilating in fear and confusion. I had managed to sound like a jungle cat, but I appeared a simple, scrawny, strange human girl. I did not blame her for her fear. Or her confusion. She maneuvered away from me, scowling at my crouched, cramped form as she walked away.

Two years ago, I would have been concerned with how she perceived me, but today, it was almost comical. If only she knew the kinds of things I'd seen.

Fear was a fascinating phenomenon. I used to be afraid of the dark, the wild, the jungle, and large wild animals. Two years prior, the zoo was the last place on earth anyone would have ever found me. But in India, I learned to see in the dark, that the wild is blessed, and the jungle is like a city—which is where I once belonged—and large wild animals are only a threat if *we* threaten them. I realized that my fears only manifested because they were misunderstood.

A slight breeze ruffled my hair and baggy t-shirt, and the chirping of birds caught my attention. I quickly glanced up to see their wings and tails flash in the sun. It reminded me of my other home—a place where bird and tiger shared a delicate relationship of predator and prey.

I turned my gaze back to the two terrified cubs, feeling a deep, burning pain in my chest. The anger and sadness that lodged there had been growing for some time.

I say that India changed me, but really, it was the tigers. And I couldn't be more thankful, even in my current state of turmoil. But I most definitely owe my trip to Sara after throwing that world-shattering Chinese New Year's Eve party only two years or so ago.

It was a lively party, with boys playing video games, girls gossiping, everyone drinking and gorging on junk food and dancing the hours away. Ten minutes remained until the clock struck midnight. As a selectively social person, I sat alone in a chair, observing everyone intoxicatingly enjoying themselves around me. I came for the sake of supporting Sara, who had thrown the party for her domestic, but traditional Chinese roommate, and to get out of my suffocating home. But this was not my crowd.

I preferred the company of one or two, and I hated to be stuck at home, alone with just my persnickety cat. She only socialized with me on her own terms. I didn't blame her. I hadn't been a joy to be around the last few months, since my mother had disappeared on a six month journalism job. Not that my mother and I had been close, but knowing she wasn't even around in case I needed her was saddening. But I always had Sara.

She stood on the other side of the room, a red cup in her hand, her short brown hair all over the top of her head from her constantly running her fingers through it. Our friendship went back seven, solid years, from the first day of freshman year of high school when we both found ourselves overwhelmed and without a friend.

The girl she was talking to walked away, and I saw Sara's face light up and grow a deep shade of red as a tall, lean young man approached her. She offered him another cup, which he accepted with a kind smile. He seemed to be a casual, at-ease person, his movements loose and genuine, his smile wide and inviting. I couldn't help a tiny smile as I watched her tap a foot on the ground behind her—a sure sign of interest.

Her romantic life had been more successful than mine. She knew what she wanted—she just needed to find it. The few relationships I'd gone through were short lived, but I'd learned what I liked with each new guy who briefly touched my life. Nothing meaningful and worthwhile—not yet. Romantic nights and time invested into one man were not top priorities for me. In truth, I didn't really understand what love did to people—probably because I'd never been in love. I was sure that it would eventually happen, but I didn't know when. Or from where.

"One minute!" some stranger screamed from another room.

I heaved myself onto my feet and stared around the crowd that was gathering in front of the television, excited to watch the countdown celebration airing on some news channel.

"Jade!"

I heard Sara's loud voice from across the room and looked over to see her waving to me over the crowd.

"Plug in the lanterns for the final countdown! I want the room to feel *authentic* and full of pizzaz." She winked at me.

I was amused by her surprising word choice. Across the room, I saw the cord to the lanterns laying unplugged a few inches from the empty socket. By the time I had the cord in my hand, they were all counting down.

"5, 4, 3…"

I jammed the prongs into the socket just as everyone screamed "ONE!"

My hand felt a tingling sensation. But it didn't just stop at my arm. The electricity ran all the way through my body, shocking all my veins and making me shudder. My hand was still holding onto the plug, and I let go just as the whole house flickered like a power outage, and I fell into blackness.

I came to with Sara and her attractive friend from earlier staring over me.

"What happened?" I asked, as Sara maneuvered me into a sitting position. My head swam, and the floor teetered.

"You blacked out and were lying on the floor whispering something about the year of the tiger," she replied, her face scrunched up in concern. "Are you okay?"

I touched a hand to my forehead, but pulled it away as it zapped my already partially tingling, electrocuted hand. "It wouldn't have been a proper electrifying party if someone didn't black out, right?"

Her friend laughed.

"I'll go get you some water." Sara ran off toward the kitchen.

"Seriously, are you okay?" the guy asked, sitting next to me. I saw his eyes linger on Sara as she moved around the kitchen.

"I'm not sure. How long was I out?"

"I don't know. It was a few moments after midnight. That's when Sara found you muttering about tigers. What's with tigers, huh?"

I had no idea what he was talking about. "I don't like tigers, so don't ask me," I replied, rubbing my face.

Truthfully, I didn't like wild animals in general, for which I blamed my mother. Between her journalism jobs, she spent her time learning everything she could. One night, while she was cooking dinner, a documentary of the deadliest killers in the wild played in the background. Unable to ignore the visual information that assaulted my eyes, I watched in terror as snakes struck with venomous fangs, sharks tore their meal to shreds, and tigers crushed the life out of their prey. I ran to my mother and hugged her waist, burying my face in her thigh to cover my eyes. She told me not to worry—they were only wild animals.

Since then, I'd done all I could to stay away from them.

Unfortunately, wild animals exist even in the city.

That's when Shianne strode over. She was tall and thin with long, straight black hair. She wore enough makeup to sell out an entire department of a store and had the most repulsive outfits. Like tonight's costume: sparkly pink tank top and blue snakeskin jeans with black pumps. I didn't know what she was trying to attract, but it couldn't have been men.

"A downed mouse. What happened, Jade? Did our celebrating knock out what little life you had?" Shianne hissed, eyeing me like a snake about to strike.

"Didn't anyone ever tell you not to play with your food?" I replied, heat flashing through my veins. I had no patience to take this from her today. Or any other day, for that matter.

She sneered at me and bent closer to put her face right in front of mine. Sara's friend put a hand on her shoulder to keep her back, but she flung his arm away. "Stay out of this, Jack." She looked me in the eyes, and I stared back, despite the way the room danced in my peripherals.

I glared at her.

She gave me one last angry hiss before slithering off.

Sara returned with my water, which I gulped gratefully, relieving some of the heat flashes.

"Do you have to pick a fight every time you see her?" Sara asked.

I frowned at her. "It's not my fault she can't handle competition. She seeks me out." It had been that way for the past seven years, since I had started high school. It began when we both showed up to class wearing the same shirt, only hers was two sizes too small. When the principal sent her home and not me—because she failed to grasp the concept that it was her belly and belly button ring showing that was inappropriate, not the shirt itself—she vowed to seek revenge and get me sent home for something. When that failed, she simply vowed to irritate and provoke me any way she could. I think she had wanted me to start a fight, but I never stooped to the level of physical violence. As for college, Shianne and I had both applied for the same scholarship for the communications program at Portland State University. Among the three applicants, I won the full amount—something Shianne couldn't let go.

"How are you feeling?" Jack asked.

"Woozy," I said, closing my eyes to try and gain some sort of stability. "I'm going to go home and sleep, Sara. I'll see you tomorrow."

She helped me up. "Don't forget we have OMSI tomorrow."

I still wasn't sure how she had coerced me into going, considering she was excited about the dinosaur exhibit since her science class had just finished a lecture on them, while I had zero interest in them. I remember her taking advantage of the loneliness that had pervaded me lately.

I steadied myself as I stood up straight. The room was finally starting to level out.

"I'll walk you to your car," Jack said.

He followed me outside into the cold air, and it felt refreshing. I inhaled deeply and watched my breath swirl white in the night. "Are you sure you want to come? I mean, I'm parked really far."

"No, I'll come. It feels good out here."

Since I agreed with him, I let him come along. Besides, I might need his help if I passed out again and lay unnoticed in the icy street.

When I got to my car, I opened the door, slid in, and rolled down the window.

"Do you want a ride or something?" I asked kindly.

"No, thanks. I have one." He hesitated and exhaled once before asking, "I was wondering about the whole OMSI thing… Do you mind if I come? It sounds like fun, and I really have nothing fun planned."

Heat flashed through my veins again, causing an instant sweat. "Sounds like a plan. I'll have Sara give you a call tomorrow."

He smiled and waved as I drove off in my little silver car, carefully navigating the one-way streets of downtown Portland. I liked the Jack guy. He seemed good-natured and kind, as well as easy on the eyes. Maybe Sara had finally found her man. The last string of boys that had been a part of her life had simply been that: *boys*. Immature. Lazy. Unmotivated. Inconsiderate. But I could already tell that Jack was more mature and grown up while also being easy going. He was a good match for her.

I stopped at a red light and waited, watching a homeless man cross the dark street with a bag of all he owned. The sad truth was that it was uncommon to not see someone curled up with all their belongings in a bag beside them.

The ragged, bearded man glanced at me while I waited. The green of his eyes startled me, an image of my father swimming before my mind. They were the same droopy shape and vibrant color. I stared as he finished crossing the street, barely noticing the light changing from red to green.

I continued up the road, doing everything I could to convince myself that it wasn't, indeed, my father. He was supposed to be living somewhere on the other side of the country. My father had stuck around as much as he could stand to, always forcing me to watch wrestling matches on the tv whenever he was responsible for watching me—a sport I unwillingly learned and now understood—but as soon as I was at an age to fend for myself, he was gone. No longer obligated to watch after me while my mother was away for her job, he fled the first chance he got. I never understood if he was running away from Portland or me or responsibility itself. Whatever the reasons, he hadn't been much of a father. Finding him living on the streets back in his hometown, though, was not something that would entirely surprise me.

The homeless man and his piercing eyes continued to haunt me as I drove up the slanting streets. Consumed with confusion and exhausted from the party and black out, I failed to notice the teens crossing the street in front of me. At the last minute, I slammed on my brakes and yanked on the steering wheel, spinning out of control.

I let go of the wheel and closed my eyes as the colors from all the lights became a dizzying blur. An instant later, my car came to a jerking stop as it hit the curb on the opposite side of the street. I squinted to make sure the kids were okay. They were safely on the sidewalk, staring at me with wide eyes. I waved at them to let know I was alright, and they continued on.

Adrenaline coursed through my veins, and the tingling feeling of being shocked had returned. I tried to catch my breath, sweating with fear and the recurrence of hot flashes. The engine of my car was no longer running, and all was silent around me, a heavy reminder of how alone I was. Maybe I should have stayed at Sara's for the night. However, the party was still going on, and I knew that I would rather be alone than surrounded by too many people.

With shaking hands, I started my car again and drove slowly back to my apartment without any more incidents.

When I walked inside, it was dark and silent. I shuddered, re-living the many times my immature father would jump out of the dark and scare away whatever sanity I had left. It was because of him that I feared the dark even more than wild animals.

I flipped on every light in my apartment and rubbed my arms, trying to shake off the feeling of emptiness that seemed to threaten to close in on me in the suffocating silence. I jumped when my tabby cat meowed from behind me. She rubbed her head against my leg, and reached up to stretch her claws against my jeans. A sure sign that she wanted food.

I sighed and glanced at the mail on the table. The ominous face of the tiger stared up at me. I snatched at the paper and read the heading. It was a brochure for the Portland Zoo. Apparently, they had gained a new male tiger to their exhibit, the newest attraction. I shoved the brochure under a magazine, out of sight. It didn't match any of my decor. Everything I owned was floral or lattice patterned. All of my artwork was of black and white cityscapes or historical fashion trends.

The single, framed picture of my mother caught my eye from the end table beside my poppy-patterned couch. I picked it up and stared at her light freckles, much like mine. She wore a pantsuit and rectangular glasses, her airplane pin clearly visible on the collar of her blazer. She loved to travel more than anything. I wondered, wherever she had traveled to this time, if she was thinking of me at all?

I set her frame back down and glanced around my apartment, realizing it was time for me to take a vacation. My mother had always pestered me about my lack of interest in travel, but I had always associated travel with her absence. However, standing alone in my quiet living room, I suddenly understood that desire to leave—to see something new.

A hot, tingling sensation shot through my veins again, reminding me of the evening I had just experienced. Drained of all energy, I fell onto the poppies and drifted into sleep with all the lights on.

It was strange, but that night, I dreamt of prancing tigers.

TRANSFORMATION

I woke to someone banging on my door. I sat up, my head throbbed from the loud pounding, and I remembered the disorienting night before.

"Morning!" Sara said cheerfully through the wood.

I flopped back on the couch and flipped the TV on. Sara allowed herself in, as I knew she would, and glared at me.

"What?" I asked, annoyed.

"Are you going to stand me up, or were you just taking your dear, sweet time?" She eyed me. "Are you still out from last night?"

"My head is killing me. What do you mean stand you up?"

"OMSI—remember? Does last night ring a bell?"

It rang a dull bell.

I heaved myself up, catching my balance before I trudged to my room. I flipped on the light and began rummaging through my closet, looking for something suitable. Through the morning grogginess, I registered the fact that it took less than two minutes to pick something out, which was a record for me. Normally, I labored ten minutes or more to pick out the ensemble for the day. Once I was dressed, I faced the mirror and let out a sigh. I grabbed a brush and tried to eliminate the snarls, but I was fighting a long-lost battle.

"Just put it up," Sara said from my doorway. I threw it into a pony and added some mascara to my wilted lashes. I grabbed my purse and coat and followed Sara out the door.

"Have you called Jack yet?"

"No, he called me. He's been waiting for a half an hour."

I did feel bad that he was waiting on us. I hadn't realized what time it was. Sara looked at ease in the driver seat, her eyes bright with a subtle excitement I hadn't seen in her for a long time. I knew it was because of Jack.

The Oregon Museum of Science and Industry was in downtown Portland, right on the river. I hadn't visited since my sixth grade class took a field trip there—when I had spilled water on my pants during lunch and my peers decided to be immature about the nature of my soaked pants. I was surprised that it wasn't that busy. Usually the place was packed with little kids on field trips and old people free from retirement. Now, it was mostly just a couple of families. More room for us to roam around. As we approached the counter, I had the feeling that the place had gotten smaller.

We paid and found Jack in the broadcasting room. They had set up a green screen against the wall and a camera where someone could pretend to be a weatherman. Jack was standing there making funny motions against the green screen. I laughed.

"You should try this. It's way harder than it looks," Jack said defensively at my laugh.

I shoved him out of camera view as I called, "Hurricane Jack has left the region."

Sara was amused, standing on the other end of the camera beside a screen that projected a map of the United States.

"A new storm is making its way through the Kansas area... Heads up for the new Tornado Sara!" I ran off screen and pushed Sara to stand on Texas.

"Action!" I said, smiling at her standing there frozen. "Don't tell me you have stage fright."

"No, I don't." She took a deep breath and held it, thinking about what to say. A few moments passed before she sighed. "I have nothing."

"You should talk about a possible apocalypse. Everyone seems so obsessed with them nowadays," Jack said.

"Yeah, beware a zombie attack in Oklahoma," Sara said with a grin. We all laughed.

"Where to next?" Sara asked, walking away from the screen and heading out of the room.

"Do they have a food exhibit?" Jack said, looking for a sign.

"Ready for the dinosaurs?" Sara said, pointing to the next room. A giant T-Rex stood at the opening, inviting visitors to come admire him. I gulped. He was big. And at one point, wild. Unbidden, a memory of one documentary my mother watched about the great predators of the Mesozoic era flashed inside my head. Raptors and the T-Rex killing their prey in a bloody display of sheer power and sharp teeth. He towered above, my head barely reaching his knee, his bony foot three times the width of my body. A rational part of me that I seemed unable to access at that moment realized there was nothing to fear from this several-million-year-dead creature, but I couldn't control the start of staggered breathing and increasing heart rate.

I trailed after them and glanced up at the ribs as we walked under them. He could have eaten and swallowed all three of us in a single gulp. I rushed to the other end of the room and sat down upon a bench. I was breathing hard, and heat flashes similar to the night before were coming again. Stupid giant T-Rex. Jack sat down beside me.

"You feeling okay?" he asked. "Want to leave?"

Suddenly, a combined force of hot and cold sensations shot up the veins of my neck. Then my vision dulled. I looked around in amazement, seeing things I had never seen before, like unsaturated colors and detail in dark corners. Everything was perceptually brighter, and I could selectively focus on areas that I wouldn't have been able to fully perceive before. And then my vision returned to normal and the corners and details blurred into darkness once more.

"Whoa," Jack and I said at the same time.

"Your . . . eyes . . . they just turned yellow!"

"Yellow?" I asked him, scared.

"Yeah, you know, like a cat's." He stared at me with wide eyes.

I was trying to keep the panic in check. What was going on?

"That's creepy," I said as nonchalantly as possible. "Let's go find Sara."

Jack followed me through the room, finding her standing over a tablet with a slab of rock that had a footprint of some weird dinosaur that I couldn't pronounce: PARASAUROLOPHUS. Or worse,

PIATNITZKYSAURUS, a seven foot tall creature with two legs and two arms, with piercing yellow eyes … I was starting to feel dizzy.

My eyes had just turned *yellow* for crying out loud! I was on the verge of a panic attack.

"Sara, you should have seen Jade's eyes!" Jack told her.

Sara looked at me curiously.

I just nodded. I didn't trust myself to speak at the moment.

"It was freaky," Jack confirmed.

I suddenly found my voice. "Just for a moment I could see . . . differently. I could see details in the dark, and all the colors in the room were dull and less particular. It was scary, as if my eyes had been replaced by eyes that belonged to someone . . . or something else." As I said it, I knew that it sounded insane, but it wasn't untrue.

Sara was staring at me like I was crazy. I knew I wasn't. I mean, Jack had seen my eyes turn yellow. I was just describing the effect.

"Do you want to go home Jade?" Sara asked, worry creasing her forehead.

"Yeah, we totally understand if you do. Don't feel bad about it at all," Jack urged.

Why did everyone keep asking me that? I was fine! Except for the minor issue of my messed up eyes. "No."

"Ok, so what do you want to do next?"

"I don't care. Let's go… to that room with the electricity balls and stuff." Despite the strangeness of my situation, I was newly intrigued by the power and shock of electricity.

Sara gave me one last look and then led the way out of the room—going back under the stupid T-Rex—and down the stairs through all the glass walls and machines the museum workers had set up.

In the room with all the glass balls and crazy electric currents, people were running their hands over the glass, squealing as the purple currents followed their fingers. It was interesting to watch, but I was wary of electricity. It seemed to be a danger around me. However, I couldn't resist as I passed an open ball. The blue lights were calling my name. Tentatively, I reached out and touched the glass. The currents immediately raced to my hand and danced in place. My whole body tingled, and then my eyes tunneled out, and I could see every strand of bright electricity clinging together. In the curved glass, I could make out two yellow-like orbs shining on either side of my distorted nose. I gasped slightly and released the glass, watching as the blue strands merged and danced in the middle again. No more yellow eyes.

I walked over to where Sara and Jack were examining a giant tower with a metal ball on top. Little peals of blue static electricity flashed and then disappeared. And I knew I was seeing it with *my* eyes. This motor, which I now could hear, created static electricity. That was beyond my mind, but still cool.

"Dare you to touch it," I said behind them, making them jump.

"No way," Sara said.

"I would if I could reach it," Jack commented, looking up to the top.

"Yeah right! You would probably turn out just like me!"

"Oh no. I really don't want yellow eyes," Jack said, sarcastically scared.

"Ha ha. Funny," I said, snidely.

Sara and Jack laughed. I gave them superior looks and stalked from the room. I could feel my hair sticking up as I passed the electric balls. Yeah, real funny.

I headed for the space room and looked at all the different ships hanging from the ceiling. The room was all dark and purple with little lights that were supposed to be stars shining in the walls. I continued through the room, staring at models of the first lunar lander and the solar system. Jack and Sara caught up with me a minute later and watched me warily. Feeling contaminated, I ignored them and headed over to investigate a picture of Earth, the sun, and other distant suns that made Earth the size of a pixel. Kind of cool and scary at the same time. It made me feel like a tiny, unwanted, and uncared for speck in the universe.

We enjoyed the rest of the day without any more spasms of yellow eye syndrome—YES for short. I didn't know how long this strange thing would last or how often it would occur. And I went to bed dreading the next day.

Portland State University isn't really that huge, but someone could get lost if he didn't know his way around. Sadly, I did, and that meant I had time to kill between classes, which was unfortunate because that's when Shianne usually found me and made my day a living nightmare.

But today wasn't going to be like that. I was going to avoid her and try to enjoy my career classes. In public speaking, I thoroughly enjoyed the lecture on ways to appear confident and prepared. That was until the YES took place. I became very distracted by all the cobwebs in the corners and the zit on my professor's face. I was also trying to make sure no one was looking at me and hoping that the YES would pass unnoticed. But to my dismay, the YES just continued on and on until I realized that I could feel a slight tingling in my neck and heart, and when I focused on trying to get rid of these strange feelings, they seemed to retract to my heart—sealed away like flood waters behind a dam—and then I suspected that my crazy eyes were their normal brown again. I was so confused. So could I control this YES thing then? Was it all in the tingling, electrical feeling? Sort of not paying attention, I lost track of time until the scraping of chairs brought me back. Still trying to figure out the reactions I was dealing with, I walked out the building's glass doors and down the front steps. I didn't manage to notice that Shianne was slowly approaching. Not until she ran into me and all my books fell to the ground in a jumbled mess and her purse spewed all its contents.

"Jade," she said sourly.

I was feeling like hitting her, which was an unusual reaction from me to her crossness.

Instead of answering her arrogant face, I began gathering my things and scooping up all the fallen papers.

"Next time don't be embarrassed by your stupidity and ugliness to wear your glasses. They won't make a difference, I assure you," she sneered.

"You know what, I'm sorry that you ran over a skunk this morning." I couldn't think of any insult that matched the level of animosity I was feeling. She had picked the wrong day to mess with me—my own body was doing the job for her.

"I didn't run over a skunk this morning." She sounded thoroughly surprised.

"Well, you don't need to impose your sourness on the rest of us."

Her shocked face was slowly turning purple, and I watched with seething pleasure as she contemplated how to get me back. My heart was racing, fueled by my anger, preparing for whatever I would need to do in order to come out triumphant in this exchange.

"Sorry, but you've clearly mistaken me for someone who gives a damn," she retorted.

My frustration and outrage were about to erupt. "If I promise to miss you, will you just leave me alone?" I snapped.

"That'd be too easy, Jade. I have to keep the mouse spinning in its wheel, or I'd have nothing to torment every day."

Suddenly, the anger and contempt burst from my chest in a rampage of emotion. I expected to scream at her, but when I opened my mouth, the anger rumbled deep in my throat, and a ferocious snarl, like a lion's growl, ripped through my exposed teeth. I slapped a hand over my mouth in the vain hope that the sound had gone unnoticed, but Shianne had heard the animal snarl. She was staring at me as if I had gone crazy. Maybe I had.

"What is wrong with you?" she hissed.

"Much less then what's wrong with you," I muttered, not wanting to open my mouth wide again, afraid I might start roaring and growling like an idiot. A few people on the steps around us had slowed in their walk, curious of what was going on between us.

"Right," she snorted. "Because I'm the one snarling like a lion. See, I knew I was right. There *is* something wrong with you. Seriously wrong."

These words hurt, though I knew deep down at the moment— buried by rage—that they weren't true. This time I felt the growl build up in my chest, but I didn't care. I denied the insanity, the extraordinary, the madness of the situation—I just wanted to snarl at her to get to the point where she would run, screaming in fright.

I opened my mouth and let the growl escape, along with a snapping snarl and a hiss, too. I clenched my jaws together but curled my lips back so that she could see that I was baring my rather unfrightening teeth, but still trying to get the point across as a growl slid through the gaps.

That worked. She hitched her purse over her shoulder, threw a terrified glance at my mouth, then started running like a maniac toward the safety of the school, tripping over the door jam and falling on her face, but still glancing back at me, as if to check that I wasn't going to eat her. I laughed at her expression, but it fell flat when I noticed the other concerned and fearful stares from the few people around me. I didn't blame them. If I had seen a fellow student roaring like an animal, I would have stared in fear, too. I went on my way to my next class, feeling a tingling satisfaction, despite the fact that I had just been growling like a wild jungle cat. I had insulted Shianne, and she was now scared of me. So this day was not a total waste yet. Just a nightmare. I had been visited by the taunting YES and now the snarling and nightmarish attack on people issue—SNAP for now. I was slowly having freakish outbreaks of cat-like instincts. This was not *normal*. For once, Shianne was right about me. Something *was* wrong. I just didn't understand it yet.

Still in reminiscence, I smiled widely as I continued down a hallway, clutching my books in triumph. However, I stopped smiling when one of the guys from my photography class stared at my mouth, his eyes confused and fearful. I snapped my mouth shut and ran to the closest bathroom in a panic. What else could go wrong today?

As soon as I knew the restroom was empty, I stood in front of the mirror and cautiously opened my jaws.

Then I screamed.

It was too terrifying not to. I mean how many people looked at themselves in the mirror and saw two-inch-long fangs protruding from their gums?

I gingerly reached up and touched it. It was so strong, so intact ... so real. I wanted to scream again. This time out of confusion and deepening fear. When were these bizarre things going to end, and why were they happening in the first place? Everything I had ever feared was suddenly manifesting as parts of my body were turning into just that.

I stared at my frightful reflection for a long time until I remembered that I had a class I was supposed to be in, and I was running kind of late.

"Snap out of it!" I murmured to myself. I could feel that interesting tingling feeling in my gums and, hoping I could control it like the YES, I pulled against the funny feelings, letting the electricity retract back towards my heart. And at once, my jaw shifted to normal. The fangs were gone, my gums feeling quite normal and numb.

As I ran to history, I tried to come up with a name for this one, but no strange acronym came to mind. I would just have to call it the fanged phenomenon. Then I told myself to get a grip on my reality. I shouldn't be having these reactions. I was a—relatively—normal human. Not some hybrid. I was snarling at people and developing fangs and bizarre yellow eyes. For once, Shianne was right. I was a freak!

Then I started worrying about my next class as I ran up stairs and down hallways. My professor was strict and he hated me and my attitude, which I had to admit, always stank in his dismal class. He treated me like a piece of crap he stepped into on his way to school and—no matter how many times he drug me against the grass, the pavement, even gravel, I'm sure—I wouldn't go away.

I hurtled to a stop outside of his door. He was sitting at his desk, the usual 'I smell something like rot' expression twisting his face. Everybody else was sitting at their desks writing out some horrible response he'd assigned. Scowling, I went to open the door, grabbed the handle and tried my best to pull the door open without being disruptive, trying to avoid detection. But the hinges were old and they squeaked incredibly loudly. I cringed as everyone looked up at me, and my professor stood, glared, and stomped over to where I stood, frozen with anticipation.

"Miss Sconsin, class has started, and you're late."

"Yes…sir." It hurt to say that civil word. "But I had an emergency… and I hurried here as fast as I could afterward."

"You do realize that this is the fourth time you've been over twenty minutes late to my class?"

"Yes… sir, and I'm sorry." Not. "But it wasn't all my fault." Really, it wasn't. It was the fanged phenomenon's fault.

"Well, I'm sorry too, because I will be dropping your participation grade by two whole letters. And may I remind you that the reports are due tomorrow, following which I shall be handing back the reports from last week… and you should probably try harder this time." He sneered at me before waddling back over to his desk. What a puffed up, shallow, ugly, flightless bat. I glared at his back as I slid into my seat and dropped my bag on the ground with purposeful disruption. The class refocused on their assignment, and I doodled on my notebook, imagining ways I could use my new-found fanged phenomenon to convince my professor to give back my dropped grades.

Still kind of ticked once class was released, I went to my parked car, hopped in, and drove to my apartment. Then I flipped open my laptop and began the paper in a biased fashion, giving him the lousiest information that was going way overboard, too much information, and a page too long, according to the average length it *should* be. I couldn't bring myself to truly destroy my own grade completely, but, feeling a savage pleasure, I printed it out, slipped it into my history book, and then went to my room to fall on my bed.

I had been through a lot, even though it was just the first day of the week. Of course, I knew that was because of the YES, SNAP, and fanged phenomenon. I was still irked and worried about the situations, but I was also tired. So I let them slip from my mind, and drifted into a light sleep that left me dreaming of the jungle and all its foul beasts stalking me for impersonating them in a lame human fashion. I had told them that they had no idea of fashion, and then remembered that I was *talking* to wild animals.

That's when I woke up and looked at my clock, which said it was only two in the morning. Grumbling, I fell back onto my pillow and into sleep that wasn't as disturbing as the last.

I was excited for the first class I had the next morning. It was my one art credit class—photography—and I had an exceptional picture I had taken over the weekend that I was excited to share. It would have been more interesting to have gotten a picture of my YES, and then I could've just told everyone it was some skillful Photoshop. However, I didn't have anything *that* interesting. I did have a picture of an intricate tree covered in icicles and strange, misshapen snow piles.

I hurried to my seat, which I now realized was beside a girl from Sara's party. She smiled at me as I dropped my book and bag beside my chair.

I smiled back. "What's your photo for today?"

"I got a cool picture of the tiger at the zoo. Then I photoshopped it to look all fuzzy around the edges and the tiger is emphasized. Want to see it?"

I nodded, remembering the zoo brochure that was buried on my table from a few days ago with the picture of a tiger on it.

She pulled it out of her bag and placed it on my desk. It was large, an 8x10. But it was interesting, and I had to admire the effect of the blurred outline, which took up all the negative space and really let the tiger shine. Something about that animal though… it was intriguing and kind of beautiful. Majestic and proud. Maybe even angry at how it had to be cooped up in the caged area. But, what did I know? I bobbed my head up and down and handed it back to her with a truthful, "It's a very beautiful picture. I like it."

She smiled at me and laid it on her desk. "Can I see your project?"

I groped in my bag for the 5x7 picture of the tree. Then I handed it to her with a smile of my own.

She acknowledged and praised the interesting way light reflected off the icicles and the intricate way they hung from the tree.

But at that moment, the teacher grabbed our attention and the class passed with ease.

I knew that history was going to be a nightmare, but I hurried there as fast as traffic would allow so I wouldn't be late. Mr. Flightless Bat wasn't in a good mood—as usual—so I sat in the back of class, taking notes and waiting in anxious silence for him to pass back our last reports.

When that time came, he started talking about how some students had been disappointing in their work, and he wished they would try harder if they wanted to pass. I think the plural 'they' and 'some' were just a pretense. I'm sure that I was the only one that wasn't 'up to scratch.' Then he started passing them all back.

Anger was already simmering in my chest from his blatant rudeness, so I knew that this wasn't going to be a pleasant experience. I just hoped and prayed that I wouldn't snarl at him with my fangs exposed.

He sneered at me when he set my paper on my desk, and I knew that it was going to be just as bad as I had anticipated. A big, red F shone brightly against the crisp, white paper. Now the anger was boiling, so I placed both hands on the edge of the desk to stop myself from jumping out of my seat and attacking him. Since when did I feel like attacking people? I dug my fingernails into the wood, holding myself in place.

But my fingernails were no longer just normally flat, hard, and short. They were long, round, and pointy, curving to razor sharp claws. I knew I was sweating with the effort of holding my anger in and because of the *claws* that had erupted off my fingers. What next? I felt like screaming. I was just about to lose it….

Thank the heavens above that the clock reached the end of the hour, and I was able to scramble through the door before anything really rash happened. I ran to the nearest bathroom and locked myself in a stall and sat upon the closed toilet seat, almost hyperventilating. I stared at my hands, feeling the electrical current pulsing through my arms and to my fingers, which still had the claws curving off them. This was not right. Was I going insane? I felt normal besides the electricity that flowed through my arms. That wasn't normal. I knew that much, which meant I was still reasoning rational explanations, proving that I wasn't crazy. But *what* then? I had no answer.

I stared at my hands again.

I think at that point I screamed. I don't remember clearly. I might have passed out.

My hands were furry—as in, real fur was starting to spread across them, orange and black.

Striped.

Now I knew for sure I was actually hyperventilating.

This couldn't be real. I must still be dreaming. People didn't turn into tigers like this. I had seen that picture earlier that morning, but that couldn't mean anything. This had started the day after the New Year's Eve party....

I froze.

I had been electrocuted on the Chinese New Year. The start of the new year had started the year of the tiger....

No way.

I think I passed out again.

When I was aware, I looked at my hands—what should have been my hands. They were paws. And the fur was halfway up my arm until it merged to skin where it had stopped at my elbow. I pulled the electrical currents away from my hands and made them hide near my heart. The paws morphed to real human hands again.

I gulped as I realized what was going on. The electricity was inside me. Stuck in my body from when I'd been shocked at the *exact* moment that it had been the new year. The *exact* moment the year of the tiger had begun. And it had to be a tiger. One of the things I was scared of most.

This was too much for me to handle. I didn't know what to do. The electricity was stuck in me. For how long though? Forever? I shuddered at the thought.

Because I knew one thing now.

I was able to turn into a tiger if I let the electricity free. It would not escape and flee from my body. It would flow through all of me and transform my human state into that of a tiger.

That thought was horrifying.

But—

I didn't pass out this time.

JUNGLE

In my apartment, I was lying on the floor. I had skipped my last class of the day because of the crisis I was dealing with. It was a good thing, too, because I sprouted whiskers and a tail on my drive home. I now needed a new pair of pants.

As I had stumbled through the door, trying to be quick and sneaky so no one would spot my tail, the electricity at my heart seemed to explode within me, and I felt it all rush through my body like a shiver of sudden cold. Every part of my body transformed into a tiger's, and the next few seconds later, I was a full-grown, fully fledged wild cat standing on four legs with clawed paws in my shabby living room. My long tail was flicking back and forth with my agitation and fear, and my ears twitched at little sounds from every direction at once, and my eyes beheld the now usual dull mixture of color and detail in dark spaces. My whiskered nose flared as powerful scents reached it: cat urine, oak, clean laundry, roses, alcohol, and sour food. I felt all the new muscle that was a part of being a tiger, and my breathing was low and heavy in my large lungs. I inhaled deeply through my mouth. For once, I felt truly powerful and strong and totally in control. I wasn't so afraid anymore, and I was curious about my strengths in this new body despite the fact that I was a *tiger*.

I rolled my shoulders and extended my claws as I stretched, my back end high and my front end low to the floor. Then I sat on my hind legs like a dog and stared around, catching my reflection in the glass of the window. My bright yellow eyes shone back at me, wide and strange. My heart skipped a beat as I caught the full reflection of my large, orange-and-black striped body covered in fur. I could make out my tail flicking back and forth across the floor as I inspected myself. It was the scariest, strangest, freakiest thing I have ever experienced. I lifted my arm, and a leg and paw lifted in the tiger across from me. I prowled over to the window and watched as the tiger's breathing sped up as the large, striped cat moved close to me. I stood so that our noses were an inch away. I could sense the glass with my whiskers, even though my breath was fogging the reflection—*my* reflection. I caught sight of my tabby cat perched on the armrest of my couch, her yellow eyes wide with outright fear and confusion. She most likely saw me as some foreign, monster-sized rival cat that had taken over her living room and appeared to have consumed her owner.

Her fear was warranted.

That's when I began to worry. I couldn't stay like this forever, could I? I didn't want to turn permanently into a tiger. I couldn't feel the electricity anymore, so I wondered if it had gone and if I was stuck like this. I pulled at all my nerve endings in my body, pulled internally from the heart, trying to reel the currents back in. And, slowly, I felt the tingling sensation from earlier as the electricity retracted away from the rest of my body and back securely behind some sort of switch at my heart. I felt myself shrink and desensitize as I became human once more, only I was naked, as my clothes had split under the immense mass of the tiger. I was still lying with my back to the floor and staring at the ceiling, thinking through the miracle that had just occurred.

I didn't know how much I could control this transformation thing. Would I suddenly burst into a jungle cat whenever my emotions got out of control? I needed space and some time to try to figure it out.

My phone vibrated beneath me, and I jumped in fright. I pulled it out of the back pocket of my pants on floor and stared at the screen. Sara inquired about my weekend. I sighed. It would be nice to act like nothing had changed, but turning into an animal uncontrollably wasn't a trivial matter. I was going to need this weekend and several more to test everything out. I had to control it, or I wouldn't be able to live a normal life.

I set my phone on the ground. I didn't know what to tell her. I could never tell her about this.

Ever.

I sat up and grabbed my phone. I sent her a message telling her I had too much homework this weekend coupled with one hell of a cold. She responded with a sad face and a get well soon. Maybe she could make plans with Jack now. I knew she didn't want me to feel like a third wheel. She had always been good about keeping her best friend close.

Unable to focus, especially on anything as mundane as homework, I went to bed early that night.

When I woke up in the morning, I panicked about school. I couldn't go back yet. What if I burst into a tiger in the middle of photoshop? What if Shianne provoked me again—not that she would after I'd growled at her with my fangs—but if I turned into a complete tiger this time, I'd be screwed. I couldn't go back until I discovered how to control it. That thought terrified me.

As much as I wanted to stay in bed, I threw the covers off and packed a bag for the day with a change of clothes, just in case. The nearest, somewhat secluded wooded area was about an hour away, which I realized was a blessing to the Portland area. I was hoping there would be a perfect spot to learn control and not be the object of some hunter's trophy case.

I ended up somewhere in the Mount Hood wilderness at an empty parking lot at the head of a hiking trail. I had never been much of a hiker, but now I could turn into a tiger, so everything was new that day.

I left my bag in my car and stood at the trailhead, bouncing on the balls of my feet. The path ahead was framed in frosted green and littered with dead leaves shrouded in white. I clutched my leather jacket tighter around me, bracing against a freezing gust of wind. I still didn't know what to expect—and I was frightened. What if there was a bear?

I shook my head, took a deep breath, and ran down the trail without looking back.

About a hundred yards in, I veered off the path and barreled head first into the wild brush. Cold, wet ferns soaked my legs and prickly fir trees scraped against my face. The city girl inside me was screaming to stop, turn around, and wrap up in a blanket forever, but something else within me said to keep going.

I kept running until my lungs couldn't handle it anymore. I bent over gasping. All around me was silence. No scurrying animals or people or cars or even Oregon rain. Nothing to provoke me or set the transformative reactions off.

I stood there, finally breathing normally. It had to be around 1 o'clock, but nothing had happened. Were the random tiger transformations done? Now that I'd completely transformed? Should I just turn back and go home like the rational part of me wanted to?

I had come this far.

I felt within me, toward the switch and regulator I managed to store the currents behind last time. Something there possessed energy. I could feel it—but it wasn't trying to escape like it had before. Perhaps I could control it. Exhaling deeply, I unbuttoned my jacket and set it on a damp rock nearby. A second later I regretted it, remembering the possibly, irreversible damage water can cause to leather garments. I picked it up and hung it gently on a tree branch. That was something I refused to lose—it was one of the most expensive things I owned and one of the only things I had ever received from my mother.

I closed my eyes and mentally—recklessly—linked the circuit.

The tingling currents wormed through my veins very slowly, enough that I could track the hot, electrifying feeling as it traveled down my arms, abdomen, and legs. I fell onto all fours and opened my eyes, the world a selectively dull, distorted, but detailed jumble around me. Wherever sunlight shone through the tangle of branches overhead, the world seemed exponentially brighter and more finely detailed than my human eyes could have ever perceived.

Suddenly, a bird chirped above me. My ear twitched, and I looked up at it in surprise. It was still February and very cold for birds. I took a step toward the tree it perched in, but froze when I heard a twig snap. It was quiet for a few more seconds, but then there were rustling leaves and more cracks and snaps. Something was coming toward me.

I bolted, stumbling over brush as I awkwardly tried to control my four limbs that weren't helped by the dangling remains of my thermal shirt and denim jeans. After I had retreated to a safer distance, I crouched low and waited for whatever was out in the woods today.

A bearded man dressed in wooded camoflage emerged, binoculars hanging from his neck. He glanced around him and pulled out a notebook, staring up at the lonesome bird.

I relaxed slightly when he didn't notice my trail of ripped, torn, broken, and disturbed wildlife I'd left in my wake. I waited until he disappeared and walked back over to where I'd left my jacket. Afraid of who would show up next, I retracted the currents like the first time until I stood shivering in the middle of the wilderness with just my leather jacket.

I traipsed back to the trail and darted into my car once I knew the coast was clear. I cranked the heat and pulled on my extra pair of clothes, wondering how I was going to test out being a tiger with bird watchers and hikers and other crazy people that didn't quit the outdoors when it was frozen outside.

I felt some relief that I apparently had some kind of control over my transformation, but now I was curious and determined. My failure at running on four legs bothered me. The muscle and mass I had as a tiger was empowering, but floundering through the forest was embarrassing, even if no one was watching.

I drove home, hoping not to be ambushed by humans again the next time I tried.

For three weekends straight, I drove out to the woods and attempted to figure out the body of the tiger. I eventually mastered the art of using my four legs as an entity, and I discovered that it was impossible to escape people. They were everywhere, doing everything—mountian bikers, joggers, wildlife enthusiasts, surveyors, loggers, hikers, campers—and I barely made it undetected most of the time.

Luckily, I knew for sure now that I could control it. Two and a half weeks of sitting in class without any outbursts had proved that. But I was still curious. The tiger within me wasn't going away, and maybe it was time to start thinking about that vacation again.

Spring break was approaching quickly.

My mother's travel pin kept haunting me, reminding me of all the experience I lacked outside of the greater Portland area. Now was my time to take a break from my busy human life and escape my city home. Maybe I could work out this tiger kink in my life if I took time to really deal with it. To let the craziness of the phenomenon sink in and give myself time to explore it and grow comfortable with it in a way that wouldn't land me in a zoo. Or a nut house.

Lying in bed, I considered where I would go. But because of what had occurred, I figured I wouldn't be going to Jamaica or Hawaii or somewhere tropical and heavily populated with tourists. To explore the possibilities and new abilities of the tiger, I would need to go somewhere where they were native, like India or Bangladesh. The only problem was I still had a fear of the wild jungle and completely wild animals.

I sat up and closed my eyes. I was slightly dizzy from lying on my back for so long, and I was nervous about booking my trip. Wearily, I pulled out my laptop, turning it on and listening to the hum and buzz as it started up. I waited anxiously as the welcome screen stared at me, and then my cat leapt up on my keyboard and mewed at me in search of attention. I suddenly realized that my cat looked kind of like a miniature tiger, only the wrong colors. She had deeper orange-colored stripes rather than black. Sighing, I opened up the internet and began searching for the largest population of tigers in Southeast Asia. There was a large population of Bengal tigers in central and north India. Resigned, I looked up cities and a half an hour later, I had purchased air tickets to Nagpur, India. I had clenched my teeth and closed one eye in nervous fear and cautiously clicked the button that said checkout to order the plane tickets. Then I had to buy a train ticket to Mansar, India, which would take me nearer to the jungles that I was heading toward.

The date of my departure was set for one week away. It was fortunate that I'd obtained my passport in my senior year of high school when my mother had planned to take me on an international trip. I'd had to cancel a week before because the last chance for the SAT had come up, and I had missed the first two. Truth be told, it would have been weird to go with her anyway. We hadn't been that close through my high school years.

I called a lunch meeting with Sara to tell her I was finally taking my vacation. I couldn't tell her the truth about my transformation, but I couldn't avoid telling her where I was going. Luckily, her last few weekends with Jack had gone exceedingly well, and it was all she could think, speak, and focus on—which seemed frivolous and perplexing and wildly foreign to me. However, the strangeness of me traveling to India didn't raise a warning flag on her radar.

"I just hope you have fun. It seems like it's been awhile since you've enjoyed yourself," she said. "Jack and I haven't discovered what not having fun is like yet."

I smiled at her, thankful for the distraction in her life, and we said good-bye for awhile. I went home to pack. I didn't pack a lot: two changes of clothes and my money for the trip. I would be spending most of my time as a tiger, so I wouldn't need a lot of clothes. I had to get ahold of Sara again to ask her if she would look after my cat. She said of course.

The week passed quickly, and in no time at all, I was in the airport, tapping my only bag—which was small enough to be a carry on—nervously and anxiously. I was terrified, but still excited. So far the plane was on time, but a part of me—the biggest part—was hoping for a delay, yet the other part of me wanted to get the travel and move into the jungle over with.

My conflicted self won the reward that both of me wanted. The plane was only five minutes late. My stomach twisting, I clutched my bag and boarded the plane. My seat was on the wing, the loudest area of the plane. Maybe that would help me to not think about what was coming.

The plane was rather large to transport us over the country, and the seats were mostly full. An Indian family sat up towards the front, and two other white American men sat behind me. I avoided everyone's gaze and stared out the window. We had a layover in New York that would last two hours to refuel and pick up a few more passengers. I would never leave the plane. As we took off, I avoided looking down, resting my head against the window, wishing for sleep to help me forget about what was coming and ease my restless state.

At our layover, a few people left and others boarded. A short, but muscular, man ended up in the seat beside me. He rearranged his position for a moment or two, trying to find the most comfortable spot. I watched him from the corner of my eye. Something seemed off about him. He wore a tight, short sleeve active shirt and a well-worn, orange bandana around his neck. A safari hat was propped on the floor between his large-muscled calves. I didn't know if it was my intuition or my animalistic sixth sense that detected his strangeness, but I avoided eye contact and rested my head against the cool glass, waiting for takeoff once again.

After we had reached a steady altitude, I sighed in relief, my breath fogging up the window pane. I hated takeoff.

"So why are you travelling to India?" came a raspy, smoker's voice from beside me.

I swiveled my gaze around and caught a flash of bright red in his retinas. My breath froze in my throat for a moment until I realized it had been from the glare of the sun through the window. And he was leaning a little bit close for my liking.

"I'm … meeting my mother there. She's a journalist."

"Mmm hmm." He stared at me without blinking. I didn't know what he wanted.

"And why are *you* going to India?" I said.

He picked up his hat and twirled it in my face. "I'm going on a safari. I'm a hiker and outdoors aficionado, and I've never been to India. I'm going to grasp nature by his essence and conquer him."

I glanced at his muddy, tan hiking boots and holey khaki shorts. "Isn't nature a woman?"

He peered at me, moving closer. I backed away slightly. "You think you're smart, huh? Nature was created by the Almighty himself—therefore, nature would accordingly be male."

"What about Mother Nature?" I asked, in spite of myself.

"You either believe in the Almighty or Mother Nature. Man or woman."

This man was a nut. I didn't reply and looked away, hoping he would understand my intentions to be rid of this conversation.

He left me alone for about ten minutes, during which he managed to down an entire plastic cup of jack and coke.

"What do you call yourself?" he suddenly asked.

Call myself. That was a new one. "Jade."

"You have a name of nature—don't squander it." He paused for a few seconds, perhaps waiting for me to ask him for his name, but I wasn't going to fall for the bait. "I call myself Oleander, but you can call me Ollie."

I couldn't resist the irrational curiosity that bubbled up. "What does it mean?"

He smiled sardonically, all his teeth showing in a creepy fashion. "Poisonous flower."

I could feel my heart rate increase. Whoever this guy was, he boded ill for wherever he was going. I had no reply for this strange and dangerous man. I looked away and leaned against the cold window again.

Half an hour later, I heard him order another drink, which he once more consumed in under five minutes once it arrived. A moment after he had finished his drink, I could feel his hot, whiskey-tainted breath on my ear. "Want to know what I'm really doing in India, Jade?" he whispered.

I remained frozen, feeling my blood rush through my veins, hearing my heart pound in my ears—waiting, almost hoping, I would suddenly sprout claws or fangs.

He was leaning against me, his lips much too close to my ear. "Hunting tigers."

I jumped with a big wave of turbulence, which rocked my head against the glass. I rubbed my forehead in annoyance. My blood was still racing, and I refused to look back at him, afraid he would see me for what I was hidden within. Taking steadying breaths, I stared out the window. I hadn't really worried or truly thought about the idea of poachers while I was in Oregon, but that could be a serious issue that I had to be prepared to face while in India.

It was all cloudy and dark outside, but we were descending onto foreign land. My stomach clenched some more as we landed down in India. This was my first time in another country.

The airport was so much smaller than what I was used to. I hurried to get away from it, to go outside and see the place where I would be living. Nagpur wasn't poorly underdeveloped. It wasn't a shabby town or village with mud huts, but it wasn't like Portland. Hindus in very colorful and traditional dress were walking about, conversing in Hindi. Meanwhile, traffic was a nightmare, worse than rush hour in L.A. This was madness.

I stayed off the streets, working my way through town, avoiding the man from the plane, who had a fancy hunting rifle slung across his back, his safari hat shadowing most of his face as he stood waiting for a cab. I clutched my bag as I searched for a bus station. Once I found it, I boarded quickly so I could get a seat by myself. I had a long ride ahead to get to Mansar. I watched scenery for as long as I could, fighting the urge to sleep. I was terrified to fall asleep and wake up robbed, kidnapped, or worse.

When I finally arrived, I disembarked and stared around. This was a busy and heavily populated city of farm houses. The lack of skyscrapers and rain reminded me how far away from home I was. This city was smaller than Nagpur, full of homes and temples, cheap little shops, and a lot less cars. But this was not my final destination. From Mansar, I caught a ride to Ghukashi, literally a village in the middle of nowhere. It was very close to a tiger reserve and jungle. There was nothing exciting there—it was the closest thing I'd seen to a hut village. I ventured toward the edge of the village where, in the distance, I could see the jungle. With one deep sigh, I turned my back on civilization and ran like the maniac I felt.

At the edge of the trees, heart pumping while my stomach anxiously twisted, I listened to the creaks of the wild place. I wanted to turn into a tiger before I ventured through the jungle. I was terrified to enter it as a human, but I wasn't going to transform out in the open. Gulping down my fear, I darted into the jungle and hid behind a tree. Then I stripped as fast as my shaking hands would allow, stuffed my clothes in my bag, and then released the electricity. It flowed through my veins, and I slowly—and less painfully than before—grew and fell to all fours. And when, at last, my tail was twitching behind me, I shook out my fur and rolled my shoulders. Then I listened to all the sounds that were making my ears twitch and flick. There was the rustle of leaves and branches as the wind blew and creatures moved. It was hard to concentrate. All the sounds and senses and smells and things to see. I was overwhelmed. Strange to me was my lowered sense of fear now that I was a tiger. I felt safer since I had the mass, teeth, and claws, and my mind was oddly clear and thoughtful. I could focus better, yet my senses had so much more strength, taking up more of my attention than before. Then again, my brain seemed to have more room to accept all of this extra information.

This was not me. This was an out of body experience—I was Jade from Portland, living in a crummy apartment in the city, going to college to study communications. I was terrified of the wild and wild animals. Yet here I was, transformed into a tiger and standing in a jungle in the middle of India. This was the complete opposite of me, but even so, I didn't feel the panic I thought I should be feeling. I lumbered forward, gazing around the trees and various species of big-leaved bushes and plants, feeling a sense of ease I'd forgotten existed.

Everything was wet or dripping, initially causing my ears to twitch in every direction, but it wasn't difficult to ignore. Too much was stealing the attention through my eyes, for never before had I considered how beautiful the jungle *could* be. I had always cringed internally at the mention of the jungle, the whole idea of it had terrified me, but now I took time to really look at it and its natural beauty. There was so much *green*. Even with dull colors, I could still see that almost everything was a shade of green—so much nature and life. The place seemed so pure with no human interference. It was relaxing and beautiful. The whole absence of fear made me feel so different, like I was suddenly a different person. This tiger transformation was changing everything about me.

A colorful frog pealed its strange chirp, and I jerked my head upward to glare at it. A rumble sounded through my throat at the annoyance of the amphibian. It hopped away, squeaking in fear.

I roared in triumph.

There was a crackle of leaves from the ground, and I automatically tensed. A drop of water splashed on my forehead from a leaf above, and I shook my head like a dog would do. I seemed to have a sixth sense; a part of me sensed the presence of another creature very close, something big. A little fear seeped into my emotions, but I felt more anticipation. I was ready to prove myself. A very large head appeared around a tree trunk. Of course it wasn't human—the face was furry with white down the sides. The nose and forehead were orange, striped black. The eyes were yellow, and they looked at me curiously and wearily.

A wild tiger.

It showed no signs of aggression, so I relaxed slightly. I took one heavy step forward.

It spoke to me.

I was shocked. I hadn't considered the fact that we would *talk* to each other.

The other tiger was female.

"I thought you were a human. I was ready to pounce. You smell strongly of their stench."

I gulped.

"I've been near the village recently," I replied, glad I had hidden my bag of clothes by a rock.

She eyed me shrewdly. "You're new to the forest here, aren't you?"

"Yes," I said hesitantly. I was afraid of what would happen next.

She prowled around me, inspecting me. "What are your plans?" she asked. "Just passing through or were you hoping to stay?"

"Stay? In the jungle? With you?" I hadn't planned on staying with the wild tigers, but there wasn't really a hotel or place to stay as a human. I had known this booking my trip. I had come to test and explore being a tiger. My plan had been to do it alone, but would this be a better, safer, choice?

"There's more than just me here," the other female replied. "There's a group of us that live here under one domain. You can choose to stay with us or move on, but if you choose to be one of us, then you'll have to meet the rajah."

The rajah. So there was a king of these beasts, meaning there was some sort of society. A hierarchy of some kind resided here. Did that mean these wild cats weren't really *wild*?

I was suddenly intensely curious about this wild society of tigers. I had come to explore being a tiger. Maybe this would be the best way to do it, with another tiger—perhaps a potential friend—to figure everything out with.

I'd already done the impossible and left home. I was in India. What did I have to lose?

"I'm interested in staying," I finally said.

She seemed pleased by my decision. "Come with me. We're mostly safe in the trees. Humans come only occasionally. That's when we drive them out." She turned around and walked through the brush, almost silent except for the thud of her padded paws on the ground and the slithering of leaves as they rubbed along her sides. I felt so strange, but powerful walking on all fours and prowling through the jungle.

"What's your name?" she called from ahead.

I had to think quickly. I didn't want to use Jade—it was so human. I was all mixed up in my thoughts and my nature. I was human. I was a tiger.

"My name is Mix," I said swiftly. "Who are you?"

"I'm Somila," she replied. "I was just about to go hunting when I caught your scent. Care to join me? We can visit the rajah afterwards."

"Um…," I replied, terrified. I was a city person, who lived off of junk food, potatoes, some random vegetables, and very well-done, finely cooked meats. I didn't hunt… at all. Nor did I eat anything raw. This was a milestone I was not sure I was really prepared for in any way.

But if I wanted to make this work, I was going to have to try it, as unappealing as it sounded. "Sure," I finally replied.

"Let's go find something vulnerable." She headed off through some bushes, her striped tail vanishing with a flick. I hurried to follow.

We had gone maybe fifty feet when I sensed something moving fast to our left. I paused as it approached. Somila didn't pause though. She turned, faced the noise, and crouched low, like my cat did when she got ready to jump.

There was a wild cat roar and something leapt through the air at the female tiger down low. My eyes followed the flight of the leaping cat, but my peripheral vision caught the female tiger pounce, and they met in mid-air, jaws open in attack form, but no claws exposed. It was playful and teasing, like when guys punched each other on the arms in greeting.

I stayed back as they crashed to the floor of the jungle, rolling around like fools. Then they righted themselves and faced me, sitting on their haunches. I sat too.

The other cat was male, and he was considerably thinner and overall much smaller than we tigers. He was also a different cat. His primary fur was golden yellow and he had blotchy, not fully circular spots dotted over the panes of his feline body. He was a leopard.

"A newbie?" he asked. "Excellent."

I swallowed.

"This is Mix," Somila informed him. "Mix, this is Shrey."

"Welcome to our home. We've needed some new cats around here. The others were tugging on my last whiskers," Shrey continued.

I didn't know what to say.

"There's one thing you should know about our jungle," Shrey the leopard began. "The leopards live on one side of the jungle and tigers on the other. The stream divides the sides, but one—Rajah Sojóma—rules over us all in the jungle. There's not a lot of us cats, sadly, but enough."

"I've heard that we're endangered," I said matter-of-factly.

"Yeah, humans label us as 'Endangered' but they're the ones who made us so," Somila replied angrily.

"We're headed that way too," Shrey said. "Nobody respects the wild anymore."

I secretly agreed.

The familiar gnawing sensation of hunger began to eat at my sides. I gave a low rumble.

"We were just about to hunt and then go see Sojóma," Somila said to Shrey. "We'll be back soon." She prowled off in search of food.

I looked at Shrey, still sitting on the ground. "You coming?" I asked.

"No, I ate a few days ago." He yawned. "But you better hurry if you want to keep up with her. She's stealthy and fast."

Panicking, I tore after her, lunging my four legs forward and backward, rushing against the jungle floor, flying through the bushes. I was just beginning to enjoy the rush of running when I ran head first into something still and solid. My first dazed thought was that I must've hit a tree. But a sharp growl switched my thought process.

I had run into Somila.

"What was that for?" she hissed. She looked angry and mean. Like a predator who would eat me.

I gulped. "I'm sorry. I was running to catch up and just forgot to slow down. I like running—" I cut myself off, almost saying "as a tiger." I couldn't afford to be stupid.

"You like running?" she asked, sounding skeptical and surprised.

"Yeah, don't you? It feels like flying."

She stared at me. "None of us really like running."

They were all crazy. "So what's the point of having four strong legs, if not to run?"

"To hunt and eat."

Well, maybe not completely crazy. "I have a confession to make," I said. Better to get it over with rather than humiliate myself later. "I can't hunt."

"What?" she gasped.

"I…came from a zoo. I escaped. I've never hunted." I was proud of my quick thinking.

"A…zoo?" She peered at me suspiciously.

"Yeah. They feed you meat already butchered. And I was born there, so I was never taught how to hunt." You could call the city a zoo.

"Alright. Watch me. Pay close attention and follow your instincts."

Somila then moved away, crouching low to the ground, slowly sneaking forward, her dilated pupils black and aware, her ears still, listening carefully. I analyzed her every movement, making sure to remember everything so I wouldn't look like a fool.

She crept along the river edge, sensing for any unaware animals that would work as lunch. She was deathly silent. Even when her body brushed leaves, barely a sound was heard, even to my super-sensitive ears. And those super-sensitive ears caught the snuffling of a smaller creature that smelled appealing. I froze before Somila did, crouching to the ground like her.

She dug her claws into the earth, ready to spring, and then she launched herself forward, flying through the air, claws and teeth exposed. Somila landed on a type of pig, a very big pig, very much like a wart-hog. It squealed until life was taken from him and then Somila looked up at me.

"Instincts," I said, understanding. It looked natural to hunt.

She nodded and then began tearing into the flesh of the swine.

I suddenly felt sick.

She swallowed a bite and said, "You can have some, if you want."

I was stuck in a dilemma. On one hand—or rather, paw—I *was* hungry, but on the other paw, my stomach felt queasy at the thought of eating a raw pig.

"It's your catch," I replied. "I'll go downstream to see if I can catch something. Save a bite for me, though, if I don't catch anything."

She nodded and I prowled off, sniffing for something that smelled even relatively appealing. I caught the scent of a fearful rodent, a venomous snake, and a large bird. The bird seemed to smell differently with each intake of air I pulled in. At first, it smelled like chicken, and then it smelled like wet, raw meat. It took me several minutes to realize that I was registering the smell with two different sides of me. My tiger instincts smelled the bird as chicken, making me long to hunt, while my human brain registered the smell as the meaty raw part of the bird, turning off any appeal the bird had as food.

I tried to focus on the smell of chicken, trying to block out my human thoughts as I crouched into the bushes. As long as I didn't *think* about what I was doing, it shouldn't bother me. Mind over matter. At least, that was my theory.

I inched forward, trying to be stealthy as I turned off my human senses and focused on my prey, letting the tiger take over.

I pounced, my claws jutting out, ready to shred the bird into dinner. It squawked as I roared and flew through the air. Feathers filled the air as it tried to take flight. My clawed paw trapped it by the tail feathers, while it flailed around on the ground in fear. I would've pitied it if I wasn't possessed by hunger and natural instincts. I bit at its neck to silence and immobilize it, and the bird fell limp. I stood there and stared at the dead bird, relishing in my success on my first hunt. Before I really thought about what I had just done and what I was going to do, I grabbed the bird in my mouth and padded back to where Somila was just finishing her pig. I dropped the bird at my feet and sat down in triumph.

"You killed a bird?" Somila asked in surprise.

"I killed a bird."

She eyed me, seeming to re-evaluate my abilities. "Birds are a rare delicacy around here because so few of us can manage to catch them.

They're usually too fast and skittish. The leopards usually get lucky because they spend so much time in the trees."

So on my first hunt not only had I managed to actually catch something, but I succeeded in catching something most tigers couldn't. That boosted my morale.

"Would you like some?" I offered. I was still hesitant on eating it.

"Oh no, go ahead. It's your catch, and I rather out-did myself on the boar." She and I both glanced at the remains of the swine.

"Alright," I replied, and before I could change my mind, I sunk my teeth into the flesh of the bird.

I managed to choke the whole thing down in ten minutes, spitting out feathers through the whole process. Somila had left me alone to eat in peace, so I didn't feel too foolish, but I would avoid birds in the future. Feathers were an embarrassing, unnecessary ordeal when eating.

I had to follow scents back to where Somila and Shrey were lounging among some many-leaved bushes. It wasn't that difficult, but there were a lot of scents to distract from my course. The sky was orange by the time I found them.

"Find anything?" Shrey asked me.

"A bird," I said conversationally.

He stared at me in surprise for a few seconds as well, and then he composed himself. "Well, I hope it tasted good."

"As well as any bird can taste," I mumbled.

"Are you ready to meet our rajah?" Somila asked, standing up.

This was my last chance to run if I didn't want to be a part this world. But somewhere inside of me was a desire to be accepted by these cats. I felt curious and adventurous. To my surprise, I wanted to know what this new world had to offer.

"Yes, let's go see him," I said, still hesitant, although I'd made a decision. I just didn't know what that entailed.

KING OF THE JUNGLE

Shrey stood up, and the three of us ventured forward, prowling in a line.

"Which side of the stream are we on?" I asked.

"The tiger side," Somila replied, her striped tail flicking in front of my nose.

"Then how can Shrey be on this side?"

Somila glanced behind her at Shrey. Their eyes met curiously, and then Somila looked at me. "Shrey and I are kind of a group known through the whole jungle. We're a package deal, allowed wherever," she explained. "The boundary line doesn't really apply to us. Only when we sleep, really."

I wanted to ask if the package deal could become three and incorporate me, but I was afraid to. Rejection from my first two 'friends' wouldn't help my slowly growing confidence.

We continued forward, following the stream. Colorful birds swooped overhead and cawed from amid the tops of trees. I could hear the slithering of snakes and lizards, and my fear rose slightly, but also the sixth sense that I seemed to be able to use could sense the spring of frogs, which I guessed to be colorful, since we were in a jungle. This place was so alive.

I could tell when we entered the main domain of the tigers because the smell seemed familiar to my nose, and I heard slow, deep breathing, and I felt in the ground beneath my feet the thud of padded paws when one walked.

"Welcome to the Sanctuary. This is where we mainly live. Only about 30 of us are in this jungle, and we share the area. But we all have a place to sleep. Just make sure you're never in Calouise's spot. He has first pick," Somila said quietly.

"Why does he have so much control?"

"He's the rajah's adopted cub. He's also the second biggest tiger in this area."

"He's also a jerk," Shrey said behind me. I tried not to laugh.

At first, it was hard to spot the tigers that were sleeping among the tall plants, their stripes concealing them within the crazy, wayward colors of the jungle, but my eyes learned to spot the difference between actual plants and big, meaty tigers.

A few of the others looked up when we passed, curiously watching me, while the rest just continued to sleep or ignored us. Even though every tiger had the same basic shape, build, and colors, every single one was distinguished differently by a specific pattern of stripes positioned on their faces and across their backs. My eyes immediately caught the little nuances between stripe patterns, allowing me to quickly identify each tiger as its own individual being. My human eyes would have assumed each tiger looked relatively the same.

A mother and her two young cubs were close by, her watchful gaze straying from her playful children just long enough to sneak a glance at me. It was obvious she was an attentive mother—unlike the mother I had grown up with. Her job received most of her attention—at least it did as I got increasingly older. But this tigress had only one job: to mother. For a moment, I almost thought I was jealous. But the fleeting feeling passed before I could give it greater attention.

There was a place up ahead that was, by all means, the best spot to lounge. A small, gentle waterfall fell into a pond with trees and a cave-like area hidden behind the falling sheet of water. A blanket of weeds and grass grew very green in the rocky cave, but a definite flattened space displayed the area of the tiger who owned the sleeping space.

"That, I'm guessing, is Calouise's spot," I said to Somila and Shrey.

"Yes. Stay clear of it and he won't rip your legs off," Shrey said.

"He sounds pleasant," I said in a small voice.

"Just stay away from his bad side and all will be fine," Somila said, rolling her yellow eyes.

She turned left and maneuvered her way toward the stream. The water was fairly clean, the depth rather shallow, and—when I had dipped my paw in it—perfectly cool. We paused at a beach, the other two looking at me.

"Before you see the rajah, you should tell us some more about you. Where did you come from?" Somila asked.

"I was migrating," I said. It was perfectly true, just not as detailed as I usually would have been.

"From?" Somila urged. They wanted more information—not exactly good.

"The north," I replied.

"How far north?"

They were killing me here.

"Far enough," I said, feeling pestered.

"Like Siberia or Nepal?" Shrey inquired.

Bengal tigers were the type I was living with, so I figured I wasn't from as far north as Siberia. "Nepal."

"That's good," Somila said, nodding at me with satisfaction.

"So are there any black panthers here?" I asked Shrey, trying to change the subject off of me.

"Not here. We're only spotted in this jungle."

"So how—" but I stopped as leaves rustled close by, and I sensed the heavy thud of large paws on the wet earth. Something big was heading toward us, from the leopard side of the river. Somila and Shrey tensed beside me, and I anxiously fixed my eyes on two large leafy bushes that concealed the oncoming creature.

Then a face emerged through the leaves, and his head was followed by his large paws, legs, and chest. He was an enormous tiger, his stripes thick and a rich, black color. He had a haughty, hulking look and movement as he prowled into the water and crossed the stream.

When he reached our bank, he paused and glanced at the package duo, water dripping from his legs and chest, then looked at me. His pupils were mostly black, the hunting, alert look easily discernible. The black eyes roved over my striped form, and then he looked at Somila.

"Who's the newbie?" the tiger asked in a deep, almost scary, voice.

"Why don't you ask *her*?" Shrey said in an annoyed tone.

The tiger's eyes snapped onto Shrey, then back to me. "Fine. Who are you?" he asked in an equally vexed voice.

"I'm Mix," I said, trying to sound confident and bold, but failing miserably.

"From?"

"Nepal." I was hoping that my voice wasn't as squeaky as it sounded to me.

He nodded once. "I'm Calouise," he said boldly.

I'd figured.

"Good to know," I replied, trying to not let sarcasm leak into my tone.

He stared at me for a moment longer than I thought normal, then he prowled off, his tail disappearing into the brush.

"He seems friendly," I said, sarcasm prominent now.

"He's not that bad," Somila said defensively.

"Because you think he's good-looking," Shrey argued.

Somila growled.

I didn't think he was exceptionally good-looking, not by my standards. Then again, I didn't know what tiger standards were.

"He's only a brute," Somila said nonchalantly, but I could sense an impressed air in her tone. I couldn't tell if Shrey did. I figured he had an idea. After all, he had known her longer.

"Come on, we should see the rajah before sundown," Somila said, urging us forward.

The thought of meeting the king of this jungle scared me. As a ruler, he must be big and strong, wise and critical. He'd be old and beautiful, lean but powerful. I discovered that he lived deeper into the jungle, which meant we'd have to cross the river to the leopard side to get to him. I suddenly felt bees buzzing in my stomach.

We waded across the water and began trekking through the other side of the jungle. Leopards could hide as well as tigers among the plants. We seemed to be in no hurry, ambling through the forest, taking our time. My impatience heightened, as did my nerves. Our slow pace was not helping me gather myself for the coming confrontation. I wasn't composing myself—I was falling apart. I worried I would leave a bad impression, which would only add to reasons for a denial of acceptance. The longing for approval, for acceptance from these foreign, wild creatures startled me, but it wouldn't go away. A part of me—a crazy part—wanted to belong with these cats. I wanted to growl in frustration; my life was turned upside down… and that insane fraction of my personality liked it.

I shook my head. Focus! That's what I needed.

We traveled for a while longer, the slope of the forest floor rising gradually until we faced a wall of old ruins. The crumbling stone was at least ten feet tall, parts of the wall missing and overgrown in jungle vegetation. It was an outside wall of some old Indian village. Somila paused, and then crouched on her back legs. She sprang upward, jumping gracefully onto a ledge before she made her way to the top of the wall. Shrey followed her, jumping just as beautifully as Somila. I was scared that I wouldn't be able to jump high enough or miss the ledge.

I anxiously shifted all my weight to my back legs, building up for my spring. Then I gulped and launched myself upward. I overshot the ledge and barely made the top of the wall. Three of my paws landed safely, the other scrambling to find a place to land. Once I had my footing, I followed the other two along the wall, glancing at the other side. There wasn't much to see. There was one building falling apart among the trees and plants. We continued along the wall, climbing up and up as we traveled to higher elevation. If we kept going, we were going to be at the top of the canyon wall that dribbled water into Calouise's pool. But then the wall suddenly veered left. We continued along a minute or so more and then leapt down some stone steps to the ground, landing in front of a large temple-like stone place, the doorway open to us. Somila and Shrey prowled on in, but I hesitated before stepping through the open threshold.

The building was wide open. There were just four walls that framed the room, the ceiling non-existent. It was large and clean, no vegetation growing anywhere inside; only stone floor, walls, and other stone formations were present besides the cats. Distributed around the room was a pair of tigers and a pair of leopards. I figured they were either some kind of guards or a large number of mates. The rajah sat on the other side of the room on a pile of stone blocks that served as a throne at the top of a small staircase.

My first impression was not even close to my expectations. The king was large, muscled, and absolutely shining in splendor. His coat was shiny and sleek, his orange bright, his stripes deep, and his chest a clean white to contrast the rest of him. His face was smooth and symmetrical, guarded. He sat tall and proud, exuding an aura that plainly warned *powerful*. I was awed.

I stayed behind Somila and Shrey, wary and definitely still nervous. They seemed relatively at ease in this mighty tiger's presence.

"Halt before Rajah Sojóma, ruler of this surrounding jungle and beasts," said a thin, female tiger from our left. We froze.

Somila and Shrey bowed, bending their front legs and dropping their heads. I quickly mimicked their actions.

"Somila...Shrey. What brings you to my quarters?" asked the rajah in a bold tone.

They split apart to reveal me, still bowed behind them.

"Come forward, new one," commanded the king.

I gulped and prowled closer to his throne, staring at him in fear.

"What do you call yourself?" he asked.

"Mix," I replied.

He eyed me. "Why are you here?"

I glanced at Somila and Shrey. "To join your territory."

He shifted his weight slightly. "What do you know about this territory?"

I tried quickly to remember all Somila had told me. "Tigers live in the Sanctuary, we attack humans if they are in the jungle, and... and... to stay away from Calouise's spot."

But to my surprise, Sojóma laughed. I wasn't trying to be funny. I was terrified and stating the first things that came to mind. I was still uneasy, unsure if he was laughing at me or not.

"Calouise's authority is so amplified. He can't claim a spot of the jungle... the jungle has its own mind. Everyone is just too intimidated to defy him."

The bees in my stomach stopped stinging, but the buzzing remained. Sojóma had a sense of humor, which was good to know. But he still sent chills that made my fur stand on end when I looked at him. I only had the guts to nod.

"You have some knowledge. Now where do you come from?"

I tried to remember… something that started with an N. "Nepal. I escaped from a zoo," I replied.

His brows rose a few inches in curiosity. "A zoo? How interesting. I did not know Nepal had any zoos."

Crap. I hadn't done all my research before I'd left for India. I didn't really know if Nepal had any zoos. But I couldn't afford to blow this bluff. "Just one."

I did my best not to flinch under his judging stare. There had to be at least one zoo in Nepal. I was banking on it with my life.

"Oh, that's right. There is one zoo in Nepal. So you escaped? Then you're not accustomed to the wild yet. I hope your transition goes well, for all our sakes."

That last line was scary enough to make a person wet their pants… if they were wearing any.

"Now, to ease that transition there are a few more rules for you to follow: if there's a lion, cheetah, or hyena in our jungle, you chase it out. They don't belong here under any circumstances. Lions are inferior, no matter what others may say, and tigers are the true royalty in the jungle. Stay away from the village because they will kill you. And stick with these two. They'll protect you and teach you as you need it."

I nodded and sighed with relief. I'd been accepted. And I had cats to help me with everything—even if it was an obligation.

I had a question, but I was still slightly scared, so I had not the guts to ask it. That was, until he spoke again.

"Any questions, Mix?"

I shifted my weight uneasily.

"Yes, Mr. Royal Sojóma, sir. Uh… how strong is the boundary between tigers and leopards because there seems to be no 'guard,' and you didn't mention anything in your additional rules."

The king eyed me. Then he laughed. "In all honesty, there really isn't a boundary. You can be on either side of the river, but there's the illusion of a boundary because of where they all choose to sleep. So they've created a tiger and leopard side. There's nothing to worry about." At that moment, a tiger ran into the room, apparently desperate to speak with Sojóma. "If you don't mind, I have prior engagements to fulfill," he said to Shrey, Somila, and me. He stood up and addressed the newcomer in quiet conversation.

I was taken aback by the sudden dismissal, but turned myself around and followed the other two out.

Once we were away from the desecrated wall, I voiced my thoughts. "He's kind of easy going, isn't he?"

Shrey looked at me for a few moments before he answered. "Yeah, for the most part. He gets scary when he cracks down on those threatening our safety, and he's fiery when he's angry or passionate about something. He used to be a great warrior when we were at constant war with the lions, but that was years ago. I wasn't born yet. Now he stays put, keeping us in check and from going extinct, both our species."

As we continued walking, I considered what everyone had said about the lions. "What did Sojóma mean when he said lions are inferior, despite what anyone else might say? And why have tigers been at war with them?"

Somila sighed. "Should I tell the story?" she asked Shrey.

"By all means. It's more about your species than it is mine."

She glanced at me before beginning. "There has always been a long standing rivalry between lions and tigers since we have coexisted. For centuries, tigers were known by the wild world as the dominant, royal species of the wild, but more specifically, the jungles."

"But lions are referred to as the King of the Jungle," I blurted before I could stop myself.

Somila snarled at me. "You believe such rubbish? Where did you hear such a lie?"

I found it difficult to swallow. "There was a ... plaque in the zoo, in front of the lion cages. I always heard the humans reading from it, talking about how incredible the 'king of the jungle' was as they stared at the lions," I lied as smoothly as I could.

She growled. "So even the humans have begun to see them as royally dominant over us. That's not acceptable. Well, the humans probably adopted this idea after lions decided that tigers didn't deserve the respect and authority of being the dominant cat of the wild world. They rebelled against our rulership, beginning the feline wars that would last another several hundred years. For a long time, the tigers managed to hold onto the ruling position throughout the world. Eventually, a new generation of lions, raised for the sole purpose of destroying the tigers' claims to any title and dominance of the jungle and wild, defeated the forces of tigers that fought against them. It was a dark moment in our history. Every wild ecosystem for thousands of miles heard of the outrageous turnover of power. Suddenly, the lions were no longer considered inferior. Tigers in every country were ridiculed and disrespected under the new regime of lion dominance."

"Did the tigers ever win their power back?" I asked, extremely curious about this animal world history that was exponentially more fascinating than any of the human history courses I had ever taken.

Somila scowled at me. "Tigers did, for a time or two, regain power. But the lions always retaliated again and again until the tigers couldn't hold them off anymore. The lions have now been in a position of royalty and dominance long enough that even the stupid humans have begun to call them kings."

"Sojóma led the last war against the lions about eight or nine years ago, but he didn't manage to win back redemption for your species," Shrey interjected.

Somila shot him an irritated look. "Don't interrupt, Shrey."

"Sorry," he replied.

"Anyway," Somila continued, "We refer to Sojóma as our rajah, our king, but outside of our community and allies, he has as little authority and respect as a regular old leopard."

"Hey!" Shrey yelled at her.

"Oh, shut your jaws, Shrey. You know that tigers are the biggest, most powerful cats in the world. Our inability to regain dominant ruling power against the lions has shamed our species. Not that leopards are shameful, but they have no claim to dominance in the wild cat world."

I glanced at Shrey, afraid he'd be offended. He met my gaze and gave a shrug.

"She has a valid point," he said.

"So," she whispered, glancing surreptitiously around her quickly before continuing, "to sum it all up: lions are undeserving, pompous power thieves that have shamed our species to the whole world."

I kept quiet. This was very important information for me to understand and adopt if I was ever going to fit into the community and wild world, however long that was. The day was almost over and it had been packed with fear and anxiety. Now I felt the need to relax and decompress.

We crossed the stream to the little beach, where Somila lay down by the water and yawned as Shrey fell beside her. I sat on my back two legs, and then feeling awkward, I laid down too, my tail trailing in the water.

"It's almost time for the moon to appear," Somila said.

"How can you tell?"

"All the animals grow louder," she whispered.

I listened intently, and sure enough, all the birds, frogs, even monkeys were making an enormous racket. I wanted to cover my ears, but I focused on the sound of the river and our breathing, pushing the racket out of my main focus. With the sounds in the background, it kind of reminded me of the city, which made me feel better. It explained why the city was called the urban jungle, among other things.

The sky darkened progressively, as did certain sounds of different animals. However, the frogs only grew louder. Shrey and Somila heaved themselves to their feet and yawned, exposing their long, rather purplish tongues in the moonlit darkness.

"You need to claim a sleeping spot," said Somila.

"And I need to go back across the river," Shrey said.

"Good night," I said before I could stop myself.

Shrey paused, glanced up at the sky, looked back at me and replied, "I guess it is a good night. I'll... see you tomorrow."

We two tigers watched the leopard splash across the river and disappear into the brush on the opposite bank. We turned our tails to the stream and waded through dark, semi-wet leaves and grasses, the scent of my new species growing stronger with every step we took.

We reached the Sanctuary, Calouise already asleep in his righteous spot and many other tigers hidden in the darkness, the sound of their slow, even breathing alerting to me to their slumber. Others hunted in the dark, sliding among the shadows in search of unsuspecting prey.

Somila headed right, leaving me to find my own sleeping space. I continued forward, searching for a section of long grass that wasn't very damp. Of course, this was mostly impossible. I felt like the only kid at camp without a bunk. A very warm, wet, noisy summer camp. Eventually, I curled up beside a large rock wall in long, cool grass. I remembered that this was supposed to be my vacation, and I rolled my eyes. Vacations were supposed to be relaxing and enjoyable. So far, this trip had been nerve-racking and potentially dangerous. I was in grass and dirt, a raw bird digesting in my intestines. But I knew that there was no going back now. I had made the leap across the canyon and this other side had so many mysteries that I knew I wouldn't gain anything by going home. Not yet.

I had never spent the night as a tiger before. The fearful portion of my personality wondered if I would turn back into a human in my sleep, but the rational side of myself reminded me that I had mastered control of my ability to transform weeks ago. I'd spent the whole day as a tiger.

Why would the electrical currents within decide to go haywire while I slept? I was betting that they wouldn't with my life.

I didn't know what tomorrow would bring, but the little bit of fear I felt was nothing compared to the intriguing prospects of what I would discover. I had found an entire new world, a new society, and I almost felt excited to face whatever was next. But first, I needed to sleep.

I forced myself to think of nothing, to shut down my mind and body. And eventually, the sound of frogs helped me find sleep, as if I was listening to cars from my fourth-story apartment.

A few rather mundane days later, after hours spent soaking in the stream and lazy conversations, my naptime slumber was disturbed as my sixth sense kicked in. My mind registered the fact that I was being watched, and I jerked awake. I squinted in the light beaming through the tree canopies and glanced around. Twenty feet away sat Calouise, his dark eyes fixed on my form. I felt uncomfortable under his scrutinizing gaze, so I yawned. Then, feeling like there was no reason to be intimidated by him, I stared straight back at him, right into his black pupils. His eyes widened then contracted. Calouise stood and turned his glare away from me, walking away into the forest. If I possessed more confidence, I would have gone after and confronted him, but I was lacking such confidence.

Instead, since I was now awake, I labored to my feet and headed to my left, which I believed was northeast. I hadn't ventured this way yet, and my curiosity was snagged.

I hadn't gone very far when I caught an unfamiliar scent. My immediate instinctive response was to growl, but I held back. All the fur around my neck was standing up. Something that didn't belong lurked behind the bushes.

My adrenaline-driven bravery overpowered my fear, and a snarl escaped my jaws as a yellow, grass-colored cat face appeared in my path.

LION SPIES

Sojóma's first rule was to take action and to chase this cat out. I growled from deep in my chest and crouched low, exposing my teeth. The lioness simply looked away and continued to pass by me, ignoring my unfriendly gesture.

As she inched by, I took a step toward her and snarled. She paused for a second, flicked her tail, and continued on. Claws pushed to the surface of my paws, and I decided to confront this trespasser.

"What are you doing here?" I hissed.

"I am simply passing through," she replied. Her tone implied that this was merely an excuse, and she was on some other mission. Her voice was slightly raspy, and it contained a heartless luster.

"Liar."

She stopped and turned to face me, full profile.

"What did you say?" she asked, her eyebrows raised and danger lingering on the edge of her words.

"Why are you really here?" I pressed. I was full of too much adrenaline and confidence to back down now. This lioness was just another Shianne.

"*That* is none of your business."

"Yes, it is. This is a lion-free territory. It's a jungle and not a savanna. Your so-called title 'King of the Jungle' means nothing here. I suggest you leave."

I had touched a nerve; she hissed. "We've won the right to rule the animal world. You can't claim it. So back down, I'm coming through." Her words were tinted with a menacing threat as she stepped forward.

"No. I won't let you." I stood firm and solid, like a wall.

Now she growled. "Try and stop me." She turned away and sprinted off.

I sprang after her, lunging forward to jump over bushes and between trees. For a tiger, I was fast, but she ran faster. I forced my strength to pump into my legs as I stretched myself out, bounding through the jungle rather than sprinting.

Halfway through my chase, I sensed another cat keeping pace with me, just out of my sight. I glanced left, searching for who it might be. One glimpse of stripy fur. I looked back ahead toward the lioness. She veered right, and I switched directions at break-neck speed, consolidating all my power into my leap across the corner she had just made.

My aim was beautiful—I was set to land on her tail, but I collided with the other tiger and crashed into a tree. I jumped to my feet and bared my teeth at this other cat who had ruined my attack.

It was Calouise. He was glaring at me, crouching low to continue the chase. I gave him one quick snarl and then sprinted after the lioness.

Our collision had only lasted a few seconds, but she was now far ahead. I bounded after her, gaining speed and ground but feeling a sharp pain in my chest. I refused to slow down, pushing myself forward. I could see her whole body now . . . she was one giant leap away ... I prepared to pounce and ...

She froze.

I soared over her and into the stream. Her satisfied expression lingered in my mind as I scrambled, sopping wet, onto the bank. She was ten feet away, watching me gasp as I stared at her like a begging puppy. I felt defeated and cheated. But I wasn't going to completely give up.

"I must say that you can run. You're smaller than that Cal cat, but you have more strength. Still, you couldn't catch me."

I wanted to tear her smug face off. "Get out of here before I *do* catch you."

"You're too tired to even jump at me. But, you're not the only cat in here. I have my own matters to attend to. Just remember that my species is superior to yours, and that it should be *me* telling *you* to leave this jungle." She turned to leave.

"You're only superior by circumstance, and one day, that'll change," I murmured after her.

She flipped around and roared—screamed—at me. I considered returning the gesture, but before I could act, Calouise sprang from the bushes and clawed her back. She hissed and snarled, moving out of reach of his exposed claws and teeth.

I found enough energy to roar back at her. She pounced at me, and I mustered every little bit of power I contained to stand on my hind legs and bat her down, my paws shoving at her head, claws scraping down the left side of her face.

She thudded down, landing on her side, blood from the gashes dripping down her face. After scrambling to her feet, she gave an anguished hiss and said, "This isn't over," before scrambling away, disappearing between the various undergrowth.

I was back on all fours, and I drew in ragged breaths. Calouise stood perfectly still five feet away, staring at me intently again.

"Where did... you come from?" I asked him.

He paused before replying, "The bushes."

If my mind and body weren't so exhausted, I would have replied with deep-rooted sarcasm. "Back where you started chasing her, where did you come from?"

"I saw her running and didn't see you, so I chased her."

"I discovered her; she was mine to chase out." Somewhere deep within me, there was a well of relief and gratitude for his interference. On the surface, though, I only felt cheated. I had discovered her—it was my responsibility to deal with her.

"I didn't see you," he repeated with a single blink. "It was a mistake."

For a brief second, I was astonished. Calouise, the Jungle Prince, had just admitted a mistake. I also registered the fact that he didn't apologize for it.

"Next time, let me try on my own. If you realize I'm in pursuit, let me finish." I couldn't prove I was worthy to live in the jungle if I always depended on help.

He watched me for a two whole seconds before nodding and prowling away. He was not a man—cat—of many words.

I drug myself along the stream bank all the way to the beach where I found Somila lounging. A single ray of sunshine illuminated her face in the late afternoon. Once she sensed me approaching, her eyes drifted to my sagging form before I collapsed onto the dirty sand. I didn't have the energy to even gulp water from the stream beside me.

"What happened?" Her words sounded casual and curious, as well as totally unconcerned.

"There was a lion… she was intruding… I chased her and… Calouise ran into me… the lion and I fought shortly and now… she's gone." Air wouldn't satisfy my lungs after I sucked it in. I was beginning to feel light-headed.

"What? There was a lion? A female one? What did she look like?" Somila asked with sudden urgency, leaning towards me.

"I don't know. Yellow? Brown? She looked like a lion."

"Did she say anything to you?"

"Yeah… she said that the we had no right to rule or have authority and that they'd won it over a fight. She also said I was fast."

Somila hissed. "Who cares if you're fast? It matters that she was *here* and that she mentioned the title. Did you say anything to her?"

I gulped with fear. Had there been something I shouldn't have said? "I told her to leave and when she didn't, I said she didn't belong here. I called her a liar and said her that their title and authority meant nothing to us … um … yeah."

"After that?"

"She got mad at me and ran. So I chased her."

Somila rolled her eyes. "Where is she now?"

"After Calouise attacked her and I smacked her to the ground, she took off. She's gone."

I could tell Somila was really thinking hard because her face was all scrunched up.

"Oh yeah," I said, remembering a small detail. "She said, 'This isn't over' before she ran off."

Somila jumped up and said, "Follow me," before hurrying towards the Sanctuary. I struggled after her, my legs sore and wobbly. She marched right up to Calouise in his almighty spot and faced him with a determined scowl.

"Mix says you saw the lioness."

Calouise glanced at me and nodded.

"Who was it?" Somila demanded.

"Zoriach," he replied without any hesitation.

Somila gave a snarl and turned away from Calouise, heading back toward the stream.

The name seemed to hold some significance that had angered Somila, but I was afraid to ask what it meant. She hurried forward, plunging into the rushing water, crossed to the other side, and then began to run. I don't think she registered the fact that I had been running *a lot* today, and I simply couldn't run anymore. A rumbling groan escaped as Somila's tail disappeared between two leaves ahead of me. She'd left me alone, on the leopard side, tired and unable to run. How nice.

The many trees blocked the partially sunny sky from view. Birds twittered on the branches, searching for grubs or watching me with a wary eye.

I stumbled along, racing a slow-moving lizard in the branches convoluting above me. I felt no pride based on the fact that I won by a whisker.

And then my whole world turned upside down in a blur of green and white. Once I righted myself, I focused on my attacker. Shrey was flat on his back, laughing so hard that the birds had taken flight, squawking in annoyance. I watched their vibrant bodies and colorful wings soar away while Shrey settled down.

If he were human, tears would have been streaming down his face. But since he was a leopard, he simply shook his head and looked at me, his eyes bright like fireflies.

"Sorry, Mix," he said, holding back a laugh. "It was just too good an opportunity to pass up. That'll most likely be the only time I ever take down a tiger on my own."

"Glad to be a part of the 'honor,'" I said, rolling my eyes.

His whiskers twitched with a smile.

Somila appeared from my left and sat stiffly before us, her eyes shrewd.

"We have much to discuss, so stop fooling around."

Shrey and I looked at her, all humor gone.

Somila looked at Shrey before saying, "Mix had an encounter with Zoriach."

His eyes grew wide. "She was here? But why? She's already the source of our shame and reason for the world's lack of respect."

"Your guess is as good as mine," Somila replied.

Silence drifted upon us as they pondered. I was hesitant to speak my thoughts, but I knew I needed to be bold. I took one deep breath, which was shaky, and said, "Maybe… she was on the lookout for another spurt of fighters hoping to overturn the odds."

I could see their raised eyebrows and silent, thoughtful expressions as they considered this. My idea was shot down by Somila.

"It would make sense if it weren't for her spies."

"Spies?"

"Yes. She's sly and paranoid. Her fear of losing power and authority has pressured her into setting up spies all over the jungle, keeping tabs on anyone who shows signs of starting a revolution."

"What are her spies?" I asked, glancing around the tree-tops.

"Mostly birds. Some bugs travel with news and fish messengers swim through channels of water to deliver their tidings. I'm sure there're snakes and apes we *can't* trust as well," Shrey said gravely.

A creeping sensation rose up my neck. I could feel invisible eyes watching me.

"Do we have spies on them?" I asked.

"We have some birds that carry frogs over to watch for longer periods of time before birds return and bring them back. They all report to Sojóma," Somila replied.

I felt a tiny bit reassured to know we weren't blind.

"Zoriach must be anxious to come check on us herself. She must expect trouble," Somila said curiously.

"Has there been a hint of preparing to fight again?" I inquired. "She might have a reason to be paranoid."

"No one has thought of challenging her clan in a long time. Not since we lost eight years ago," Shrey replied.

I didn't even pause to think—like I should have—before saying, "Maybe it's time for a revolution. Let's reclaim and redeem our ruling power."

Both sprang to their feet and shushed me before staring around as if waiting for someone to swoop down and attack us.

"One whiff and she'll launch an attack," Somila said quietly, sitting down again.

I was no expert, but I felt Somila could be just as paranoid as Zoriach. I looked at Shrey, who was staring at the ground. Neither seemed willing to talk about the idea of fighting.

The sky and surrounding forest were growing dark. I stood and, after one glance back, started toward the tiger side and Sanctuary. A feeling of boldness and longing to be accepted combined to form an overwhelming power of wanting to make a stand. The instinct of authority, the new circumstances, and the building power were driving my mind to the conclusion of a revolution to strip the illusion of power and superiority from the lions. I hadn't been in the jungle or wild world very long, but the encounter with Zoriach had shifted something within me. Her complete refusal to acknowledge me with any kind of respect just because of my species had lit some small flame of rebellion. But it seemed that everyone in this jungle was too skittish and afraid to even talk about the idea of revolting. The human within me—Jade— reminded me that this entire cat civil war could be forgotten and left behind with a relatively simple decision.

However, as a powerful tiger slowly becoming accustomed to and integrated into this world, I was intrigued and kindled with rebellious fire. Zoriach's condescending attitude and words still echoed in my head: *my species is superior to yours.* In reality, it wasn't a simple decision at all.

I felt stuck in the bitter situation.

The stream was glittering in the pale moonlight that filtered through the canopy. It washed along in a soothing manner, light reflecting off the surface in a mesmerizing fashion. I did not want to disturb this flowing ebb of water on its peaceful track through the jungle. As I thought of this, I understood how Somila felt. She didn't want to ruin the society that was flourishing without quarrel in this small part of the world.

Sighing, I crossed the river and looked back. Ripples from my body spread away from the initial disturbance until washed downstream and out of sight. I was sure that Somila was afraid of the ripple effect. It would take a long time for the damage of a feud to wash away. I could see it with any war.

When I found my sleeping spot, Calouise was waiting there. He sat majestic and tall, still like the calm before the storm.

"What do you want?" I asked him, starting to grow annoyed by his strange staring and appearances.

"To talk," he said simply.

I stood baffled. Calouise was the 'strong but silent' guy. He didn't say much, but he wanted to *talk*. I didn't feel this conversation would go far.

"About?"

"Zoriach."

"What about her?" Suddenly, I was curious. There perhaps was a cat who was willing to talk about Zoriach and the problem that she was.

"She needs to be challenged."

I was completely taken by surprise. I sat down and stared at him in shock.

"Why?"

He didn't even take time to think about it first. "It's been too long since a fight, and we deserve the superiority. It was ours to begin with."

It was the most words I had ever heard him speak at once, and they were filled with power and passion.

"I agree."

"Do you?" It was his turn to be surprised.

"Yes, but Somila and Shrey don't. They're too afraid."

"There's no need for fear. It's a chance for redemption, authority, and glory."

Glory. This was the most interesting conversation I had enjoyed in a long while, not the least of which for conversing with a male tiger in a jungle in India.

"Tell them that," he said simply after my lengthy silence.

"Yeah," I replied quietly. "I will."

He stood and prowled away without another word.

GUTS, GUYS, AND GLORY

I couldn't get the idea of glory out of my head for days. In reality, it was more likely closer to a full week before I mustered the guts to bring up the idea of revolution once more. I spent those days bonding with Somila and Shrey, which only made it more difficult to decide when to puncture our blossoming friendship with the weight of Calouise's words that I carried. I myself didn't fully understand where the foolish bravery and desire to fight for a title I had never owned manifested from. Spending my time as a tiger seemed to be getting easier and more comfortable, which could have been a reason why I felt a compulsion to challenge the condescending lions. Every day I walked on all fours and perceived the world from the tiger's point of view. I spent most of my time among my new friends, their habits affecting me in ways I didn't even realize yet.

I was starting to think like I was only a tiger. And I wasn't sure if this was something I truly wanted. But I knew it wasn't something I completely opposed. I was functioning in a new world and it was much too interesting to forgo. I would have to accept whatever consequences came along with it for the time being, including thinking like a true tiger and partaking in the rituals that accompanied living in this wild world.

When I finally confronted Somila and Shrey about the idea of revolution—after many troubling, silent encounters with an expectant Calouise—I told them what Calouise had said to me.

"Why can't you just leave it alone?" Somila hissed at me.

"We're tigers. It's a part of who we are—to feel empowered, to question any authority that claims to be above us. Obviously, Zoriach is not considered worthy to be called 'King of the Jungle.' Fearing her, remaining under her shadow, makes us cowards," I said, attempting to reason with her.

"It doesn't matter how I feel. I'd rather live. You haven't heard the stories. Many tigers and leopards died the last time we were in open war with the lions. And we *lost*. You are not our ruler or leader. So please drop this topic and move on."

Shrey seemed unsure. "Mix has a point," he said quietly to Somila.

She turned and snarled at him, her teeth exposed in vicious anger. "We challenge Zoriach, and we die. Get it?"

The two of us nodded in fear of losing a limb. But deep down inside, I still had the nagging sensation that something had to be done.

Somila and I went for a walk in the early part of the afternoon. We strolled along the edge of the river northwards. Strange red-leafed plants grew in bunches along the riverbank. I was trying to pay attention to the scenery, but Somila kept stealing my attention to gossip. I guess every girl has the need to gossip, no matter what species.

"Mix? Are you even listening to me?"

Her annoyed voice penetrated my concentration on the very strange red plant. The vibrancy of the red reminded me of the blood dripping down Zoriach's face the day I scraped my claws across it.

"What?"

She sighed.

"Seriously. What did you say? I'll pay attention."

She gave me one skeptical look before saying, "How many times have you actually spoken with Calouise?"

I tried really hard not to roll my eyes. "Only a couple of times."

She glaringly searched my face for some hint of a lie, but I had nothing to hide. I guess she didn't detect any secrecy because she gave a hearty sniff and continued the gossip. "Calouise and I have a … a history."

A history! This was beginning to feel like high school. "Really, how so?"

She watched a colorful frog hop across our path before answering. "Well, it was a lot like chasing each other. I'd show interest, and then he'd show interest and so on. Of course, he's above my station. He's the 'Prince of the Jungle' and I'm what you'd call—"

"A peasant?"

"Exactly."

I'd sensed some of this my first day here when Calouise had walked across the river and Somila had spoken defensively for him against Shrey.

"So are you still playing chasing games?" I asked.

"No. Not really. He, or rather *I*, lost interest."

Now I really did roll my eyes—it seemed the appropriate response to such a trifling conversation. The many games and attempts to uphold certain reputations in regard to relationships was not something novel. It was rather mundane and somewhat petty, at least from my perspective, to pretend that what had happened didn't occur.

"What do you think of him?" she asked me.

There it was: the defining question. My answer would define what kind of friend or enemy I was to her. But in all honesty, I wasn't really sure. My first impression of mean and haughty had been replaced with mysterious in the way he always seemed to be silently staring at me, like he was sizing me up. Or estimating my abilities. Or judging how well I was fitting in.

"He's strange and quiet," was all I could say.

"Yes...," she replied, her eyes out of focus. "And strong, too."

I felt the urge to roll my eyes and laugh at the same time. The river gurgled past, dull under the grey sky. The air was full of monkey calls, bird chatter, and bug sounds. It had taken a short amount of time to become accustomed to the constant vibrations of the jungle.

"Mix, I have a flea."

I gave her a perplexed glance. Fleas were common of house dogs and cats. Were they common on tigers too? I immediately felt a crawly, biting sensation on random patches of my body.

"Just one flea? Don't they come in groups?"

Her raised brows expressed confusion in response.

I suddenly felt stupid. Was this a tiger idiom I needed to learn? "Why don't you tell me about this ... this flea?"

Her puzzled look morphed into one of resignation. "He's been obsessed with me for about a month now."

"Who's he?" I asked, realizing that this flea may not be, truly, an actual biting insect.

"His name is *Jasper*. He thinks he's sneaky when he's following me, but I've caught him on many occasions."

"I haven't seen him yet," I said, glancing around surreptitiously.

"Jasper is very sneaky," she said simply.

We both paused in our stroll along the river and listened to the sounds around us. I pinpointed several frogs in the surrounding bushes, but nothing to suggest we were being followed by a stalker tiger.

"He's not here now," Somila commented, "but keep yourself aware and you'll see him soon enough."

I was barely paying attention. We were close to the Sanctuary. Calouise's spot was empty, but that didn't surprise me. He was a roamer, quiet and stealthy, observing alone, his presence troubling.

That's when I noticed that I couldn't see anyone. It looked like the Sanctuary was deserted, but I could sense the other tigers nearby. They were hiding, not just camouflaging, but truly hiding out of sight. From what? I wasn't sure, but I suddenly grew very apprehensive. The sudden silence of the jungle around us was unnerving. I crouched to the ground and slid along on my belly, creeping along the jungle floor.

"Mix! Hide!"

The urgency in the voice caused me to spring up and leap toward a tree. I curled myself into a ball at its base and held my breath, eyes and ears peeled for the danger.

A few moments later, a rushing sound and annoying bird caws flew in with the wind. A couple seconds more and the jungle was rent with cawing, flapping, black birds swooping in all directions. Crows circled trees, dived to the ground, swooped through grass. It was some kind of organized mayhem.

In all the commotion, a snake fell from a tree and landed with a thud and hiss on my back. I leapt up in shock and fear, the snake sliding from my back to the forest floor, and I was out in the open as the crows screeched around me. They were so loud and annoying, obscuring my vision as they spiraled in all directions. Amongst their incessant caws I could hear their words spinning around me. *Weak. Inferior. Long reign the lions. Cowardly. Menial. Remember your place. Rebellious. Insubordinate. Man-eaters and insurgents.* These stranger birds were invading the Sanctuary, our home, and hurling insults at us while we crouched and hid in obvious fear. I knew we did not deserve this—but at the same time, we were exactly what they called us if we remained hidden and afraid. I didn't know what would result if I reacted against these monstrous birds, but impatience and anger overlapped my anxiety, and I began swatting at them, roaring when they dropped like rocks to the ground.

When eight crows lay either injured or dead around me, the remaining simultaneously joined together in an organized rank and flew off, cawing until they were far enough away that we couldn't hear them anymore. I stood panting as other cats emerged into the open. Black feathers littered the ground around me.

Everyone was looking at me in surprise. Then some tiger I'd never met yelled, "Yeah! That was some hard-core retaliation!"

"Shut your jaws, Jasper," hissed Somila.

"Why? It's time Zoriach finally saw some rebellion. We're obviously all too scared to act, but Mix isn't."

I stared at him, unsure what exactly he meant. I had simply decided not to take insults from a bunch a birds. I hadn't considered that Zoriach had sent them herself.

Somila growled.

"It was courageous. One step toward glory," said a deep voice I had no trouble recognizing.

"Yes. That took some guts," said Jasper, nodding his big orange head.

"Wait. Those crows were Zoriach's?" I asked, hoping for clarification. I'd heard one of them screech *long reign the lions*, but I had assumed that they simply supported their rule, not deployed by the ruler.

"Yes. She sends them once and awhile to scare us and see who's crazy enough to rise up and retaliate," replied Somila, something like a warning coming from her strained voice.

I wanted to feel fearful that I may have jump started the crazy cat war, but all that registered on my emotion track was anticipation. A few faces looked pleased at my actions—like Calouise, who had appeared from nowhere yet again, and Jasper's—but others looked angry and afraid. Somila's was both scared and furious.

"This isn't the time to become noble. Zoriach is obviously worried if she's made a personal visit and sent a swarm of crows to check on us. We need to lay low for awhile or she's going to come at us hard and wipe us out." Somila glared at me. "You're still a newbie. You need to be careful. You can't just come here and start a self-righteous rebellion against *our* enemies. It's not too late for us to kick you out."

The adrenaline-charged anticipation was wearing off. I was beginning to feel fear and now rejection. I had spent so much time trying to fit in, and now I was becoming a threat.

"I'm sorry," I mumbled.

"Don't be sorry because their ears are back," Calouise said.

I looked around. He was right. Most of the ears on the cats around me were flattened to the tops of their heads.

"Look, let's just lay back and keep quiet for awhile. We've shown some rebellion, now we can let it stew. Let's not be hasty or stupid," Shrey said very calmly.

Somila was more than willing to agree, I felt compelled to agree, and Calouise only agreed with a surly growl.

The crowd of tigers dispersed. Those who were proud gave sanctimonious nods before leaving, and Somila glared before turning her back on me. Eventually, it was just Shrey and I left facing each other in the relative quiet.

I felt void of all emotions; they were locked up somewhere for now to revisit at a later date. Instead, I stared blankly at Shrey, unable to even feel my legs.

"So…," I began, desperate to break the silence.

He said nothing.

"What do you think? … About all this?"

He rolled his neck from side to side and peered at me. "I'm not sure."

"So you're … not mad at me?" I asked hopefully, my voice higher than usual.

"No ... I'm not upset. But I'm not necessarily happy with you either."

I nodded. I could accept that ... I hoped. After a lengthy silence, I turned to leave, but he stopped me with a question.

"Do you believe in fate?"

I could feel my brow furrowing—I *hated* these kinds of questions. The deep, philosophical ones that could take a lifetime to sort out.

"Why?"

He shrugged. "I was just thinking that maybe you're here for a reason."

If anyone had asked me the same question a few months ago, I would have gave them a stone cold 'no.' However, somehow, my transformation and move to India seemed to be revealing something greater to me. This wild world, the oppression from the lions, the simmering feelings of rebellion—they were all new and very compelling. Perhaps some larger force like fate was propelling me forward. Realizing this—almost understanding and accepting this—scared me, as if I wasn't in control of my path through life anymore.

Or had I chosen my destiny by coming to India? A destiny to play a part in the war between tigers and lions that could win them—us— back the graces of respect and royalty.

"Then again, maybe this is all just a coincidence," he said when I didn't reply.

Could that be true, too? Was it simply coincidence that right after I arrived and decided to stay Zoriach appeared? Was it pure chance that Zoriach's arrival and my collision with her had pushed the concept of revolution to the forefront of everyone's minds? Even for me, that seemed unlikely. Like an echo, I could hear my mother's number one excuse for everything that happened in our lives: everything happens for a reason.

I wanted to shake my head. It was all too much.

"Can you believe in fate if you believe in coincidence?" I asked him, partially serious, but also joking, attempting to lighten the mood.

A smile shot across his face. "Can you believe in choice if you believe in destiny?"

It was as if he was in my head.

Shrey walked away without another word. I made my way to my sleeping spot, relatively oblivious to the golden light beaming through the canopy. My mind was befuddled by Shrey's troubling words. This was the exact reason that I hated philosophy. It called into question morals, beliefs, and character. It challenged the core of your being.

I slumped to the ground and spent the rest of the evening trying to clear my head, but to little avail. Instead of thinking about philosophy, I ended up thinking about how I didn't feel like myself anymore. I wasn't the sassy, fearful, *city* girl anymore. I was more methodical, brave, and emotional now. But I couldn't decide if this was good or bad, and my brain was too exhausted to consider the pros and cons of each new trait. Eventually, I drifted to sleep under the influence of frog lullaby.

It took me a few moments to realize why I felt so worried when I awoke. But then I remembered that I had made an outright move of rebellion, and that had caused unease and anger in my fellows. This had me worried about rejection and the threat of an attack from Zoriach. A little bubble of happiness came along as I thought of Calouise, Shrey, and Jasper, who were all on my side. That was until I realized they were all males—all equipped with a Y chromosome and wired with a desire to fight.

Lie low. That's what everyone had agreed to last night. With the threat of rejection and war looming over my head, I figured that it would be best to not start a new fight in the lion versus tiger century-old battle.

After the damage I had caused from the night before, I decided it would be best to avoid Somila. She would surely still be angry with me, and after the befuddling conversation with Shrey yesterday, I figured I should leave him alone, too. I did not want the company of Calouise even though he supported me. I had no desire to deal with his weirdness. There were no other tigers I was on speaking terms with aside from Sojóma, and he wasn't the type of cat I could just go see and have a conversation with.

Feeling quite alone, I heaved myself to all fours and padded out randomly into the jungle. I thought of home and my tabby cat, who must have thought I abandoned her, and Sara, who might been have wondering where I was and when I was coming back. I'd been gone about two and a half weeks. The scary thing was that I had no desire to return home. Portland and college all seemed like a distant dream. Unreal, fantasy, a former life. My experience as a tiger in the jungle seemed so much more a reality to me. This crazy, magical, *unreal* event that had happened to me felt truer than my human life. This realization brought me up short. It terrified me to realize that I was okay with living as a tiger and not going home.

I needed a shrink.

If my thoughts and decisions were this messed up, then my brain needed help. But seeing a psychiatrist would require returning to

America and paying a bunch of money that should go towards student loans. Better to be unstable and live like a wild animal in the jungle.

My brain was fine.

Suddenly, my sixth sense picked up on something. I could feel it watching me. But I could tell that whatever it was meant no harm. The energy it possessed was not tense.

But I was still new at this.

"Who's there? And what do you want?" I demanded.

Some bushes behind me rustled and a tiger emerged. I recognized him from the night before.

"Jasper?" I asked, my brows scrunched together.

"Yes?" he replied tentatively, like a kid caught spying on his parents.

"Why are you stalking me?"

"I'm not stalking ... just observing our new, fearless warrior."

"Hang on a minute. Number one: I'm *not* fearless. Two: I'm no warrior. Three: following and watching someone without them knowing *is* stalking."

"What do you mean you're not fearless? Yesterday you started a rebellion, and a few days before you chased Zoriach and threatened to fight her."

Perhaps in those moments of adrenaline I hadn't felt fear, but I sure as hell felt it now.

"Look, Jasper, I'm not starting a rebellion. It's not safe—and it's not my intention."

"Why? Because of what Somila says? Let me tell you something about Somila: she's nice, but a complete coward. If you asked her to talk to Calouise, she'd never do it."

I frowned. "She talked to him the day Zoriach appeared."

He didn't skip a beat. "That was because she was worried and angry. If you want her on your side and ready for action, she has to be riled up and thrown into it. If she thinks about it too long, she goes all girly and backs down."

Go all girly? Was he implying something about me or girls in general? "If you like her so much, why do you point out all her flaws?"

Jasper gave me a clear quizzical look. "Like her?"

"She told me you stalk *her*."

His shoulders rose and fell. "Like I said, she's nice… and she has a sleek coat."

I rolled my eyes and began to turn away from him. Now he sounded like the typical guy.

"Wait! Don't go just because I said she looks nice. You look nice, too."

I shot him a fierce skeptical look over my shoulder.

"You do," he insisted. "You're strong, like a weapon."

I wasn't sure whether I should be flattered or offended. I could be a 'weapon.' What was that supposed to mean? "Look, I don't want to be a weapon, and I don't want to be your 'girl.' Got it?"

He was immediately on the defensive. "I didn't … I never said *anything* about having a girl. What gives you that impression?"

"Let me see… the compliments and praise, pointing out Somila's flaws and then my attributes, more compliments, acting all defensive, stalking me. They're all indicators."

"You females always read too much into everything."

I began to walk away.

"I just wanted to be friends. You looked like you needed company," he called after me.

"Thanks, but no thanks." I headed for the water, making sure I gave the beach a wide berth as to avoid Somila and Shrey.

I felt as if I had burned all my bridges. Somila and Shrey were no longer, for the time being, my good friends, I'd just blown off Jasper, and there was really no one else left. It reminded me of the time Sara and I didn't talk for a month in high school over a guy that was not so good for her, but she refused to listen. Thinking of Sara and home was a reminder that I had somewhere to go back to if I wished. But was that what I really wanted—to cut ties, count my losses, and go home?

Nothing was waiting for me at home. Sara had Jack, my mother was traveling as usual, and school would always be there. But this world, being a tiger, had so much to offer—opportunities to rebuild myself, to be brave, to make a difference, to transform my personality in addition to my physical form. Those opportunities had so much potential that I didn't *want* to go home yet, despite the uncertain situation I found myself in. I'd need to find a way to rebuild the bridges I'd managed to burn.

I would let things play out, staying among the tigers longer. Strangely enough, this didn't bother me too much. The fact that it didn't bother me bothered me more than anything else. I felt mixed up.

Oh, the irony.

I crossed through the water to the leopards' side and aimlessly wandered the terrain. Leopards—I'd come to learn—preferred to spend time in trees. They were considerably smaller than other 'big' cats, and the trees supported them as well as gave them an advantage against prey and other predators. Shrey probably spent more time on the ground than all the other leopards combined.

I began to pay attention to my surroundings when I rammed my head against a stone wall. Skull throbbing, I looked up. It was the plant covered wall we had walked along to see Sojóma. I jumped on top then leapt down to the other side. The one desecrated building was forlorn and crumbling. I decided I would stay here. It was a good solitary place to not worry about bothering anyone. Of course, just as I laid down, my stomach rumbled. It'd been a good week since I last ate. The fortunate part about being a tiger was I only felt the need to eat about once a week. I only had to kill something and swallow its raw remains once every few days. I still endured moments where the entire idea of it disgusted me to my core, but at least I didn't need to eat everyday like a dog or house cat. I would resist the urge to hunt for as long as possible. Some innocent creature still had a few hours to live.

I was growing comfortable in my solitude when a voice made me jump out of my fur and to my feet.

"Mix."

I spun around in a flash. "Who's there?" I called.

It was Sojóma, standing impressively on top of the wall with his vibrant, sleek coat aglow from the sun. My brain scattered: what was I supposed to do? Bow? Stay silent? Leave?

I stayed motionless and quiet as he descended the wall and stood right in front of me.

"I must say that it is nice to not have subjects constantly bowing in my presence."

Fear and shame turned my veins to ice. Was this his subtle way of saying I should show more respect or was he serious?

"I'm sorry, your majesty. I've been stepping out of line all over the place." I bowed my head.

"There's no need for an apology. Now, this stepping out of line … what exactly do you mean?"

As awkward as it seemed in my head to have this kind of conversation with the tiger King of the Jungle, I felt comfortable in his radiant presence.

"I'm sure you heard, but a week ago or so, Zoriach paid a visit. I chased her down. But I also said some things that could cause damage in the future."

"What did you say?" he asked calmly, lying down to be comfortable. I simply sat. The expression on his face seemed to reveal that he already knew what I had said and done. But I decided to humor him. He was the rajah, after all.

"I threatened her species and the crown." I waited for him to say something, but he remained silent, so I went on. "Somila and Shrey became anxious and paranoid, and when I mentioned the word 'revolution,' they silenced me with a threat of rejection. I felt the urge to fight for what is rightfully ours, but they told me it wasn't worth it. Calouise supports me. So does Jasper. Somila is terrified. And yesterday, when the crows flew through, I couldn't stand their insults and lies, so I swatted at them and killed a few. That was the last straw for Somila. She basically told me to back off or leave. So, in fear of being ejected from the jungle, I am here, in solitude, where I can't cause any damage." With the conclusion, I collapsed in exhaustion on the ground facing Sojóma, realizing I'd just overloaded the king with information.

He studied me before replying, "You are unknowingly brave. Bravery comes to you when you find yourself in a situation that calls on it. The others, those who are fearful of revolution for our benefit, have not found themselves in serious situations that require bravery. From seeing the actions you've performed from unconscious courage, I can only imagine what you're capable of if you consciously took action. You could be a valuable asset to our jungle."

I didn't like the implications of where this could be going. "It was a result of foolishness. I didn't know better. Besides, all the other cats are afraid of a fight."

"Sometimes it takes new circumstances and new blood to help them realize what's for the best." He gave me a searching look. "You certainly have both, but what remains is the final question: are you up to the task of leading them to revolution?"

He said exactly what I'd been afraid he'd say. And what was I supposed to say? 'Sorry, can't. I'm really a human from the city, and I'm already in way over my head.' That wouldn't be productive. I had already made the impossible decision to go to India and live in the jungle. I knew that I wanted to continue discovering what this world had to offer, as well as find out what I was capable of. So what was one more crazy decision in the scheme of things?

"Depends on if you can agree to support and guide me. I'm a newbie, and I wasn't always wild. I'm going to need help to push them toward battling." I didn't even realize the words I was saying until it was too late. It didn't help that his powerful presence was a source of intense pressure to impress him.

Sojóma smiled. "I'd be more than willing to help. I agree that it's time to put Zoriach in her place."

I felt more reassured. His willingness to talk to me, support me, and help me made me feel as if he was the father I'd always longed for. Someone who believed in me, even when I didn't believe in myself.

Funny, but this morning I had firmly decided to stay out of all this business. Now, I had just agreed to be the spark that would cause a wildfire. And now I felt like the weapon Jasper had mentioned to me earlier.

Oh, there was the irony once more.

It's astounding how fast the world can turn upside down.

We sat in silence for a few minutes, until my stomach rumbled and broke it.

"You need to hunt," Sojóma observed.

"I know. I just prefer to wait as long as possible."

His head tilted sideways in curiosity.

"I only eat when I have to. I don't enjoy killing the creatures of the jungle."

"That's an intelligent, kind decision, but it looks like you're reaching your 'long as possible' mark. I'll hunt with you, if you like."

"Don't you have servants who do that? Females?"

Sojóma gave me a fierce look. "You are confusing me with a lion."

"Oh … I'm sorry," I replied quickly.

"Forgiven. I actually enjoy hunting my own food. It allows me to traverse my domain and keep an eye on things."

My smile was lost in an echoing boom that vibrated the trees. It sounded like a gunshot. Both of us sprang to our feet and ran to the wall. Sojóma reacted faster than I did. He was already stationed on top of the wall by the time I clambered up.

"What was it?" I asked.

"Human." He said the word like it was poison in his veins. "A human with a machine meant to kill."

"Aren't we in a protected area?"

"Some humans are too greedy to abide by their own laws."

Translation: poachers.

"That was near the Sanctuary, wasn't it?"

"For certain," Sojóma replied in his deep voice.

"Should we—"

"Yes. Come with me." He jumped off the wall and began to run through the brush in one swift movement. I hastened to follow, sprinting with my four powerful legs to catch up to the king and assess the damage. When we reached the stream, he leapt over it and disappeared into the greenery on the other bank. Not wanting to mess up, I simply splashed through the cool water and left a wet trail behind as I entered the Sanctuary. Everyone was in a frenzy. The shot had rattled them, and they were all rushing to a specific spot. They all stood in a tight, many-layered circle. I had to push and shove and receive some snapping snarls to get to the front where I could see what was going on. I ended up between Sojóma and Somila, all of us staring at the tiger in front of us, his jaws clamped on a bloody human arm.

Jasper had ripped off the poacher's arm.

All the eyes of the tigers and leopards around us seemed to swivel onto Sojóma, waiting for his reaction and guidance. I could feel some of their eyes on me, too—even Jasper's.

And I thought about how terrifying it would be if he found out what I really was.

MAN EATER

Jasper's eyes were still black two hours later while we tried to talk to him. He seemed frenzied. His breathing was heavy, and he twitched often. And his black, dilated pupils reminded me of my cat when she would crouch into attack mode.

"Jasper, what happened? Why did you bite his arm off?" Sojóma demanded.

"He was human," Jasper replied hungrily, his pupils dilating further, which I thought was impossible. I suddenly grew scared. I had to make sure I didn't transform any time soon or I'd lose an arm or worse.

"What's wrong with him?" I whispered to Somila.

She shook her head.

"Did the man harm you?" Sojóma asked Jasper in a slow, deep voice.

"He tried to...but I took him down before he could hit me." Jasper met my eyes with his deep, black holes. "He tried to kill me, so I tried to kill him. The blood... so warm. The taste so... intoxicating." Some drool dribbled down the side of his mouth.

I no longer felt any desire to eat.

"Jasper. I want you to go drink water and then lie down in the stream to calm down. And to wash the blood out of your fur," Sojóma commanded.

Jasper licked his cheeks thoroughly and then did as he was told, his tail twitching as he walked away. Sojóma watched him with a frown.

"What's wrong with him?" I repeated.

"It's very rare," Sojóma replied without looking at me, "but some tigers develop the taste for humans, usually once they've tried them. It is much more common that tigers only attack humans because the tiger is old and weak and humans are easy prey. I'm afraid we're all going to have to keep a close eye on Jasper. The last thing we need is a war with the humans."

I suddenly found it very hard to swallow.

Sojóma turned to face me. "Weren't we just about to hunt before all this horror interrupted?"

I could feel Somila's eyes burning a hole in the side of my face.

"I… I actually don't feel hungry anymore." This was entirely true.

"If you don't eat, you'll be eaten. We may be at the top of the food chain, but scavengers will believe you're a delicacy if they find you passed out due to starvation."

"Go on, Mix. You don't want to be eaten, do you?" Somila asked mockingly. Our friendship was on thin ice.

"Alright, alright. I'll eat something."

"Some is better than none," Sojóma remarked.

I wondered if being poetic was part of the kingly job description.

We stayed on the tiger side of the water, hunting in a southern part of the jungle that I had yet to traverse. It was more or less the same as the rest of the jungle: trees, bushes, grass, and plenty of life. As Sojóma began to move slowly and stealthily, I had an urge to show off. Somila's and Shrey's reactions when I had caught the bird seemed to be a goal; I wanted praise from Sojóma for what I could accomplish, especially since he was expecting so much out of me.

I knew climbing a tree was out of the question. My bulk was too much for the tall and scrawny trees that were common here. I moved closer to the water where birds of prey liked to try and catch fish. Those birds were about to live up to their name. I crouched in the grass as quietly as I could and waited, remaining still for a large chunk of time. Just when I was about to give up and catch my own fish, a large brown bird landed and settled itself on a branch hanging just above the moving water. It was one giant leap away. If I made no mistakes, I could catch it.

The powerful blood of the tiger surged through my body, the electricity responsible for my condition charging my nerves so I could feel it for the first time in a while. My muscles tensed, my whiskers twitched, and my ear flicked at some distant noise behind me. I allowed no thoughts to distract me as I prepared to lunge.

"You're going to miss!" a voice screeched.

I leapt into the air, the bird squawked and took off, leaving some feathers, and I came crashing down into the river.

"I called it!" Somila yelled from the shore.

Submerged in the cool water, there happened to be a wriggling fish near my mouth, so I bit down to kill it. Irritated by my failure and Somila's sabotage, I walked up out of the river right beside Somila.

Sopping wet, I shook all of the water onto her. Then I dropped the fish and glared at her.

"Why are you here?" I demanded.

"I felt the urge to follow you."

"Why?"

It was a few moments before she surrendered the truth. "I... wanted to make you look bad for Sojóma."

I'd figured.

"I don't understand why he likes you so much," she added. "And Calouise has a thing for you, too."

"And Jasper," I added, in spite of myself. My irritation was too great to hold back.

She seemed surprised... and angry. "Jasper too? That's...that's... just so—"

"Unfair? Let me ask: why do you care?" I was about to fold my arms when I remembered I was on four legs. "Because you told me he was a flea. He was a stalker and annoying, but now that he favors me instead of you, you're jealous and mean?"

"I don't know what to say."

"Look, you don't have to worry because I don't care for Calouise or Jasper. You can have them both. Sojóma, on the other hand—"

"Paw," she interjected.

"Huh?"

"On the other *paw*. We don't have *hands*. That implies thumbs."

Had I really just said that? She was staring at me, one eye glaring. I attempted to move on from my slip up. "Sojóma and I are kind of working on something together. Plus, I like talking to him as his own...*cat* rather than king."

Somila's body language suggested she wanted to fold her arms too. Then I wondered what she would look like as a human. I imagined straight red hair and a pale face with golden eyes. And in the current setting, her eyebrows would be creating a very definable V as she stared at me.

"Listen, Somila. I'm not going to start a huge rebellion any time soon. But I encourage you to think about it. Your mind is safe from Zoriach and all her spies. Consider who you are, what you are, how you feel about her kind and their 'title' that should be ours. Consider how many allies we have, how many of us there are, and how well you think you could fight against Zoriach's cronies. Think about how good it would feel to say 'I'm king of the jungle and I proved it!' All I ask is that you think on it."

"What do you know? You're a newbie, raised in a zoo!"

"I know that I don't like being treated like a prisoner or dirt. I know that I feel powerful and that I have the right to be better than a lion. And I know that those who fight for a right that they deserve will conquer, even if they are lacking in numbers."

She was silent.

"I didn't come here with a plan to overturn your world. Things are just happening, and they're not all my fault. Think for a few days, and then we can talk." I paused. "And stay away from my food." I grabbed the now muddy fish in my jaws and walked away from her without another word. Her petty attempt to make me feel foolish was nothing compared to how I felt about playing a role in the upcoming revolution.

I needed more than Sojóma and Calouise's support to engender an emotional drive and desire to take Zoriach's title and pride in the tigers and leopards around me. Somila was going to be my greatest challenge. She was very strong in her fear, enough to ostracize me from the community to avoid any kind of confrontation with the lions.

When I reached the bushes, Sojóma appeared from behind one. I knew at once by his expression that he had listened to the whole conversation.

"That was a very moving speech," he complimented.

I only stared at him with the fish dangling from my mouth.

"If it ends up convincing Somila, then we should have no problem with any of the others."

I gave the tiniest of nods.

"I'll let you go enjoy your catch. We'll stay in contact, Mix. Relax into the many ebbs and energies of the jungle for a little while." Sojóma smiled and walked around me into the grasses and out of sight. I let the fish fall to the ground. It was caked in mud and covered in bits of tree. Despite my previous hunger, I really felt no inclination to eat the fish. It didn't smell appealing either. With a sigh, I left the fish behind, all trace of hunger gone. Sojóma must not have been ready to have me rile everyone up quite yet, which was fine with me. It would give me more time to figure how I was going to do it. In the meantime, I really needed something to preoccupy myself with.

The river was gurgling. I walked back through the grass to the bank. It was empty; Somila had left. I collapsed onto the muddy sand and stared at the light reflecting off the ever-changing water, which sparkled. Little dazzles of light blinded my eyes every few seconds. I couldn't look away, mesmerized by how much light I could perceive but how little color came through these eyes. I could see the water had a blue tint, but it was dull and unstable. The foliage around me was a collage of green shades but not really as vibrant as it would have been with my human eyes. I was able to appreciate the amount of plant life, but it wasn't the same.

Still staring at the water, I considered my human form and life, the elevated light levels and dull colors a reminder of what I now was. I'd spent several weeks as a tiger without any reversions to my human body. I wasn't particularly missing my human self, but I felt a curiosity to see what would happen if I tried to turn back. My tiger transformations had become increasingly easier and less painful and uncomfortable every time I had tried them during my attempts to test my abilities in the Oregon wilderness. Of course, I couldn't completely transform back into a human right in the middle of the jungle among cats and animals that knew me as a tiger. But I could try to only transform my paws back into hands.

I surreptitiously glanced around me, looking and listening for anyone who could possible walk up on me. I was relatively alone, with the exception of inattentive birds and other small creatures that I wasn't worried about. Carefully, slowly, I searched within me, consciously feeling for the nerve endings in my toes. They didn't reappear for a few moments—moments that began to feel like minutes as the fear set in. I couldn't find the tingling, electrical currents. Holding back the panic, I pulled further and harder, willing the currents to retract. They reappeared, prickling along my suddenly transformed fingers and hand as well as along my arm. I stared at my wrist where my striped fur transitioned to peachy skin, wiggling my fingers as the prickly sensations were wearing off. It had been difficult, but I had managed to do it. I could still go back to being a human if I needed—or wanted—to. I released the currents, and my paw and claws returned.

To pass my time, I took to stretching my neck so I could count my stripes instead. It was quite difficult; I could only see from my shoulders to my tail, so any stripes on my neck and head went unaccounted for. However, I did notice a clump of matted fur covered in dirt on my left paw, and before I could stop myself, I began to lick it clean. My tongue was like the scratchy, rough backside of a sponge used to scrub tough grime. It felt relatively pleasant on my fur, but I was sure it would feel as if barbs were being dragged across my skin if I licked my human arm.

As I groomed myself, a brief flurry of motion caught my eye. Someone on the opposite bank was sneaking very deceptively along the river. I paused, crouched lower, and watched carefully as a male tiger slid into the water and crossed to my side of the river without a single splash or barely a ripple. Just before he slipped out of sight, I realized it was Jasper. He was sneaking off in the direction of the humans. After the eventful morning, I knew he couldn't be up to any good. I didn't know whether to follow him alone or go find Sojóma. The odds of Jasper taking a simple stroll were low. And my hesitation had already given him a head start. If I could prevent something bad from happening, I might be able to win a few favors back.

I jumped to my feet and followed Jasper's scent. It was faint, and I really had to strain my nose, but I could detect it. A few minutes later, I had caught up to him. He wasn't moving fast, but he was definitely moving intently. His tail was twitching, his ears poised, his body and legs tense as he crept through the brush. I followed him all the way to the edge of the forest. It was late afternoon, the sun behind us, the village ahead a mile or two. He stared at the distant town, tail still flicking from side to side. He was thinking, calculating. There was only open, dusty grassland between us and the village. He had nowhere to hide if he decided to sneak up on the village. There was no way I was letting him ruin everything because he couldn't control his bloodlust. We didn't need a secondary war between humans and tigers. And I couldn't sit back and let Jasper make a poor name for us tigers as monsters. We were so much more than that.

He took a step forward.

I launched from my hiding place and scrambled forward to put myself between him and what lay ahead.

Upon my intercedence, his posture quickly transformed from the patient consideration to vicious attack mode. His teeth suddenly were bared, and he swatted at me with his clawed paws. I dodged and returned the gesture, knocking him upside the head. He gave a horrible snarl and glared at me with each eye like an abyss.

I gave my own aggressive growl and made sure my teeth were visible. He didn't back down. Instead, he took another threatening step forward. I slowly circled to his right side, his dark, wary eyes glued to me. I froze for a few seconds before I leapt at him. My jaw and paws rammed into his flank and knocked him to the ground. As he struggled to get up, I placed both my paws on his side, forcing him to stay on the ground, his breath staggered.

"Listen Jasper! I can't let you do this," I said angrily as he tried to snap at my leg.

"Who are you to stop me?" he growled. Any affection he'd had for me was gone.

"You can't attack the humans."

"Why not!?" he screeched.

"It's weak, Jasper!" I yelled as he tried again to shove me off. "Humans are weak and pathetic. They don't care about us. They're easy prey for the old and sick cats, but not for you. You and I are young and fit. We don't need to hunt them."

"I don't care!"

I pushed harder on his side, moving one paw to his throat. He coughed and sputtered under the pressure.

"Listen, you idiot!" I snarled. I had to make him grasp the concept, make him realize what kind of doom this would bring upon us if he went through with it. "You are making our whole species look weak! Do you understand? You're going to be the weak link if you go through with this."

He couldn't move his head, but his eyes swiveled to peer at me.

"I am not the weak link," he gasped.

"Then get your hide back to the Sanctuary and stay there!" I took my paw off his throat and eased up on his side. He slowly got to his feet, his left side matted with dirt and dust. I cautiously watched him as he glanced toward Ghukashi and then heavily padded back into the trees. A single sigh of relief escaped before I followed him.

The rest of the day was relatively uneventful after that, and I seriously doubted anything else could top my talk with Sojóma and Jasper's attempt to raid a human village. As the sky grew dark, some cats settled down and others rose to hunt in the darkness. Our eyesight was impeccably refined at night compared to the day due to our large pupils that allowed so much more light in. Thanks to my tiger eyes, I'd never be afraid of the dark again.

My mostly human brain still required me to sleep at night, so I curled up in my spot and welcomed the relaxation and relief of sleep.

I jerked awake, pulled from a deep sleep, as I was shaken and yelled at.

"Mix! Wake up! Hurry! We think Jasper's gone after the humans!"

I blinked once and saw the details of Somila's whiskers.

"Wait, what?" I asked a bit dazed. It was still dark—very dark, right in the middle of the night.

"Jasper's hunting humans!"

"No! He tried to do that this afternoon. I stopped him." I jumped to my feet and shook out my fur, forcing my blood to flow back into my numb legs and paws.

"Well, he's been gone awhile. It might be too late," Somila said as we took off into the forest.

"It can't be. We have to try."

"Calouise and Shrey and a few others are already after him."

"We have to hurry!" I pulled ahead and sped between the trees as fast as I could. My legs were still heavy from sleep, but I forced them to move, forced my paws to thud and pound against the earth. At the edge of the forest, I scanned the open land for any light color revealing a tiger or leopard. I couldn't see anything especially helpful. Somila caught up to me, very winded.

"I don't see anything," I said angrily.

"They're already... on the outskirts... of town," Somila said between breaths.

"Quick!" I took off again, flinging dust and dirt behind me.

I could hear Somila groan as she ran behind me. Even a small smile was impossible in my current state of worry. We weren't cheetahs, so it took a little bit longer than a few minutes to catch up with the others. I found Shrey right away, hidden in a bush right on the edge of the village. I crouched beside him.

"What's going on?" I asked him. Now my breathing was ragged.

"Jasper's in the village," Shrey replied.

I gazed toward the small town, searching for a hint of Jasper's form somewhere in the darkness. I spotted him slinking between buildings, hiding in the shadows. He was being methodical and patient, but he was entirely determined.

"We're all afraid to interrupt him. He's not himself," Shrey added in the silence.

"Someone has to try," I whispered.

"And risk one of our lives? There are billions of humans and maybe a few thousand tigers."

I glared at him. "And there are thousands of leopards. More of you than me. *You* go stop him!" I growled.

"Hush," Calouise snarled as he strode by.

"Someone has to stop Jasper," I said irately.

"The humans will deal with him," a voice said behind me. Shrey, Somila, and I turned to look at who had spoken. Sojóma stood tall and firm in the darkness behind us.

"You mean you're going to let him die?" I said, shocked.

A scream erupted from the village. A snarl and several other screams tore the silence of the night. Then light blazed as other villagers awoke. Torches and lanterns appeared everywhere. I gazed at Sojóma expectantly.

"We either lose just him or risk losing many of us. We banded together against our nature to improve survival. As unfortunate as it is, I would rather lose Jasper alone than lose several of us as we attempt to stop him." Sojóma's voice was deep and grave, but I sensed the authority radiating from him.

As I turned to watch what happened in the village, I grappled with his wisdom. It made sense, but the idea of standing there and doing nothing felt wrong. But we all stood there and watched the events unfold like a horror film we couldn't escape. Jasper stood in a human doorway, covered in their blood, some tissue hanging from his jaws, blood dripping onto the dry ground, creating a dark pool. The village men surrounded him, some holding torches, others spears, and the rest held shotguns. I don't know what the men with spears were thinking or if they realized they were holding weapons of the wrong era, but Jasper saw their weakness. He leapt at a man with a spear, batting it aside with a paw and landing on top of the man's chest.

The man beneath Jasper screamed something I could not understand just as Jasper ripped out his throat.

The four men with guns all aimed at Jasper, and we all heard the thunderous sounds as an innumerable scattering of bullets sunk into our kin. Jasper's snarls and growls immediately were silenced. He fell limp on top of the dead spearman. Somila and Shrey looked away. They got up and walked away, heading back toward the jungle. I stayed put, my eyes transfixed on the scene before me. One gun man shot one last round into Jasper's head to ensure his death. Then the men lifted him off their fellow and carried him away and out of sight. The rest of the men picked up their fallen brother and, with tears in their eyes, they carried him away to his family, the light fading with them.

Sojóma moved forward to sit beside me as Calouise left for the forest. I felt tormented and depressed. Two of my species had died. Never before had I seen such brutality by animal or mankind. I'd seen a bloody battle on TV, but that had never been real. I'd seen drug deals and school fights, but never murder. I was in shock.

"The family of the dead man will take Jasper's teeth and make amulets out of them. They'll symbolize brutality and then protection from the man eater—the tiger. They will only ever see us as monsters," Sojóma said sadly.

I said nothing.

"Mix, you must realize this was bound to happen."

"He tried earlier this afternoon."

"And you were able to stop him, for the time being. But please understand that no matter what you did, Jasper would have eventually done what he has done tonight."

"Why must we be enemies—tiger and human?" I asked without looking at him.

He sighed. "We've been enemies since we existed. We both hunted the same prey, thus we were competitors. Sometimes, we hunted each other. They wanted our hide and we wanted their flesh. Our animosity has only evolved as their sophistication has. Now they threaten our home and our prey. They prey upon us more than we prey upon them.

Despite their size and ability, they have become the dominant species. Their killing mechanisms much outnumber and overpower ours. You saw what they did to Jasper."

"It was horrifying," I said numbly.

"I advise you to be ready for more, Mix. If we plan to war against Zoriach, we have to be prepared for death and brutality on every level. We face losing much more than Jasper." With that, he stood and prowled away across the grasslands, vanishing into the trees.

DECISION

Jasper's death rattled us for several weeks. Despite Somila's insistence that she didn't like Jasper, it was evident how untruthful this was as she dealt with his absence. I knew that deep down she had reveled in his pursuit of her. It was attention from a male without asking for it. She had appreciated it, even though she'd denied it. Now that attention and affection was gone. Somila hadn't eaten anything substantial for days.

And neither had I. For weeks actually. It wasn't the specific loss of Jasper, but rather the deaths and idea of mortality that disturbed my sleep and diet. No matter what I did, the images of Jasper ripping out the man's throat and then the men shooting Jasper dead would not leave me alone. None of the males understood Somila's and my attitudes, but we didn't care. We were united again in mourning, and I was pleased to have her on my side once more.

On a positive note, no one had mentioned a thing about rebellion and warring against Zoriach since the death. It hadn't even crossed my mind. Sojóma's last words to me were locked away in an untouched region of my brain. He had said to prepare for more death and brutality.

It was those exact words that made it so hard to hunt. How could I kill an innocent creature that didn't deserve to die? I'd been eating what I could find already dead, like a vulture.

Sojóma found me one day eating from a leftover dead deer that some other cat had left unfinished.

He wasn't very happy with me.

"Mix, you must stop moping around. When's the last time you hunted something on your own?"

I swallowed what was in my mouth and stared at him, expressionless. "About a month ago. Why?"

"You are not a hyena. You don't scavenge for your food. You're better than that."

"Why does this animal deserve to die? I don't see why I should kill something innocent."

"Why does the rat die to the snake, the chicken to the wolf, the fish to man, the deer to tiger? It's the way of the world, the circle of life."

My mind immediately jumped to *The Lion King*. Then my inner nature cringed at the oxymoron.

"We are privileged to be higher on the food chain," he continued. "We are less populated to control the populations of animals below us. If we didn't eat deer, they'd continue to multiply and destroy the world's greenery. It's a delicate system that we are lucky enough to be a part of."

Who could argue with his wisdom?

"If it helps," he added, "hunt only older deer. Don't kill the young ones. They'll repopulate later in life."

Don't kill Bambi, got it.

We sat in silence for a few minutes before I asked, "What do we do about poachers?"

He sighed. "Don't rip off their arms. That only angers them. Kill them before they kill us, I suppose. They're such horrible creatures."

I didn't know if he meant poachers or humans in general.

"If they don't kill us, then they poach our territory."

I guessed he didn't like humans in general. "What can we do?"

"Remain loyal to our species," he said simply.

Fabulous. Loyal to tigers or to humans? He wasn't making my situation any easier.

The rest of the day was rather unexciting, like most others, except I hunted a boar *myself* for dinner.

The next week was more eventful. I lay by the river, the water drifting by as usual, the sun lost behind clouds and the canopy. Shrey sat by me. We were discussing zoos and their purposes. Of course, as a wild animal, he didn't understand the concept of a zoo at all. Since all those who knew me in the jungle believed that I had escaped from a zoo, I had to speak against the institutions of zoos. But I couldn't resist pointing out all their positives.

"They cage wild animals," Shrey repeated.

"Yes, and they encourage breeding of endangered species, like us."

"Then why did you escape?" he asked matter-of-factly.

"Because the zoo I was in didn't have anyone for me to breed with. I was alone and the zoo didn't attract very many visits. It was useless."

"Zoos are useless. It's just another tool for the humans. We're on display for them to gaze at day after day," he replied, shaking his head.

"There aren't poachers there, though."

"Why do you defend the zoo?"

"It was my home, Shrey. I lived there for most of my life. Whether you like it or not, I came from one." I'd never been so passionate about a lie.

"I'll respect that then," he said simply.

We fell into a comfortable silence accompanied by jungle noises that had become as normal as city street noises. But that silence was ripped as feral snarls and angry roars sent birds squawking. Shrey and I jumped to our feet and hurried to the source of outrage. Two tigers were quarreling over something I couldn't see. Fangs were thrust into necks and claws slashed at faces. One tiger grabbed the source of conflict and made to run off, but the other seized it in its jaws. Then they were pulling, a tug of war that began to tear the object. It split with a horrid ripping noise, and I saw clothes tumble onto the ground. My clothes. My bag had just been torn in half.

I was frozen in panicked distress, unsure what to do.

Now my jeans were the object of choice for the tug of war. I watched with sadness as the fabric tore from their claws as they pawed at it suspended between their muzzles. Eventually it tore apart at the knee, and they went at my t-shirt. For a moment, I panicked that they might recognize my scent. But then I remembered how differently I smelled as a human compared to when I was a tiger. I watched helplessly, glad I'd packed one I didn't care too much about. As soon as they tugged, it ripped from their jaws. Cotton was no match against tiger fangs.

After it was all ripped to pieces, they sniffed at it and wrinkled their noses.

"Human junk," one commented.

"It's worthless now," the other said.

Yes, it was worthless now. If I needed to change back, ever, I was in trouble.

After that, everyone dispersed, mumbling about terrible humans.

"This isn't good," Shrey commented. I looked at him curiously. "Them finding human objects in our jungle."

"No, this isn't good at all," I agreed, although for entirely different reasons.

Two days later, another scuffle broke out. I ran up to a horrifying scene. Two tigers, different from the last time, were battling each other over food. The dead hog lay several feet away from their current location of demolition. It was a large-scale cat fight. They stood on hind legs and tried to tear each other apart with teeth and claws. They rolled on top of each other, snarls and growls erupting from their throats while fangs flashed in the sunlight.

When I saw the trails of blood falling from them onto the ground, I knew something had to be done. There came a brief moment where both of them stood facing one another, blood dripping, teeth bared, shoulders hunched, growling menacingly. I shoved my way between them and snarled.

"Enough of this," I growled. My posture mimicked theirs, lacking blood. I turned to glower at the one I couldn't see, but as soon as I turned my head, the other lunged at me. The claws raked at my back, the jaws clamped on my ear. I was knocked to the ground, disgusting snarls released from my chest.

I pushed against the ground, my claws digging into the earth as I snapped at my attacker. I was able to bite at his neck, not enough to kill, but definitely enough to injure. He fell below me as I held a paw against his flank. At that moment, the other tiger jumped on my back, scratching my shoulders and biting my other ear and neck. I roared in pain, but pushed off the flank of the tiger on the jungle floor to stand on two legs, off-balancing the second attacker, causing him to fall hard on the ground with a thud. Then both of them were on their feet, on either side of me, snarling between angry breaths.

"ENOUGH!" a loud, imperious voice rang.

We all fell silent and looked up at Sojóma, who stood a few feet away over the hog, surrounded by onlookers. "What is this? The three of you fighting over a hog?"

"Actually, Mix was—" began Shrey.

"Silence!" Sojóma commanded. "I want their explanations,"

I glared at the tiger on my right.

"We were fighting over the hog, sir," he said. "It was my kill."

"I'd been hunting it for several minutes," said the other, "when he came along and killed it."

There was silence for a few agonizing moments.

"Why are you here, Mix?" Sojóma finally asked.

I swallowed. "I tried to stop the fighting, but it only grew larger, sir." More silence.

"The two who fought over the hog, Mehan and Jokane, if you cannot work out who the hog belongs to, then it is mine and neither of you will enjoy it. You have until I return to make your decision," the rajah said.

They nodded in understanding.

"Mix, you will come with me," Sojóma added.

I grimaced, but obeyed. As I followed the king from the fight, I heard murmurs and flutters from the audience we had attracted. I blocked out their words, afraid to hear anything negative. I had been doing so well at not causing any disturbances. He led me to the water, where he sat on the bank, tall and foreboding in my current state of fear.

"Clean yourself up," he directed.

Into the stream I went. It was cool and rather refreshing on my hot and slightly bloody back. I dipped my head under and felt relief on my sore and torn ear. There was a gash there. It would probably scar. When my head resurfaced, I took a breath and then shook myself. I remained in the water as I looked up at Sojóma. After all our conversations and time spent together, I'd believed we had become friends. But as I gazed at him above me, I was reminded of his position and power. It was like growing close to a parent or teacher, and then something bad happened and I remembered that they have all authority over me.

We gazed at each other. I refused to break the silence, out of defiance and respect. At last, he spoke. "Once again, I've underestimated you."

I didn't know if this was good or bad. It was like that a lot with him.

"You went in and took initiative. You tried to stop Jasper, and then you tried to stop their fight. No matter the outcome, your actions are much more impressive than any of the others. You've taken on responsibilities that everyone attributes to me. Everyone else has run to collect me rather than sort out the problems themselves."

I had no idea what to say. No sassy comeback or respectful comment came to mind.

"Now, while I appreciate your attempt to split up the quarrel, I ask you to let it be in the future. Tigers are not meant to live in a pack as we do. When we live too close together, we fight. It is only natural."

"Understood," I replied, water dripping from my chin like a child.

"Please do not think I'm upset with you, Míx. On the contrary, I'm surprised and proud. Never have I met a tiger as intense and passionate as you when you're in action, on guard."

I guess that was what some of my fears had become—they had transformed into a passion and intensity hardly seen before. I wasn't entirely sure what that meant for me yet, but I was okay with it. Anything that rid me of my fears was essential and useful, allowing me to grow and transform. I already knew things had changed within me. I'd always been a bold person, able to stand up for myself, but that was always among humans. I was growing comfortable enough with the tigers and wild world that I was standing up for myself as well as other tigers.

"For an animal who's never been wild, you possess fantastic instincts."

"Thank you, Sojóma, sir."

Sojóma could see that boldness within me as well. I knew he could. It was my strength and audacity that he was relying on in the potential war to come. We both knew I wouldn't stand down and cower in the face of repressing enemies—it was I who wanted to restrain that impulse and he who wished to exploit it.

He stood up, his crisp, white chest shining with the reflection of light off the water. "I'm excited to see where you take us."

And he was gone.

I dragged myself out of the water and licked at a gash on my leg, thinking of Sojóma. He saw and said a lot of insightful things. I wondered how someone could achieve that kind of wisdom. He wasn't that old, but I knew he was weathered. Shrey had said that he had been a great warrior years ago. Since we had agreed to work together and he already seemed to understand a great deal about me—more than I thought he did—I was glad that I had his support. It would be near impossible to succeed on my own, especially when a part of me— probably some rational sliver within me—still felt like running from it all.

The bushes rustled, and then Shrey and Somila appeared.

"What did Sojóma do?" Somila asked, her striped face twitching in anticipation.

"He asked me not to interfere with food quarrels."

"That's it?" she asked, disappointed.

"Yes, that's it. I didn't do anything wrong," I reminded her.

"He seemed angry," Shrey replied.

"He was angry at the other two and authoritative with me."

"What kind of word is that: *authoritative*?" he asked, suspicious.

I didn't like him questioning me. "It's a psychological word."

"What do you know of psycho—lo—gy … What? Stop speaking human gibberish. You're a tiger!" he said angrily.

I did not like where this was headed. "Who came from a zoo! I came from the human world," I shot at him.

"Let's cool down," Somila said quickly, glancing at our hostile postures.

"I'll never support a zoo or humans," he growled.

"You don't have to. But respect that I came from them."

"It doesn't matter where you came from, but what you are."

"Where I came from made me who I am!" I shouted. He had no idea.

"You're a tiger. No matter where you came from, you are a wild animal!" He took a deep breath and stared at me, waiting for my reaction.

My anger was suddenly gone, replaced by curious exhaustion. Shrey was right. And he was wrong. He would never understand my internal conflict, the two sides that made up my personality. But they couldn't coexist anymore. I'd been unconsciously fighting the urge to let go of all my human ties and, at the same time, fighting to find an excuse to leave all this madness and return to my home in the city. I had to decide, to pick, which life I wanted more.

I remembered the difficulty I'd had transforming my paws back into human hands. Had it been hard because I'd been a tiger for such an extended amount of time or because of something else? Because somewhere within I was resisting returning back? If it was time-related, I truly had to make a final decision. If it wasn't … well, I still had a decision to make before I became too invested—if I wasn't already.

This was not a decision to be made in an instant. But I was out of time.

Somila and Shrey were still waiting for me to say something.

"Look, right now I'm a tiger. That's why I live in this jungle. Please realize I will have human tendencies to accompany my wild instincts. That's all I've ever known." I hadn't made a decision yet, but I knew the clock was ticking.

"Just… don't use human words we don't know. It's unfair to everyone," Shrey replied. He seemed much calmer.

"I will do my best."

He gave me one last disturbed look before prowling across the stream and disappearing into a tree on the opposite bank.

I could feel Somila staring at me. I waited for her to speak.

"Sometimes I wonder how Shrey and you could get along so well. Then one of these fights occurs, and I realize that you two are actually normal."

For the briefest moment, I felt like laughing. I was anything *but* normal, but she didn't need me proving her wrong today. "Yeah… normal," I replied without much emotion.

She seemed to debate whether or not to say something before she asked, "I'm hunting tonight… do you want to join me?"

I'd never hunted at night before, even though it was common for tigers. I was curious how much easier it would be to stalk prey when my eyesight was at its best. After having the talk with Sojóma, hunting wasn't so dreadful anymore. And whenever I hunted hungry, animals became appealing as food rather than sources of disgust. I was glad of the transition the more time I spent as a tiger. Without it, I would have starved.

"Yes, I think I will," I replied.

Her slumped over posture perked up a bit in happiness. "Then we'd better nap now."

We woke up just after sunset. The frogs were louder than ever, chirping incessantly. I wondered how I'd ever slept through it.

My eyes adjusted to the darkness, and I could suddenly see a whole new world. The lightest things were so easy to see, detailed and effortless to focus on. Dark things were not nearly as hard to perceive as it would have been if I were human. It was like I'd put night vision goggles on, only I didn't have a green sheen over everything.

My poor prey. It didn't stand a chance.

I could feel my instincts kick in as I maneuvered between trees. I felt powerful, and as I heard a rustle of leaves in our hunting area, I grew excited. Many of us cats were out that night, and this was the first time I'd ever felt positive anticipation about hunting.

As I prowled around, I caught sight of Sojóma. He caught my eye and gave me a nod of acknowledgement and an approving twitch of his whiskers before his face was focused and poised once more. His presence was reassuring and comforting.

Deer enjoyed nibbling the grass. Somila and I walked to the edge of the jungle and crouched low, searching for a lean, long-legged animal. It took a few minutes before I caught sight of movement. A doe was nibbling at the grass by her knees. My blood pumped fast as I began to creep through the grass, careful to make barely a noise.

Suddenly, birds exploded from the trees. Roars echoed, and the doe bolted. I whipped my head around and stared back at the jungle. I hoped it wasn't another food fight because I'd already begun sprinting for the trees. Something told me this was more important than food. Every other cat that had been in the vicinity was running to my left, toward the scene of commotion. I merged to join them, passing them as I powered my way through, running like someone's life depended on it. I could feel the hurried, frenzied energy in the air.

I was at the front of the throng now, the first to burst between two bushes and freeze at the sight I emerged upon. Damaged brush, dark blood, six lions—all female—and Sojóma. Sojóma on the ground, limp, bloodied, broken, and without breath. The rajah, our king, fallen.

Only astonishment and then blood-boiling anger registered in my brain. This couldn't be happening—it couldn't have happened. I needed him. We all did. It had to be a joke, a ruse, a gag. I stared with tormented horror at his unmoving body, waiting for him to stir.

But he didn't.

Sojóma dead.

Zoriach stood in the middle, three long scars down the left side of her face from the last time we met. They were faint, but I could see them, even in the dark. I began a vicious growl. I wanted her corpse.

"Now, young one. You knew someone had to pay for all of your recent ruckus," Zoriach said patiently.

I glared at her. "You've only started a war, Zoriach." If the other lions weren't there, I would have already lunged for the kill.

"Oh good, you know my name. This makes it so much more *personal*." She leered at me. "We knew war was coming. Now we're on the offense." She seemed very satisfied with herself.

"We have the home field advantage," I hissed. She now stood before a wall of tigers and a few leopards, but there weren't enough of us to even the odds against the five assassins she'd brought with her. The rumble of growls intensified. It reminded me of thunder.

"Fighting will not take place here." She seemed about to laugh. "We'll return home, and if you want to foolishly challenge us, you'll meet us on our turf."

"That's halfway across India," snarled Somila.

Zoriach's black eyes swiveled onto Somila. "I've made the trek twice. If you want to fight that desperately, you'll do the same."

She and her fellows turned to leave. Just before they were out of sight, I called, "I will find you Zoriach. And I will make you pay for what you have done."

All I could see was the gleam of her eyes in the night. "We shall see." And they melted into the darkness.

My blood was still pumping fast. I could feel my heartbeat thudding in my ears. As I looked down at the slain rajah, I wondered if tigers could cry. I could feel the urge, but no tears spilled. His majestic body looked so small without his life, his soul, to fill it. Already, his fur appeared duller, his body shrunken, his glassy eyes unmoving and inanimate. While I gazed, I could see the father I'd never had. His wisdom, his aura, his kindness. I had grown fond of his advice and dependent on his guidance. He was supposed to be my advisory benefactor, supporting me—helping me—doing what was necessary to bring redemption and glory once again for the tigers. But it did not matter now. Our untold, nonexistent story had a tragic ending. He was gone. Now I was alone on my journey to convince the rest of them of the importance of challenging the lions.

Perhaps Sojóma's death had done the job for me.

I looked away and saw that most of the other cats were staring at me, some of their gazes angry, others curious. In that moment, with all their eyes upon me, I realized that many of them blamed me for his death. I'd challenged Zoriach. Twice. Three times now, after tonight. This had been her retaliation.

But this was exactly the reason she had be stopped.

Somila still stood beside me, her gaze neither accusatory or angry.

"I'll fight," she said, her quiet voice gruff. "I'll fight for you, for Sojóma, for our redemption."

I was proud of her decision.

And I'd made mine.

I decided to fight for the tigers. I'd fight for the tigers' right to rule and for our king. I'd forget about humans for awhile and remember how much I hated the lions.

Fit for a King

The rage that had consumed me on the night of Sojóma's death had receded some. We all mourned our lost rajah. All of us, tiger and leopard alike, forgot about the world for a few days in remembrance of Sojóma. We buried our anger over the humans. We vaulted our vengeful fury saved only for the lions until a later date. We bottled our happiness for a brighter day, and we sobbed internally for the loss of another brave, majestic, wild tiger.

It was hard for me to comprehend death, to grasp the idea that those who died left this world. We all believed the dead did something: a portion of the world believed the dead did nothing—gone from the world with no soul or spirit, thoughts never to exist again; some believed the dead returned in another form; and yet others believed the dead continued on in another world and life separate from the rest of us mortals. I discovered that tigers believed the body of the dead decayed to help renourish the earth, and the life-spirit of the deceased, as they referred to it, was released into the atmosphere to fuse harmoniously with the energy forces that propelled the courses of the natural world.

I knew I couldn't fathom death as the complete end—an end with no light, thought, memory, or misty existence. If Sojóma reappeared on Earth as something else, I was terrified and hopeful at the same time. Above all, I imagined him in an afterlife looking down on us. I did not know if there was a heaven for the animal kingdom, but I also knew that Sojóma had been more than an animal. He had been wiser than a lot of humans, so how could he not be among great kings of old?

For four days we mourned him. Then it was time to let him go. Even though it was the animal kingdom, we had a ceremony for his passing. It would be the day to end open lamenting and say goodbye one last time. Life would move on after his ceremony. It needed to.

I kept myself out of the ceremony arrangements. I did not want to put myself where I did not belong. I knew nothing of how a tiger death ceremony went. We all let Calouise and all the cats who had lived with Sojóma handle the arrangements.

I'd rarely seen Calouise since his adopted father's death. I was unsure if they had been close at all, and I was afraid to ask. He was next in line for the throne, so I was sure he had enough stress and grief and other heavy emotions weighing him down.

The day the ceremony took place I followed everyone else. The procession crossed the river in silence. It grew as leopards joined the ranks seamlessly. We didn't stop walking or slow down or speed up. It was smooth and sad and flawless. Without a sound, we passed through the jungle until we came to the familiar stone wall that always appeared out of nowhere. One by one, we vaulted over the wall like a band of thieves. But all we would be stealing was time; time out of our lives to honor one who no longer had any time at all.

When I made it over the wall, I looked upon a beautiful sight. In front of me stretched a long line of flowers that blocked my path. Cream-colored, blue-violet, yellow, red—all jumbled together in beautiful chaos. Appropriate to their name, Forget-Me-Nots and a strange, red and yellow flower that reached upward with twisted petals like a claw lined a pathway that led to crumbled remains of a long forgotten stone edifice. Upon an outcrop of stone lay the body of Sojóma. Sunlight streamed through the trees behind him, almost a spotlight on his elevated form.

I watched as Shrey walked up the floral path with an orchid in his mouth. When he reached Sojóma, he laid the flower down on the stone beneath him. On the forest floor and surrounding stone around our rajah's raised body lay flowers dropped by his friends and subjects. I'd never been to a funeral before, but the vision before my eyes was so precious, so artful and majestic, that it was truly a funeral fit for a king.

I grabbed a Calla Lily from the piled line of flowers and made my way up the path. The closer I stepped to his body, the stronger the urge to cry grew. This was the day to accept he was gone. He would never return to us, to me. This thought swam in my head as I stepped up to his platform. I gazed up above me to where one of his paws stuck out over the edge of stone. Without proper thought, I jumped up to stand on the stone ledge beside his body. It had begun the decomposition that snares all dead bodies, but I could still see his splendor and power sealed inside his once pristine coat.

I placed the pure white Calla Lily under his paw and pressed my nose against his cheek. I did not know if my actions were disrespectful, but they felt right to me. I gazed upon his face one last time before I leapt down and sat beside Somila and Shrey to wait out everyone else's flower placing. While I waited, I peered at the red-yellow and claw-like flowers that lined the pathway.

"Somila, what are those flowers with the Forget-Me-Nots?" I whispered.

She glanced at them. "They're Glory Lilies. We call them Tiger Claw. They're hard to come by, so they're very sacred."

I didn't say anything else, but I thought about how perfect they were for Sojóma's funeral.

After every tiger and leopard had placed a flower below his resting place, Calouise stood before us and spoke. "It's a sad matter to lose a rajah, but more tragic to lose him to slaughter," his deep voice rang. "Although it is custom to outline his achievements in all his life, I find it hard to really sum up who he was in just his accomplishments. What can I say? He was a great warrior in the last Feline Battles. Even though we lost, he never gave up hope of one day gaining redemption. He was a great rajah after that war was over. He was a steadfast father to an orphaned cub—he raised me to be wise and discerning and a defender of our species. He brought tigers together under one canopy. He defied the laws of nature that we had lived by for all of time and found a way to make us live together in peace. He's protected us and stood up for us and made the hard decisions that others could not have made. Sojóma cared about everyone and never hurt anything that didn't deserve it. He killed only for hunger and battle. He lived for our survival. And we will live for his memory."

The speech dug deep into my chest and tore at my emotions, begging for the tears to fall. Every face around me looked as I felt: overwhelming sadness and loss. The emotion was building inside me, threatening escape any way it could. I retracted a line of electricity from my eyes and watched as my vision grew strangely bright and vibrant before it was blurred by a curtain of water. And as the curtain spilled, I made history for tigers: I cried, and tears splashed down onto the dirt below me.

"Words can never convey our emotion properly. We will miss you greatly, Rajah Sojóma, King of the Jungle."

Silence.

It did not last long enough.

"I shall take his place now, ruler over us and our species. I do not expect to fill his paw prints well, but I'll do my best. And as your rajah, I declare war upon my father's murders and all their supporters. However," he paused to let murmurs die down. I wondered if it was hard for him to speak this many words at once. "I will not lead you to battle alone. It was my father's wish—and mine—that Mix shall assist me with leading us to war. She is strong and passionate and has already come face to face with our enemies on several occasions. She knows what is at stake and what it is we are fighting for."

I felt ready to pass out as all eyes flickered to me. The tears were gone as were the bright colors. I couldn't lie. Deep down, I had expected this, but it was still shocking. It felt as if the weight of the animal world was suddenly on my back. If I hadn't already agreed to help Sojóma, I might have still run from it all. But my bag of clothes was destroyed, Sojóma was murdered, and I'd made a decision to stay. I had to find a way to swallow the fears and doubts and find my strength.

Luckily for me, Calouise spoke again, and all their eyes fixed on him.

"Mix is now second-in-command. Please respect her. Now, let us have a final moment with our fallen rajah."

We all sat in peaceful, heavy silence and looked up at him one last time. It may have been seconds or hours, but no one moved, nothing made a noise, the sun beamed through the canopy, and we said goodbye.

Nearly everyone had left. It was dusk, and Shrey and I still lay in the funeral lot. Calouise was there too, speaking to a small group of leopards. I figured he had done more speaking today than in his entire life.

I hadn't been able to leave with everyone else, exit with the crowd, blend into a mob. It didn't seem a proper way to leave such a sight or occasion. Shrey had stayed beside me, although I didn't know why. We hadn't spoken yet.

"Did you know," Shrey began quietly, "that Sojóma never mated with anyone?"

I gave him a quizzical look. "Is that strange?"

"Yes, it is. Tigers don't mate for life. He could have been busy breeding more of your species. It… just seems odd for a male so concerned with the status of your species."

"Maybe he never found the right female." I sounded pathetic, even to myself.

He looked at me like I was crazy. "Us cats don't breed because we find the right female. We find a female able to bear healthy cubs."

"I'm still learning," I replied defensively. "Where I came from, animals bred with those in proximity. But they at least had a relationship since they lived so closely together. I don't know. I guess it is odd for a wild cat. Maybe he wanted to fall in love."

"What is that—some human way to breed? We don't fall *in* love. We just love. Love until it's no longer needed. We love the female, the cubs, and then we leave when they are ready to move on. Then we love another."

"Interesting." I knew that my human brain could fall in love. But it was strange and good to know that a real wild tiger would not fall in love with me. Not a normal one, at least.

"Have you ever loved someone, Shrey?" Maybe it was too personal a question, but I was curious.

He gave me a calculated look. "Several times. I have no issues populating my species. As long as my body will allow me, I'll love every female on this planet if I can."

Any female that got his love was lucky. Too bad not every female deserved his love. "That's a great act for your species, Shrey."

His puckered face suggested that this conversation was not over, just shifting.

"Have you loved, Mix?"

What an odd question, now that I thought about it. And it was a bit personal now that it was flipped onto me. Whoops. "No. I came from a zoo that had nobody to love me, remember?"

He nodded. "You should get busy. You're young and healthy. You can save the tigers one cub at a time."

As awkward as this conversation was, he had a point. It was just so hard to realize that love from a tiger was temporary. Everything I'd ever known about love came from the human world—books, movies, television, media reports of couples celebrating their 67th wedding anniversary. We mated for life. We loved for life. I shook my head. I didn't see myself ever being comfortable enough for mating in the wild.

Shrey wasn't waiting for a response. He was staring at Sojóma with sadness. "Goodbye," he whispered. He gave me a sad smile and walked toward the wall.

I watched Calouise and the leopards until he nodded and they prowled away. Then our eyes met. His had the most yellow in them that I had ever seen in his eyes before. I didn't look away; I didn't back down. He had just put me second in charge. Time to find that courage and use it.

He strode over and stood before me, not looking away either. He didn't say anything.

"I suppose you want a thank you or something," I sighed.

"No."

He was back to his old self.

"Then what do you want?" I wasn't hostile, just exhausted and not in the mood for a long, monosyllabic conversation.

"To tell you that I didn't want to take over. I tried on several occasions before Sojóma died to convince him to find someone else. I've never wanted to rule. I'm grateful for what Sojóma did for me, but I never wanted his authority."

For a cat who had never wanted to have authority, he had come by it very well. Everyone was intimidated by him. "And? This concerns me because?"

"After he died, I tried to convince the dignitaries to let you take over. They refused to let a newbie who had barely lived in the wild to rule over everyone."

I agreed with these dignitaries.

"I think they were more selfish about that decision than necessary," he added. It was strange to hear a personal comment and opinion coming from him, especially about cats that seemed to have some sort of authority and worked alongside the rajah—almost like colleagues.

His comment, though, seemed appropriate. People in power being selfish? It didn't seem too improbable. "I don't want to rule, either."

"You are full of courage and authority, even though you don't acknowledge it. You've been afraid and domesticated for a long time, but you have the skills necessary inside you."

It was strange how differently some of the cats perceived and treated me in the animal world. In the world of humans, I'd been a relatively quiet nobody. I stood up for myself, but I attempted to keep to myself whenever possible. Sara had been my only close friend, and she certainly did not see me as a bold person, capable of leading anybody to do anything, least of which to war. The question was whether or not I could believe in myself the way Sojóma and Calouise seemed able to do. Perhaps compliments would help me achieve that confidence. But, for the time being, I tried my best not to let the praises distract my focus on our conversation."Why don't you want to rule?"

The yellow in his eyes disappeared a little. "I just want to be a tiger, Mix. I only want to roam my territory and hunt and mate and die in peace." He sighed. "What do you have against being a ruler?"

"I know nothing about how to rule a group of wild cats that don't belong in a group. I'm hardly wild. I hardly understand the general lifestyle of these cats here, let alone the normal lifestyle of a single tiger."

His droopy, sad face reminded me of how emotional even a jungle prince could be. "Only Sojóma could pull off controlling a group of wild cats in one territory. Only he had the patience and power to convince all of us that this was the right way to save our species. But I'm less sure. Fewer cubs are being born every year, and we've been living together for over eight years."

"Encourage breeding. As our new rajah, explain the importance and necessity of bearing cubs. If we go to war, some of us will die. A new, young generation *has* to exist before we face Zoriach."

"This is why you should rule us," he said simply.

"Because of my ideas?"

"Yes."

I wanted nothing to do with ruling a band of wild tigers and leopards. I was still trying to wrap my head around leading them to war. "I have no problem giving you my ideas. Take them and use them. You possess the aura needed to rule. We can work together, but you have to be the face of the authority."

He peered at me through narrowed eyes, which eliminated all yellow left in his sockets, gauging how stubborn I was going to be on my decision. "Fine," he sighed at last. "It's a deal." He paused, looked around us, and then whispered, "And feel free to boss around the dignitaries. Prove to them how wrong they were."

They didn't seem so wrong to me, but the idea of messing with people who loved power a little too much excited me just a little too much.

"Come with me," Calouise added as he began to prowl away. It was dark now, stars were barely visible through the canopy, Sojóma's body a faint shape in the darkness. I looked back at his dark, broken form before following Calouise's tail to the wall, up the wall, along the wall, and all the way to what had been Sojóma's fortress. The open ceiling revealed the starry sky thanks to a lack of vegetation. The tigers and leopards that had lived with Sojóma remained, sitting like monuments on either side of the stone blocks that resembled a throne. These cats were the disapproving dignitaries, and they looked quite impassive as Calouise entered the building. Those masks morphed into narrow-eyed annoyance when they spotted me walking in.

Calouise stopped walking and stared up at the visible sky for perhaps a minute. I stood there awkwardly waiting, unsure what to do. The dignitaries were trying their best to bore holes into my head. Nothing happened.

"This place is more peaceful than the Sanctuary," Calouise suddenly commented. "You should sleep here." He turned to face me.

"With you and those cats?" I whispered.

"Yes. You're second-in-command. You should stay here with me ."

"You were second-in-command and slept out there, under a waterfall."

"Behind it," he corrected.

I glared at him.

"I already said: I didn't want to rule."

"I don't either!" I hissed.

"Shh! They don't need to hear you say that," he whispered, glancing behind him.

"I don't want special treatment. I didn't ask to be second-in-command or to lead the war."

"It doesn't matter. It's been thrust upon you."

"I know, and I'm trying my best to accept that. But I don't want to sleep here. Besides, how can I earn everyone's trust if I appear too snobbish to even sleep in the Sanctuary?"

"They have to respect you." He was staring deep into my eyes. He really wanted me there.

"I don't just want their respect. I want them to like me, trust me. How can I lead these cats to war if they don't trust me? I don't want cats that dislike me to follow me in battle."

His dark eyes roved my face. I could only tell because slivers of yellow appeared when his pupils shifted from side to side. "Sleep in the Sanctuary if you wish. You are always welcome here," he said quietly. He faced the dignitaries and called loudly, "Come down and meet Mix, my friends."

Friends was a loose term.

They glared at me and Calouise, tails flicking behind them in agitation. "She should come to us," replied a harsh female voice.

Calouise growled and took a step forward. "She's second-in-command. Get your tails down here."

They didn't flinch like I wanted to. They didn't twitch a whisker. In unison, they rose and climbed down the steps, stalking closer with their noses high. I had visited this fortress once or twice and had never been acknowledged by them. All the times I had spent with Sojóma, and they had never made themselves known to me. And the way they looked down at me made me suddenly dislike these dignitaries. Calouise seemed to be right about them. I'd done nothing to offend them, but they already seemed to hold a grudge against me.

They sat before me, refusing to stand in my presence. I stood firm and looked each of them in the eye. None of them broke our eye contact as I stared into each set of dark eyes. They were resolute and absolutely every bit as stubborn as Calouise's description of them had implied.

"Introduce yourselves," Calouise's deep voice rang.

The farthest tiger on my left with the deepest glare opened her jaws first. "My name is Nashur, and I am head advisor to the rajah," she said clearly, perfect pronunciation. She had a thin face, especially for a tiger, and thin stripes to accompany it. As a human, she would've been a crisp, trim business woman.

The leopard all the way to my right spoke. "I am Cyan," he said in a rough voice that did not match his smooth sounding name. "I am the chief advisor in any regard to the lives of leopards." I was surprised that there was a dignitary simply for telling the rajah how to deal with leopards, as if our species were completely different. It seemed a useless position.

"And I am Saltir," said the leopard to the left of Cyan. He was the smallest leopard I'd ever seen. "I deal with all of our spies as they come and go with information."

The smallest male in charge of espionage. I wasn't sure if it was poetic or ironic. The last cat was a male tiger, small for a tiger of his gender. He alone seemed to hate me the most. His stare was piercing, and his tense face was not inviting or warm.

"They call me Trapir," he growled. His voice was gruff and scratchy, like a smoker's. "I am in charge of all fighting."

Now I understood. Trapir felt threatened by me. Calouise had put me in charge of the war. I was encroaching on this tiger's territory and expertise. But that wasn't my fault. I had been appointed head of war. I'd never asked for it.

For a group of cats that'd never met me, they were adept at intimidation. If Sojóma hadn't just died, I would have shrunk in fear to these high-nosed, vain animals. But with his death so fresh in my heart, all I desired was to verbally attack them for their aloof and demeaning manners. Zoriach's actions had stoked the fire within me and there wasn't a chance of it being extinguished.

As much as I wished to attack them one by one, I refrained for the sake of saving some of my dignity.

But I couldn't contain it all—I hadn't developed *that* good of self control quite yet.

"It's a delight to meet you all," I said, my voice much too sweet and kind to be sincere. "I've heard so much about you all that I just couldn't wait to finally have this meeting, face-to-face." I eyed them one by one again, making sure they understood I was not to be intimidated. "I'm sure each of you has heard plenty about me. After all, I am the chosen leader by both Sojóma and Calouise, the cats you so devotedly serve."

Nashur was glaring at me, my diplomatic mask not lost on her.

"The disdain you all displayed just a few moments ago will not be tolerated by me. I'm not to be underestimated by a bunch of doting servants that lack any real power." I'd lost track of what I was saying. Emotion and sass were spilling from me like a dropped carton of milk. I'd lost control, Sojóma's slaughter—his absence—eating me from the inside out.

Nashur's thin face was wide with shock, her jaw slightly open, her nose flaring. "You... you don't know anything!" she said loudly, but with control.

"Sure I don't," I replied, holding back the sneer. I couldn't completely burn these bridges.

"Who do you think you are to come in here and judge us?" snarled Nashur. I had rattled her world. "You do *not* know us."

I growled at her. "Who are you to judge *me*? You four decided that I wasn't good enough to rule in Sojóma's or Calouise's place. You don't know me either."

"We know that you act rashly, without advice or proper thought," commented Cyan. "We've seen the result of your actions. One of them lies dead, out there, on top of the rock."

I shot him a look that would've killed. "Sojóma commended my actions, and it was Zoriach that killed him, not me."

"Sojóma, dear him, could sometimes be foolish," Nashur replied angrily. Her little 'dear him' didn't fool me. I could almost hear the unspoken words in her mind: *Look what it cost him.*

"I don't allow anyone to disrespect me. In fact, I usually just get harder to control. I may be rash and a newbie, but that does not define me." I looked at Calouise, who was hiding in the shadows, either a coward or wise cat.

"Watch your back, Mix," Nashur growled as I turned to leave.

"I'm not afraid to prove myself to you," I replied without looking back. I knew she understood that my words meant I'd fight her if that was needed to prove my worthiness—I was a tiger, and I wouldn't back down.

"And thank you, Calouise, for this lovely introduction," I called as I stepped through the doorway.

Trapir

For a week or two, I avoided everyone. Although Sojóma's ceremony was over, I still needed time for final processing. And I wasn't simply processing Sojóma. I now had a war to lead. The emotional drive did not pose a problem—Zoriach had put the nail in her coffin by killing Sojóma. Physical fighting was instinctual, but also strategic. I held no skill when it came to strategy in fighting, especially fighting to kill. Understanding wrestling was not going to be enough to allow me to fight to the death. I knew who I needed to go to in order to learn, but I had zero desire to spend time with someone who seemed to hate me.

On the other end of the spectrum, I couldn't get rid of Calouise. As usual, he didn't say much, but he lurked in the shadows, monitoring me. I wasn't sure if he was worried about me and my isolation or if it was his job to look after me. Either he was lousy at being sneaky or I was just really alert to his presence. No matter the circumstances, I didn't talk to him. I'd hardly spoken to anyone since the incident with the dignitaries. Somila had tried numerous times to engage me in conversation, but I was an expert at cutting conversations short. Shrey had attempted to talk a few times, but he took the hint better than Somila did.

After my reclusive bout, I spent some time with Shrey. His idea of hanging out didn't involve pestering me about every emotion and thought that had rattled around my brain for the past week.

"Be prepared for a lot of new cubs," he commented casually as we lay on the bank of the river.

This was similar to the conversation we'd had at Sojóma's funeral about love and mating. I'd noticed the females around the sanctuary acting more seductively and invitational here and there in the last few months. The instinctual drive to mate couldn't be repressed, but the community I found myself in seemed to handle being in heat in a more sophisticated way than I expected the rest of the animal kingdom did. Wild tigresses typically called out and marked trees with their scents to seduce hormonal males. Bloody battles would ensue if two males came upon an inviting tigress at the same time. However, in this jungle, females went into heat, began acting more invitational, and the males attempted to win them over, almost like courting the tigresses. Usually it was the stronger, better-suited male that won over the female, but whatever way they handled mating in our community, it avoided brawls and blood baths.

I couldn't suppress being a female, but when the times came, I discovered my human mind was still very adept at controlling the animal instincts that didn't serve purposes in their moments. My body may have been alerting me to my readiness to bear cubs, but my mind was far, far away from such considerations and concepts. But I understood the importance of having more tiger cubs. Each new tiger life was potential to rebuild our species.

"Oh yeah? Is there any way we can encourage breeding? Because, in case you haven't noticed, our species is kind of in trouble," I replied.

"You're supposed to be the one that's persuasive. Don't you have to rile us up to prepare for war?"

I shot him a scornful look. "I don't want to worry about that right now. I have… ideas formulating in my head." That was half true. "But on the breeding subject, we should come up with some way to force males and females to be near each other long enough to begin to consider mating."

He peered at me. "Like putting us in a zoo?"

I didn't like his tone. I glared at him. "No, not a zoo. A social gathering of some kind."

"We aren't humans, Mix," he said sternly.

"Thank you, Mr. Obvious."

"Well, sometimes it seems you forget." He repositioned himself as he lay on the ground, leaves crackling beneath him.

"Yeah, yeah. I've been working on it."

He sighed. "Mating will occur. I have no concerns about the actual action. It is not guaranteed that any cubs will be born, however. That is out of our control."

"How many tiger cubs were born here last year?" I asked with genuine curiosity.

"Twelve were born, but only five have survived so far."

"That's it?"

"Survival of cubs is not very high. That's why your numbers aren't growing."

"What about you? Shouldn't you be out there with females?"

He shifted his weight only slightly. "I've done my part for this week."

I was suddenly uncomfortable with this conversation. "Right," was all I could manage to say. The painful silence was broken when Calouise materialized on the opposite bank. For once in my life, I was grateful for his appearance.

"Mix," he called across the water. "We need to meet. It's a professional matter."

With a heavy sigh—one that could have crushed a rabbit—I heaved myself to all fours and crossed to his shore. He gave a nod of acknowledgement to Shrey and then a whisker twitch to me, which was as closest to a smile I'd ever seen him have, before venturing through the brush. I kept pace with him as the world around us grew steadily darker with the coming of dusk.

"So, Calouise, what is this professional matter?" I asked conversationally.

He looked at me when I said his name. "You can call me Cal." He paused for a moment before looking in front of him again.

I was well aware he had just attempted to make our relationship more casual, but I didn't reply.

"We have to begin war preparation. No more delaying. Anger will fade if we wait too long. Someone else will have to be attacked to rile them up again," he continued after my silence.

"I understand. But… you do realize I'm new at this? I lack experience in any kind of war."

"Yes," he said simply.

"You're not worried about that at all?"

He glanced at me. "No. War is about passion. No one can properly fight without powerful emotion. You have the emotional drive. You just need technique and strategy."

"And I'm going to learn from who?"

"Trapir," he replied without meeting my eyes.

My heart skipped a beat and my stomach twisted over itself. That cat scared me. His glare, his constant tense posture, his quiet but gruff voice. If anyone made me fear for my life, it was Trapir. I had no desire to ever offend him.

"Fabulous," I said after my panic leveled off.

"Don't fear, Mix. He's been hardened by a brutal life. He's lost much, but he has learned a lot."

"For some reason, that doesn't make me feel any better."

For a moment, I thought I had heard the quietest chuckle.

When we reached the fortress, the jungle was dark and appropriately noisy. In the opening of the canopy that surrounded the building, stars glittered between wispy black clouds. No moonlight was visible, but my eyesight was still excellent. My first impression was slight relief—I didn't see any of the dignitaries. But a few seconds later, Trapir entered the fortress, followed by Saltir. Cyan and Nashur were not anywhere nearby, for which I was grateful. It was mostly Nashur that angered me. Everything about her made me shed.

Saltir didn't pause, but walked away from us to lie down behind the stone throne. Trapir stopped before Calouise and me and waited for one of us to speak. I looked at Calouise. He nodded at me, inviting me to talk first. I had no idea what to say.

Trapir gave an impatient huff and glared at me. I swallowed my fear and opened my jaws, "I need instruction on fighting strategies. You're head of all fighting, so naturally you're the expert. Therefore, I come to you."

His troubling gaze searched my face and then glanced at Calouise. He was thinking—judging me and my abilities, as well as Calouise's judgment in placing me as second-in-command. At last he said, "Fighting is instinctual. You don't need me."

His response irked me. I had put my pride and fear on the line, and all he had to say was that I didn't need him. He wasn't getting off that easy. "Listen—I know you don't like me, and believe me when I say that I didn't want to do this either, but here I am. I need more instruction—I need to learn how to hone my instincts and develop a strategy so I don't make a mistake and die. I can fight. But I want to effectively kill and that requires careful strategy."

I saw the slightest of twitches from the tense muscles around his glaring eyes. He was listening, maybe even curious. So I went on, "I understand you have no respect for me—I've never done anything to prove my worthiness to you, and you barely know me. I don't know you either. Yet here we are. War is coming, and I know that *I'd* like to achieve victory. The other tigers and leopards won't follow me if I can't earn their respect. Knowing how to fight will bring me one step closer to being worthy of their respect and my position as a leader in this war. It isn't about just helping me. It will be helpful to us all if I can be an effective, respected, trusted leader. So will you help or not?"

Trapir's gaze grew even more curious as opposed to disapproving. Calouise shifted his weight anxiously beside me, and I waited with impatience for something to happen.

"Alright," Trapir said at long last. "I'll teach you."

The tiniest of sighs escaped from Calouise as he relaxed. I was relieved and slightly surprised that I'd managed to win him over. The possibility of winning over the rest of the community seemed an even greater possibility now.

"Brace yourself and square up," Trapir commanded.

I shot Calouise a perplexed look and then a panicked one at Trapir. "Wait, we're starting already?"

"I don't see why not. No time seems any better." He crouched and focused all his energy in my direction.

"But…I'm not prepared or ready. I don't know what to expect. I don't know what to do—" I couldn't finish the sentence because the wind got knocked out of me. Trapir had lunged at me, rammed his head into my chest, slammed me to the stone floor, and pinned me under his front paws. As I regained my ability to breathe, I could feel my heart rate increase and my temper spike. I was alert and provoked now.

I twisted out from under his paws and kicked at his face and flank as I rolled onto my side and then my paws. I tensed and crouched just slightly, baring my teeth. He was poised across from me, his whole body tight. Ready.

Without much thought, not sure what to do, I pounced, and he met me in the middle. I attempted to strike at his face and neck with my paws, but he managed to dodge and somehow I ended up on my side pinned beneath him once more.

"Too basic," he shot at me, digging into my flank.

I growled in response. He let up and returned to his previous spot, his black eyes not leaving me. I rolled back onto my feet and prowled to where I had started, facing Trapir. Calouise was in the distance, near the throne, carefully observing us with his ever-watchful gaze.

I fixed my own eyes on Trapir's dark form across from me. "If that was too basic, what should I do?" I called impatiently.

"Anticipate the basic and then attack differently."

This cat was going to get me killed.

"'Cause that's so easy," I muttered quietly to the night.

Trapir was in his crouched position, ready to go again. I mimicked him, this time waiting for him to make the first move, ready to anticipate as he instructed. He didn't move for a long while, not so much as a twitch. I tried not to blink, afraid that an infinitesimal moment of lost concentration could be the moment of surprise.

Unfortunately, I couldn't fight the urge to blink forever, and indeed, he chose that precise instant to attack. Luckily, blinks are quick. I was able to position myself properly to be able to block a basic attack to the face. But as I stood up to push his paws aside, he dropped to the ground and drove his big, hard head straight into my chest. I fell over backwards, unable to breathe, gasping like a dying, wounded animal. As I struggled to pull in oxygen, Trapir looked at me with no expression.

"That wasn't…basic," I gasped.

"Most cats you will face will fight on a basic level. It's instinctual and absolutely normal. But there will be some, such as myself, who will have more experience, and they'll be well above using basic, animalistic fighting techniques."

"I appreciate the warning *after* I've been knocked flat on my back," I snarled as I sat up.

"I have learned that experience is the best educator. Words usually pass straight through the head as if no brain resided inside."

"I'm not your usual tiger," I replied.

Calouise laughed from his observational perch. Actually laughed. Of course, it was at my expense. I shot him a dirty look.

"Again," Trapir commanded.

"Are you crazy? I can hardly breathe."

"War doesn't wait for you to catch your breath."

"It's not a war yet. I'm conditioning myself."

He glared at me. "You came to me for help. If you want it, then prove it. One more time!"

I let out an aggravated huff. I shook out my fur and then began to circle towards him. He reacted immediately, falling into perfect sync, circling just as I was. His pace matched mine, even when I sped up, making it impossible for me to ever catch up to him. My only chance was to leap across our circle and hope to catch him off guard...even a little bit.

After seven circles, I was beginning to see that Trapir couldn't be caught off guard, at least not by someone as inexperienced as myself. My tactic changed as we endlessly circled. We reached the point of the circle where I stood able to see Calouise. Without relaxing a muscle, I took my eyes off Trapir and looked into Calouise's glowing ones in the darkness.

I gave him one wink, by which point Trapir had already decided my switch in eye contact was his chance to strike.

But this was all a part of my plan.

He took a bound and a leap, but when he was airborne, I rolled over, flipped around and pounced on him as he landed, in surprise, empty-armed. He fell to the floor, pinned on his side by my front paws. There was a second of frozen triumph, but then I lost my footing, fell and found myself trapped by teeth at my throat from my adversary. Somehow he'd escaped and gained the upper hand.

He let me go and backed away slightly as I sat up. "That was progress," he said quietly.

"I don't understand how you got out from the pin," I said angrily. I'd *had* him beat.

He eyed me carefully before replying. "When you're pinned by an enemy, pay attention to their stance. Usually the front two paws will concentrate all the pressure on you and the upper half of your body as they hold you down. Once they believe you're secure, they'll go for the kill, teeth aimed to rip out your throat. But that second that they've believed to have won, you use your unpinned part of your body, generally your back legs, to kick at their stomach or to knock their own feet out from under them. You can almost always escape, it's just knowing how and when."

I made quick mental notes of his instructions, realizing at the same time that he was actually instructing me. "Okay, I'll make sure to try that."

"You need to master it. It'll be the difference between life and death."

"Then let's go again," I said, tensing my legs.

He shook his head. "The hour is late, and we've done enough for tonight. We'll practice more another time."

"Oh, so now that *I'm* ready to go, you're all done?" This cat's double standards were starting to get on my nerves.

"Not everything in life is convenient and open to your availability and desires. Quite the contrary."

I glared at him and then at Calouise, who still lurked in shadow by the throne. "Alright, as you wish. Should we meet again tomorrow?" I did my best to sound polite rather than frustrated and rude.

"Only if you feel like you need to. I'll be around…" his voice trailed off, almost sad.

"You'll be around?" I asked with sarcasm, irked by his lack of interest. "Alrighty, then I guess I'll see you *around*." I turned away from them all and padded out the doorway into the soothingly noisy night. I'd made it to the crumbling stone wall before I heard the dull thud of pads against the earth. Calouise had caught up to me, as I figured he would. His mysterious character was strangely predictable. I stopped walking and looked up into the canopy, vaguely hoping I could catch a glimpse of a star, but the dense trees and drifting clouds made it almost impossible.

"What do you want, Calouise?" I sighed.

He stood beside me, staring about the brush. "Did that seem helpful at all?"

Another sigh. "Towards the end, when he actually began to give me strategic tips, that was helpful. But his passivity is slightly irritating. *Come back only if you feel you need to*—what's that supposed to mean? If I don't go back, I look like a prideful, selfish—" I struggled to find the right word.

"Lion," he interjected. "They're an excuse and filler for anything nonplus."

"Right… and if I do go back, it appears that I lack confidence and ability, shedding doubt on my potential skill to lead us to war."

He didn't say anything, just stared at my face.

"I mean, what is Trapir's issue? You said he's had a hard life. What has he been through to make him so annoying and dislikeable?"

He remained quiet a bit longer before replying simply, "That's not my story to share."

I gave an exasperated humph. We stood in relative silence for another minute. The frogs and crickets chirped. A gentle breeze rustled leaves. Creatures of the night disturbed the air.

"What should I do?" I asked quietly.

He replied without skipping a beat, "Stay with me tonight in the throne room."

I shot him a bewildered look. Something about the intense and serious tone he used to offer such an invitation suggested that this was not simply about sleeping. "What does that have to do with my Trapir issue?"

"It doesn't. It's something to do."

"Calouise—"

"Cal. I already said to call me Cal, Mix."

I squinted at him sternly. He wasn't dropping this idea, and he was attempting to make our relationship more casual and friendly than it had ever been before. I was afraid to assume what he wanted, but the unwavering gaze he held upon my face, waiting for my answer, left very few possible options of what he could be offering. "Look, I'm not looking for or wanting that kind of connection. I have enough to deal with as it is." I hoped that was sufficient enough to turn down anything he was offering without sounding rude, especially since I wasn't completely sure what he *was* suggesting.

The contours of his face drooped only slightly—enough to indicate his disappointment. "You're the one who said to encourage breeding."

At last, my assumptions were confirmed. He had just offered to *mate* with me. My mind was spinning in three different directions: as a female, a part of me was flattered; as a biological tiger, I felt an instinctual inner curiosity of what would come from such an interaction; but as a humanistic rationalizer, the thought of mating with a wild tiger seemed out of the question. I wanted to fall in love with someone, not just love like a wild animal.

As much as I had allowed myself to become integrated into the wild animal world, I couldn't quite reconcile the idea of mating like one. But, of course, I couldn't tell him what was going through my head at that moment.

"Yeah, but—not with me. I have to lead a war—I can't have cubs!"

"Don't explain, I understand," he replied quickly, restoring emotional walls I'd never noticed existed before.

"I'm sorry…," I said, not realizing until now how much this had meant to him. I had figured his offer was purely instinctual, even though I supressed my biological drives in this area. I did my best to not be invitational.

"Nothing to worry about."

"Calouise—"

"Cal," he insisted.

"Jungle Prince! I'm sorry to reject your mating offer, but this is not the time—not for leaders and officials like us." Our eyes met, and in that short moment, I saw a glimpse of some of his emotions and desires and thoughts communicated in the dark masses that were his ever-dilated pupils. Looking into his eyes, I had a crazy thought that perhaps, just maybe, his offer to mate had been motivated by something more than just a biological, hormonal instinct. That his emotional disappointment was because his motivation stemmed from something else.

But I didn't know him well enough to even give such a thought credence.

"I get it, Mix. Trust me. I completely agree." He flipped around and disappeared as he always did, but this time, his absence was heavy and full of confusion and mixed up emotions and uncertainty lingering in his wake.

"UGH!" I collapsed on the damp dirt and gazed into the darkness. Mating with a wild tiger felt like the definitive final act that would solidify complete release of all human thinking and rationalizing. It would be an utter surrender to the wild, animalistic nature that resided within me—a nature directed and motivated by pure instinct. I may have had a tiger body, but my brain had remained the mostly human thought processes it had originated as. Could it stay that way? Would giving into my wild animal nature cause me to lose the last human piece of me? Or could I simply surrender the human for the moment until I rose above the base instincts to find myself once more, much like I did when I hunted? For the time being, I decided it wasn't worth testing out, especially since I didn't even know how much I liked Calouise, let alone the idea of mating with him. And I wasn't prepared for any consequences that could arise if I traveled down that path.

I found myself wishing the night was a lot murkier and actually dark. So, for the first time in months, I decided to retract some electricity from my occipital lobe. I remembered the struggle to transform a couple of months ago when Jasper had died. I faced a similar problem this time around. I probed with my thoughts, trying to control the circuits, compel them to reel back inward so I could see as a human again. It took a minute or two, but eventually I found the end of the nerves and forced them to allow my human eyesight to dominate my tiger body. The world around me dissolved into darkness and dullness. I refused to think anymore and found refuge in the solace of sleep.

I woke up the next day alone, out in the middle of the jungle. The wall was to my left, and the sun was directly overhead, its beams penetrating the canopy with great precision. I'd slept until midday, and as I sat up, my body stretched and made a point of making known all the sore spots from last night's training.

I stared around me, still trying not to think about all that had transpired the night before. Everything was so vivid. The greens were a lush, bright alive color, and birds' feathers stood out strikingly bright in tree branches. My own fur jumped out and caught my attention. It was so *orange*. For a few moments, I gazed about, my groggy brain not fully understanding why my vision was so oddly different. Then I remembered that to help myself sleep, I'd resorted to human eyes. With little effort, I released the stored currents within me and blinked twice as all the colors faded slightly, but my world brightened as I took in more light.

I had two options, and talking to Calouise was not one of them. I dared not even let myself approach that subject yet. No, I had a choice between hunting for food or going back to see Trapir. Like I'd told Calouise, going back to Trapir appeared weak, but not going back appeared arrogant. I knew I needed my instruction in order to be successful as a leader and fighter. It looked as if I needed to swallow my pride and face the old cat again.

As for the decision to hunt, I wasn't starving, and if I did go see Trapir, it would probably be best not to approach more training on a full stomach. I could hunt afterwards. Mustering my courage, I stood up and stretched, spreading my toes, exposing my claws, feeling my large muscles find momentary relief from their soreness before I sauntered toward the fortress, hoping that Calouise would not be there. And if Trapir wasn't there, I was going to be irritated and angry.

When I reached the doorway, I paused and peered inside. Calouise's unmistakable form lay sprawled across the throne, his eyes closed. It wasn't uncommon for jungle cats to sleep through the day, but Calouise had never acted like a common tiger. Finding him sleeping was not a big shock, though. After what had gone down between us last night, I didn't blame him for sleeping. It meant avoiding thinking and facing reality, even if only for a few hours.

Saltir was still inside, pacing behind the throne. Nashur was there too, stationed at the right side of the throne, Calouise's tail inches from her face. I didn't see Cyan or Trapir. I wanted to leave quickly in order to avoid any confrontation from any of the three cats, but before I could disappear, Nashur called my name.

"Mix! What a delight!" Her high voice couldn't have been more false. I glanced at Calouise's sleeping body and saw his tail twitch, but he didn't wake.

I felt like calling her a lion…but that would create a fire that would surely awaken Calouise. Not to mention dig a deeper ditch between us.

"I was just leaving," I said, turning away from the doorway.

"So soon? Why don't you tell me what it is you need?"

"That would just make your day, wouldn't it? Me relying on you? Let me be the first to inform you: I don't need you."

She glared at me and glanced at Calouise. I was sure she didn't understand his sudden strange sleeping habit.

I saw the opportunity to strike in the most diplomatic manner I could muster. "You're probably wondering what's the matter with our new rajah, but I can assure you that I know exactly what's wrong with him. And it's none of your business."

She twitched slightly, but held her composure as she replied, "It's my business if he chooses to share it with me. I am his advisor. He knows he can come to me with any problem and receive advice. I'm not worried at all. As for you, if you don't have a genuine reason to be here, I request that you leave."

Her formality did not mask her animosity, which suited me. As long as I always had the upper hand in our relationship, she could hate me until the end of time.

"Well, I was here to see Trapir, but seeing as he's not present, I shall indeed leave. Keep your head in the canopy, Nashur. It keeps our encounters *arousing*." I walked away from the doorway and circled around to the back of the building. Perhaps when he'd said *around* he truly had meant somewhere around the fortress. It was an overgrown meadow surrounded by foundations of once-existing walls that had crumbled away long ago. The sky was clear and visible above, not a cloud in sight. As I stood staring at the sky, I caught movement out of the corner of my eye. From out of the grasses rose Trapir, his ever-hard face glued to mine. We stood in silence for a while, dragonflies and bees dancing around us, clearly visible in the open space of the meadow.

He spoke first. "I am truly surprised to see you, Mix."

"Why is that? Did you think I was too proud to come back?"

"Not prideful. You're one who likes to triumph on your own. You're very independent and desire to succeed without a lot of assistance. I know because I am the same way."

"You almost sound like him... like Sojóma," I said quietly.

Trapir looked down and back up solemnly. "Before he died, he talked to me about you. He saw greatness in you. He believed in all your potential. I saw that yesterday when you stepped up and asked for someone to teach you. It showed that you have good qualities that drive you forward through life."

Something about the way he said it, the huskiness and roughness in his voice, the emotion that leaked out between his tough walls—he and Sojóma had been closer than simply king and dignitary.

"Sojóma was an amazing tiger. A great rajah and a great soul," I said softly.

"I know. He was my brother."

My brain went blank. I'm sure my face displayed apparent shock. "Wait! Your brother?"

"Yes. He was my younger brother. I never desired to rule, so Sojóma took the job and appointed me head of warfare. Sojóma was a much wiser, selfless cat than I. He saved my life back in the first feline wars. A true warrior."

"Your brother." I was still hung up on that small piece of information. "You're the older brother, and he saved you in war, and you're the one in charge of fighting? How did that come to be?" I didn't want him to think that I saw him as incompetent for his position, but I was curious how he had managed to come by it.

He sighed. "When we were young, Sojóma and I were both skilled fighters. We wrestled often and fought for our territories, always coming out as the victors. We had remained close, even before he began the community living.When we went to war against the lions almost ten years ago, we lost much." His face hardened, but his eyes remained glassy and sad as he continued. "I loved many tigers, but only one did I ever truly bond with. We had been together for several years before and during the Feline Battles. She was killed in the last war by Zoriach. I was huddled over her body when two lions took the chance to attack me, too. Sojóma was there—he materialized from nowhere and saved me. I didn't—appreciate it for months until I learned to accept that she was gone for good." He drew in a deep breath and closed his eyes for a few moments, appearing to compose himself. A bee landed on his ear and his ear twitched, shooing it away.

"After the acceptance of her death ... what happened to you? How did you move on?" I felt intrusive asking, but he had already shared so much, and I was ready to latch onto any information that would help me deal with loss.

"That's when my grief morphed into anger, and fury has burned in my body ever since, desiring a chance to avenge her. And now Zoriach has only dumped dry wood onto the vengeful fire by taking my brother, too. I became a fighter—a warrior with the sole purpose to kill those that had taken everything I'd ever lived for."

I was waiting for the tears to come, but then I remembered that tigers didn't cry. His dark eyes met mine, and we were united for a time in grief.

"I loved him," I said before I could stop myself, "like a father and for who he was, how he lived and sought the good in all." My entire perception of Trapir had morphed. Now I could see the heaviness that pressed on him at all times, requiring him to always appear strong.

"Everyone but Sojóma seems to have underestimated you, including myself. I apologize and ask that we can try to approach an understanding relationship."

"Of course. I appreciate the opportunity to get to know you better. You don't come off as such a stuck-up hard ass now." I added a wink, afraid he would take that the wrong way.

He didn't get angry, but his eyes narrowed slightly. "You're a strange cat, Mix."

"So I've been told," I sighed. "Now, are we actually going to get any training done today, or should I come back another time?"

"If you're still up for it, then yes, we will train today."

"Great, so do you have anything specific to teach or are we just winging it again?"

He shook his head and shoulders, getting his blood flowing again, almost as if he was shaking the heavy conversation and memories away. "Last night wasn't just random attacks. I was assessing your abilities and skills. You have the basics, but you're a fast learner with little fear. All that's left is advanced skills to fine-tune your instincts." His tone was very mechanical, focused on our business, no trace of emotion left in it, the previous conversation a blink of the past.

"Alright...so what's the plan now?"

"We are going to face off, and I want you to perceive and anticipate the exact moment I'm going to attack. Dodge or defend as I leap, rather than after I've leapt."

"You want me to *guess* when you're going to jump?" I asked skeptically.

"Not guess—perceive."

He squared up and grew tense, his eyes narrowed and black. I tensed up, focusing my senses on his taut form, waiting, attempting to *perceive*. I wasn't sure what to look for. A few seconds passed. Flies buzzed about us, Trapir remained relatively motionless. My focus was slipping. And of course, he pounced when I least expected it. I barely had time to jump and roll out of his line of fire. Once on my feet again, I turned to face him, ready for whatever criticism he had for me.

"Your turn. Attack and I shall perceive it ahead of time."

"No criticism?" I asked quickly, confused.

"Not yet," he replied, almost a twinkle in his eye.

I shook my head, but did as he instructed, channeling my energy into my muscles and focus. I didn't really think, but rather allowed my instincts to shift my body with my enemy's, allowing instinct to propel me forward with paws raised and claws exposed. Trapir did not meet me in the middle with defenses. As my feet leapt forward, he had already jumped to my right and then pounced into my flank as I flew through the air toward a location he no longer occupied. I fell, he pinned me, and I found myself bested and out-maneuvered once again.

"Ugh!" I yelled as he let me up. "That's so frustrating. So what's the secret?" I growled.

"I discovered your tell, Mix."

"My tell? Like in poker?"

"Poker?" His brows were raised slightly.

"Never mind poker… but a tell, as in finding a tick or twitch or something that gives away when I'll strike?"

"Precisely."

"So what's mine?" My voice was a bit rushed.

"As I had expected, yours was not similar to most other tells. A great number of cats share the tell of one momentary body freeze before they strike. It's their final pause before the attack, the split second they need to lock onto their target. Generally, you would watch their eyes or tail. Advanced hunters have mastered staying almost completely still until they leap while others have trained themselves to always be moving so that their prey can never truly anticipate the exact strike."

I was growing impatient.

"Which brings me to you, Mix. You stay moving, but just barely. Your body naturally adjusts itself to stay locked onto your target. You move and freeze, move and freeze—nothing special there to signal your moment of attack. Your tell is almost imperceptible. It took me two days to really catch it. Your nostrils flare."

"Is that hard to perceive?"

"To an untrained prowler, yes. For a fighter? It depends. They'll be more likely to spot it while any other cat may never figure it out."

"So do I need to learn to hide it?" This was probably the most urgent question at the moment.

"It's not imperative. If we find ourselves running out of ideas to work on, we can definitely consider it."

"So... what's your tell, Trapir?" I asked facetiously.

He peered at me. "I couldn't tell you," he replied curtly.

I hadn't expected a real answer.

Rise in Numbers

I trained with Trapir on and off for almost two more months—right up until we were ready for war. Not long after I first met with Trapir, I had to swallow my pride and meet with Saltir. That tiny little leopard made me feel small when I saw how high up in a tree he was lounging, waiting for me outside of the stone fortress. When he spotted me standing in the grass below him, he lazily but lithely sauntered down the convoluted branches. It was not my choice to spend time with this tree frog of a cat that I could kill with one good swat to his head, but Trapir had insisted that I understand how to liaison with our spies and runners, especially since I was like the general in our upcoming battle. I guess more of a commander. I had never been one to follow military rankings closely.

When he was finally on level ground, although several feet shorter than me, we were able to talk. Technically, he was my teacher and he had been in a position of power the last time we had met, but this time it felt good to be the one looking down on him.

I didn't want to waste any time. "Alright, Saltir. Who are our spies, and when can I meet them?"

His pinched face was scornful. "You have to be more discreet. Zoriach has spies in here, too."

I did not appreciate his condescending tone.

"Then why did you say to meet here? I figured, *based* on what we're discussing we would, you know, meet in a *secure* location." There were just some personalities that I did not understand. I was irritated. I'd maybe seen Somila and Shrey twice in two weeks. Calouise was giving me the cold shoulder—not that I blamed him—but I missed company that wasn't always based on preparing for a battle.

He didn't reply to my snippy remark, but walked away from our meeting spot, away from the fortress and deeper into the trees. He spoke quietly as we walked. "Most of our spies are birds because they're fast and reliable. They bring some frogs with them. Those frogs stay for longer periods of time to collect more information, and then they try to catch a ride back."

"Try?"

"Birds and frogs are prey, Mix. We are talking about the lions' territory. They kill anything they can, especially if they suspect that it could be one of our spies. We always try to be discreet."

"Discreet. Yeah, got it." So I stopped talking, waiting for him to say something once we reached a secure location. We walked for a few more minutes before he stopped and finally said something.

"This spot should do."

"How is this spot any more secure than the last one? How do you know?" I was trying very hard not to growl in outright irritation.

"Well, first off, you never meet with spies anywhere near a highly populated and well known place. The enemy's eyes are more likely to be near the Sanctuary or throne because that's where most of us spend our time. The farther away from others, the better."

"And you picked this spot out of any other because…?"

"This felt secure."

"Oh, but ten yards back, that spot didn't?"

His small eyes narrowed. "Don't question me, Newbie. I've been doing this job a lot longer than you've even been wild. If we can even call you wild now."

I'd touched a nerve. "Alright, small fry. So how do these spies of ours know where and when to meet you?"

Most of that had gone right over his head.

"What did you just call me?" he snapped.

I growled in response.

His replying growl exposed his teeth and scared off several birds. He had a lot in him for such a little cat.

We did not hear the pounding of paws over our aggressive noises. But we sensed something coming and our heads both whipped around to see Trapir and Calouise burst into our midst. Their growls were short and angry once they realized it was Saltir and I causing a commotion.

"What is the meaning of this?" Trapir rumbled. For a moment he reminded me of Sojóma, bursting in on food squabbles ages ago. He would have been disappointed in me for being antagonistic. It seemed Trapir was too. I relaxed and dropped my head, feeling shame—but only because I'd upset cats that I actually cared for. "I apologize. It was my fault." Kind of.

"It takes two to quarrel," Calouise said curtly, not looking at me.

"You're both dignitaries, so start acting like it!" Trapir snapped. He glared at us.

"It won't happen again," Saltir assured them.

Trapir gave an angry snort and disappeared with Calouise.

I glared at Saltir.

"Let's just get this over with so we can leave," Saltir said.

"Agreed," was my reply. "Look at us, agreeing on something."

He didn't respond, but continued to walk deeper into the jungle. I followed reluctantly.

"Obviously, that spot has been compromised," he said.

It took every ounce of willpower to not start name-calling again. "So … how do the spies know where to meet us?"

He stopped walking and looked about before replying, "You're really unobservant, aren't you?"

I bit my tongue. By end the of the hour, I might not have any tongue left.

"I've been marking trees with a special sign that our spies know and trust. Each dignitary has one. You'll have to have one as well."

"Do I get to pick the sign?" I asked, afraid Nashur would be in charge of it. She'd give me something stupid and demeaning, no doubt about it.

"Yes. It must be distinct enough to stand out from common scratch marks on trees, but also subtle enough to avoid curiosity where it's not wanted."

I thought about it while we continued forward, considering what I'd want my mark to look like. I knew already I wanted it to have a subtle 'M' shape. As we walked, I carefully watched as the little leopard quickly brushed his paw along the bottom of a tree and left four crossing scratch marks that looked like a misshapen snowflake. It was, indeed, subtle but unique.

"Here, this should do," Saltir said, stopping—hopefully—for the final time.

"What now?"

"We wait for them to arrive. They know to wait in the trees around our territories until one of them spots one of our fresh marks. Then they spread the word to gather."

I was actually intrigued to learn about this hidden network of communication and cycle of spies and messengers within our community. It was another layer of complexity and beauty in this wild home of mine that I could appreciate.

While we waited, I scratched some signal prototypes into the dirt, trying to find an 'M' shape that didn't look too human or too much like an English 'M.' I was getting close to liking a variation of an 'M' shape that subtly looked like chicken scratch, when they appeared. They arrived in relative silence, a cluster of birds, rodents, frogs, and geckos. They were good at their job, at least the stealth portion.

"Welcome all. Thanks for meeting promptly. This meeting has two purposes. As usual, I'd like to hear any news, and additionally, to introduce Mix, our newest... dignitary and second in command, under Calouise," Saltir said.

I felt his comment about being under Calouise was unnecessary. All their eyes shifted to peer at me. I didn't know if I was supposed to say anything or not.

"Hello," I said tentatively, glancing uncomfortably at Saltir.

The spies didn't reply, but simply nodded.

"What news?" Saltir finally said, directing their attention off of me.

An olive-yellow, black-streaked bird chirped up. "Zoriach's pride has recently grown. Four cubs have been born among them."

"There has also been a rapid increase in the amount of prey disappearing," an osprey chimed in.

"How much of an increase?" Saltir asked.

"More than can be accounted for with the addition of four cubs."

"Hmm ... I wonder ... Any other important observations?"

Then a giant squirrel with the longest and coolest looking multi-colored tail I'd ever seen spoke up. "Darting among the trees, I've found traces of new and other cats in the lions' territory. I've spotted only a few, but there's evidence of more."

"And the stripy hyenas have gathered in more of a group closer to the lions," a frog added.

"What other cats are new to the area?" I suddenly asked.

The squirrel looked at Saltir. "Your dark brothers."

Saltir's eyes widened, and I could see his fear.

"Dark brothers? Like, what, black panthers?" I asked in confusion.

"Yes, as much as it hurts to say. I can only imagine the kind of deal Zoriach had to offer in order to persuade them to join against us."

"Would they have normally allied with lions? Or with us?"

"Neither. They'd need a very strong reason to join either side. But since it's Zoriach, her offers could not have been benign and simple."

I looked back at the spies gathered before us who had remained quiet during our exchange. "Do you have anything else to report?"

"Zoriach knows you're coming, she just doesn't know when," an orange-and-brown speckled gecko said. "She has cats guarding their territory, constantly on patrol, as well as sentries and spies littered across the country, all waiting to inform her of your movement to attack. She means to not be taken by surprise."

"Well, we'll have to find a way around that, now won't we? I'll devise some sort of plan." As I said it, I knew I'd need Trapir or Calouise's help. "In the meantime, we need reinforcements. If Zoriach has hyenas and black panthers, we aren't going to stand a chance. Saltir, who can we send as messengers?"

He looked at me, a sudden change in his expression. Not irritation or anger or even surprise that I'd taken control of their meeting.

It was admiration.

"These creatures are at your disposal to command. They are trained to travel and observe and deliver information."

I could hear the pitter patter of water falling on the leaves overhead as I pondered what to have them do.

"I need a third of you, mostly birds, to fly out and find any other clusters of tigers or leopards you can and—"

"Beg your pardon, but most other cats are nomads. You're unique to live in a community of tigers and leopards successfully," a slender, forked-tail, soot-colored bird said, clinging vertically to the side of a tree.

"Either way, find as many as you can. This is why I want birds to find them. I want all of the fast flyers that can spot and catch the nomads to find them. Let them know that we plan to battle the lions for their power and make them pay for their oppression and bloodshed. Tell them to join our cause. Convince them to fight at our side to put the lions in their place."

Several bird calls rang out in agreement.

"Not to be the bearer of bad news, but why would nomadic leopards come to your aid? This is between lions and tigers," an irritating frog asked.

I glanced at Saltir, but he didn't say anything. "We have leopards already here. They should want to back them up."

"He has a point, Mix, as unfortunate as it is. We don't have anything to offer the leopards to get them to join us. We won't strike nasty deals with them," Saltir said.

I growled. "I'll talk to Cyan. We need as many cats as we can find. That's going to rest on your shoulders, messengers. The rest of you... return to Zoriach and continue your excellent work."

The spies began to dissipate, sliding back up the trees or flying off with the geckos or frogs. Before they all disappeared, I had an idea. "Wait! I need two of my messengers to accompany me when I speak to Cyan."

The osprey and the forked-tail bird remained behind as the rest took flight in a beautiful flapping of wings and darting between branches.

"Will Cyan be available to talk?" I asked Saltir.

"He's almost always available," he replied.

I decided not to claw into that one. Then I laughed at my own cat puns that had become more and more a part of my identity. "You two fliers, come with me. You can ride on my back as long as you watch your talons."

The osprey gave a flapping jump and landed between my shoulders, but the smaller bird leapt into the air and flew above my head.

"I prefer to be airborne, Commander."

I was taken aback by the title, but I liked the sound of it. "What do you call yourself, if you don't mind?"

She darted around my head, not wishing to land. "Swift, Commander."

"You're a very elegant bird, " I said as we began to head back to the fortress. The rainy jungle rang with its usual hum of activity, but under the comforting sound of a spring shower. It almost reminded me of home, but the squishy mud that sank when I took a step and oozed between my furry toes was enough to overshadow any thought of home.

I paused at the threshold and took a deep breath. My heart was pounding as I considered spending an extended amount of time in Calouise's presence. I also did not feel particularly excited to talk to a cat that I hadn't had any contact with since I had endured the uncomfortable confrontational meet and greet with him. I had never understood his purpose until now.

Saltir had already entered, as had Swift.

"Is there a problem?" said a deep voice behind me.

Of course Calouise had to be somewhere he could observe me gather my bearings.

"No, I was just about to enter," I said, the osprey shifting his weight anxiously, his talons digging into my fur and flesh. I took a step forward.

"Wait. Please."

He'd even used please.

"I'll meet you inside," I whispered to the bird on my back. He took flight, his talons now jabbing into my spine. "What do you want, Calouise?" I said with a sigh.

"I told you to call me Cal."

"I don't believe we're on such familiar terms, your Majesty." I bent my front leg in a small bow, but I saw him cringe at the formal address.

"Don't call me that again," he growled quietly. "And don't bow either."

I snorted. "Is that a command or request?"

"A request … for now."

"What do you want?" I repeated. "I actually have an agenda to follow today."

"Can we talk later then?"

Talk. With Calouise. It felt like an oxymoron.

"Yeah, sure." I stepped through the doorway, Calouise close behind me. "Why are you following me?"

He raised his brows. "I live here."

"Right." I felt the rush of blood to my cheeks and looked away before I could find out if tigers blush.

Saltir had convinced Cyan to meet with me, and he sat waiting, the osprey perched on Saltir and Swift clinging to the side of a stone block.

"Mix, I'll admit I'm surprised," said Cyan in his sandpaper voice.

"I'm sure you're just as thrilled to see me as I am you."

He glared at me. I could see his claws push out from under his paws. "Why are you here?"

"I'm in the process of recruiting other cats to aid our fight, but I've been warned that leopards outside of this forest won't be too sympathetic or interested in our cause."

"And?"

"I want to know what you can do to persuade nomadic leopards to join us."

He raised a single brow. "You expect me to help you when you are responsible for the death of the rajah? You started the war, and that is not our community's or the other leopards' fault."

"Zoriach oppressed us, *all of us*, and *she* killed Sojóma. This is about all of us, tigers and leopards, and our common enemy— Zoriach and the lions." I hissed.

"You started this animosity."

"The lions and tigers have been fighting for centuries. It's time we stop acting like cowards and stand up for ourselves. I will do everything I can to make this right. I'm not one to be underestimated, and I plan to win this war and exact vengeance for our loss, and that's not possible without more numbers. So can you help or not?"

"This started because you threatened to take Zoriach's power away from her. So she retaliated by taking Sojóma. While we here in the jungle may care about losing Sojóma, nomadic leopards won't give a panther's paw about any of this. That's the cold truth, Newbie."

I snarled at him, my shoulders tensing. "I'm Commander of this army and war. You'll not address me so informally, Leopard!"

Saltir growled in response to my insult against the leopards. I glared at him. If he wanted to back Cyan, then he'd get more hostility from me. I could sense Calouise tense up beside me, ready for action. I glared at

Cyan. If I didn't need him to win the war, I'd have laid him flat and left an irremovable reminder that I was not to be underestimated and belittled.

Calouise stepped forward, his black glare deeper and more threatening than mine by a long shot. "Last chance, Cyan. Will you send these two messengers out with a message to persuade the other leopards or not?" he growled, bearing down on the smaller leopard.

Cyan's angry glare exposed zero yellow in his eyes as he stood firm before his king. "No. There's no reason to."

I released a frustrated puff of hot air and turned away from them both, my claws scraping on the stone as I turned to face Saltir. "Do you have *anything* we can send to the leopards that might bring them here?" I was conscious of trying not to let my voice sound desperate and weak, even in my irascibility.

When he remained silent, glancing between Cyan and Calouise and myself, Calouise turned his imperious stare onto Saltir. "Are the snow cats still in the community up in northern India?"

Saltir anxiously glanced at me, but I knew he wouldn't ignore a direct question from the rajah. "As far as I'm aware, yes."

"And the clouded community in Nepal?"

"I believe they have disbanded," he replied, avoiding my gaze.

"Thank you," he growled. "You two fur brains are dismissed. Winged messengers, follow."

Both the birds took to the air and followed us out of the doorway, around the back of the fortress, and into the meadow. The osprey perched on my back again, and Swift circled our heads.

"I apologize for their behavior," Calouise began. "Neither of them seem to grasp the importance of this war."

"It's not the war, it's answering to me. I assume you have some kind of plan?"

"For many years, Sojóma and a snow cat called Mehish were friends. When Sojóma created our community living, Mehish decided to attempt it as well with a small colony in the mountains."

"So they're our best shot?"

"Yes, but nomads are good, too."

"Yeah, but if Mehish has heard about Sojóma he may be more likely to war against Zoriach. What about the … clouded community?"

"A small cousin of our leopard neighbors. They couldn't make community living work. But they are not an impossibility."

"Alright, I want the faster flyer of you two to fly towards Nepal and do all you can to recruit nomadic leopards."

"That will be me," the osprey said above me, making my ear twitch.

"Swift, your job is to contact Mehish and do all that you can to get him and his cats to join us."

"As you command," they both said, and they flew up and out of sight.

"Now we wait," I said.

"And hope," he replied.

I nodded and turned to leave, but he stopped me.

"You said we could talk," he said gruffly.

"We just did," I said, hoping he'd take me seriously.

"I have something else to say."

I sighed. "Go on."

He shifted his weight, seemed to debate whether or not to sit or stand and finally decided upon standing. "I didn't mean to offend you."

I knew he was referring to his mating offer, but I didn't know what to say. He hadn't offended me. I just was scared… and confused. The act of animalistic mating would never be acceptable in the way my mind processed love. But as I recalled back to the first official offer from him, I remembered the emotion and deeper well of personality I'd managed to see in his eyes. It had not been the typical emotion and functioning of a pure wild animal. He was something more, which was the most important idea for me to consider in our potential future, whatever it entailed. *If* we ever mated, it would be at a point where I had enough evidence to know that Calouise and I were on the same humanistic cognitive level. I had to know he could fall in love with me if anything between us was going to work. But I was getting ahead of myself. I didn't even know how I really felt about him at this point.

On another note, I certainly was not ready to have any tiger cubs in the wild, wild jungle. I had a hard enough time imagining having kids—human kids—at all.

And there was always my fantastic feline figure to worry about.

But he didn't need to know any of this.

"I wasn't offended…," I finally replied in honesty, but I felt as if he needed some kind of rational tiger-esque reason for my refusal. "I'm just… not ready to have cubs. Not when mortality rate it so high and war is upon us."

His black eyes softly roved my face for a moment or two. I sort of lost track of time.

"Can we stop avoiding each other?" he said at last.

I expected to feel apprehension at not avoiding him, but I felt expectant instead. "I think that would be… fair." Fair? My vocabulary had severely failed me. However, there was a certain amount of relief settling upon me. Avoiding him had been a hassle and a stressful burden.

I thought I saw his whiskers twitch in a satisfied way.

"Calouise, your majesty!" a voice called from somewhere out of sight.

"What is it?"

"It's Näni. Her last cub is coming," a tiger said, emerging from my right.

"I'll be along," Calouise said in his deep voice. He didn't rush, but ambled off in the direction the other tiger had come from.

I followed him, curious. "Why does this concern you?"

"Sojóma intended us to be like family. He dictated that it's the honor and royal privilege to be present when new cubs are born and to bless them."

I was intrigued, but I found it hard to imagine Calouise being soft enough to bestow a blessing. I had to see it for myself.

I figured Näni would be in the Sanctuary, but we were traveling north, away from the Sanctuary and any other traces of our community area.

"Why is she so far away from everything?" I asked as we began trekking through thick growth and grasses and trees that were relatively unmarked by our presence. A few old scents registered on my nose, but too old to be of any concern.

"No matter how we live, we cannot suppress a thousand years of instinct. Our females will find a secluded, protected area to give birth and raise the young cubs."

"If she is so protective, how will she react to us being there?"

"Aggressively."

"Should we wait?" I asked, unable to hide the anxious squeak in my voice.

"She's been birthing for two days, alone and left to instinct. Today, the last cub will be born, and we will approach slowly and cautiously so as to not alarm her. She knows this community's rules."

We walked at a leisurely pace for a few more minutes before my ears detected heavy breathing from somewhere out of sight. Ahead was a cluster of tree trunks with long, thick grass surrounding it. I could just make out the tip of her ear as she stood and repositioned herself before disappearing in the grass again.

I felt such an urge of curiosity—I'd never seen anyone or anything give live birth before—and I also felt a tingle of fear.

We got within 15 feet of her before she registered our presence. She growled and flashed her teeth in the instinctive, warning way. I looked at Calouise. He stopped approaching and sat down slowly and cautiously. I did the same.

Most of the grasses around her had been flattened during her process of labor. Two tiny little tiger cubs with spiky, striped fur crawled around, lying almost on top of each other. They didn't move much, their eyes closed. Their mother, Näni, stayed close to them, but kept shifting around, her sides and legs heaving and flexing. Her last cub was about to enter the world.

It came in a membrane-like bubble as she labored and pushed it out of her. She squatted as close to the ground as she could, the bubble popping and the newborn laying on the ground, its fur wet and matted in substances I didn't want to identify. But it was a beautiful process to witness and the cub was so small and adorable, almost like a little tiger stuffed animal—only wet.

Näni scooted around and began to lick and groom the newborn with her rough tongue. The cub's eyes remained closed, and its movement was limited, but it was beautiful new life.

"It's so small," I whispered.

Näni's eyes were almost black as she gazed at us, her tired body huddled around her cubs in a sheltering way.

"I'm only here to bless them," Calouise said gently to the protective mother.

"And I'm only here as an admirer," I added, afraid she'd attack me.

Her eyes swiveled between the two of us. "Be quick so I can be left in peace," she said in a type of agitated hiss. I could sense her struggle to hold back her motherly instincts.

Calouise approached them slowly, his body alert, but his expression gentle. When he was within a foot of the new cubs, Näni backed off just enough to expose the newborns' heads. Calouise licked his paw and then very carefully placed it on top of each cub's head. Then he bent closer—still proceeding with caution, Näni's eyes never leaving his form—and whispered something quiet to the little cubs. My sensitive ears couldn't even pick it up. He lifted his paw and bowed once before he backed away, and Näni curled around her babies in relief and exhaustion. I caught her shoulders slumping as we walked away.

"What did you think?" Calouise asked me as he padded by my side.

"It was … something. A good something, though," I added with a half smile that I wasn't sure he saw.

"It's hope."

"Yeah, it is. Hey, what did you say… for the blessing, I mean."

He gave me a sideways glance, very coy—which I didn't think tigers could manage. "Wouldn't you like to know?"

"Well that's why I asked," I said, realizing he was not only having a full conversation, but dragging it along like he didn't want it to end.

He turned to walk east, towards the edge of the jungle. "Keep walking with me, and I might tell you."

I hesitated and shifted my weight. We stood only a few hundred yards from the Sanctuary, where I knew Somila and Shrey would be. I had been hoping to spend time with them and ask them about the leopard situation that had come to light that morning. But, up until now, I hadn't realized how much I *enjoyed* talking with Calouise. I appeared to be one of the only cats he actually held steady conversation with. And as much as I resisted admitting it …

I had missed him.

I internally shied away from that kind of thinking. I felt complete terror at the idea of emotional attachment to Calouise, or anyone for that matter. I was scared at where it might lead and, also, of how easily I'd be devastated if he moved on. If he managed to fall for me—if we mated and even built a relationship—what would happen after? I give *birth* to *cubs*? I'd be a tiger mom raising cubs in a jungle.

It was that kind of human thinking that was screwing with my ability to be more like normal tigers. Of course I could manage to raise tiger cubs—it was natural.

But what if I ever needed to return to the human world? Would I have to lose and leave them all behind?

Building a relationship—even a potential family—here and having to leave them …

It wasn't what I wanted.

And that scared me more.

I had remained motionless and silent for the quick thirty seconds it had taken for my brain to process that mess, but Calouise was waiting patiently, his crisp, white fur almost shining silver in the patches of light that managed to filter through the dense, wet canopy.

I stepped forward in his direction, and we fell into a comfortable, matching stride.

"Took you long enough to decide," he said without looking at me. I thought I detected disappointment in his quiet, deep voice.

"I had to make a choice to ignore my other plans so I could spend this time with you." As soon as I said it, I knew I was travelling down the path I feared most.

This was confirmed by the half-raised cheek and bright yellow eye glance that gave away his pleasure. "I understand. I've had to neglect a council meeting or two in the last few days, as well."

He's not a normal cat, my inner voice squeaked. As much as I wanted to believe it, I remained cautious. I'd only heard of one tiger ever falling in love, and that had left him in a world of pain. Even if he were capable of it, I didn't know Calouise's motivation or final intentions. He had offered to mate, but why and what that meant to him were still a mystery.

We walked leisurely for a while before we spotted the edge of the jungle. I made to turn back, but he continued forward, passing the treeline, and stood tall and majestic at the edge between the trees and grassland. The yellow and green grass waved lazily in the slight breeze while birds darted in and out of sight. He took a deep breath, and in that moment, I saw him. I saw his great size and strength, his beauty and power, and his emotion and might. He was King. King of this place, King of us, and King of the jungle.

"You belong on the throne," I whispered, standing just behind him.

He looked at me, his yellow eyes shining.

"You're Rajah," I added. I felt, in this moment, referring to him in the culturally specific title would convey the deeper meaning and emotion I was experiencing.

"Come here, beside me," he whispered.

I moved to stand beside him on his right, also staring out over the grassland. The sky was mostly grey, but the sun peeked out whenever it could find a break. I looked over the scene and felt a wonderful sense of peacefulness and contentment.

Calouise gazed at me—I could feel his eyes on my face, and I refused to meet them.

"You belong here, too," he said.

"I'm not a rajah," I replied, still not looking at him.

"But you could be a rani—a queen."

"*Your* queen?" I asked, looking down at his enormous paws, avoiding his gaze.

"Not necessarily."

For some reason, that disappointed me—my heart had cringed slightly at his reply. But I felt greater embarrassment for having asked the question in the first place, especially when I wasn't really ready to hear his answer. I couldn't even be mad at myself for the disappointed feeling. I had asked, but I'd also rejected him in the past. He could just have been on guard like I was trying to be.

I sensed him look away. He began to walk in the direction of Ghukashi.

"Wait! You're walking towards the village… in broad daylight."

"I won't be seen. I'll be seeing."

His response didn't surprise me—over our months together, I'd come to realize he was an observer. He seemed to take pleasure in spending his time watching. He didn't just watch me, but other cats in our community under his domain, and I wasn't surprised that he had some strange desire to observe the land outside of the trees.

I took a hesitant step forward.

"There's a lot of world beyond the jungle, Mix. You won't see it if you stay afraid."

I shot him a dirty look. He already knew me too well. "Alright, " I replied reluctantly. Across the grassland we headed, my senses on full alert. "You realize these people are killers."

"After he tried to kill them. Jasper became a killer, too."

"Only because another man tried to kill him first."

"It's true, the world appears to run on killing," he said, his tail flicking the yellow grass behind him. I had to keep telling myself not to tense up every time I heard the gentle swoosh and rustle as the grass and little creatures hiding in it were disturbed. "We kill to eat, we hunt to survive."

We continued, prowling through the grass for a few hundred yards in silence. The village's huts were in view, and I felt my pulse beginning to race as we moved closer and closer.

When we were about 100 yards from the nearest hut, Calouise stopped and crouched low, almost disappearing in the long, yellow, and waving grass. I mimicked him.

"There's more to life than survival," he whispered, gazing toward the village. I followed his line of sight and caught sight of the five humans.

My body immediately froze, ready to defend or attack, but as I continued to look, I realized it was five children, their dark Indian skin shining golden in the momentary sun. Flecks of black earth flew into the air as they kicked a ball between them and danced around in delighted laughter. They weren't half bad at dribbling and passing, kicking up more dirt as they constantly adjusted their positions in their makeshift circle.

I watched them with fascination for a solid amount of time before a mother called them in for dinner. Calouise still remained at my side, relaxed and apparently at ease, even with the proximity of the village.

"The sun is getting low. We should go back," he said quietly.

"Yeah…." I stood up slowly and carefully prowled in the direction of the trees. "You said life is more than survival. Maybe that's true of humans, but tigers—"

"Tigers are more than raw instinct. You should know that from experience."

I looked back at him, his paws making the slightest thumps behind me. His eyes were their normal deep black again.

"Maybe we would be surviving better if we relied more on instinct," I whispered, thinking back to Shrey and his talk about mating and simply loving.

"Perhaps." It took a couple hundred more feet before he spoke again. "Life wouldn't be worth living if we didn't enjoy it."

"You're a tiger—a wild animal. What do you enjoy that's above instinct?"

"So are you. What do *you* enjoy?"

We had reached the edge of the trees where the endless creaks, caws, and chirps felt comforting. I pondered his question trying to keep my human brain from interfering with my answer.

"That's not how it works. I asked you first," I said, trying to buy time.

His dark eyes were boring into mine in a way that made all my courage flee and my own eyes dart away in emotional terror.

"Walking and talking with you," he replied.

I didn't expect that one. I also didn't want to sound rude or be untruthful by not responding with something that reciprocated his enjoyment. It had most likely taken a good deal of effort to admit it to me. Or maybe it had cost him nothing because, unlike me, he wasn't fighting his feelings. Or even embarrassed by them.

"I do enjoy my time with you, as well. I also really like running."

"That's unusual."

"So I've been told."

"It does prove my point," he said smugly before he stepped under the protective cover of trees.

I shot him an irritated glare, but I don't think he saw it. I followed him back to the Sanctuary, unsure if our conversation was over. He still hadn't told me what his blessing had been.

I nearly bumped into his rear end. He had stopped and was looking to his left. I scooted up close and peered in the same direction. Three little tiger cubs—only a couple months old—ran around, pawing and biting and passing a ball shaped mass. They gave wimpy, squeaky roars when the ball rolled out of reach or was taken by another cub. I watched with fascination and adoration. I had seen cubs play many times. They loved to pounce and wrestle—practice with instincts they were unable to control yet. But this scene was more than instinct. The cubs played with the ball and each other. Just like the human children had done only an hour ago. It was proof of Calouise's point that life was about finding joy, about living in happiness rather than simply surviving.

I shivered when I felt his whiskers tickle the side of my face as he whispered in his mesmerizing voice, "The finest blessing is to know that you are a tiger, and with that comes a great power and potential to continue our legacy as kings, defenders, protectors of the jungle. Tigers must not simply survive; we must live, and it begins with you when you grow up strong in order to discover that which makes you happy."

The last look he gave me that night was soft but triumphant in the fading light. I let him disappear without saying anything else, left alone with the new knowledge tumbling around in my head. Calouise had proved a beautiful and important idea, but I had witnessed something more in studying both the children and the cubs.

What was more important to me was the realization that our species weren't so different after all.

CALCULATION

Yesterday afternoon felt stolen—a brief lapse of time that seemed more like a dream in the harsh reality I returned to. Harsh was a rather dramatic term. It rained more often than the previous months, which initially surprised me since it was approaching summer months. The consistent pitter patter on the leaves and ground felt like home.

I wasn't particularly fond of sleeping in mud or waking up soaked to the bone, but the rain was familiar, and the dew droplets that clung to my fur were beautiful when the morning light hit them. I relished the coolness of mornings once the afternoon hit. While it may have been wet, the air grew hot and humid. It was my first India summer.

After spending an unexpected afternoon with Calouise the day before, I made it a priority to spend time with Somila and Shrey that day. I was apprehensive to see Somila. We hadn't held a steady or interesting conversation since Sojóma's death. I was to blame for that, but I had no idea how she would react to my sudden recovery and willingness to engage in conversation. Of course, Shrey would be stoic and care-free about it all. I had talked to him more than Somila in the last few weeks, so I hoped Somila didn't feel too jealous. I would also need to keep my time spent and feelings on Calouise to myself as best as I could. I didn't need that to claw a deeper gash in our frail relationship.

I leisurely prowled to the beach area around midday to find it empty. Somila and Shrey could be anywhere since I hadn't informed them beforehand that I wished to talk. Truth be told, I missed their friendship, and I planned to wait on the bank for them all day.

I didn't wait long. Shrey appeared on the opposite side of the river, slowly sliding down the side of a tree. I wasn't used to seeing him in trees since he usually spent the majority of his time on the ground with Somila or me. He disappeared into the brush before he emerged on the opposite bank.

"Hello, Mix," he said in a cheery tone. He splashed across the river and shook off the water into my face in his old playful way.

"I'm already wet enough, you lunatic!" I called, turning my face away.

He gave me a momentary, piercing glance. "Lunatic is too… human. Try something else."

"Lion is too insulting, isn't it?" I said, trying to hold back the sarcasm.

"Normally, that'd be only a huge insult to a tiger, but under the circumstances, yes that's too harsh for my innocent action."

I rolled my eyes. "Alright, you panther, stop shaking your water on me. The sky has done enough of that already."

He started to laugh, but it was a laugh at my expense. I could tell by the twitch of his whiskers.

"What's so funny?" I demanded.

He was laughing too hard to explain.

"He's laughing because you're complaining about the drizzles we've had," said Somila from behind me. I started at the sound of her voice.

"Drizzles?"

"Yes, drizzles. Monsoon season is almost upon us. You can complain about being wet once it has stormed for a week straight." She said it with a sardonic smile.

I shivered. "And how long does monsoon season last?"

They gave me quizzical looks.

"I was raised in a zoo, remember? Whenever the weather was less than ideal, they had a warm, dry place for me to stay."

That seemed to satisfy their curiosity.

"It lasts a couple months," Somila replied. She sat down beside me, her paws sinking a little in the soft ground. I chanced a glance at her face, expecting to find a glare after my lengthy silence and isolation, but her face was relaxed. Even kind. "How have you been, Mix?" she asked softly. She was acting nicer than I had expected. But I wasn't letting my guard down.

"I've been better. The last few weeks were rough. But each day is an improvement."

"I guess that's… good. I know you and Sojóma talked a lot."

I couldn't even detect a jealous undertone.

"Yeah… we all miss him. And on top of that. I've been training with Trapir for weeks. I've been sore and tired."

"Well, you're going to need to start training us here pretty soon."

"What? Don't you already know how to fight? I mean, I was raised in a zoo. You both are naturally wild." If they didn't feel able to combat, this was going to change my entire battle plan.

"We can hunt. We can kill. We can brawl. But truly attacking another cat with the intent to kill and surviving … that's not hardwired in all of us. Before we strike Zoriach, we should all go through some sort of training from someone who knows what they're doing."

"My plan was to attack once our reinforcements arrived, but if you feel unprepared—"

"So we are getting reinforcements?" Shrey asked suddenly, sitting up straighter, but sinking deeper into the squashy earth.

"Not definitely. I've sent out messengers with requests."

"To who?"

"To nomadic tigers and leopards, Mehish and his leopard community, and clouded leopards up north."

Shrey let out a defeated sigh.

"What?" I snapped.

"We're doomed," he replied.

Somila glared at him. "No, we're not. We'll definitely get nomads. Even five more would greatly increase our odds."

"Yeah, nomadic tigers. We won't see any leopards," he said kneading the mud with is claws, avoiding my gaze.

"How do you know?" I asked him before I could stop and think.

His face suddenly grew dark and fierce, and I felt like cowering into a ball. "I'm a leopard, Mix, in case you've forgotten. This war you're fighting? It's between tigers and lions. It's really between you and Zoriach, but both of you have support from your species. Leopards have *nothing* to do with this. We here in *this* jungle are fighting because Zoriach took our rajah and threatened us all. But Mehish and other nomads won't want to get involved. It's not their fight."

"What do you mean this is about Zoriach and me? The feline wars have existed for ages," I asked, offended by the selfish accusation.

"True, but those ended years ago. This is happening because you challenged her and she's taking her revenge. She wants to hurt *you*."

"Then why wouldn't she just kill one of you? Why kill Sojóma?"

"Because killing Sojóma not only hurt you, but also hurt us. Zoriach is sick and bloodthirsty. She thinks she can annihilate all of us if she incites us all," he said.

"Well, she just might achieve that if we don't get help."

"I wouldn't count on it," he said with finality.

I didn't want to believe him, but if he was right, we were doomed.

And monsoon season was coming.

"Why?" I accidently said in my defeated way.

Somila had remained silent for awhile, sitting slumped over, her eyes carefully watching us, her tail flicking back and forth, brushing against wet, leafy bushes as she sat in the middle of our tension.

"What do you mean?" Shrey said.

"I mean, why is Zoriach doing this? Why does she hate us? She already has the appearance of dominance and royal authority in the animal world. Why is she determined to destroy us?"

"Because you challenged her. Zoriach is paranoid and easy to anger," Shrey said slowly and deliberately.

I almost hissed at him. "But *why*?"

Shrey opened his mouth to respond but Somila shot him a glare and then looked at me. "Zoriach is… She was raised differently than normal cats," she began patiently. I was taken aback by the maturity she displayed. "Of course she grew up in a pride, but her parents were from a generation that were raised by lions who lost repeatedly to the tigers. Their hatred of us was not only passed down to Zoriach, but it was actively infused into her personality. Then in the last war, her father was killed by Sojóma, and her mother was fatally injured. Zoriach snapped at that point. She killed Trapir's mate and many others. We suffered a defeat we hadn't been prepared for. Tigers had been oppressed and made to feel inferior for a half a century, since the last time they'd controlled the domineering power, but they had expected to win that rebellion. The tigers left licking their wounds, ready to rest and wait for another chance to strike. That's when Sojóma began the community living. It was almost ten years ago. Shrey and I weren't even born yet. Ever since that victory, Zoriach has been constantly on alert, spying, sneaking, and preparing for us to revolt and take back everything."

"But wasn't killing Sojóma enough revenge for her?"

"It might have been if she had killed him right after the last battle. But she's lived eight years past her parents' deaths with vengeance and distrust in her heart. The only revenge and peace of mind she'll receive is eliminating all of us."

This was very important, useful information. Disheartening, but useful. I was angry no one had thought to share it with me before now as commander.

"Well, we are indeed doomed if reinforcements don't arrive. We are coming up on monsoon season, and none of you feel confident in your ability to actually battle." I attempted to sound sarcastic, but there was too much truth and fear in that gloomy statement to let sarcasm take control.

"I hope you have a plan, Commander," Somila said in a serious voice, but I thought I heard the held back sarcasm in her statement as well.

"I did, or at least, part of a plan. Until now."

"You should come up with something soon. Everyone is wondering when we will actually be moving forward with battle plans."

I shifted my weight uneasily, disturbing a clump of grasses that housed an agitated frog. "A lot is happening behind the scenes right now. I'm waiting for news on reinforcements. Then I'll know what kind of plan I'll need."

"You're going to need a drastic one," Shrey said. "Because reinforcements aren't coming."

I growled. "You don't know that with certainty. Zoriach has black panthers—*your* dark brothers. I should be able to recruit other leopards."

"Just be prepared for anything," Somila said calmly. "Maybe you and Calouise can come up with something."

"What do you mean?" I asked, feeling my throat tighten. "Why him?"

"Relax, Mix," she said, holding back a laugh. "You're his second in command. You two can bounce ideas off one another."

"I… haven't really talked to him in awhile. I might be better off—"

"Except yesterday," Shrey said in a scathing tone.

"Back off, Shrey. He's not as horrible as you seem to think he is," Somila snapped. "I'm sure their conversation yesterday was a first in a long while."

I thought I saw her wink. Was that it? No more jealousy?

"Yeah. He was showing me some of his kingly duties in case… he dies in battle. Or Zoriach assassinates him, too." Saying it out loud hurt more than I expected. What if he died? What if Somila died? Or Shrey?

What if I died? I wouldn't just be leaving behind these cats that I loved, but I'd never be able to return to the human world either. Sara, my mother, my tabby cat—we'd never see each other again. I had two lives to permanently lose.

I could feel the beginning of panic and the endless what ifs designed to send me running in utter terror, but I shut them down. I would not die. That's why I'd been training with Trapir for so long. I would be ready to battle and win. But would the cats I cared about be able to do the same?

I needed to make sure everyone received training, or we were all going to die whether we had reinforcements or not.

"I'm sure Calouise will be fine. He's a big cat. He can take care of himself," Shrey grumbled.

"It does look like I'll need to talk to him again. We need some kind of plan…"

"Just keep us in the loop, Mix. We're your friends. And allies," Somila said.

I sighed. "Why didn't I just kill Zoriach when I had the chance?"

"What chance?"

"At the river. Or when she killed Sojóma. She was right there…"

"You couldn't have killed a frog the day you chased Zoriach through the jungle. You barely made it back to the beach. She had done nothing horrible yet, either. As for the day she killed Sojóma… you weren't ready.

I believe a part of her wanted you to attack her, but she would have torn you to pieces. Zoriach is a killer."

"Yeah, well, the next time I see her, she's dead."

"That's sort of the point of going to war against her," Shrey said.

I gave him an angry glare and an irritated hiss.

"What's with you today?" Somila asked him, flinging a pawful of muddy dirt at his face.

"I don't know," he replied defensively, shaking and wiping the mess from his head. "I… just don't like Calouise. And…I think you're both being too positive about reinforcements. And I really don't want to die," he added quietly.

"Well, death is sort of the result of war," I said.

His tail twitched, brushing some leaves and flinging water in my direction. "Okay, okay. I'll make sure everyone receives some training before we face her. As for Calouise… you have to stop getting upset every time we talk about him."

"Why?"

"Because we're not going to stop talking about him," I said, raising my brows as Somila nodded beside me.

He let out an exasperated huff. "Females. Alright. Just don't complain to me when he turns out not to be all that he seems."

"What's that supposed to mean?"

"All the females think he's something extra special because he's the jungle 'prince,' when really, he's just an ordinary, hormonal male tiger. He will love like all male cats love and move along to the next. He doesn't care more than any other cat, he doesn't show any more emotion than any other cat—less than others actually—"

"Based on what evidence?" I suddenly asked. Did Calouise have a dark history I needed to know?

"Females talk. I've heard complaints about his aloofness and inability to express joy... at all. His love is quick and lacks passion. He's just a pretty face and an empty shell."

I felt a flood of relief and a rush of apprehension. I already knew Calouise was able to connect—that he cared about me. He could have lied yesterday about what he really enjoyed, but the way he looked me in the eyes, the sound of his voice whispering in my ear, and the persistence with which he tried to talk to me, spend time with me, be with me.... He'd have to be one hell of a liar if none of it was genuine. But how many females had he carelessly loved?

"Mix, you are in the wild, and he is wild animal," I mumbled to myself, too quiet for either Shrey or Somila to hear. My brain had a valid point, which was only slightly disappointing. I was growing comfortable with the way of the wild world. Perhaps that's why calling *myself* Mix didn't seem to bother me. Jade was someone else, someone back in the states that I'd lost contact with.

"He's not an empty shell," I said definitively.

"But he does have a pretty face," Somila said with a smirk in my direction.

"Were you like this when Somila liked him?" I demanded at Shrey.

"Yes, he was," Somila said with a pointed look at Shrey.

"Maybe he's changed. Maybe he was waiting for—"

"Don't say 'the right female!'" Shrey growled, jumping to his feet.

I stood up. "Trapir had one he really and truly loved! Don't tell me it's impossible!" Suddenly my claws were buried in the damp earth.

"It's… very rare…and weird!" he spat.

"But maybe that's what he's looking for!"

"How would *you* know what he's looking for?"

"I… don't know. It's just a hunch." I relaxed my shoulders and retracted my claws, keeping a watchful eye on Shrey across from me. "But stop making him out to be a bad cat. He's not what you think he is. He's my friend, just like you are."

He stared at me with a pinched face for a solid minute without speaking. I glanced at Somila, but she just shook her head. Rain started to fall above us as we waited for his response. Shrey and I been bickering a lot lately.

At last he seemed to relax, shifting his legs closer together and shaking out his fur. "Fine. I'll think the best of him… for now. But the minute he becomes all that I said he was, there'll be no more sympathy from me."

Half a laugh escaped through my hard face at his final statement. Deep down, he only got upset because he cared. At least that's what I wanted to believe. "Thank you," I said curtly.

He sat back down. I remained standing. "I think… I'm going to take a walk. Cool off."

Somila finally stood and stretched. "I'll join you, if you don't mind."

For once, I didn't. "Okay." We walked upstream, away from the Sanctuary, and Shrey, and most of the other cats. Rain kept falling, finding its way through the canopy and splattering on all of us below. Nothing felt more like home than the feel of water soaking through my coat.

We were at least 100 yards away from Shrey before Somila decided to talk, as I knew she would. That part of her hadn't changed at all.

"So what did you and Cal really talk about yesterday?" she pried, the old, familiar tone of gossip in the air.

"I told the truth," I replied, my voice uncontrollably higher than normal.

"Yeah, right. Come one, Mix. Gossip is essential to a successful female friendship."

"That's debatable. I did tell you the truth. Or at least half of it."

Her raised brows demanded more information.

"Look, I don't know why you want to talk about this. Last time we talked about males around here, you got angry and jealous, and then one of them died!"

She rolled her eyes. "Don't be so dramatic. That's my job."

"I thought you wanted him. I don't want to ruin our friendship."

She took a deep breath as her pupils dilated slightly. "I'll always have a hot spot for Cal, but I've moved on. I found another striped coat that makes my whiskers quiver. If you want Calouise … and he wants you, then go for it."

I was taken aback, but also pleased. And still terrified. "Alright, well thanks, I guess."

"Sure. We females have to make sure we don't find more causes than usual to start problems in our small community. But that doesn't mean you escaped talking about what *is* going on with you and Calouise."

I felt uncomfortable. I had never been one to enjoy girl talk. Spilling my deep thoughts and emotions out into the open seemed vulnerable to me. But maybe talking about them would help me figure out all the fear and confusion I felt about him. "I don't know what to say. I mean, he's offered to mate several times, but I've turned him down each time."

Her eyes were really wide. "Really? He's offered? More than once? And again after you turned him down already?"

I just kept nodding.

"That's unlike him. I don't think he's offered before, but rather just agreed to others' offers. So he's been persistent? He must really like you. That's unusual."

"Is it?" I asked, carefully stepping over a snake that slithered across our path.

"Well, yeah. If we get rejected even once, we usually move along to the next available mate that catches our attention. It's about simple enjoyment and reproduction. Love and attachment never play a role in mating… well, rarely."

"It does in other species," I said defensively. Humans were very good at love and attachment. Most of the time.

"What species? Humans? Right. What do they call it?"

"Falling in love," I replied, almost defensively.

"Right. I've heard stories about humans. Some of them love just like tigers do according to some nomads I've come across."

I couldn't disagree with her. Not entirely. "That's uncommon for humans. Usually they are committed to one and raise offspring as a unit."

"All of this from a zoo, huh?" she asked skeptically.

I glared at her. "Yes. Those humans would visit. As for tigers, perhaps attachment and being 'in love' is the uncommon thing when it comes to our love."

She shook her head. "Maybe you're right. It's true, Trapir *fell in love*. You seem able to do so. Maybe you'll get lucky with Calouise and he'll be able to fall in love, too."

A part of me hoped so. Still, another part of me didn't want to have cubs and raise them in a jungle.

"Anyway," Somila continued, "so why have you rejected his mating offer if you like him so much?"

"Because… I'm supposed to lead a war. Cubs are out of the question right now."

She gave me a sad look. "Yeah, I guess that makes sense. Just don't hold out on him forever, okay? If you two care for each other, don't miss your chance to connect. You only live so long, and there're only a few chances to do what makes you happy."

A fish jumped beside us as I considered what she said. Did I want to take that chance with Calouise? Would being with him, loving him, choosing him, make me happy? That wasn't something I could answer right away.

"Enough about me. Tell me about your new interest," I said, trying to hide the desperation in my tone.

Her entire posture perked up, and her eyes dilated a little in excitement. "Well, he's no Calouise, but he's got the most attractive V stripe on his head…."

Our conversation lasted another hour or so before we ended up back in the Sanctuary. We had passed by the beach, but Shrey was already gone. Somila stretched and yawned, her tail curling above her head.

"I believe it's time for a nap. Sujit with the V and I are hunting tonight," she said with a smirk.

"Is that all?"

She bumped into my shoulder in a playful sort of way. "We'll see."

"I'll see you around, Somila." I gave her a half smile.

"Yes, I'm sure we'll have plenty to talk about in the next couple of weeks."

I didn't reply, but I figured she was probably right. I knew I needed to talk to Calouise. All the new information I'd received on Zoriach and monsoon season and reinforcements needed careful consideration and planning. I couldn't do it alone.

I also had the new information about Calouise, which made me want to talk to him in a friendly, personal way, much like yesterday. A part of me still wanted to wait and see. I knew it was the smart thing to be cautious and patient, but the emotional me wanted to be reckless and fall in love with the tiger prince of the jungle.

I decided to sleep on it for a night or two.

I passed by Calouise's old waterfall spot and glanced inside, expecting to see it dark and empty. Instead, I stopped in my tracks and squinted at the flash of orange and white that snagged my attention from behind the water.

"Who's there?" I called. My voice echoed into the cave and sounded much more confident and bold than I'd planned. Whoever was inside didn't respond right away, so I stepped forward and poked my head through the curtain of water. It fell like a sheet of cool ice that melted the instant if made contact with my fur. I shivered as it ran down my back in slithering trails.

My eyes adjusted quickly to the dim light of the cave and then fell upon Calouise, lying quite relaxed in his old sleeping spot.

"Well, I'm surprised to find you here," I said calmly, stepping through the water all the way and shaking it off, listening to the small splats and echoes the droplets made as they were flung from my back against the walls.

"Why is that?"

Another small, uncontrollable shiver ran down my spine as his low, deep voice echoed gently back to my sensitive ears. I hoped he didn't catch it, but a part of me already knew he had.

"You're always in the throne room now."

"That doesn't make this place suddenly off limits," he replied, gesturing beside him for me to sit.

I hesitated only slightly before deciding there could be no harm in it. "What if this spot was claimed by someone else now?"

"Nobody has."

"How do you know?" I was sitting, considering lying down as well, but remembering how much of my body would be in cold, wet vegetation and rock, I remained upright.

"Because it's my spot."

"But you sleep in the fortress."

His look of sarcastic exasperation almost made me laugh. "Technically, this is no longer my spot. Symbolically, it will always be mine. In their heads, this is my spot."

"Alright, you big-headed prince. Careful, or someone will think you're arrogant."

He flashed me an alluring smile. "I'm not a prince, but a king."

I couldn't resist the laugh that escaped this time. It was strange to see this humorous side of him. Strange, but attractively intriguing. I guessed today would be an intimate talking day instead of strategic.

"And what were you doing over here?" he asked conversationally.

"I was finishing my day with Somila and Shrey."

"The one you put off yesterday for your rajah?"

"Indeed."

"Well, I'm grateful for yesterday and glad you had your chance to speak with them today." He gave a slight head nod in appreciation.

I stared at him with what must have been a stupid expression of admiring wonderment that I hopelessly fought against revealing. Each day with him unearthed another layer of his complex personality, but that only made him more irresistible.

And it sucked.

Just as much as it was thrilling.

I desperately wished to ask him if he was special—if he was able to defy his nature and fall in love—but that would be a perilous thing to do.

"Yeah, it was nice. I haven't talked much since Sojóma's death, so it was refreshing."

His sympathetic look made me shift my weight and want to change the subject.

Before I had the chance to do so, a tiger ran by the cave calling for Calouise in an urgent manner. Calouise reacted and leapt through the waterfall in an instant and chased down the cat looking for him.

I stood and carefully walked to the mouth of the cave, petrified of what information I was going to hear next. Who was the latest victim of Zoriach's sick need for revenge? I took a moment to steady my breath.

Calouise was running back toward me, his shovel-like paws flinging wet dirt behind him. He skidded to a halt in front of me, but only for a second. "We've lost a cub. Maybe another." And he was gone again, running towards the stream.

"Wait!" I screamed after him, also taking off. It wasn't difficult to follow him. His tracks left sharp divots in the earth. I left a parallel set beside his as I sprinted. Being smaller and faster, I caught up in a few seconds, running beside him in no time. We were going upstream where the water rocketed over boulders in violent rapids but then whisked around a corner to a slow, marshy channel.

Calouise slowed down enough to catch his breath and then continued in a type of jogging trot. I matched his pace.

"Not to sound insensitive, but why the panic and rush? The community lost a lot of cubs last year."

He whipped his head around and gave me an angry chuff. "It is *always* a tragedy to lose cubs." His eyes appeared blacker than usual.

I swallowed the fear that had just caused my throat to tighten and continued to follow him until he stopped. He lifted his nose and inhaled deeply.

"It's dead. Good." He leapt forward in continued pursuit. A small breeze ruffled my face and fur, bringing with it the distinct smell of blood. Whatever was dead had been a carnivore.

A few instants later, we came upon a wholly frightening and stomach-turning scene. A monstrous crocodile lay limp, the back of its neck area ripped open and torn to bloody scraps. Its enormous jaws were ajar, its many large teeth exposed and rather red. A few feet away the ravaged and mangled tiger cub lay in a tiny heap, his jaws open too, but in way that clawed and tore at the heartstrings. His fur was matted and muddy-red. The crocodile's immense jaw force had crushed the baby in an instant.

A male tiger stood not far from the croc, the white of his maw dripping red.

"You took him down on your own?" I asked.

He gave a stiff nod.

The initial shock was wearing off, and an agonizing wailing sound captured my attention. I looked around to see a shaking tigress grooming another cub, his body also matted with mud and blood, but still alive. He'd have some scars later in life. The wailing came from a third cub, her tiny, piercing cries heartbreaking as she called out to her dead brother. She nosed at his limp body, confused and worried by his lack of response.

I had to look away, to get away, away from the sad, painful reminder that danger lurked around every corner and life was precarious, especially for us threatened tigers. It wasn't just humans that killed us, but other predators too. Crocodiles killed cubs and humans killed us all.

Either way, we couldn't escape our condemned fate.

I was running—running without any purpose but to leave. I lunged between tree trunks, dove under low branches, and leapt over bushes. I ran until my paws hurt so bad that I had to stop. Standing at the edge of the river in unfamiliar territory, I tried to catch my breath. I'd run so long, I had ignored the painful but necessary process of breathing. Now it was pure agony to draw in the short, loud, seemingly useless bursts of oxygen.

I eased my throbbing paws into the cool water in the hope for some kind of relief. Even the cold and painful state of my body couldn't overwhelm the crushing images of lost life.

They were only babies, a few months old. Had they deserved to die? I could hear echoes of Sojóma's voice explaining to me the circle of life and how everything must be consumed by something. But even he had told me to avoid the young—to let fawns live so we could have more deer. Didn't other animals have any kind of compassion?

I shook my head. I was in the wild jungle, and I had—needed—to find a way to handle this if I planned to be successful in war. I gathered my resolve and faced the devastating images and truth of death and brutality. They washed over me, battered against my heart, but I refused them entrance. I would remain strong.

I was interrupted as the clamor of resounding crashes and pounding paws reached my ears. For the briefest moment I felt fear, but then I remembered running off and leaving Calouise back at the scene. I hadn't expected him to follow me, not this far. Did he really care for me that much?

Sure enough, he appeared, charging around a tree and stopping just in front of me. He released a large breath in what appeared to be relief.

"What are you doing here?" I asked wearily.

He sucked in a few more breaths. "You ran off and didn't come back."

"And that means you have to follow me?" I felt flattered and annoyed. Would I ever be able to be alone again?

"I wanted to. Are you alright?"

"Yeah, I'm fine." I walked back up onto the bank and stood awkwardly in front of him, his penetrating gaze searching my face. "Thank you. For checking on me."

"You're welcome."

"I think I just need some alone time, if that's okay with you."

Rather than look concerned, his face returned to the hardy mask he usually bore that concealed his emotion. "Whatever you wish."

I brushed by him, careful not to actually touch him, but close enough to feel electricity. It was similar to the currents I felt within me when I transformed, but this electricity was more external, on the surface of my skin and ends of my fur. There was a strong desire to touch him, so strong that I almost lightly touched my shoulder against his back hip. I refrained and avoided looking back, prowling away with my mixed emotions. Still consumed with sadness, it felt strange to experience the intense energy that was flaring between us. It would have been strange despite the circumstances, but it may have felt more intriguing and exciting if I hadn't just witnessed the current atrocity.

He didn't follow me. I sensed his motionless body until I had wandered too far away. I wondered what thoughts he was thinking—if they were about me or the lost cub or a jumbled mixture of both. Maybe he needed alone time, too.

I found my way back to the Sanctuary and my original sleeping spot. I stared at the compacted mass of grass and leaves from my time spent there. That had been my frightened, stay-out-of-the-way, newbie spot. It had become a spot of comfort. But looking at it now, it didn't feel comforting. I walked away from it and meandered along the stony cliff face until I came upon the waterfall. This had been Calouise's spot, and he was right—most of the other cats still considered it to be his.

I knew better. This spot was now unclaimed. It was secluded and beautiful and considered a place of privilege. I was second in command. I was battling and beating my fear. I now possessed all of Calouise's previous authority and power.

This spot would now be mine.

I moved around the falling water and entered the cave space. There remained a permanent indentation from when Calouise lounged there, and somehow, that indent appeared much more comforting than my old space.

I curled up in the center of the spot, noticing the indent was larger than me, and stared unseeingly at the shimmering water. The images of the dead cub still assaulted me, as did old memories of Jasper and Sojóma. I knew the idea of loss would never be easy for me, but I knew that soon enough it would become part of my everyday life. Accepting it would be beneficial to survival, but the emotional side of me knew that acceptance of the normality of loss and death was not a good thing. I had to find a way to put a stop to the unnecessary deaths. There wasn't much I could do to stop the humans from harming us, but I would do all in my power to bring an end to the rivalry that cost us so many lives.

Tigers wouldn't just survive.

We would rule.

NOMADS

I was running. Sprinting through the jungle almost blind. My peripheral vision wasn't working, and neither was my night vision. I could barely see, but I couldn't slow down. The urgency I felt couldn't be stifled. I had to reach my destination.

A wall suddenly manifested, but I was prepared. Without thinking, I leapt onto it and ran along it. My heart was thudding in my ears.

I couldn't run fast enough. Strangled roars and cries of agony assailed me as I desperately tried to move closer to the source. Each bound became increasingly difficult, as if greater weight was being added upon my shoulders or my paws were sinking into relentless pools of monsoon mud.

Somehow I ended up where I needed to be. I stood before the stone fortress, the smell of blood overpowering. Something warm oozed over my paws, and I looked down to see a pool of deep red. My breath froze in my chest. I followed the trail up to the doorway and then gasped in sorrowful horror at the mangled remains of Somila. A few feet away lay Shrey, his small, dotted form so much smaller in death. Blood dripped from his teeth and paws, but also from his neck.

"Shrey?" I croaked. I gently nudged his limp body. He didn't stir.

Horrified, I looked around. The throne room was dark—blacked out even with my tiger eyes. I could just make out another unmoving body at the base of the steps. I hesitantly stepped over to it, panic building inside my chest.

The striped flank had several severe gashes dug into it. The neck and throat were torn, but the face remained untouched. I recognized it at once, and the strangled scream of grief and denial was lost in the suffocating darkness.

Calouise lay dead before me.

The agony that was crushing every internal organ within me was unmatched by any physical pain I had ever experienced. I fell beside his body, refusing to believe what I saw.

A sinister laugh broke through the thick curtain of silence. It echoed above, around, and inside me, turning my veins to ice. At the top of the stairs, I could make out the blocky throne. Zoriach perched there in arrogant triumph, her yellow eyes glowing brighter and brighter as the darkness thickened.

Just before the crushing night engulfed us, her eyes flashed red.

I bolted awake, my breath impossible to catch, heartbeat racing. I could still hear her voice ringing in my ears, despite the sound of the water splashing into its pool. I couldn't control my panic, the images of Calouise and Somila and Shrey and their pools of blood and the red of her eyes blinding me. Even if it hadn't really happened, it was about to become a potential reality. They had been dead, and I couldn't bring them back. They had been gone, and Zoriach was to blame. Even if I killed her, I couldn't have saved them.

It was only a dream.

An all too real one.

I had to check on them, make sure they were all okay. Just before I sprung out into the open, Somila and Shrey prowled in front of the waterfall, having a light conversation in the early afternoon. Their cheerful attitudes seemed out of place compared to my state of fear. How could they be so carelessly oblivious to the fragility of their lives? That one moment could be their last…

They wandered out of sight, unaware of my presence. It was okay though. They were alive and well.

I only felt the slightest relief at their safety. Somila and Shrey were still alright. Calouise, however, was out there somewhere. I didn't yet want to address the meaning behind my emotional reaction to finding Calouise dead, but I did want to see him. I had to—I wouldn't be completely reassured of his safety until I saw his dark eyes alive and alert, resting on my face.

I stood up and stretched, my muscles sore from remaining tense and stationary for so long. I wasn't sure where to start looking for Calouise, but the throne room seemed to be a good starting place. Truthfully, I *really* didn't want to go over there. The idea of pooling blood and blackness and Zoriach's red eyes still scared the hell out of me. And I had absolutely no desire to talk to or deal with the dignitaries today.

I hoped I would find Calouise along the way.

My adrenaline still rather thick and prevalent, I ran from the cave and toward the river, careful to avoid the beach. Finding Calouise was the only thing I desired to do.

It wasn't raining, but it was humid. Clouds dominated the sky, and the air tried to strangle my lungs as if the night hadn't done enough.

I plowed through the river water, grateful for the small, cooling relief. It was hard to be an animal that didn't excessively sweat. Without shaking the water off, I plunged ahead through the brush, quickly scanning the area around me, listening and looking for anything that resembled a large tiger. There were plenty of leopards lounging in trees above me, but hardly anything on the ground. Their calm, even breathing seemed to reflect a state of easy relaxation I was not privileged to on a regular basis. I only felt the slightest twinge of jealousy.

I approached the wall and stared up at it, admiring its resilience to the crushing will of time. It stood even after all that had fallen around it. How long would it outlast us?

With a sigh, I jumped on top of it and found stable footing to look around. I couldn't make out the fortress, but I saw the trees that surrounded it. The line of the river cut a path through the forest, winding this way and that. The trees stretched on and on ahead of me with no end in sight, a blanket of green.

"What are you seeking?"

The sound of his voice sent sparks of fire through my veins. The ice was gone. I released the breath that I hadn't realized I was holding and looked down to see him lying quite at ease below me in the old ruins I loved to hide in when the world threatened to collapse on me.

"That doesn't matter anymore," I replied, jumping down and walking over to him.

"It must. You looked so intent."

"Let's just say I found it."

"It?"

I glared at his insinuation. "Alright, you."

He sat up a bit straighter, unable to hide his pleasure. "Why were you looking for me?"

I didn't know if I should tell the truth or not. Would he make fun of me if I told him I'd had a nightmare that scared me so bad I ran out in the jungle to make sure everyone was okay?

I would have.

"Calouise, do you know how to fight? Like in battle?" I decided to ask.

"Call me Cal."

"You didn't answer my question."

He peered at me, as if trying to figure out why I asked him such a strange question. "Yes, I can fight"

"But I've trained with Trapir. Have you?"

He glared now. "I don't need to train to know how to kill."

I was close to offending him. "I just wanted to make sure you didn't die on the battlefield because you were overly confident and inexperienced."

He suddenly stood up and growled. "I can handle killing arrogant lions," he rumbled. "Do you want me to prove it to you?"

A little. "That's not what I meant."

He moved right up in my face, his nostrils flaring, whiskers twitching, tickling my own. Every muscle in his body was tensed, his posture hulky and sturdy, his white chest heaving as he looked down at me. I suddenly understood what Somila meant by good-looking.

I didn't back down.

"Do you want me to show you?" he asked aggressively, but not in a way that made me want to cower.

"Alright. See if you can beat me," I said. Training with Trapir, I had little practice or experience outside of his instruction. I wanted the challenge.

Calouise's head jumped back a little in surprise, but he didn't say anything. Tigers weren't like the decent men that refused to hit or fight a woman. Male tigers obtained status through demonstration of strength and dominance. It didn't matter who it was against.

He backed a few feet away and crouched just slightly, his undivided focus on every movement I made. I got low to the ground, ready to duck, dodge, or jump if he attacked first. But he didn't. He continued to watch me, moving slightly if I did, a low rumble coming from his throat. The sound wasn't menacing, but rather invitational. I flashed my teeth at him and hissed, watching for his reaction. The corner of his mouth twitched—like he held back a smile—as he returned the threatening teeth exposure.

I shifted my weight to my back legs and raised a paw, claws exposed, and lunged towards his ear. He growled and lunged forward slightly, also raising a closed paw at me.

Calouise was *playing* with me.

I squinted at him and released an angry growl for not taking this seriously.

He returned one, realizing I meant serious business.

With a snarl, I jumped at him, both paws and claws ready to smack the side of his head and neck, trying to be careful not to get too close to his main artery that I knew would kill him if I reached it. I managed to nick the side of his neck, but not deep.

He snapped at me and hissed at the mark I'd left, more hurt by the fact I'd managed to even touch him at all. He made to bite at my neck, but I stepped back, my front paws reaching up to push his face away.

As soon as both of my paws were up, he dove his huge head into my chest, pushed me back on my hind legs, and managed to wrap a paw and arm around my shoulder. I fell on my back, winded, and Calouise stood over me, one of his back legs pinning my leg down and one of his front paws pushing down on my chest.

He loomed over me, his face inches from mine, breathing heavily, his nostrils flaring and whiskers twitching. The electricity flared between us again, stronger than ever before—so strong I briefly wondered if it could spark enough to cause me to revert back to a human, but that idea fleetingly vanished as I stared into his eyes. I felt the strongest desire to press my nose to his.

I suddenly felt a greater terror than the fear I'd felt that morning. I was scared of what this electricity meant, where it could lead, what was possible. Some part of me wished to explore this more, but the fear and my reasoning left me feeling wary and unwilling to take such a drastic risk.

Before anything else could happen, he released me and backed away several feet. "I'm sorry," he said quietly.

"What for?" I asked, rolling back onto my belly.

"I ... should have let you win," he said slowly. There were pangs of disappointment, but a great amount of relief as well. I wasn't ready to handle whatever was flaring between us.

But still, I frowned at him. I knew he was lying. But I let it go—for now. "No, that was good. Now I know you can fight. Or I know that I'm not as good as I thought I was."

He chuckled. "You aren't bad. I grew up with Sojóma and Trapir."

"Right." An awkward silence fell upon us, both of us refusing to talk about anything to do with the energy and feelings between us. He had already been rejected by me enough times to keep his distance and I— slowly—was coming around, but still holding back, afraid to fall openly in love with someone who might not be able to love me back the way I desired.

What an emotional mess.

Thankfully, Saltir burst over the wall a moment later. It was one of the only times I was grateful to see him.

"Your majesty... and ...Commander, there are cats approaching in the northeast quadrant," Saltir said.

"What kind of cats? Lions?" I asked, standing up.

"No, two tigers, both male."

I looked up at Calouise, filled with hope. "Reinforcements," I said.

I saw his face tense. "Nomads," he muttered.

I turned to Saltir. "Set up a greeting party for them. I want them to feel welcome here. You and the other dignitaries. Our rajah and I will be along soon."

He stood there, staring at me, confused by my giving orders. He glanced at Calouise, looking for different instructions or confirmation. His questioning my authority irritated me.

"Am I not second in command?" I growled.

Saltir looked between Calouise and me, who I saw from the corner of my eye give the slightest of nods, giving credence to my commands. With wide eyes, he left to fulfill his duty.

I faced Calouise, knowing my expression was incredulous.

"Saltir and the rest of the dignitaries are bordering on losing their positions with their disrespect," Calouise said angrily. "But they need strong leadership and reasons to respect you. To them, you arrived here and rose to power very quickly, becoming a catalyst of another war. Don't let them get the better of you, and I won't let them continue to disrespect you."

I knew his words were wise, but I couldn't help the sarcasm. "Oh, let them be their arrogant, insolent selves. You or I could easily overpower them if we needed to."

He peered at me. "Well, at least, *I* could. Your display earlier leads me to doubt your ability to overpower anything."

I gaped at him until I realized he was being facetious. "Those red marks on your neck there would suggest otherwise."

His whiskers twitched in a smile. "You put up a noteworthy fight."

We stared at each other, eye to eye, several feet apart. I was reliving the encounter, especially the end. I bet my life he was reliving the same moment, too. Bringing up the emotional and physical tension that had sparked between us was on the tip of my tongue.

"They're waiting on us," he said quietly.

The moment had passed. "Right. Our first reinforcements."

He moved to the wall. "They're nomads, Mix. Be wary." He jumped on and over the stone and vanished from my sight.

I followed him, curious by his imminent warning. "What do you mean by that?" I asked, catching up to him.

"You said you came from a zoo?" he asked, still walking.

"I don't ever remember actually telling you that," I replied with surprise.

"Sojóma told me."

More surprise. "Were you close to him? I've never asked."

"One thing at a time," he said evasively. "You joined us having to be introduced to the wild. But our community culture has changed us— slowly—and we are not the same wild creatures we were twenty years ago. Nomads are wild. They're ungoverned and rely more on instinct."

"What happened to finding what makes you happy?"

He met my eyes briefly. "You and I and a few others have … exceeded wild inclinations and basic instinctual drives. We operate at higher levels of pleasure and values. Nomads' happiness is directly related to fulfilling their instincts."

I couldn't help note how he had included himself in the perception of greater civilization in the wild world. He saw me as an equal in cognitive and operational levels—I didn't come across as too human to him. And it was getting easier for him to open up and talk to me with more than one or two sentences at a time. His beautiful vocabulary was greatly diverse, a lot like Sojóma's. He didn't condemn me for sounding human like Somila and Shrey did. He sounded just as similar. Here was evidence that Calouise was not a normal tiger.

That was part of his allure.

"And you're worried about what?" I asked. "Them disturbing the peace?"

"More our lifestyle." He walked between two bushes, its branches springing back at my face as I followed him. "And perhaps some of our peace. They are coming for the sake of revenge. They've been mistreated and abused out in the wild, on their own, ridiculed by other species for the shame all tigers bear."

"We'll keep an eye on them," I tried to reassure him. I didn't understand the source of his anxiety. Did he truly care and wish to protect our community that much?"

"When you say 'we,' you mean you, right?" His tail flicked back and forth in front of my nose.

"No, I'm not going to babysit nomads. That's what Nashur and Cyan are for."

"Ha!" he laughed loudly. "Clever."

"Glad you approve. So, tell me: how close were you and your father?"

He froze and twisted to look at me, all humor gone. "He was my adopted father. I shared no blood with him."

He had reverted back to blunt, simple statements.

He remained silent for a moment longer, then continued walking again. I remained behind him, afraid I'd angered him.

"I'm sorry if I offended you," I said quickly.

"Not offended. The distinction, to me, is important."

I trotted forward and walked beside him, waiting for him to continue.

"My mother died after she weaned my sister and me. We were alone a few miles from Sojóma's newly established community, but not a part of it. My father had been banished from the community after starting too many fights and killing another male over a female. He found us alone in our den, recognized us as his offspring, and wandered off to live his lonely life. He was wild to his core. Left to fend for ourselves, my sister only lasted a week. After her death, I left the den, searching for food, refusing the temptation my dead sister now was in my state of starvation."

I felt the urge to vomit at the very thought.

"I ended up within range of Sojóma's reigning territory, weak. He stumbled upon me perhaps an hour later. He gave me food, taught me to hunt and fight, and how to live peacefully and cooperatively. We weren't close emotionally, but I'll forever respect his actions and uncommon wisdom."

Calouise did, indeed, truly care about the community. And his personality appeared more complex every day.

A question bubbled to the surface of my mind, but I bit my tongue, unsure of the response he would have if I asked. But I threw caution to the wind and overpowered the voice that told me to hold back. "Shrey told me Sojóma never mated... do you know why?" I stared at him, waiting for his reply, ignoring the leaves that whipped my face and soaked my fur.

"You ask strange questions."

"And you're lousy at evasion."

He sighed in resignation. "He told me that everyone he ruled was like a cub to him, and the thought of mating with a tigress and then abandoning her and the cubs for another always disturbed him. He believed the best chance for survival was to build relationships and community. Strength in bonded numbers."

"It sounds smart."

"It sounds human."

For a moment, I wondered how he would know the lifestyle of humans, but then I remembered that he had observed the nearby village, just a small example of how humans clustered together.

I had also noticed that the word human seemed difficult for him to say.

"Humans are vile—but—their way of bonding doesn't seem atrocious and appears to make them happy." He lingered on the word *happy* momentarily, and I suddenly realized that Calouise, with his advanced upbringing and elevated level of thinking, was left searching for something to bring him joy. He was beyond the basic satisfying of instincts for pleasure, and so, constantly searching for something more.

He was looking for love.

If only he would get there himself and figure it out.

Our time for talking was up as we approached an unfamiliar area of the forest. The four dignitaries stood like a many-patterned wall in front of us. Just beyond them were two very large male tigers, their yellow eyes bright in the shady afternoon.

I let Calouise step up between the dignitaries—who parted—to talk to them, but he gestured with his big head for me to join him. I walked over, but Nashur, being the lovely cat she was, refused to move for me. I shouldered and shoved my way between her and Calouise until I stood tall, right beside him.

"Ah, Calouise, so good to see you alive, well, and in charge," said the first cat on the left, his white fur rather yellow and dirty. "I was sorry to hear of Sojóma's passing. He was a legend."

"Indeed, I hope you are well, Pravin," Calouise responded.

"And who is this hellcat by your side? Did you finally convert to a life of commitment?"

"This is Mix, my second-in-command and Commander of our forces."

I stood up straighter as they eyed me.

"A hellion with true authority, huh? I should have known Calouise not to be a committed cat. He's too tiger to settle for one hellion."

"I'm not a hellion," I snapped.

"Relax," said the other male at last. "Every tigress is a hellion."

I wanted to snarl at him, but I refrained. We needed these repulsive cats.

"We hear you're massing a force to take on Zoriach," Pravin commented, sensing danger.

"Yes, are you interested?" Calouise asked.

"We're always up for killing a few lions. What do you plan to do?"

"Avenge Sojóma, take back power, and put the lions in their place," I growled.

"You're an ambitious hellion, aren't you?" he said in a slightly impressed tone.

I took a step forward. My claws were exposed, teeth bared. I refused to take insulting remarks from anyone, especially an outsider.

He looked me up and down, determining my ability to do any damage. "Alright, *Commander*, what do you want with us?"

"I want your hatred of lions and ability to kill. I sent for you nomads because I knew you'd be invaluable to us and our cause."

"Is that supposed to be an insult?" Pravin asked savagely, stepping closer, claws suddenly visible. "Invaluable? Is that supposed to make us want to help you?"

"I had hoped it would. It means incredibly valuable and important," I replied as calmly as I was able. "We need you, and if you want to take any revenge on lions, you need us."

Pravin glared at me and stepped back, but his claws remained ready.

"When do you plan to attack?" the other male asked.

"As soon as monsoon season ends," I replied, glancing at Calouise. I still hadn't talked to him about my plan.

"That's a couple of months from now," Pravin said. "What are we supposed to do until then?"

"We're all going to train. And travel. We have to attack Zoriach on her turf."

"And you want us to just live here with you until that time?"

"To the best of your ability, yes," Calouise answered.

The two nomads exchanged looks. I'm sure they were questioning whether it would be worth their while to stick around. At last, the unnamed tiger spoke up.

"We'll stay and fight, but we won't stay in your communal pit."

I looked at Calouise with excitement. We had two more to add to our cause. He still appeared apprehensive.

"That's fine," Calouise replied curtly. "Make this outside territory yours, for now."

They both nodded. "Let us know when all the fun begins," Pravin said before walking off.

The other tiger's eyes lingered on me for few seconds longer before he turned and prowled away. It was long enough to make my skin crawl.

"Thank you for doing as you were told, you're dismissed," Calouise said to the dignitaries. They all left, disappearing between the trees, except Trapir. When they were out of earshot, he spoke.

"So we finally have a plan?"

"A very rough one," I said. "Train through monsoon season as new reinforcements arrive and set out for Zoriach towards the end of summer."

"Were you ever going to ask me about training everyone? Or did you plan to do it all yourself?" He seemed offended and irritated simultaneously. I didn't realize this was so important to him.

"I *was* going to ask you, but I only decided on this plan two days ago. I'm sorry for not being prudent enough to come to you right away." Honestly, I needed his help.

He snorted.

"So would you like to help me train them all or do you want to leave me to do it all by myself?"

"I'll help you," he said grudgingly. "But it has to be basic technique."

Relief flooded through me, relaxing some of the muscles that housed my stress. "Fair enough." I turned to Calouise. "What do you think of this plan?"

"I think it's appropriate."

That was going to have to be good enough.

Trapir nodded to us. "Let me know when you want to start." He ambled off, leaving Calouise and I awkwardly together once more among the silent shrubbery and trees.

"Well, my plan is working so far. I think we'll get a lot of nomad tigers to join us. It's just the leopards I'm unsure about," I said nervously.

"Don't count them out yet."

"Shrey and Cyan don't think any will come."

"If you're going to take the beliefs of Shrey and Cyan, you aren't going to accomplish much."

I felt a bit more hopeful. "You think they'll come?"

He didn't reply right away, but seemed to choose his words carefully. "I think they'll show up, but I have doubts that they'll join us."

"That's all I need." As long as they showed up, I felt confident in my ability to persuade them to fight with us.

"I hope you're right."

So did I.

LORD OF THE LEOPARDS

The emotional tension between Calouise and me remained unsolved. Both of us were consumed with being diplomatic, accommodating, and authoritative with all the diverse nomads. I kept sending the messengers back out—after they returned and rested—to find more cats to send our way. I would accept every tiger in India if they could get to us in time.

The arrival of other nomads was not as eventful as the first one, with one exception. About a week after Pravin and his disturbing, staring friend arrived, our first female joined us. Nashur and I were supposed to welcome her before Calouise got there.

"You want me to go with *her*?" I asked him in disgust. "You know she hates me, right?"

"And you, her. I think you can handle a sassy tigress," he responded, distracted by a messenger he was supposed to be meeting.

"There's only room for one witty, tenacious female in this jungle," I said.

"Then put her in her place and cooperate to do what is necessary."

"Do you understand the concept of hate?"

"Do you understand the concept of duty?" he growled.

That one hurt. "Indeed, your majesty," I snarled.

I suddenly had his full attention. "Don't call me that."

"Is that a command, now, instead of a request?"

His brows furrowed in anger. "No." He sucked in a deep breath. "Please—" he said it painfully, "cooperate with Nashur to get the job done. I'll be there soon."

His formality stung me, but I didn't know if he felt truly upset with me or was trying to remain professionally cordial in front of the messenger.

"I'll do my best, Jungle Prince," I said quietly, walking away with my head down. Perhaps I'd disappointed him by my immaturity.

"Mix," came his deep voice, so low I almost didn't catch it.

I looked back at him.

"I'm not a Prince, but a King," he said softly. He gave me the smallest of smiles, and I returned a full one.

Nashur waited for me at the wall, perched ever so properly, her eyes on the partially sunny sky.

I jumped up beside her. "Let's get this over with," I mumbled, walking past her.

"Nice to see you again. Aren't you excited to do this together?" she called from behind me.

"Not particularly. Save the niceties, Nashur. We'll need them for later."

We moved in silence through the brush. I followed her, unsure of where we were meeting this newcomer. She led me east, deep into the jungle on the leopards' side.

"Have you met many nomads, Nashur?" I asked.

"I thought you said to save the niceties," she snapped.

"I'm not being nice, just conversational."

"Well, shut your muzzle. I have no desire to talk to you."

I considered incessantly talking to drive her crazy, but Calouise's request to do my duty and cooperate hovered in my mind. I refrained and continued on in silence.

At last, we reached wherever we were supposed to be and waited, standing side by side. A few painful minutes passed by.

"I don't approve of how Calouise is ruling," Nashur suddenly commented.

Of course not. "You don't want to talk to me, remember?"

"Will you just stop being difficult?" she hissed.

Never. "What's wrong with the way he's ruling?" As far as I was aware, Calouise devoted plenty of his time to ruling, blessing cubs, traversing the community, maintaining a presence.

"He hardly ever partakes in actually overseeing his kingdom. He's never present for councils. He's always off somewhere."

"Did you ever consider that he might be *off overseeing his domain*?"

She glared at me. "You think you're smart, don't you?"

I raised a brow.

I could see the irritated growl building, but before she could release it, the snap of some twigs and movement of leaves caught our attention. Both of us looked up, trying to catch a glimpse of the newcomer.

She came into view, slender but not small, her coat sleek and clean. She sniffed the air and clawed at the bark of a tree—an action I'd come to know as leaving a mark and scent to alert others of your presence in the surrounding area.

She wandered over to us, her gait seductive, one paw crossing in front of the other, her back end weaving side to side.

I glanced at Nashur. I suddenly felt a great urge to intimidate this female.

Nashur was watching her carefully, her gaze shrewd and wary. She and I were both—for once—on the same page.

"What a welcoming party," she cooed. Her voice was the sound of chocolate and honey. "Where is Sojóma? I was hoping to express how much I'd missed him."

"Sojóma's dead," I snapped, forgetting I was supposed to be accommodating.

She gasped. "What a shame. The only cat to ever deny me… I was still hoping to change his mind."

"I sincerely doubt you would've succeeded," Nashur said through a closed mouth. "He kicked you out for a reason, Sarga."

I stared at Nashur in surprise.

"Well, perhaps I'll be rejoining you now that he's gone, huh?" Sarga said, moving closer to Nashur in a threatening way. A part of me wanted to see if a cat fight would break loose, but I didn't know who I would want to lose.

"If Sojóma banished you, I'm sure Calouise won't let you back in," I said tensely.

"We'll see. Calouise hasn't been one to deny me before," she whispered.

I growled.

"Mix!"

I whipped around, spotting Calouise a few feet away. Out of the corner of my eye, I saw Nashur and Sarga both straighten and appear civil.

"We're supposed to be greeting our guests," he said a dangerous, dark voice.

"I apologize," I said through gritted teeth.

He eyed me, his brows curious rather than angry. Then he spotted Sarga before us, and I caught the slight dilation in his eyes. He stepped between Nashur and me and stared down at her.

"Calouise … I almost didn't recognize you," Sarga said sweetly, looking up at him in an innocent way. "But, I should have known—only the cutest cat in India would grow up to be so … powerful and mighty."

If she wasn't careful, I was going to rip her throat out.

"It's been a long time," he replied.

"Apparently, just the right amount of time," she said quietly, taking a step toward him.

Both Nashur and I stepped ahead of Calouise with equally menacing growls.

"Well, Cal, I see you didn't follow in all Sojóma's paw prints." She glanced between us and winked at Calouise.

"Why are you here, Sarga?" he asked, ignoring the spectacle unfolding around him.

She sighed at the change in topic. "I want to put Zoriach and the rest of her miserable species in their place."

"Good. Then I hope you're willing to remain in this area until we are ready to attack."

"I've waited this long already, I can wait some more," she hissed.

"Perfect. Stay close." He nodded to her in a business-like way and turned to leave, both of us following him.

"I'll stay as close as you want, Cal," she called as we walked away.

She wasn't going to last long as this rate.

We all headed back to the fortress in silence. I knew Nashur had her eyes on me most of the time, but I refused to meet them.

At the fortress doorway, Calouise paused. "Go on ahead. I'll be there momentarily," he said to Nashur.

She glared at the pair of us before disappearing into the throne room.

Calouise gazed at me, the intent stare that used to haunt my steps back when I was a newbie. "Thank you for defending me," he said quietly.

"Nashur did, too. Why aren't you thanking her?"

"I don't want her to get the wrong idea."

"What about me?" I asked, staring unflinchingly into his eyes.

"Does me thanking you give you any ideas?" he asked, raising his brows.

I searched his face, looking for a hint. "Thanking me in private does."

His expression softened slightly. "I hope they aren't wrong ideas."

His cryptic language was killing me. "I'm going to nap before I hunt tonight. See you later?"

He seemed to teeter between asking me a question or not. I raised my brows, inviting him to do so.

"Do you … still sleep in the same spot?"

"No, actually. I moved to an unclaimed spot that was much nicer. It's behind a waterfall."

He looked surprised. "That's my spot."

"We already established that it wasn't yours anymore. It's mine," I said with a smile.

"If you ever decide to move again…"

"I'll check with you for the best spots," I assured him.

He nodded and disappeared into the fortress.

I made my way back to the Sanctuary, wondering if he'd been about to offer a sleeping spot in the fortress again. Would I have said yes?

I curled up in my spot and tried not to think about Calouise and Sarga and everything Sarga had said. I knew it would only make me mad and possibly insecure. I tried to shake the image of the disturbing way she walked. She oozed invitation. For the briefest moment, I considered how I came across to the males and other females around me. I tried to not appear invitational, afraid of where that would lead, but suddenly, I was curious how I'd appear open and attractive to male tigers. Was is just the seductive prowl? Was it about coats? Or scents? Or the size of the tigress? Growing up in the human world had left me with only human ideas of what attractiveness and sexuality were supposed to look like. In the wild world, I didn't have such a clear idea. I knew Sarga's appearance was meant to attract the males, but I would never stoop to that kind of blatant activity. She was almost trying too hard.

Nevertheless, I, personally, was going to have to keep an eye on her …

About a week after Sarga arrived, we had welcomed six nomads. I was starting to feel really optimistic. Calouise and I both started attending council meetings to discuss issues about the nomads and the next steps to take towards war. They were, for the most part, horribly and incredibly fruitless. None of the dignitaries could agree on anything, much less approve of any ideas I offered. Calouise increasingly supported me, reminding them—on multiple occasions—that my opinion, overall, held more weight than any of theirs.

I quickly grew tired of these meetings, especially when I had other things to do, like hunt for the first time in two weeks or attempt to think of ways to sneak up on Zoriach's territory. And I had gained no new or useful information from the councils after the first two. Nashur argued against everything I said. Cyan refused to cooperate, and Saltir hardly had anything to contribute since most of the spies and messengers were gone and busy. Trapir appeared as disinterested as myself. We had already agreed upon when to begin training everyone, and all he had to do was wait until that time arrived.

Nashur was complaining about Sarga and Sarga wandering through our domain, seducing every male in the vicinity, threatening peace—or whatever peace we managed to hang onto. I was only half-listening, watching Calouise from the corner of my eye, waiting to share a look with him that expressed a common boredom or exasperation.

A bird the color of daffodils and olives fluttered into our midst and landed in front of Saltir, folding its black-streaked wings. Everyone stopped talking to listen to what it had to say.

"Both Saltir and Cyan have been requested at the northwest edge of our territory."

"Who has requested?" I demanded, suddenly alert and attentive. Who could possibly want to see Saltir and Cyan? Unless …

"Their presence is required immediately by Lord Mehish," the bird said, glancing at me.

My breath caught. My heart raced, and I turned to look at Calouise, barely containing my surprise and excitement. "We must accompany them," I said eagerly, rising to my feet and shaking out my fur.

"You were not requested," the yellow bird chirped, fully facing me now.

"But … I'm the Commander. I was the one that sent for him after those two skeptics said he'd never come." It took every ounce of self control to not let my voice get higher and whinier.

"Mehish prefers to talk first with leopards. It's just his custom. I'm sure you understand," said Cyan in a calm, elevated voice. He tilted his head, a look of smug victory evidently plastered on it.

I glared at him.

"Mix and I will wait here. Send Lord Mehish our regards," Calouise said quickly.

Cyan nodded and followed Saltir and the bird out the doorway.

"Should Mehish decide to speak with us, I prefer if it was only Mix, myself, and the leopards," Calouise said, looking at Trapir and Nashur.

"Whatever you wish," Trapir replied, bowing his head. He walked out without another word.

"Why does Mix get to stay," Nashur asked, trying—and failing—to hide her jealousy.

"She sent for him," he said simply.

"But I'm your chief advisor," she whispered.

I saw his tense face twitch in irritation. "Mix is leading us to war. Would you like to take that job?" he growled.

She glanced at me with a sour face. "No."

"Good. Remember that the next time you feel like being disrespectful and disobedient. Now go."

She didn't waste any more time, but departed, leaving us alone to wait.

I flexed my claws in and out, trying to relieve some of my anxiety. "Do you think he'll want to talk to us?"

He sighed. "Nothing is for sure."

"But he's here."

Calouise remained silent and padded away to lie against a wall. I didn't pester him, but did my best to wait patiently, pacing around the room to pass the time.

After what felt like a half hour, I finally sat beside him and sighed. "He's not coming."

"Why do you care so much?"

"I don't know. Because I don't like Zoriach?"

He frowned at me. "No, that's not it."

"How would you know?" I asked defensively, shifting away from him.

"You cared before Zoriach made you angry. I remember."

"What do you mean?"

He leaned back and stared at me. "I told you not to be afraid."

I was surprised he remembered that. It was the first day we had ever spoken to each other. It was also the first time I felt the desire to be a part of this crazy, intricate, beautiful, wild world.

"I won't deny that I've been terrified, but I want to prove that I belong in the wild, with the tigers, with you." The last part slipped out before I could catch myself, but deep down, I knew it was true.

He was staring into my eyes, only a few feet away. "You don't have to win a war to prove you belong," he said quietly.

If only I could believe him. "Nobody in this jungle seems to think I'm capable of doing so. The dignitaries scoff at me, the nomads poke fun at me. Even Somila and Shrey have doubts."

"But the nomads came. And stayed. Somila and Shrey still talk to you, accept you. The dignitaries accept no one. You belong more than they do."

I wanted to ask him why, but I feared his answer would be too biased to be a source of any true comfort. I still had the desire to prove myself. Perhaps some of them felt I belonged, but I wasn't born here, I hadn't fought with them—all I'd managed to do was create conflict and chaos.

He gave the answer even so, as if he could read my thoughts. "You are a tiger. You've brought fresh air and energy back to us. That has more value than anything else. You've reminded us who we are," he said quietly. "Nobody would've dared to threaten Zoriach before you came along, even though we should have. You've proved yourself more than any of us."

I recognized the objective spin he'd attempted to gild his words with, which allowed me to accept them as a type of truth, but I knew his words originated from a biased background. Even still, I felt a bit better. I gave him a small smile. "Underneath that tough, aloof exterior, you're actually warm-hearted and sentimental, aren't you?"

He turned away from me. "Only with you," he said seriously.

I wanted to say more, but I suddenly saw his tense and poised posture. He was listening intently, all his senses directed towards the stone doorway.

Focusing my hearing, I detected the distinct sound of claws scraping against stone. It caused hairs on my neck to rise—it was the equivalent of fingernails and chalkboards. There was a light thump—some cat jumping from the wall to the forest floor—followed by several more thumps. At least four cats were coming our way.

More than just Cyan and Saltir.

Calouise immediately jumped to his feet and stood tall and straight as a king.

I reacted a second later, also getting to my feet as Cyan and Saltir emerged from around the arched, stone frame. They moved to stand like sentries halfway between Calouise and me and the entrance.

I held my breath in anticipation.

He appeared dramatically, purposefully stepping into the room, his posture tall and expression proud. His grey-spotted body was lean, but he wasn't small—at least by leopard standards—yet his head almost looked small in comparison to his fluffy body and tail. His alabaster fur was thick, but sleek and well-groomed. As a snow leopard, he was a strikingly beautiful cat.

He prowled to stand a few feet from us, a smaller leopard trailing behind him, alert to the situation, but his head bent as a subordinate.

Calouise gave the slightest of head bows. "Lord Mehish," he said with respectful acknowledgement.

"Rajah Calouise," Mehish replied, bending deeply at the knees. His eyes briefly flickered onto me.

I felt an urge to introduce myself, but I had a feeling that would be out of place. A few agonizing seconds ticked by until I opened my mouth to speak, but Mehish cut me off.

"I am accompanied by my head advisor, Moranaha, but he will not be invited to speak freely."

This cat took formality to a new level.

"Beside me is Mix, Commander and my Fifth Paw. She is free to speak as much as you or I," Calouise responded, an authority in his voice that I still wasn't accustomed to. I also was intrigued by the title of 'fifth paw,' but I would ask him about it later.

Mehish's shrewd gaze was fixed on me, probably questioning my position and authority and right to speak, but I refused to shrink.

"You sent for me," Mehish said, addressing Calouise.

"I did," I said, much louder than I'd intended. "We're going to war against Zoriach and the lions, and we need your help."

His expression only shifted slightly, revealing his displeasure. "I don't see why that involves me or any of my cats. This feud is not new and it has always been between tigers and lions. Leopards have no claim to being king of the jungle—we never have."

I did my very best not to glare at him. "We're outnumbered. Zoriach has recruited panthers and hyenas. We've only managed a few nomads. If you don't help us, we're all going to die."

"And what would I and my cats receive in return for service? We win no titles, we don't want land. You have nothing to offer."

"Our continued friendship," Calouise said.

Mehish gave a sardonic laugh. "Am I to understand that if we don't help you, we are no longer friends?"

"Yes. For the time being," Calouise replied bluntly.

All humor had vanished from Mehish's white face. "You would have me sacrifice my species for the sake of friendship. I refuse."

I couldn't hold back anymore. "Zoriach killed Sojóma! Will you do nothing?"

His fiery eyes swiveled onto me. "Sojóma's death is a tragedy. But I won't aid in frivolous battle that has nothing to do with me or my cats." He looked between Cyan and Saltir. "I'm astonished you two are willing to partake in this nonsense."

"Sojóma was our rajah," Saltir replied quietly.

"And Zoriach threatened all of us," Cyan said.

Mehish stared around at each of us, and I could see that his decision was final.

"I'm sorry I can't help you," Mehish added. He did sound sincere, which upset me more.

"Why did you come here, then?" I asked desperately.

Mehish sighed. "Because I felt obligated as a friend to Sojóma, and I was curious. But I won't let that be our demise."

"But you would let this be ours," I said stiffly. I growled in frustration and bitter letdown. What we were going to do now? I'd been so sure of my ability to persuade him if only he showed up.

I had miserably failed.

Mehish's face hardened. "What happens to you and your species is your choice. You don't have to fight Zoriach."

Calouise repositioned himself beside me. I knew he was getting angry; he just did a better job at controlling it than me.

"We can't back down now—that'd be weak," I responded. "Besides, it wouldn't prevent Zoriach from picking us off one by one anyway."

"I'm afraid that's out of our paws. We can't be of use to you."

The panic struck me as the reality sunk in. Each breath became shorter and shorter, the doom before us a blazing problem I didn't know how to solve. I had to keep it together at least until the Lord of Leopards departed.

"If this is your final decision, then I request you leave us in peace so we can come up with a survival plan," Calouise said in his formal, diplomatic tone.

Mehish bowed slightly. "I hope you all come out of this mess." He acknowledged me by making eye contact a final time before turning around and padding away and out into the jungle, his advisor following, their white tails vanishing as if they hadn't been there at all—like ghosts.

Calouise seemed to relax beside me, but my stress level had increased immensely. I rolled my shoulders in an attempt to relax, but they immediately tensed back up. There was no way we tigers alone could take on the lions, panthers, and hyenas. I hated that Cyan, Saltir, and Shrey were right.

I hated being wrong.

"The only thing I proved today was my worthlessness as a leader," I said out loud and at large. I didn't care who heard me—word would spread like wildfire. There was no avoiding the obvious truth.

"Enough," Calouise snapped. "You would let this one setback be our end." He paced in front of me, his striped tail flicking back and forth in agitation.

"We're outnumbered," I responded as loud as I could without actually screaming. Birds perched overhead took to the air in alarm. "I'm not magically gifted in the art of warfare like some of you seem to think." I stared at each of them that remained. Trapir and Nashur's faces had appeared at the doorway. "I don't have any answers."

Whatever little strength that was still in me broke in that moment, and I slumped to the ground waiting for the tears that I expected to manifest.

They didn't come. And I remembered I had four legs, paws, and a tail.

Sunlight broke through the trees and flooded the open, nonexistent roof overhead, reflecting off of the damp stone and lightening the room, despite the mental gloom that pervaded it.

"No one expects you to have all the answers," Trapir said, breaking the silence.

I glanced down at him from where I lay at the top of the steps, surprised by what he'd just said.

"We don't expect easy victory," Saltir added.

"Hell, none of us even expected a leopard to show up, let alone join us," Trapir said.

"But ... he's not going to help us," I replied. Did no one understand that?

Calouise maneuvered to stand on the steps in front of me, his unusually yellow eyes level with mine. I couldn't refrain from meeting them. They sparkled in the sunlight.

"We don't give up," he whispered softly, but confidently. He said it just loud enough that I knew everyone could have heard him. I don't know how long we stared at each other in sunlit silence while his words battered against the solid weight of pre-emptive defeat that had taken hold of my soul. It took awhile, but eventually—perhaps because of the soft way he said it or the sympathetic look in his eyes or the determined face he held before me or even the sunlight—-the words beat away the dejection and took control of my resolve.

I sucked in a deep breath and sat up a bit straighter.

"Alright," I said quietly to him. He took a few steps back as I stood up. "I'm not giving up. We aren't going down without giving every last drop of genius and strength we possess."

I saw Trapir and Saltir's nods of agreement, Nashur and Cyan's grudging acceptance, and Calouise's half smile of approval. It might have been a picturesque moment except for the outburst of roars and cries of fear and pain that arose and assaulted all of our sensitive ears.

The horrifying sounds were distant, somewhere out in the jungle, but terrible enough to block out any perception of sunlit hope. I bolted down the steps, across the stone, and out the doorway. Sprinting, I refused to look back, even though I knew everyone was behind me, doing their best to keep up. It was all too familiar—the roars, the running, the blood-coagulating terror. What was waiting for me this time?

With One Eye Open

This is unbelievable," Cyan muttered.

"More like a tragedy," Saltir replied.

Calouise hadn't said anything.

We all stood in a misshapen circle around the bloodied and muddied, matted lifeless remains of Mehish, Lord of the Leopards. His advisor appeared to be somewhere between supreme grief and rage.

"This is outrageous," he growled. "If we would have just stayed out of this mess in the first place …"

I released a low rumble at him. "Are you saying this is our fault?"

"If you hadn't asked for us, we wouldn't have been here," he replied angrily.

"It was your choice to come or not," I snarled, taking a step toward him.

Calouise moved to stand between us, his eyes on Moranaha. "Mehish's death has nothing to do with us."

"Then whose fault is it?" he hissed.

"How should we know? Weren't you with him when it happened?" Nashur asked.

I investigated Mehish's body while Moranaha attempted to explain why he had been absent from his lord's side, apparently having had to deal with a bowel emergency. Besides the general mess of mud and blood, I could make out dark, muddy footprints on his neck and flank. They were large—too large to belong to a leopard or panther. The prints were barely larger than mine.

"It was a lion," I said, interrupting whatever they were still talking about.

Everyone looked at me.

"How do you know?" Moranaha asked skeptically.

"The paw prints on the body—they're large enough to belong to a lion or tiger. If Zoriach suspects your presence to mean you are allying with us, she would do all in her power to prevent it."

He still looked doubtful, as if he suspected one of us was the assassin.

"Saltir," I said, "Gather some messengers and have them scout the forest and surrounding area. Tell them to look for anything moving faster than a hunting prowl."

Saltir didn't hesitate to follow my command this time. He gave a stiff bow and spun off, for once in a hurry to get something done. Perhaps he was on his best behavior because we had company, or maybe it was because he actually cared about finding out what happened to the lord of his species. Truth be told, I didn't care what his motivation was.

"We'll find out who is behind this," I assured Moranaha.

"Get word to me when you do," he sighed. He laid on his belly and crept toward Mehish's body, nosing his small, white head under one of Mehish's limp legs.

"What are you doing?" I asked.

It took him a moment to reply as he wriggled under Mehish's chest and lifted the body up over his back. "I'm taking him home."

I couldn't help the moronic stare as I watched him struggle under the larger leopard's dead weight that was awkwardly and unevenly drooped over his back.

"Is he really that stupid?" I whispered to Calouise.

"Why do you think he wasn't permitted to speak?" was his quiet reply.

I fought a smile. "What are you thinking? You can't take him there."

"Of course I can."

"No, you can't carry him halfway across India by yourself. You can barely carry him as it is. You wouldn't make it past a village carrying him, let alone fight off another assassin should it come back around."

"I must try. I won't leave him here to rot and be forgotten. He deserved more than that."

"I can send Cyan and another tiger to accompany you and share the load," Calouise said in resignation.

I shot him a worried glance. We needed those cats.

"But I need them to return at once. Without the leopards, we can't spare any potential warriors," he added.

Moranaha sighed. "I do appreciate the assistance."

"Cyan, recruit some tiger nonessential to us here and be on your way," Calouise said, the essence of finality apparent. He waited for Cyan's signal of acceptance, and then Calouise looked down at Mehish's body one last time. "It is a tragedy," he said simply and sadly before silently prowling away without another word of salutation or dismissal.

"I'm sorry for the loss you've incurred here today," I said to Moranaha in the most diplomatic way I could think of. He seemed taken aback, but I was already a few feet away, not waiting for a reply, anxious to follow Calouise and figure out what the hell we were going to do. As soon as I was out of the group's line of vision, I ran to catch up with Calouise.

I followed his distinct scent of fresh jungle rain back to the wall and crumbling remains of the building that seemed to be our spot. He sat there, staring at nothing, waiting—I figured—for me. I walked over to him and sat down in front of him, moving my head until I caught his attention and stare. We remained in silence for a while, neither of us sure what to do or say. Not ready to disturb his potential thought processes, I studied his posture. He did not sit erect and upright, confident and in control as per usual. Instead, his shoulders were slack, his back arched in a slump, his tail motionless. It was the closest I'd ever seen him portray a position of defeat.

The sun that had radiated through our canopy earlier disappeared behind some very sinister looking clouds, and I waited with resignation for the day to become worse.

"What do we do now?" I said at last, unable to wait any longer.

"Elaborate," he said bluntly.

"The leopards aren't coming, Mehish was just slaughtered in our jungle, and we still have to come up against Zoriach despite everything else. So what now? How do we overcome it all?"

He shook his head. "I don't know."

"You're the one who told me not to give up," I said angrily. I couldn't—wouldn't—do this alone.

"I don't have a plan. I don't have all the answers either."

It was the first—and only—time I ever saw worry, panic, fear, and desperation in his expression. Whatever walls or masks he usually upheld were down.

It was unnerving.

But I felt gratitude that it was with me he was willing to share this vulnerable moment.

"We have to do something," I whispered.

"Please share any ideas."

"I only have one."

"That's one more than me," he said.

Thunder crashed from above and shook the tops of the trees, sending water droplets down upon our heads. I shook them off and met his uncertain gaze.

"We start training. And more ideas will come to us. But we need to start preparing everyone for battle or there really, truly, is no hope," I said. "If we're lucky, each one of our cats will be able to kill at least three of hers before they go down."

The downpour began right at that moment, an onslaught of water cascading on our fur and the ground and remaining stone. The symphonic pounding and pattering accompanied by the booming thunder was amplified in the fast-falling darkness.

In our thundering silence, I realized that this time it wasn't me appearing weak and desperate and afraid. I was the one consoling the usual solid rock of support in my life. It was strange and curious and kind of poetic in the way we were able to be there for one another. In particular, I was proud of myself for reaching a point where I had enough confidence and a good enough relationship with someone to be a source of support for them. I carefully studied his face, waiting for him to find his solid foundation once again.

Lightning flashed and briefly illuminated Calouise's shadowed face. He no longer looked uncertain and afraid.

He was determined.

The next morning, we—or rather Calouise—called for a population conference. Every tiger and leopard under our command was mandated to appear. They were supposed to meet in the throne room, where the dignitaries and I sat on either side of our king and waited while they all piled in.

I looked down and saw Shrey sitting front and center, staring up at us expectantly. Behind him, I caught sight of other cats getting shoved aside or splitting apart to let someone through. A few seconds later, Somila emerged, shouldering Shrey aside to sit beside him. Then she, too, looked up at me, a half-smile stretching the side of her face.

On the other side of the room were the nomads. Pravin and his once unknown friend—Dekovin—stood in the very rear of the company, as close to the doorway as was possible, while cats still filtered in. Sarga sat on top of a piece of stone, a foot or so above everyone except us, standing out, as usual.

At last, almost everyone was there, the stench of wet animal fur astronomically unbearable in such tight quarters. The mass of assorted stripes and spots caused me to blink a few times, the effect dizzying.

Calouise gave me a signal—my cue to grab everyone's attention.

"Thank you all for joining us here. Our rajah has some important and crucial news to share with you."

The hum and buzz of the room grew silent and what felt like a thousand, bright, hot spotlights swiveled onto the five of us.

I heard the smallest of sighs come from Calouise before he began. "Many of you may have heard, but Lord Mehish was slaughtered in our jungle yesterday. He was here to determine whether or not he and his leopard community would aid us in the coming assault on Zoriach. It is doubly unfortunate that, after refusing to help us, he died by the forces he had just pledged to stay away from.

"Mix and Saltir sent out scouts to discover who the killer was. As we had suspected, a scout reported seeing a young male lion retreating north from our Sanctuary. This lion wasn't some random traveler. It was Singh, Zoriach's Fifth Paw—her personal spy and killer when she's too cowardly to do the work herself."

The leopards released outraged roars, while many tigers growled. If there was anything Zoriach could be complimented on, it was that she knew how to make enemies.

It was my turn to speak. "The leopard cousins aren't coming, but that doesn't mean Zoriach is going to leave us be. We need every one of you and anyone who joins us to do what we must to get rid of the lion threat. So every day between tomorrow and when we set out for Zoriach, there will be training provided by Trapir, Calouise, and me. We know you can all hunt, but we want you to be able to battle and kill."

The meeting concluded with some excited roars and chuffs. The recent murder brought on unprovoked by the enemy had re-boiled our blood. Zoriach and her worthless allies would not go unpunished.

The day after our successful conference, our training areas were overcrowded. Trapir trained inside the throne room, Calouise in the meadow behind it, and I in the grassy area on the other side of the stone wall. Trapir had informed us that we should start with only the basics, making sure they could dodge, counter attack, and successfully take down and pin their enemy long enough to give the killing blow. There were too many of them and not enough time to teach the little nuances and maneuvers of the experienced warriors.

In my grassy area, numerous cats encircled a small clearing where two cats faced off. At first, the cats in my arena were hesitant to attack one another. When I finally coaxed them into getting used to the idea of batting at each other, they were slow and tentative, afraid to hurt each other. We weren't going to win a war with scaredy-cats.

"That's it," I said in exasperation after the third round of relatively nothing accomplished. "You're all going to be slaughtered the instant you step foot onto the battle field. This is training, not play time." I stepped into the center of the ring. Somila stood across from me in the crowd, her eyes wide and curious about what I was going to do next.

"Somila, come here and face me," I commanded in a firm, but friendly tone.

Her eyes grew a bit wider as she hesitantly stepped up and stood casually in front of me.

"Is that your fighting stance?" I questioned, striding around her, trying to be a source of intimidation.

"No, but I—"

"Do you want to learn?" I pestered.

She scowled at me—a good sign in this moment. "Yes."

I was near her back legs, which were not tensed or ready for any kind of action.

"Then you've got to be—" I kicked out at her back feet, almost knocking her to the dirt "—prepared."

She was alert now, her posture in an active stance. I had irritated her. She was now staring at me intently while I circled her, wary of my next attack.

Knowing she wouldn't be ready, I leapt at her without warning, catching the back of her neck and shoulder, dragging her down with my weight and momentum. She landed hard on the ground, an angry snarl escaping her clenched jaw. But I had already rearranged myself to have her pinned, my teeth at her neck, ready to kill.

I released her, and she stood up, breathing hard from the surprise ambush.

"Our enemies won't wait for you to be ready. They'll take you as soon as they see the opening," I concluded.

Somila shook out her fur and moved to stand back in the ensemble surrounding me.

"Who's my next pair? I want to see real action. We aren't killing each other, but it's time to stop being nice."

A few seconds of silence went by, and then Mehan jumped into the arena. "I'll do it," he said.

"I can take him," Pravin replied with confidence, emerging from the crowd.

I stood back, watching as both of them settled into their tense, hunting stances.

"I'll make this more interesting," I called. "Whoever wins will remain in the ring until he's beaten."

There were some smiles, nods, and excited cat calls. Perhaps they had needed some kind of motivation to attack one another. Now it was about competition instead of just attacking each other unprovoked. I couldn't resist smiling as Pravin swatted at Mehan and drew blood, causing a collective gasp among the intrigued onlookers. Mehan retaliated by hitting back, where in turn, Pravin ducked, and Mehan struck again, slicing a deep gash in Pravin's ear. After that, they tore into each other, wrestling, scraping, biting until the trampled, once green grass appeared rather gory. At one point, Mehan had almost pinned Pravin, but Pravin, being a more experienced fighter as a nomad, managed to maneuver free.

Eventually, I had to do something or the fight would never end. "You have one minute to end this fight. Find a strategy that will allow one of you to overcome and 'kill' the other."

They faced each other, both sporting long, livid gashes on various planes of their bodies. The audience started chanting, rooting for a winner. Pravin snarled when he realized his support was not as collective as Mehan's was, but Mehan was a member of our community. I caught sight of Dekovin, standing a few cats away from me, his eyes locked on Pravin, his mouth forming a chant to support his travel partner. Several other of our nomadic allies were in support of Pravin, which didn't surprise me. Sarga, as well, was chanting Pravin's name, but I had a feeling that her support was more about how Pravin showed his masculine prowess than because he was a nomad like her.

In a matter of roughly 30 seconds, Pravin had Mehan down in the mud and grass, a dirty paw holding down his head, fangs poised to make the killing stroke.

"And that's officially the end of round one!" I called.

Pravin eased up on his adversary and strutted around the arena, drinking in both the jeers and praises as they came. Mehan slouched off, his fur matted in a mess of mud and blood, a sour expression twisting his face. I had brief, thoughtful hope that what I had created here wouldn't come back to bite me in the ass tomorrow with vengeful fights taking place elsewhere. Those needed to be saved for Zoriach's cats.

"Alright, who's ready to take on Pravin?" I said, staring about the crowd, hoping for a volunteer.

"I'll take him down," Jokane growled, prowling to the center of the arena.

Pravin shot him a smug, but skeptical look.

I watched with guilty glee at how well my plan had managed to incite them to fight one another.

The fight began in a similar way to the last. The crowd cheered and growled, chanted and snarled as each cat had moments of gaining the upper paw. After the span of around five minutes, Jokane triumphed over Pravin, which excited the audience more than I could have ever expected.

"What's all the noise?" came a familiar, deep voice from behind me.

I swiveled around and saw Calouise attempting to squeeze between tigers that were focusing solely on the victor. "I've added an element of incentive and entertainment to my training."

He managed to shove his way through until he stood beside me, staring out over the arena where Jokane stood proud and cocky. I half expected him to start flexing his muscles.

"What is this?" Calouise questioned.

"Just watch," I instructed. "Alright, next challenger!" I called to the crowd at large.

Jokane stared around, daring anyone to attempt to take him on, strutting around in a circle, further flattening the disturbed grass.

Across from me, two tigers parted and revealed Sarga. She stepped into the arena and prowled forward, facing Jokane, her muscles already taut, her usually confident and seductive gaze suddenly fierce and focused. Jokane let out a disbelieving laugh at his next opponent. I shared a glance with Calouise, both of us surprised by her decision to challenge one of our larger, stronger males—and take it seriously.

Mistakenly, Jokane remained relatively relaxed, humor still glowing in his yellow eyes. Sarga was crouched low, her tail twitching from side to side as she eyed him. I watched her mostly black eyes shift from his face to his torso to his legs, gauging where to strike first.

As much as I would have liked to have a female take down a male, I possessed zero desire for Sarga to excel and win at anything. She didn't need any increase of status or prowess. She was infamous enough.

It was over in a matter of seconds. Foolishly off guard, he was tackled to the ground by Sarga wrapping her front legs around his neck and her back legs around his torso. He tumbled over, and she dug her claws deep into his neck right at the main vein. Any struggle would have caused her claws to splice through his skin and make him bleed out. The onlookers collectively gasped at how quick she'd managed to take him out. I caught Calouise's impressed expression from the corner of my eye and couldn't help the twinge of envy that sparked within me.

Sarga had released Jokane, who slunk off, embarrassed by his defeat.

"This goes to show that you can *never* let your guard down or be too confident," I yelled over the noisy group. Sarga shot me a challenging smile. I didn't know if she knew how I really felt about her or if she just was smug and wanted to take me on. Before I could decide anything, Nashur materialized beside me. She was was staring at Sarga with the deepest glare I'd ever seen—she hadn't even glared at me that horribly before.

"So who's the next challenger?" Sarga asked, strutting around in victory, much like the previous winners.

"You've turned this into a game," Calouise commented with interest.

Nashur peered at the two of us. "I'll fight her."

I couldn't raise my eyebrows high enough to express the amount of shock and surprise I was experiencing. I didn't think Nashur *could* fight, let alone be willing to partake in the game I had constructed.

"Be my guest," I said, scooting aside so she could step into the arena.

The two females stared each other down, mentally tearing each other apart. Suddenly, I felt excited about the prospect of this training exercise. I was about to witness the showdown of the tiger century.

"This is a sick game," Calouise said, his eyes glued to the two squaring off.

"But so much more entertaining than just training, right?" I looked at him, perplexed. "Wait, why aren't you training in your own area?"

He managed to tear his gaze away from them to look at me. "I'm done for the day. I only managed to give them a demonstration before we had to stop."

"You really think that's going to properly prepare them to kill lions?" I asked him with a frown. "This is our only shot."

"Yes, I understand, but my group and I heard all the roars and cheers, so I led them over here to see what was going on. We couldn't focus with all the commotion." He stared into my eyes, the beginning of a smile pulling up one of his cheeks.

I rolled my eyes. "Tomorrow, it's back to business. *Teach* them. Help them."

He moved his gaze back onto the two tigresses in the middle as he said, "Yes, Commander."

I couldn't resist the smile that spread across my face.

Sarga and Nashur had incited the crowd. Most of the males were rooting for Sarga. I could see Nashur's supporters were mostly leopards and other females that felt threatened and uncomfortable with Sarga and her troubling presence. I knew this fight was going to be a demonstration of power between the two of them—between the powers of the truly wild lifestyle and community leadership status. Watching them, I honestly didn't know who I wanted to see take a bigger beating. I half wanted to jump in there and take them both down myself.

Sarga attacked first, swatting at Nashur's head. Nashur dodged and growled. Sarga wouldn't be able to catch Nashur off guard like she had with Jokane.

"Remember, this is about who is the fastest and most effective at delivering the killing stroke," I called, hoping to see some crazy action happen quick. "This is a training exercise, after all," I said a bit quieter.

Calouise laughed.

Nashur had attempted to pull her adversary down the way Sarga had beaten Jokane, but Sarga maneuvered out of the hold and bit Nashur's back leg. She whipped around and clawed Sarga in the face. In the momentary second that Sarga was surprised by the blood that had been drawn, Nashur tackled her to the ground. Before Nashur could make the kill though, Sarga kicked with her back legs, shoving her off.

Seeing Nashur on the ground, a vivid red gash in her flank, I suddenly felt a surge of unwanted pity. Nashur was trying to defend her community, her power as a female member in this community, and perhaps regain some respect. As much as I disliked her, I would rather have Nashur win this one.

Sarga stood over Nashur's fallen form, taunting her prey before making her final move. But Nashur reached up, wrapped her paws around Sarga's neck, and pulled her throat to her exposed teeth in one quick, battle-ending movement.

Despite how much I hated the idea of it, I was impressed by Nashur's efforts and victory.

"And there's a lesson to you all that you should never wait to kill your enemy, not even to gloat or taunt. Be swift and get the job done," I said at large amongst the cheers and jeers.

Sarga forced herself onto her four paws and glared at Nashur. She wasn't going to take this defeat well.

"That's all for today. More tomorrow—come face the champion!" I called, hoping to lessen some of the dangerous excitement that was flaring up. I watched Sarga stalk off, her body movements not fluid and suggestive for once, but tense and jerky.

Several tigers went off in pairs, talking with bright eyes and twitching whiskers, planning for tomorrow. Nashur still stood in what had been the middle of the area, panting and staring at Calouise and me. He smiled at me and then strode over to the winner of the day, probably to congratulate her and make her feel like her fight hadn't been in vain. He was better at being diplomatic than me.

A few yards away, Dekovin was watching me with a very focused stare. When I caught his gaze, he decided to prowl towards me, his tail flicking back and forth behind him. Unsure of what he wanted, I allowed the muscles in my legs to tense, prepared for action, just in case.

"That was a pretty clever idea you came up with today," he said quietly, his voice deep and thick, like he'd swallowed tree sap. "I thought this communal living had made you all weak, but you cats proved yourself worthy opponents, didn't you?"

"We're all on the same side, Dekovin," I replied, taking a step back. He was still moving slowly closer and closer.

"Yes, but now we know that fighting with you all will not be a total waste of time." His eyes flickered between my eyes and legs as I stepped back again. "You're a powerful cat, aren't you?"

If he didn't back down, he was going to gain a few new scars. I was being anything *but* invitational to this sleazy cat. Apparently my defensive posture was coming across as an invitation to him, and he continued forward, taking another step toward me. A rumbling growl began in the back of my throat. He was a lot bigger than I, but I was prepared to do some damage if needed.

Suddenly, Calouise was next to me. He stepped between us, standing firmly before Dekovin, his lips curled back, his teeth barred, a terrible snarling, ripping noise erupting from his clenched jaws. Dekovin responded with a challenging growl, but Calouise hissed with his mouth wide open now, teeth clearly exposed as a threat.

I had watched in videos and documentaries how big cats and other species fight each other over a female, but that was usually after the female had purposefully attracted them. What I had before me now was not two cats fighting over me, but rather one cat defending me. This may have been something new for the animal world, but as I watched Calouise intimidate and threaten Dekovin, I felt a mixture of irritation, appreciate, and desire. I'd been prepared to defend myself, and I was only slightly annoyed that he hadn't given me the chance to do so, but I couldn't deny how it felt to have him protect and defend me. I didn't know if he did it because he simply cared and saw that I may have been in trouble, or if it was because he felt like he had to protect what he considered his. I didn't want to leap to conclusions, but if he was jumping out there in the world to protect me because I was his—in his mind, at least—then perhaps he could love me after all. Maybe he already did and couldn't express it in any other way but defending me from nosy, hormonal male tigers.

That was something to be explored in the future.

In the meantime, I eyed his protective form and defensive snarls with a type of thrilling pleasure. As much as I told myself not to draw any conclusions, I couldn't help the swell of pride, desire, and emotional intensity that arose within me. I saw this act as one born of deep emotional attachment.

Dekovin's eyes roved over me and then flickered back to Calouise, who still stood aggressively in his way. He relaxed slightly and backed a few feet away.

"Can't let a hellion fight for herself, can you?" he hissed.

"She shouldn't have to against a nomad like you," Calouise growled.

"You didn't even give her a chance to express if she was interested or not," he said.

I stepped around Calouise and faced Dekovin, my stance planted strongly in the muddy earth. "I'm not. Now leave me be or I'll attack you without Calouise's assistance."

He shot me one final glare before swiveling around and prowling off into the damp brush.

I turned to look at Calouise. He was fairly relaxed now, but breathing a bit harder than normal from the exertion.

"You didn't have to do that. I was capable of handling him myself," I said firmly. As much as I had loved the gesture, I didn't need him or anyone else to think of me as weak.

"He would have put up a hard fight." He glanced around us, taking in the relatively empty space in the walled off meadow we talked in so often. Only Nashur remained, sitting away off in the center of the matted mess that had been the arena, her watchful gaze carefully studying us.

"Why do you care?" I pestered. Maybe he would give me an honest, revealing answer—but my hopes weren't high.

He was still breathing heavy, his eyes staring into mine, their deep black inviting me to get lost in them rather than keeping me away in warning. He remained silent as large rain drops began to fall in the trees above, splashing to the ground around us.

At last he replied, "You're important."

I sighed. How very generic. My eyes shifted in Nashur's direction. Perhaps her presence had prevented him from saying what he really meant, but there was nothing I could really do to make her leave.

And the moment had passed.

I began to walk towards the wall, exhausted from the day and weather and circumstances. The amount of stressors upon my shoulders seemed to keep growing.

"Do you think Sarga will cause trouble after losing today?" I called back towards him.

"Not any more than usual," he said.

I jumped a little, not realizing he was right behind me. "Should I be worried about Dekovin? Do you think he'll try to find me tonight?" I whispered, unable to keep the fear inside.

"Do you want me to stay in the Sanctuary tonight to keep an eye on the place?"

For a moment, I thought he was being sarcastic, but his face was entirely flat and serious.

"No, that's not necessary. I'll just sleep with one eye open," I assured him. I didn't want to appear weak by having a bodyguard—the rajah, nonetheless—stationed to watch over me while I slept.

"You're always welcome in the throne room," he said politely.

"Thanks, but my waterfall suits me just fine." I jumped to the top of the wall and stared down at him. "I'll see you tomorrow. We have a lot more training to get done."

"Yes, indeed." He turned to walk away, but then stopped and said, "Rest well, Mix."

I didn't reply but watched him and Nashur disappear in the direction of the fortress. A part of me was tempted to follow them, but I couldn't handle the emotional pressure and temptation that would await me there if I decided to sleep in the throne room. I especially couldn't handle the looks and judgment from the dignitaries that would be bound to follow if I suddenly changed my mind and slept among them.

I went back to my waterfall spot, the jungle growing increasingly darker as I journeyed. My ears were alert, listening for any sound of a prowler on my trail. But there was nothing out of the ordinary.

I curled up in the cool indentation and listened to the sound of the water falling and splashing into its pool. Today had been mostly a success, but there was still so much to do and prepare for before we could head out after Zoriach. With that stress lingering in my muscles, I fell into an uneasy sleep.

Snow, Clouds, and Mist

The following day's training went as smoothly as I could have expected after the eventful showdowns before. The crowd that surrounded me had increased exponentially in comparison. Everyone wanted to participate in my exciting, nontraditional training rather than Calouise's and Trapir's regular and rather mundane training. When Calouise noticed this, he knew I couldn't manage to train them all in the way I had been before. We would never get through everyone enough times to prepare them adequately.

He decided to also train them in a competition-based fashion, drawing half of my trainees to his arena in order to help instruct everyone, even if it was accomplished differently than Calouise's normal mode.

Nashur managed to win two rounds in a row before she was defeated by one of our males in the community. I watched her slump from the arena, exhausted and disheveled. She ducked her head as she passed me, but I caught the glimmer of relief to be out of the center of attention and attack. She hadn't been raised a killer.

The training fields remained busy for the next two or three weeks, cats returning to continue to hone their skills, master their opponents faster, kill more effectively. By the third week, rain and downpours were nonstop and the arenas were a mud pit. Only the serious trainers kept returning, including Somila and Shrey. I was proud of them for their dedication to improve and prepare themselves for what lay ahead.

Everyone grew excited whenever Calouise or I participated in the brawling and training, jumping into the arena and dragging ourselves through the mud, growing dirty alongside them. I think it inspired them to see their leaders beside them, fighting and preparing together. We were a community—a type of family—and we had to be a functioning unit of destruction, not a mass of chaotic mess. Shrey was wrong: the war on the lions wasn't about me and Zoriach; it was about all of us tigers and leopards alike, rising up and defeating the degrading bully that shadowed over our species, shaming us, belittling us, making us look defenseless and pathetic. We wouldn't take it anymore. We had to regain our respect and authority in the animal world to stop feeling powerless and unimportant. Welcoming the nomads and training warriors brought us a few steps closer to achieving that victory.

Almost three weeks since my encounter with Dekovin on the first training day and every time I saw his lanky body or beady eyes, I shivered with the memory: his thick voice; his dangerous, dark eyes; his hungry expression—they lingered in my mind until the flashback of Calouise putting himself between Dekovin and me ruptured the disturbing memory. I clung to the way he roared in furious passion, dug his claws deep into the soft earth, and glared savagely at the cat who was crudely interested in me. I told myself Calouise wouldn't have done that so aggressively for anyone else. I knew he cared about everyone in our community, but not enough to put himself in potential danger to defend a cat who he knew could manage to communicate her interest or lack thereof without difficulty.

I had never been one for soppy adoration or romantic gestures. The idea of constantly thinking about someone had always seemed a distraction—a waste of time to me. I had never understood the purpose or inspiration behind love stories and songs—it had all seemed so foolish to me.

But I was catching myself in dazes as I walked, my thoughts entangled in memories or fantasies about a tiger prince of the jungle. Dreams of him wormed their way into my slumber—he was usually shrouded in mystery, his form blurred, but his eyes always bright and watching me, much like they always were in reality. Back in my early days in the jungle, I considered his constant, watchful stare disturbing and unnecessary, but now I found myself searching for it, feeling comforted and reassured whenever I caught his dark eyes gazing in my direction. The deep black of his eyes did not frighten me the way Dekovin's did.

They never had.

A part of me disliked the girlish responses I was experiencing. However, the greatest side of me was entranced and pleased to finally understand that love and romance weren't a joke or a waste of time. They brought a sense of contentment and delight that I had not anticipated.

And I hadn't even admitted to myself my feelings, let alone discovered if he had any such reciprocating affections whatsoever.

It was such a disaster, but one I didn't mind wading through.

I sat on the stone wall, overlooking and overseeing the diehard trainers at each other's throats in the pouring precipitation. Calouise sat beside me, his tail swishing back and forth behind us, brushing mine every few seconds. It tickled and caused me to be all too aware of his presence, which was a problem I faced even when he wasn't beside me or touching me. I still had never had the guts to say anything to him about how I felt or tease apart his own emotions, but I'd been subtle here and there, trying to find what I could when I had the opportunity. Up on the wall, we were relatively alone, the nearby cats on the ground below us very much focused on the two that were fighting.

His tail tickled mine again.

"Doesn't it bother you?" I whispered suddenly.

He turned his head to look at me, his face very much twisted in perplextion. "How horrible they are at killing one another?"

I released half of a laugh. "No. When your tail touches mine. Doesn't it mess with your senses?"

His remained mostly serious, but I caught a twitch near his nose. "Not at all. Does it bother yours?"

I stared past the training pit, gazing unseeingly into the murky green of the jungle trees, trying to think of something to say. "No, not really. But shouldn't you be more careful?"

"Of what?"

I forced myself to look into his eyes. "Someone seeing you being so informal with me."

He raised his brows. "I did not realize that my tail swishing from side to side was considered informal in relation to you."

I let my face display my annoyance. "It's the brushing of my tail, not the swishing itself." He was forcing me to be obvious, to say it out loud, to lay it out in the open between us. He was clever, but I wasn't stupid.

"I don't think any cat would notice something so trivial, but—" In a quick instant, his tail was caught on mine, almost looped around it. "—*that* they might consider informal."

The air was suddenly too warm, even for India. I pulled my tail away and wrapped it securely around my self. "Are you crazy? What if someone saw? They might think…"

"Think what?" he questioned, his expression playful.

"I … don't know. That we are more than we seem." It was becoming more and more difficult to not reveal anything that he hadn't revealed to me. I wouldn't be the first—I would remain stubborn to that.

He looked away, also out over the overcast jungle. "We already seem to be more than we are to them. They see fearless leaders and powerful rulers when we are really just two tigers who sit upon stone and wear a face of authority. Our power exists only because it is them who gives it to us."

He was right, but … "That's not what I meant." Below us, Somila overpowered Jokane in the muddy arena, her fur matted and indistinguishable from the ground. I could feel Calouise's eyes on me, and I met them reluctantly.

"I know what you meant." He turned his gaze to the arena. "And I don't care what they see or think," he whispered quietly.

I had to stop the smile that threatened to spread across my face, forcing it to explode within me, causing a burst of hot pleasure and excitement to seep through my veins.

In the arena, Shrey triumphed over Somila, much to the glee of the surrounding leopards. I didn't resist the smile that bubbled up this time.

"It's encouraging to know that a leopard can take down a tiger. He'll have no problem destroying lions," Calouise commented.

"Good, because leopards are the only allies we have," I replied, accepting the change of topic.

He didn't say anything, but continued to watch the happenings below as another leopard squared up against Shrey.

I shook off the water that had collected in my fur as I had remained relatively motionless. The downpour and monsoons were so common now that I had managed to grow accustomed to being drenched to my core, but the feeling of rain soaking into my fur made me feel heavy and weighed down, like I was turning to stone.

Calouise didn't even flinch as droplets of water flung across his back.

"We have less than a month now until we set out for Zoriach. Do you think they're ready?" I asked him.

Before he could reply, I heard rustling in the brush behind us. It wouldn't have bothered me except for the persistence of noise reverberating up to us. I swiveled around on the wall and crouched into a position ready to pounce. Calouise mimicked me, a rumble deep in his throat. Whatever was moving towards us was not someone from our community. It was multiple someones, and they were making no intention of being quiet or polite to the jungle and its occupants.

Through the cascading sheet of water, I could see a grey and white face emerge, blurred by the rain. A second later, a sandy-colored, blurred cat appeared beside the grey one.

Rather than hostile, I was shocked and confused. I glanced at Calouise, who was also looking at me with disbelief. Were we really seeing what I thought I saw?

I jumped from the wall before Calouise could and padded over to the newcomers, still wondering if my eyes were deceiving me. When I stood about five feet away, I stared in open awe at the two cats that were facing me. Moranaha was planted firmly in the muddy ground, his thick fur dripping wet, his paws and legs plastered and caked with mud from his journey. Beside him stood a sleek stranger. Her legs and back were patterned with very large giraffe-like spots. It reminded me of a tortoise shell. She was just as small, if not smaller, than her snow leopard companion, thinner and just as wet as Moranaha appeared to be.

Calouise had managed to make his way over to us.

"What are you doing here?" I gasped at Moranaha, forgetting about diplomacy in my utter shock. "And who are you?" I asked the stranger.

"Still just as blunt," Moranaha commented.

"She deserves an answer," Calouise replied boldly. I knew he had no patience for useless conversation when it came to diplomats.

Moranaha said nothing, but looked over at his companion, inviting her to speak first.

She took a step forward and glanced between the two of us. "I'm sorry, I thought Calouise was the rajah here," she said, attempting to be polite.

I desperately fought to hold in my less-than-diplomatic retort.

"Mix is my Fifth Paw and Commander of the war on Zoriach and the lions. She is just as important as I, if not more so," Calouise responded with his imperious voice.

Her eyes swiveled from Calouise to mine as she addressed me. "My name is Alsandi, and I am the former rani of the community of clouded leopards in Nepal. I and a few nomadic fellows have come to join your ranks against the lions."

I wasn't aware that I was staring at her like a gaping lizard until Calouise nudged me in the shoulder. "What made you decide to come?" I managed to choke out.

"When a single group of cats led by one monster manages to kill two of my great friends and leaders, I find the courage to step outside of safety and reason in order to do what is needed. Neither Sojóma nor Mehish deserved to die the way they did, slaughtered and paraded as a joke around the animal kingdom by the lions. Too long have the lions selfishly and abusively remained in a position of power. It is time the tigers were back on top, looked upon as pillars of peace and graceful dominions of authority once more." She gave a slight bow to me as she concluded her short speech. The few she had spoken of now emerged from the dense brush, their yellow eyes glowing in the gloom. At least six of them.

The well of hope that had sprung up at the sight of them was now overflowing. This was more than I could have ever dreamed of—not only that they were here, but that her words had been so well spoken and stained with truth, I felt that I would have fought for *her* if our roles were reversed.

"I, too, have come to help the tigers restore their positions of power in the animal kingdom. What the lions did to Sojóma and Mehish was unacceptable and inexcusable. I am here with the best warrior cats I could find to help you all put the lions in their place," Moranaha said. After his words, five more burly snow leopards appeared from behind him, their once thick and majestic fur matted and flat in the monsoon winds and rain, but their white faces glowering with anger and determination.

Thirteen. Thirteen leopards from across the country that were now a part of our ranks. They may not have been as large or deadly as a single tiger, but they were killing power nonetheless. It was so much more than I had allowed myself to dare hope for.

"You cannot imagine how grateful I am to see you all here. You leopards just may be the factor that ensures our victory," I said, full of sincere gratitude and relief.

"How long until you leave to attack?" Alsandi asked.

"Less than a month," I replied. "We've been training every day for the last month and a half or so, strengthening our bodies and skills."

"That sounds appropriate."

"Yes, and Mix has turned our training into a game," Calouise added. I thought I detected a hint of playful mockery in his tone.

Both Moranaha and Alsandi's brows rose with confusion.

"A game?" Alsandi questioned.

"Trust me, it's not as silly and useless as it sounds," I replied defensively.

"I would like to see this training game," she said, stepping forward.

"Of course, follow me. You and the other leopards are welcome to join." I turned around and made a muddy path back to the wall. We jumped to the top of it and looked down upon the arena where two leopards were dueling. Calouise and Alsandi sat on either side of me.

"The purpose of the game is for two cats to face off and see who can take out the other most swiftly and effectively. Whoever wins keeps fighting until they are defeated," I explained, hoping to capture the fun but also the important training aspect of it as well.

"It has been immensely successful," Calouise added.

I knew that he truly like this idea and thought it fascinating and useful. His praise to outsiders really solidified his opinion and my success, though.

I looked at Alsandi and Moranaha, who sat on her other side, searching for expressions of approval. I couldn't have them running back to their safe homelands simply because I was unconventional.

She watched with careful attentiveness as Shrey dominated his adversary. Now Mehan was facing Shrey, a matchup that would have ensured Shrey's end a month ago. If he won now, there was no denying that my method was a success. If he lost …

I would worry about that if the moment came.

Mehan was easily almost twice the size of Shrey. With the first swipe of his paw, Shrey was thrown to the ground in a splashy thump. But Shrey was clever and fast, and he knew how to use his size as an advantage. He had mastered this in the last two weeks that I'd been observing him. As Mehan prowled to stand over him, Shrey belly crawled as quick as he could, digging his claws and paws into the soft earth, pulling his small, low body under Mehan's. Before Mehan could catch him, Shrey wrapped his front legs around Mehan's neck and placed his teeth at his jugular. It reminded me of how Nashur had defeated Sarga. Both of them knew how to use their smaller size to lend to their triumphs rather than defeat.

I shot a smug smile over to the leopard leaders that had arrived today.

"I'm impressed. A leopard that can kill a tiger—a male tiger, at that. This game must do what is necessary," Alsandi commented.

"Indeed," I replied with confidence.

"You're welcome to join them," Calouise said politely.

"Perhaps tomorrow. We have all traveled a long way for many days in horrible weather. I think we would prefer to hunt and sleep first," Moranaha said.

"Whatever you need," Calouise replied.

They all gave small bows to him before hopping from the wall and prowling into the shrubbery in search of a resting place.

I couldn't contain my excitement as I met Calouise's eyes. "They came! I can't believe it."

"You were right. All along."

I smiled. "Yes, yes I was. Where's Cyan?" I spun around widely, hoping to find the irritating cat nearby in order to gloat, no matter how unprofessional it seemed. This was a small victory that we greatly needed, and I wanted to rub it in his furry face.

Calouise gave a light chuckle. "I think he'll feel shame enough when he realizes he was wrong and lost to you."

I sat back down and gave him a reluctant look. "Yeah, I guess you're right."

"I have to be right sometimes. I am the rajah, afterall."

The loud clatter and swoosh of rain had begun to dissipate slightly. I could make out parts of the jungle farther than ten feet away now. With the momentary ease of downpour, I caught sight of a few birds rising above the treeline in order to travel without being pelted back down to the ground. During heavy rains, the jungle that always seemed to teem with life felt very lethargic and calm, a great deal of species patiently waiting out the storms before venturing out to eat or socialize. The atmosphere would have been different on its own with the change of season, but an excess layer of calm and patience seemed to preside over the creatures of the jungle, especially when it came to the tigers and leopards. The days to confronting Zoriach were counting down, each day dissolving into the next, faster and faster as the departure loomed closer.

"I think we really have a chance now," I whispered to Calouise, who still sat beside me on the old stone wall.

"We always did," he replied, not looking at me.

"But the leopards solidify the odds in our favor," I said. He didn't understand how sure I'd felt that we were heading to our ultimate defeat; how worried I'd been, unable to sleep restfully because of my disturbing dreams; how desperate I was to not fail the tigers. I wasn't sure he would ever fully understand because I didn't know how to explain it to him. But he cared: cared about the status of our species, cared about the community, and cared about me—that I knew with certainty.

"Have you devised a plan of attack, yet?" he asked, switching the subject, as I had expected he would.

"Honestly, I have been trying to think of a way to take Zoriach by surprise, catch her unaware and unprepared. But, I don't think that's going to work. Her network of spies stretch from here to Gir. There's no way we could make it there without her being alerted."

"So what is your idea now?"

I sighed. "Since we have the leopards, I think the best option is to just travel in one large pack, come at her full force, intimidate her with what we have managed to recruit and build. We'll meet each other on the battlefield and really fight to see who deserves to hold the power in the animal kingdom."

He was studying my face, his pupils swiveling from side to side, slowly, calculating. "Do you have any doubts about who really deserves to win?"

"No ... I just know that life has no certainties."

His face hardened and the rain began to pour again. "There is certainty that we all will die. But what we choose to do with the life we have determines all outlooks."

"You don't have any doubts?" I asked, remembering his fear and dejection a few months ago after Mehish had died.

"I've never doubted our worth and right to have power and authority. Fears about our victory? Yes, that I have been afraid of for a very long time. Way before you joined us. But it was you and your passion that reawakened everything we already knew but didn't want to face. War is scary, but I believe we have a chance."

"I'm terrified," I admitted.

He gave me a sad smile. "I would be worried if you weren't."

We didn't discuss my attack strategy again, a mutual agreement and acceptance in the air between us. Instead, we oversaw the rest of the training, reengaging and instructing when it was still necessary. Most of the cats in the training area knew what they were doing now. They just had no other outlet for their fear and tension as they waited for the day of war.

In the following weeks, I ended up fighting and training more often as well. The amount of anxiety and fear and energy that coursed through my body in an hour would have been enough to drive a person to emergency therapy, but the animal world offered so many other outlets for my emotions. Sometimes, when the anticipation and terror were too much, I simply ran. I sprinted through the brush, splashing through muddy pools and puddles, ignoring the stinging whips of leaves and branches, desperate to relieve the energy. The first two times I bounded away into the jungle, Calouise followed me, concerned for my well-being. I appreciated his care, but it took me a long time to communicate to him that I needed to be alone and free to run, to attack a bush or tree, to get out the overwhelming sensations of feeling out of control. The third time he tried to follow me, I threatened to rip off one of his legs if he didn't leave me be. We both knew I didn't have the ability to do so, but he finally understood the message.

The training areas filled again in the final week before we set off. The clouded and snow leopards had periodically been participating in the training exercises, unsure how they liked the game aspect but still willing to prepare themselves to kill efficiently. A couple of them really enjoyed the competitiveness of the game. As they were smaller cats than all the tigers, and even most of the regular leopards, they found great satisfaction in improving their abilities to take down cats bigger than them.

Three days before we departed, I was pacing in the meadow, not really watching Alsandi and Somila train, too distracted by my own thoughts and anxiety to give them my full attention. At this point, they knew what they were doing. I was simply a mediator.

Calouise sat on the other side of the meadow, his tail flicking from side to side, the only sign that revealed his inner emotional state of less than calm. A partial ray of sunlight illuminated one side of his face, causing a sparkle in the blackest part of his eye. The monsoon rains had been gradually shortening and relenting. When the sun did appear, the drenched jungle was enveloped in evaporating mists that hung in the canopy and trapped a great amount of heat for us below. Somehow, the humidity was worse than the torrential deluge we had experienced for the last three months.

From somewhere out of the mists, Sarga materialized. In all honesty, I was surprised she lasted as long as she had, still hanging around, still not pregnant, still willing to go to war. But I still didn't like her.

She wormed her way in the direction of Calouise. Suddenly, I had no problem focusing. I watched warily as Sarga approached him, and his attention shifted as he turned to look at her. He remained sitting, but she stood in front of him, lucid and inviting.

A different kind of fear twisted in my stomach. Calouise and I had still never been explicit about our feelings. Of course his previous mating offer had once been an explicit communication of intention, but that was months and months ago. Our relationship had grown and developed considerably since then. But I was still too afraid to admit my human-type love for him, and I felt that he didn't know how to handle that kind of emotion, let alone name it and admit it to me. We were exceptionally close, but exclusivity had not been established. And as much as I suspected his feelings for me, I still had doubts.

And Sarga was a walking invitation to any male.

I didn't want to be *that* girl, but the jealousy and possessiveness that arose within was like an unstoppable wave of the sea. I watched them talk, debating whether or not to interrupt them. Of course Calouise was free to talk to whomever he chose, but Sarga was a special case.

I held back for a few more moments, still pacing, my eyes locked onto them from across the meadow. The two fighting—whoever they were—flickered in and out of my peripheral vision. I expected Calouise to shake her off, act aloof and blunt as was his custom, but then I saw him laugh. Not just chuckle, but sincerely laugh.

Envy suddenly erupted from some dark place within me.

"Now you know how I've felt every day since you've arrived," came a sad voice from beside me.

I couldn't tear my eyes away from Calouise and Sarga, but I recognized the voice without hesitation. "I doubt we feel the same," I replied.

Nashur remained standing next to me, and I could sense her eyes on me as I stared at the other two. "Perhaps not quite the same. But when you arrived, you had everyone's attention: Sojóma, Calouise, Trapir, the common cats. I've always been shunted aside, overlooked, unappreciated."

I didn't know how to reply without completely insulting her. And I had no energy to put effort into a sincere and honest answer that wouldn't drive her away. She had opened up to me, but I had no desire to reciprocate any kind of open relationship with her.

When I didn't reply, she turned to walk away. "I see the way you look at him, and I've seen how he watches you. I wouldn't worry about Sarga, but I wouldn't let her do as she pleases either."

"You're a strange cat, Nashur," I said before she was out of earshot.

She disappeared into the pervasive mist without another word. My eyes were still on Calouise. I wasn't going to go interrupt. I didn't want to let envy rule me.

But then Sarga moved closer to him, her tail curling around his neck.

A growl rumbled in my throat. I prowled over to them, my paws sinking deep in the soft earth as I walked with purpose, my large footprints imprinted in my wake.

"I hope I'm not interrupting," I said as I approached, hoping with great sincerity that I was most definitely interrupting.

Sarga's deeply dilated eyes diminished slightly as they swiveled onto me. "Actually—"

"Of course not," Calouise said, smiling at me. "Sarga was just asking me if I wanted to take a walk to stretch my legs."

I glared at her. "How nice," I said scathingly.

"Would you like to join us?" Calouise offered.

I met his gaze, which was warm and inviting, but his tense posture communicated his uncomfortable feelings in this situation. Sarga was glaring at me, her scorching gaze ruthless.

I considered his invitation, realizing that while he was extending me the courtesy to come—as he most likely wanted—he was also considering her offer, planning to accept. Why else would he have invited me if he wasn't planning on going? With her.

Anger was starting to take over, and I had a decision to make here: join them on a repulsive walk through the jungle or save myself their company. He could choose to ignore her on his own if he wanted. Or choose to accompany her. I was going to leave that up to him, and I had made previous plans to go on one final hunt with Somila and Shrey before our trek across India. "A walk sounds great, *but* I have prior plans to uphold right now," I told them somewhat sadly, although not because I was missing out on the walk.

"I'm sure they'll appreciate spending time with you," he replied sincerely but with a hint of disappointment. I wanted to be able to trust that disappointment.

Sarga glanced between us, her expression quite suspicious—most likely wondering how he could possibly know my prior plans—but I was firm in my avoidance and still waiting for Calouise to make his choice.

"I'll see you later?" I asked him.

"If you wish. I won't be gone long," he replied kindly.

Somehow, his words washed over me like ice rather than with warmth as I knew he had intended.

I wanted to leave without saying another word, but I couldn't do it. I cared too much to be blatantly rude.

"Are you ready for tomorrow?" I asked him before walking away.

I expected him to return a positive answer, one full of hope and optimism, an appeal to anticipation and victory and glory—it was something I needed.

"Tomorrow is the beginning of the end," he said solemnly. "It's hard to be ready for an end."

I swallowed with some difficulty, suddenly overcome with the weight of his words. No matter how I looked at it, he was right. It was either the end of oppression, the end of the lions, or the end of ourselves. And if Sarga got her way—if Calouise chose her—it was the end of us. There was no certainty except that something would come to its end in the next few weeks. Tomorrow marked that beginning.

We parted, and I wandered toward the Sanctuary, my appetite inexistent. I knew Somila would be waiting near the waterfall, but I was half tempted to not appear. We had talked briefly here and there in the last few months, but my responsibilities as a dignitary and her intense schedule of training had kept us busy but apart. With all the stress I had, all I really wished to do was sleep, where all my worries and fears could be set aside for a few hours.

But responsibility did not rest the way stress did.

And I had a responsibility, as a friend, to Somila.

She was, indeed, stationed beside my sleeping space, sitting straight. I couldn't help but notice how her muscles were toned and her body appeared strong.

"You look good," I commented as I approached.

"All thanks to your training program," she said with a smile. She eyed me. "You've looked better."

"Try leading a band of cats to war." And watching someone you care about walk off with another.

Her eyes drooped a little in what I hoped was sympathy. "I can only imagine the pressure."

I sat beside her, my posture much more slumped than hers. "I never thought I would be here," I said before I could stop myself.

"Me neither. When you joined us, I thought you'd be just another cat. And when you started talking about taking on Zoriach, I thought you were crazy and might cause our final downfall. And then Sojóma saw something in you I didn't understand. And then Cal. The lions have been oppressing us for far too long. Until an outsider like you came along and saw that something had to be done."

"I feel like everything just happened and I was left to find my place in the thick of it all. I never saw myself as a leader."

A squirrel skittered purposefully through our midst, searching for some kind of sustenance.

"Maybe not at first. But you're a natural leader, not a follower. You just needed to step into it and embrace it. I feel better knowing that you are the one leading us through this. You have what it takes."

I managed a smile. "I couldn't be here without all of you to support me."

She nudged my shoulder. "That's what friends are for."

I took in a deep breath, looking up, where the last rays of the day streamed through the canopy. Perhaps Calouise's decision would leave me free to focus on what needed to be done. We were going to war in the morning and everyone was depending on me. This night would be my last night as simply Mix. Tomorrow, when I led them from the safety of the jungle, away from our home, toward their possible doom, I'd be something greater than just a tiger or just a girl. I would be someone who writes a chapter of history, possibly for both worlds. I wouldn't just be another lifeform on this planet, but someone making a difference.

I would fully become someone with greater purpose—someone who could bring redemption and glory back to the tigers, saving what pride and majesty we had left.

BEGINNING OF THE END

The journey across India was not uneventful. I had come to learn that Gir was almost directly west of where we lived, a good week and a half or so walk from our Sanctuary to their illusionary doorstep. The trek wasn't really the problem.

It was avoiding any trouble with humans.

As a former human, I didn't think there would be very many issues with traversing through the back ends of farmland. We very well couldn't walk along the main roads, a band of forty or fifty tigers and leopards prowling with purpose, out in the open. It would have raised a lot of strange questions and drawn an unwelcome crowd of curious researchers or greedy poachers. But I figured farmlands would offer a safe area to travel. Afterall, Zoriach and several of her friends had made the journey a number of times.

It became clear as we actually began traveling that it would be an understatement to say that I was wrong. From my perspective, seeing a tiger or even a group of tigers crossing through my backyard or farm would have been a moment of sheer awe. I would have enjoyed watching them, been curious and tried to document the phenomenon. I think that's what a lot of people in America would have done.

But in India, tigers and leopards on farmland are just as unwanted and unwelcome as tigers and leopards on the roads. The amount of times we were yelled at, had things chucked at us, and shot at was innumerable. Since we were seen as a threat to their livelihood, there was no sympathy from the Indian farmers.

Of course, it didn't help when we started to feel hungry. Walking all day long was exhausting and burned a lot of our energy stores. Normally, I would only have to eat a large meal once a week or so. However, one meal was not enough to last us a full week. It barely lasted the smaller cats among us three days. The larger cats, like Pravin and Mehan—even Calouise—started to feel the pangs of hunger by the end of day two. The unfortunate part about the long stretch of farmland was that forest and jungles were not anywhere nearby. Our hunting options were scarce. When we started to get hungry, we had a plentiful amount of livestock options around us. But I knew that hunting the goats or sheep or cows would only worsen our name. The whole point of going to war against the lions was to redeem ourselves. How could we claim to be a species of greater dominance and power if we were petty thieves of humans' livelihood?

This was hard to stress to the especially hungry cats. The nomads, in particular, didn't seem to grasp the importance of what I was saying.

"Those animals exist to serve the humans. Why can't they serve us, as well?" one of our nomadic allies questioned me. The sun was beginning to go down on the third day since we had left the Sanctuary.

"Because they belong to the humans. The wild world is ours. We can take as we please when it doesn't belong to someone else," I replied, trying to rationalize with a bunch of irritated, exhausted tigers and leopards who were glaring at me with great frustration.

"But if we don't eat, then all that's left is our dead bodies. What's worse, dead tigers or a few dead goats?"

I growled at them. "If we kill their animals, then we become the monsters they think we are. We are not monsters, and we are not thieves. If you want to be a part of this troop, then you'll follow our command and hunt creatures that do not belong to the humans."

I received some more argument, but the majority grudgingly agreed. That night, we did lose two nomads. They couldn't handle our strict rules and decided to hunt the goats anyway. Calouise banished them without hesitation. It felt good to have him support me. It almost made up for him walking away with the most dangerous female in our group. Those supportive actions made me feel like I was on the right path, that I had what it took to actually lead this ensemble to some kind of victory. But it still hurt to watch two of our reinforcements disappear. Every cat was precious to our cause.

Most of the time, we journeyed by night, the cover of darkness a safety blanket that we took advantage of. During daylight hours, we split into smaller groups, the majority of us resting, laying low in whatever tall grasses and shrubbery were nearby, concealing ourselves from the danger of being spotted. Others hunted, unable to stomach the pangs of hunger any longer.

It was during one of these restful days that I was resting beside Caliouse, staring out over the vast yellow grasses that had long ago gone to seed. Calouise had been his normal self, remaining friendly and close. Since his walk, I'd barely seen Sarga, and Calouise had acted no differently towards me. Either nothing had happened between them or our relationship was not what I had thought it was. I had no way of knowing, and I was too afraid to ask—afraid of the answer and what he might read into my curiosity. Perhaps we would never go further than friends, which was a painful idea, but it was impossible to resist him completely. He was my best friend, if nothing else.

He was not asleep, or even restful. His watchful eyes gazed over the land, observing and learning as he always did.

Neither one of us had really slept much on this trek. As the leaders, we had to keep an eye on everyone and our surroundings, sentries and protectors. We tried to take turns, but both of us were too anxious to achieve rejuvenating sleep. I always seemed to bolt awake after only an hour or two, struggling to catch my breath from the nightmare or my hypervigilance that appeared to keep running even when I slept.

"You should rest," I said to him, the sun starting to descend into evening. The hum of crickets was just beginning.

"I can't. I always have disturbing dreams," he replied almost absent-mindedly, distracted by something I could not see.

I couldn't stifle the yawn that followed. "Still, I know you're tired."

He managed to tear his gaze away from the distance and turned to look at me. "I'm not the one yawning."

"You should try it."

He turned away again and sighed. "I should try to sleep, you're right."

I gave him a smug smile.

Yes, he was still my best friend.

He settled himself a bit more comfortably into the dirt, below the tops of the waving grasses, concealed and relatively safe. Within a few minutes, his breathing leveled off, deeper and slower, calming and reassuring as I listened to it. He had become my source of calm, a presence to ease my stress, even if he didn't completely eradicate it.

Focused on his breathing, trying to relax my own tension, I didn't catch the energy that was rushing towards us, not until it was within a few feet and emerged in the flattened circle of grass we had created in our attempted slumber.

The small child rammed into my flank, unable to scream as he fell backwards, his eyes wide, the wind knocked out of him. I could see the blatant terror in his facial features. When he finally caught his breath, he began to scoot back, slowly, as if hoping his careful movements wouldn't provoke anything from me. Calouise was still asleep by my side.

I didn't want this child to fear me. Our reputation as man eaters could never be swayed if we didn't find ways to interact with humans on a kinder, gentler level. The boy had stopped moving, his ankle caught in a tangle. I could hear his breathing rate increase, his fear rising as he stared at me, realizing he was trapped.

I inched forward slowly, keeping my eyes locked onto his, hoping he could sense that I meant no harm.

His eyes had grown even wider—which I hadn't thought possible—as I moved closer. I consciously made an effort to not show my fangs. I didn't want him to think I was hungry, even though I was. But I would never eat a human, no matter how hungry I was. Especially not a terrified child.

I was crouched only a few feet away from his tangled foot. I gingerly reached out my large paw and tore the grasses wrapped around his ankle. He pulled it free, his eyes darting between my paw and my eyes. I could still see the apparent fear contorting his face, but his eyes were more curious now. I remained still, not wishing to frighten the poor child anymore than he already was.

The boy stood up, standing only a foot or so away from me. His chest was level with my nose as I lay in front of him. Slowly, cautiously, he reached a hand out, his fingers trembling slightly. Just as carefully, I pushed my nose against his palm. The fear on his face vanished, and a cautious smile replaced it. I licked his hand once, and he giggled.

The night around us was maturing, the stars beginning to appear in the purplish sky. The boy pulled back his hand and turned to leave, a hesitant smile stretching his face. The fear in his eyes had not disappeared, but he was not without curiosity. He waved once, and I gave him a friendly chuff. A moment later, he had disappeared back into the long yellow grass. Perhaps there would be one less human out to kill tigers in the coming years.

If only I could change them all.

We were camped a few hundred yards from Zoriach's territory. At sunset, we had arrived and decided to try to rest one more night before entering the warzone. We bunkered down just before the edge of the treeline that bordered a more open grassland area. Our surroundings were fairly dull—a washed out monochromatic blur of brown and yellow, much like the distasteful color of lion's fur. Smidgens of greenery were here and there. The closer to the small mountains, the greener it became. It was very dry and hot when the sun was high, but the evening was comfortable enough.

Calouise and I both knew that Zoriach was already aware that we were this close—that tomorrow would be the day of reckoning. I arranged a wall of five or six tigers to stand sentry in the scrawny trees that surrounded us. Zoriach and her cronies wouldn't be able to touch us until we were ready. This battle would begin on *our* terms.

I also insisted that we stay in a tight group for this last night. The closer we were, the less likely anything horrible could happen to any one of us before the morning. Strength in numbers, just like Sojóma had always believed. The nomads weren't too keen on the idea, but they agreed. They had already come this far—they really didn't have any other choice.

I didn't leave them with one, anyway.

I sat among the sentries, unable to sleep knowing the lions were out there, somewhere in the falling darkness, hungry for our blood. Zoriach wouldn't rest until we were dead—I couldn't rest until she was defeated. I shivered slightly, almost as if I could feel her breath at my neck.

"Anything of interest out there?" came his voice. He settled comfortably beside me, a pillar of strength.

"Just a bunch of scaredy-cat lions hiding in the brush," I replied, trying to keep the fear out of my voice.

"You should get some sleep before tomorrow."

"I can't possibly sleep."

He didn't reply but sighed in a sad sort of way.

"Are you alright?" I dared to ask, not really expecting a true answer.

He finally turned his head to look at me. "I feel just like a cat who's going to war would normally feel the night before the battle."

I gave him a small smile. "Not all bravery and positivity in that head of yours, huh?"

He briefly met my eyes but couldn't seem to hold my gaze. "I'm always afraid," he admitted.

"Of what?" I pushed, pawing at the dusty ground.

He stood up at that moment and turned to walk away. "Wouldn't you like to know," he said mysteriously, a hint of a tease deeply imbedded in his tone. He prowled back toward the communal sleeping area, his pace slow and steady. I could tell he was lost in his head, unable to focus or relax. He couldn't even sit still next to me for longer than a few minutes.

I didn't blame him.

I wandered back in the direction of the gathered group, watching most of them squirm while they tried to sleep. Some of them whispered to each other, others didn't even pretend to be sleeping, their eyes wide open and glowing in the falling sunlight. I could see Calouise many yards away, talking with Trapir.

"It's a sight, isn't it?" came Sarga's voice from behind me. "All these cats gathered together for something greater than just themselves."

"What do you want Sarga?" I asked, trying to not growl. I had to keep my own problems contained.

She sat beside me. "Honestly, I was wondering if you knew how to get rid of an annoying flea. I may have been *too* invitational to him, if you know what I mean."

I could feel her looking at me, but I couldn't meet her gaze. I most definitely, very much disliked her. "Why would you come to me for that kind of advice?"

"You're a strong female. I've seen how some of the males look at you. Dekovin, Mehan, Cal—they give me barely a whisker twitch in comparison to you. Especially Cal."

She suddenly had my full attention.

"Let me tell you about Cal: after I literally begged him—as if I was chewing his legs off or something—he agreed to walk with me to dispel an all too interested male who had been following me around all afternoon. And in those two minutes, I discovered how dull of a cat he is. He's a pretty face but an empty shell. Conversation with him was mind-numbingly boring. I don't know how you stand to be around him every day."

My heart was racing, and her words seemed to be reaching me as if from far away, like an echo. He hadn't wanted to walk with her—not willingly. He'd hardly spoken to her—given her almost zero attention. It felt like some of the pressure and tension that had been weighing on me for days and weeks was lifting. Of course, the immediacy and inescapable reality of the war looming before us still left a considerable weight on my shoulders, but Sarga's words were a source of relief and freedom. Calouise hadn't chosen her—he'd simply agreed to help her as the good rajah he was.

She was still waiting for my reply.

"I don't know. I guess I just haven't paid close enough attention before," I said, barely conscious of what I was saying. I was feeling unexpectedly grateful for this conversation, but I was also done. I wanted to talk to Calouise. I felt a bit of remorse for what I had assumed and how I may have unconsciously acted toward him. If I was lucky, perhaps he hadn't noticed anything strange, and we could—or I could—return to our normal interactions with our undercurrent tensions and unexpressed emotions.

"Well, at least I didn't pursue him. Saved myself there, didn't I?" She gave me a knowing look, expecting me to agree with her. In a way, I did. She'd saved herself from my anger and severe disappointment.

"Yes, it seems you did," I said quietly. Sarga still wasn't leaving, and I remembered that she had started this conversation by asking for my advice. "As for getting rid of unwanted attention? Don't ask for it and stay strong. Be confident and assertive. That's all I got."

"Thanks, I appreciate that. Well, try not to stay up all night. It's not worth it if you're alone. And it's especially important that you're rested for tomorrow, Commander."

"I will do my best," I replied.

She stood up and sauntered off. I didn't watch her leave, but rather swept my gaze over the cats, searching for him.

He was still talking with Trapir, and I realized that my and Sarga's conversation had not actually lasted very long. However, it felt as if it had dragged on forever as I had processed everything.

I watched them talk for a few moments, feeling a warmth settle over me. I'd been fighting my feelings for so long, afraid to admit to them, afraid to show them. But I didn't want to be afraid of that anymore. The jealousy, the pain, the relief—they'd all been such strong emotions, and I understood why now.

I wanted to speak with Calouise before the battle in the morning, but I'd let him finish whatever business he had with Trapir first. Maybe I could even sleep for a little while, and we could talk in the morning.

Despite my insistence that everyone sleep in the same spot, I wanted to be alone. I wanted to be able to breathe and pace and stretch and relieve the remaining anxiety without disturbing the others who could miraculously sleep with some kind of ease.

Before I could find a more secluded area, Shrey walked up to me, his yellow eyes glowing slightly in the little light that remained.

"Where are you headed?" he asked me, concern apparent in the spotted features of his face.

"Somewhere quiet and a little more alone," I replied. His expression was too kind to lie to.

"Is that safe? I mean we all know Zoriach isn't one to play by any rules. She's probably just waiting for one of us to wander off alone."

"I'll be fine," I assured him. I moved to walk past him, but he stepped in my path.

"We'll be alright, Mix. You've trained us well. We're ready. We just need you to lead us." He made eye contact with me, his brows high, pointedly trying to reassure me.

"I know," I replied. He was a good friend.

He let me pass with a slight bow. I nodded to him and continued forward, little puffs of dust pluming around my paws with every step I took. I already missed home.

I found an area of dusty grass that wasn't completely dead or yellow, but still a tiny bit soft with green. The sun's setting rays pierced the sky overhead, the clouds bathed in fiery orange. Somehow, the color of the sky was comforting. It was the color of my species.

My constantly swishing tail suddenly bumped into something unexpectedly solid. Unbidden, I whipped around, my teeth bared and a growl rumbling in my throat, ready to kill. But I came face-to-face with Calouise. I let out an irritated huff and relaxed from my hostile stance.

"If I was a lion, my tail would be between my legs," he commented quietly. His black eyes sparkled in the final light of the day.

"That's reassuring. What are you doing here? Why did you follow me?" I stared into his eyes, not afraid anymore of what he might see in mine.

But he didn't seem able to hold my gaze again. He stared down at his paws where he repeatedly retracted and pushed out his claws, kneading the earth. He pulled in a steadying breath and took a step forward. "I wanted to find you before the fight tomorrow morning. I want to talk now, just in case…" He paused and looked up. Our eyes met, and I could see the tiniest flicker of fear in his eyes, but also something more, something deeper and desperate to escape. He seemed surprised, too, to find our faces less than a few inches apart. We hadn't been this close face-to-face since the day he had laid me flat on my back.

"There is no just-in-case," I whispered.

"But if there is, I want you to know … you are that which makes me truly happy."

I expected to feel surprised, but I only felt warmth. And a sense of joy. He was staring into my eyes, waiting for my reaction and response. I moved to gently press my forehead against his. It was the first time we had purposefully touched in a romantic way since we had met.

"I love you, too, Cal."

I closed my eyes and stood there in comfortable silence, head-to-head with someone I loved, for an indescribable amount of time. He was right—just in case we didn't survive the fight, at least we had this time before it all ended. At least I now knew, without dispute, that he *could* fall in love and he had done so with me. At least he knew that I loved him the same. At least we had finally admitted the truth to each other after all this time, before it was too late.

We remained there, together in the grass, long after the sunlight had faded into the black of night.

I awoke as the rays of dawn streamed across the eastern tree line.

His warm body was still beside me. I could feel his flank rise and fall with his steady breathing. I looked at his face, relaxed and free in a way I'd never really seen before. He never appeared so open and calm when awake, when his mind was constantly buzzing and thinking, maintaining his walls that housed his emotions.

I heaved myself to my paws and padded a few feet away, staring up at the sunrise. Strange how much had changed in the course of a night— a span of a few hours. Strange how the prospects of war and the possibility of death seemed to dissolve all walls and inhibitions. Strange that from impending war, love was able to be revealed, able to fully bloom in the safety of darkness and trust.

I heard Calouise stir but didn't turn to look at him, not sure what he would be feeling or thinking now that it was morning. Now that he'd gotten what he had wanted for so long, perhaps he was done with me— confirming my deepest fear. Another strange aspect of war—the shifting of terrors. I now feared death and loss more than anything I'd ever feared before. My old panic inducers seemed an obliterated memory.

I heard him stand up and shake out his fur. My heart was thudding in my ears, waiting for him to make a decision that would define the finality of everything between us.

I listened to the soft thumps his padded paws made as he walked across the dusty ground. A few seconds later, he stood beside me. I could barely contain the relief and sense of contented joy that arose with his presence.

"We have a war to attend today," he said quietly, not looking at me, also gazing at the sunrise.

"Couldn't we skip it?" I whispered half-heartedly. "Lie here all day and stare up at the sky?"

"We can do that tomorrow."

I finally turned to look at him, his eyes already on me. "Promise?"

"Promise."

"I guess it's time to wake them all up," I said with a sigh.

"Most of them should already be awake. It's time to inspire. And lead."

I gulped in terror.

"I'll be by your side," he said in his comforting deep voice.

Somehow, that made all the difference.

We both turned away from from the climbing sun and headed toward the area our community was gathered in. Calouise was right: most of them were wide awake, pacing around each other, their many patterns a beautiful array of dizziness.

I spotted Somila a few yards away and bounded, with what felt like thousand pound weights attached to my paws, over to her. "Can you rally the sentries? I have something to say before we attack." I found it hard to swallow. The reality of what was about to happen seemed to be truly sinking in.

She nodded and ran off, disappearing into the treeline.

"Is there anything you'd like me to do?" Calouise asked from my side.

"Can you get everyone's attention? I just need a moment," I replied quietly.

He gave a swift nod as well and prowled forward, calling all the cats to attend and attempt to focus their restless energy on us.

The moment went by quicker than I had expected. Somila returned with a pawful of tigers that had taken turns keeping watch, keeping us safe through the night. They converged into the gathered mass. I stepped forward, trying to see them, but they all blurred into an orange and gold horde. Maybe that would make this easier. I couldn't see their fearful faces.

I sucked in a deep breath. This was it: somehow, I had to inspire.

I really wished I had thought about this speech more in advance.

"Today, we have the opportunity to make history and impact our future." I looked out over them all, trying to focus on these cats who were my family, who had followed me here, who seemed to believe in me. Their faces were anxious, but they appeared expectant. I needed them to believe in themselves now. "Out there, just beyond the trees, waits an enemy that has opposed us since we've come into contact with one another." This was really going to test my memory of tiger and lion history. "For over half a century, they've held our seats in the positions of power and looked down upon us. We've been oppressed and ridiculed, attacked and bullied. The lions have not been worthy cats of authority. Their accumulated title 'king of the jungle' is undeserving and misplaced. True leaders, worthy kings, do not invade others' homeland and murder their kin. True kings do not belittle the creatures of their kingdom. The animal kingdom is vast and varied, but the lions are unable to respect that. They're selfish, prideful, and unworthy to wield authority. Today, we will show not only the lions, but the rest of the animal world, that the tigers will not stand for injustice and dishonorable acts from those that claim to be rulers. Tigers once ruled with dignity and grace. The lions overthrowing us years ago does not lessen who we are and what we are capable of. Today, we take back the power. Today, we fight for our right to be kings, to lead and watch over the animal world in the manner we were always meant to. Today, with the rising sun, we will attack like beams of righteous light and reclaim what belongs to us!"

The resounding roars shook the sparse trees about us. Somewhere during the speech, I'd found a thread. Somewhere along the way, our purpose for this war resurfaced like it never had before. The energy before me set my heart ablaze and gave me a source of strength. The fear from their faces was gone, even if it wasn't dissolved within them. Remembering the sinister looks from Zoriach, the heartless murders of Sojóma and Mehish, the paranoid, hateful nature she possessed—we were here to put a stop to it.

They were still roaring, expressing their own excitement. Fear could be dispelled—at least temporarily—with purpose.

I looked at Calouise, whose eyes were glowing with his own internal fire. "You're the leader I could never be," he said with admiration.

I smiled, filled with a fire to achieve great victory.

Beaten, dead, defeated

Calouise, Alsandi, Moranaha, and I stood at the front of our forces, just in front of the treeline before the expansive grasslands, the sun at our backs.

Zoriach and Singh stood at the other end, perhaps fifty or sixty yards away. She was surrounded by a mass of umber lions, blackened leopards, striped hyenas—at least fifty or more. It was no lie—we were outnumbered, but not enough to send us running. I was confident in my family's ability to take on the enemies. Every one of us was capable of taking out at least two or three of her cats.

I could hear the rumbling symphony of a hundred wild cats in the air, their breathing and anticipatory growling resounding around us. For the briefest moment, I felt the stirrings of panic and terror race through my veins, but they were gone as quickly as they had come.

Fear would not rule the day.

Zoriach appeared to wish to say something. I had already given my inspirational speech. There was nothing she could say that would make us flee.

"I'm surprised you made it this far without cars, or humans, or any other creatures that look down upon you impeding your path," came her rough voice.

I knew she was trying to incite us. What she didn't know was that we were already riled up, ready to fight. Calouise was stoic enough not to respond to her. He would simply allow her words to fuel the fire within him.

I was doing my best to do the same. I wouldn't give her the benefit of my response. I'd speak in actions only.

"It seems almost sad that you and your friends have come halfway across India simply to die here and reestablish what the world already knows: tigers are weak and not worthy to hold authority. The lions are king of the jungle, and we will prove it to you today and every day after that you tigers try to foolishly rise up and challenge our power. We will put you in your place again and again until you've all learned the lesson." She concluded her sentence with a taunting snarl.

A tiny part of me had hoped we would face each other and she'd back down with her tail between her legs. That perhaps she was *possibly* smart enough to give in before it was too late.

But her words fed the largest part of me. I, and those backing me, had come here to earn our stripes, to earn our way back on top, and to silence our oppressors. Tigers were anything but weak. And we would prove it in battle.

None of us said a word. Instead, with a shared look between Cal and me, we both opened our jaws and roared at her, letting them hear our voices, our strength, our power, our authority. All those behind us joined in a moment later. I would say the sound was deafening, but it was rather motivating in a way that words could never be.

With a final snarl, I crouched. Across the savanna between us, Zoriach sprang forward, bounding in a frenzy toward us, her amassed troops right behind her. The pounding of their paws was like drums of war.

I leapt toward them, Calouise at my side, Alsandi and everyone else at my tail, our own cacophony of paws thundering in answer.

I expected to run straight into Zoriach, to meet her head on and finish this quickly, but despite my speed, I was overtaken by Trapir and Moranaha. When our forces collided, I barely glimpsed Moranaha tackle Singh before I was engulfed in a sea of bristling fur and snapping teeth.

Two black panthers had decided to face me. With our collision, one of them had rammed me from the side as the other clawed at my face as a distraction. One powerful swipe of my paw put the first one on the ground, momentarily incapacitated. I turned to the other at my flank and brought him to the ground by the neck, my teeth sinking into his jugular not a second later. The metallic taste of iron seeped onto my tongue, enough to cause pause in my reaction time, enough to make me briefly question what I had just done. That was until the other black cat jumped on top of me, his teeth tearing at the back of my neck.

I flung myself to the ground, landing on the other cat as he was pinned to the dusty earth. An angry growl escaped from between his jaws, but I silenced him a moment later.

I briefly surveyed my surroundings. I'd managed to kill the two against me, but I could already feel the itching trickle of blood that was sinking into my fur, running along my skin. A few yards away, Calouise was battling a lion and hyena, the smaller one trapped beneath one of his back legs while his remaining paws fended off the attacking lion.

Shrey was up against a black panther and a hyena, but even as I watched, he killed the hyena and overtook the panther.

We had lost a few of our own already. Moranaha had not lasted long. Singh had managed to kill him, blood pooling under his small, limp form. Somila now faced the bloodied lion, her own muzzle no longer clean and pure but tainted with red.

I did not see Zoriach as I quickly scanned of the scene, but my observation was interrupted as a male lion leapt at me, his bloody fangs exposed. I dodged his advance and turned to face him as he whipped around. I crouched low and bared my own fangs. I waited for him to strike, remembering my training, carefully waiting for his tell.

His entire body froze once before he lunged at me. I side-stepped and tackled him, dragging his large body down to the ground, my claws digging deep into his neck, catching the fatal artery. His warm blood splattered across my face, but I didn't have time to let the disgust register. Another lion, this time female, landed on my back, her claws slicing deep just below my shoulder blades.

I roared in pain but managed to stand on my hind legs, and she toppled off of my back. I maneuvered to land above her. Her paws batted at my face, claws scraping along my cheeks, but my teeth were at her throat before she could do any more damage.

Four of them. I'd already killed four of them. They lay like sacks of meat around me, lifeless and empty. The smell and taste of blood overwhelmed me, and I couldn't help the human response to vomit. My whole body involuntarily convulsed.

I felt so weak.

But strength could not fail me. I saw Somila fall, a panther's teeth ready to take her out. I was already running towards them, her paws and claws keeping him at bay, struggling to hang on, to live.

I leapt at him, arms open, wrapping around his middle, pulling him off as we were propelled forward by my lunge. We landed hard on the dampened, red-stained earth, but the struggle was over in an instant.

I left him broken in the dirt and turned to face Somila as she labored to her feet.

"Thank you," she choked out between heaving pants.

"The battle is not over," was all I could manage. She nodded, understanding. She couldn't give up yet. She couldn't be done, give in, let go of her strength. Not quite yet.

I watched her suck in a steadying breath before lunging after a hyena that had managed to overpower one of the snow leopards.

Alsandi whisked by, her own face and paws streaked with red, chasing a lioness. I would have been disappointed if I found any one of my cats without red upon their body in some form.

"This ends now," came her raspy voice from behind me.

I twisted around, my lips curling back, my teeth bared in pure hatred. She was responsible for all of it. She'd killed Sojóma. She'd sent the assassin for Mehish. She'd belittled me and perpetuated the lie of our weakness and unworthiness throughout the world. She and her miserable species.

"I'm surprised you didn't take me from behind. It would have suited your cowardly style," I hissed, unable to remain silent anymore.

We fell into a prowling, circling pace.

Her yellow eyes narrowed, her slitted pupils dilating only slightly. "It has to be a fair fight between you and me. That's the only way to settle this once and for all."

"Yes, let's finally finish this. I should have ended you that day in the jungle."

She released a derisive laugh. "You wouldn't have survived such an encounter."

"Well, you aren't going to survive this one," I snarled. I lunged forward, my claws exposed, but she reacted too quickly, her own paws striking the side of my face, drawing blood. I could feel it drip onto my paws.

I was going to have to be patient to beat her, but the longer we circled, the greater my anger and hatred grew. I leapt at her, both paws out, slamming onto both sides of her face. I managed to trap her head long enough to bite down on her ear and drag her to the ground, but she twisted from my grasp.

She was anything but a simple enemy.

Zoriach jumped at me as soon as she was free, her own arms wrapping me up and bringing me to the ground. I kicked at her with my back legs and claws, trying to tear at her stomach or thighs.

For a moment, I was pinned. A great fear of death washed over me as I looked into her eyes, a triumphant expression beginning to warp her features, but that was all I needed to knock her own feet out from under her. She toppled, but before she hit the ground, another tiger tackled her from the side, both of them rolling in the dust and dirt, their snarls and growls indistinguishable from one another.

I pushed myself to all fours and ran over to them. I wasn't going to let someone else take on Zoriach alone.

Trapir and Zoriach stood facing each other, both of them sporting long gashes and scratches. Trapir's muzzle was stained red, globby blood dripping from his chin. I ran to stand beside him. I did not challenge any claim he felt he had when it came to killing Zoriach. She'd murdered his brother and love. No one had a better claim of vengeance on her than he did.

He seemed to have no qualms to my presence or aid. And I was eternally grateful for his assistance. Between the two of us, Zoriach's chances of survival were dwindling closer and closer to zero.

I squared up next to him, our growls a harmonious, terror-inducing song. For an instant, I thought I saw a miniscule glimmer of fear in Zoriach's face, but her determination replaced it a second later.

"Your end has come," I hissed.

"You've lost most of your reinforcements," Trapir snarled. "I killed at least six of them." He stepped toward her, claws disturbing the dry earth.

"I took out five of them," I said, also prowling forward. "See, you've underestimated our strength. Tigers are powerful and skilled in combat. We are not meant to be pushed down. We were designed to fight and rise above."

Trapir and I stepped forward in unison, and Zoriach actually took a step backward. I caught Trapir's sinister grin upon the realization that we had shaken her. Both of us crouched, ready to finally end it.

Zoriach had a choice: run or fight. For a moment, I thought she would run, and I was prepared to chase her down. But she surprised me and tensed into a fighting stance. At least she would be a worthy opponent. She'd go down fighting.

I circled around as Trapir prowled toward her. Her eyes flickered between us. I knew she was unsure of who to keep an eye on, but that was an advantage for us. I was about to strike when another lion—a bloodied male—burst into our midst. He jumped between Zoriach and me, and roared, fangs glinting in the sun. I stayed low to the ground, creeping toward him, not taking my eyes off of his face. I was only a few feet away when he decided to roar once again. If he was trying to intimidate me, it wasn't going to work. As his jaws opened wide to allow his roar to escape, I struck at his throat. In a quick instant, he fell silent and limp, blood spilling from his exposed neck.

Trapir had pounced on Zoriach as I incapacitated the male. They were engaged in swipes and bites, trading off, grappling with each other, drawing blood with almost every strike. With one swift movement, I bounded over the dead lion and leapt on top of Zoriach's back, my teeth sinking into the back of her neck as Trapir knocked her to the ground. Her agonized scream was silenced with a sudden, precise bite administered by Trapir.

Zoriach was beaten, dead, defeated.

Trapir and I looked at each other, both breathing heavily, both covered in gashes and blood of our enemies and our own.

I looked to the bright sky, and I roared as loud as my sore throat would allow. A roar of victory and strength. Trapir joined in, our voices resounding through the air, filling the battlefield with our triumph.

Most of Zoriach's forces had already been taken care of. A great deal of death surrounded us. I didn't see with clarity who had survived, and I didn't see Cal either, but I didn't have time to search. The few lions and panthers that remained were rounded into a small group in the center of the grassland, their paws sinking into the pools of blood that dominated the landscape.

There was only eleven of them left, most of them lions. They'd surrendered when their leader had been slain. These were the smart ones. We, the victors, stood in a circle around them, our dark, wet, stained muzzles bearing down on them. I glared with as much energy as I could muster.

They all had witnessed our strength. Zoriach was dead, their forces depleted. This wasn't just a defeat, it was a demonstration of our power. Tigers were the kings of the jungle, the dominant cat, and the defeated cats would do well to spread the word. We would rule the animal world with dignity and grace in a way the lions could never manage.

I stepped forward to deliver a final message. "You and all of your species would be wise to remember all that happened here. Tigers overthrew the lions. And if you forget, we will not hesitate to deliver a reminder," I growled.

Their fearful faces nodded, their yellow eyes darting between each of ours.

"Go! And tell the world the tigers are back where they belong!" I yelled. Our circle split apart, allowing them to disperse, most of them running away as fast as they could, some of them stumbling over the dead forms that were scattered across the land.

We roared after them, roars of relief and joy that we had survived and won.

I felt like I could breathe for the first time in months. I sucked in a deep breath, letting my lungs expand, dispelling the overwhelming tension and fear like never before.

But it did not last long enough.

The fear returned slightly as I looked about me at the survivors. Their joyful faces gave me momentary happiness, especially as my gaze fell upon Somila and Shey's red-matted faces. Both of my friends had survived.

What caused the fear was my inability to identify Calouise's face. At least fifteen or twenty cats surrounded me, but none of them were him.

"Where is he?" I blurted before I could stop myself. "Have you seen him?" I pleaded to Somila, to Nashur, to Alsandi.

But it was Shrey who spoke. "Mix, I'm afraid ... he's fallen. Calouise is dead."

I looked at him, the fear gone, a cold numbness stilling my heartbeat. "W-what?" Suddenly, I laughed. I couldn't prevent the hysteria that bubbled from some dark depths of my heart. "No, really," I choked out between the laughing fits. "Where's Calouise?"

This time it was Somila. "Mix, he didn't make it. He's gone." She moved to step toward me, attempting to be comforting, but I backed away.

"No!" I shouted, the hysteria gone. The cold nothingness was gone too. My heart was beginning to race, my breath suddenly short, my lungs unable to expand. Even my legs were starting to shake. "No!"

I turned away from them all and ran across through the grasses, searching each inanimate form as I went. So many lions, hyenas, black leopards, snow leopards, regular leopards, clouded leopards, even tigers surrounded me. So much death and destruction.

So much blood.

I felt like I was drowning in it, suffocated by the dead bodies of my kin. Each face I came upon sent a jolt of tingling ice and then white hot fire through my veins. Each face that wasn't his sent another spike of stomach-turning energy through my body. We'd lost so much, but I still couldn't find him.

Mehan's face, Pravin's features, Sarga's form, Moranaha's body, Cyan's spotted mass. Countless, nameless others.

And then Calouise.

I found him almost on the outskirts of the battlefield, his large, once majestic form decimated in blood soaked mud, torn apart by our enemies' claws and teeth. The tiniest sliver of hope that he may still be breathing withered at the sight of him. His breath was gone. His lifeforce snuffed out. His dark eyes glassy, yet dull. I stared into them as I felt my innards crumble. I collapsed beside him, shaking uncontrollably with unshed sobs and tears, feeling as if steel clamps had taken hold of my lungs and a knife had torn open my heart, the blood spilling—trapped— inside of my chest. The physical pain could not escape me the way it would if I'd been human, so it was forced to erupt internally, burning away everything inside until all I felt was searing fire. Our victory meant nothing because the rajah—our king, my love—was gone.

We may have won the battle, but we—I—had lost so much more.

RANI

The entire jungle seemed dark upon our return, despite the rays of sun that beamed through the scattered canopy. The flattened patches of weeds and grasses dotted throughout the Sanctuary reminded us that this was our home, our sleeping spots waiting just for us—our own beds as sources of the deepest comfort.

The trees of our jungle were an umbrella of safety. Stepping beneath their protection was like being engulfed in a parent's welcoming arms. The open terrain of Gir and all the land in between had made us feel exposed, as if we were walking targets, which we probably had been. It was a miracle none of us died on the road.

I laid behind the waterfall, unaware of the world, stuck in my head. We had debated for a long while what to do with all of our dead. The snow leopards had left their fallen behind, their numbers too few to carry them back to Nepal. The clouded leopards felt the same, but they were more nomadic than their cousins, so leaving behind their dead did not feel like leaving behind a part of their immediate family.

After our victory, our nomadic tiger allies dispersed. Alive and victorious, they suddenly were free to roam the world as the powerful, ruling big cats of the earth. No longer would they have to worry about humiliation or oppression. They did not feel any obligation to bury or take their dead with them, either.

Our own community struggled to agree. I refused to leave Calouise behind. Our rajah had not fought and died for us simply to be left to rot in the lions' homeland. It wasn't even an option. I did not feel as strongly that we had to carry home the others we'd lost from our family. There were so many of them. What would we do with their rotting bodies? They had not been the ruler of our community—they didn't have a place to be laid to rest as Calouise did.

Outside of my insistence that Calouise was coming home with us, I did not argue or take part in the discussion about the rest of the dead. I had no energy to even care about it. I remained by Calouise's side until they'd made up their minds: we would only take our rajah, no one else. In truth, we really didn't have the strength to bring them all the way home.

I had wanted to be part of the carrying party, but Somila and Shrey had both insisted that I walk unhindered, leading us home while other, more able cats took Calouise's body upon them. I felt that this was ridiculous and insulting to my abilities and strength, but after a day of trudging towards home, I understood what Somila meant by more able cats. I could barely carry my own weight, let alone the larger body of Calouise.

When we made it home, he was set upon the same rocky outcrop Sojóma had been laid upon so many ages ago. I refused to look at him— at the disheveled, decomposing mess he had become from the week-and-half long journey home. That mass of flesh and fur was not Calouise.

It had merely been the vessel that had housed his spirit and soul—which was now gone.

The inability to shed tears was fundamentally challenging. I did not know how to release my grief, so it remained within me, weighing me down as if I carried the weight of his body, his duty, his responsibility, his absence and death alongside my own exhausted weight and unshed emotions. With every step I took, I was unable to detach my paw from the ground, so the earth came with it. Every step became heavier and heavier, until all I could manage to do was collapse. My muscles ached and seared with pain. My heart bled the tears I could not spill. My stomach and lungs had shrunken so that every breath was short and coarse, my appetite quite inexistent.

I had never known pain like this.

Calouise's ceremony was tomorrow. I understood the role I needed to play. When Nashur and Trapir and Saltir requested a council to discuss the plans, I came along simply to appease their wishes. Their nagging would have been worse than sitting in and listening to all they planned to do. Flowers, procession, words of send-off, rites of transition, coronation, final farewell. I listened and agreed to it all. I already knew that nothing they ever comprised would be an adequate good bye.

"Mix, did you hear me?" came Nashur's strained voice. She had been kinder to me lately, but I attributed her sudden amiability simply to the loss of the rajah. She had no one else anymore. "You will have to make an ascension speech."

"What?" I said, looking around, trying to regain focus of my surroundings. We were in the throne room, birds perched on the tops of the stone, their twittering voices a sound of song in the late summer. "What for?"

"You'll be Calouise's replacement," Trapir said gently.

His replacement? He couldn't be replaced. There was no such thing. "No, I can't."

Their sympathetic looks made me angry.

"He was rajah. Isn't there a cat next in line?" I said desperately.

All of their yellow eyes were upon me, their expressions soft and concerned.

"Calouise never had any cubs," Nashur replied quietly. "His line is no more. You were his fifth paw, the commander of our forces, and the tiger who led us to a victory we have not been able to achieve in over half a century. No one is better suited or worthier to rule us than you."

The sincerity of her words pained me. The one cat I always counted on as a target for the release of negative energy was all kindness and compassion and doting. It was unnerving and anything but helpful. I couldn't help the glare.

"I am not Calouise, and I could never fill his paw prints," I snapped. It was an insult to his memory to think that I could.

"We don't expect you to be Calouise," Saltir finally said. "You are Mix, the one who rescued us all."

"No one is forcing you. But we can think of no one better," Trapir said.

I stared at him. "No one better? What about you? You were Sojóma's brother, Cal's uncle, the tiger in charge of training us all, which is what secured our victory."

"I am not a ruler," he said simply.

I growled in frustration. Several of the birds took flight. "Neither am I."

"Not yet. But you are a leader," Saltir responded.

I released a puff of air, hoping to expel some of the tension that weighed upon every part of my body, but all it did was make me feel weaker. "I don't know what you want from me. I don't know how to rule. I was only able to lead because I had Calouise by my side. I wouldn't have been able to do it on my own."

"No one expects you to do it alone," Nashur replied. "I am chief advisor. I am here to serve you." She squirmed a little in the spot she sat, avoiding my eyes. "I know we have not really been paw to paw in the past, but … you have proved me wrong in my opinions of you. I see your worth and potential."

Perhaps if I was in better a place, I would have been touched by her sentiment. But all I felt was a mixture of pain and uncertainty. How could I possibly rule the community? We had just won a battle to secure our power in the world. If I ruled the largest community of tigers and leopards in the world, I became an authority figure beyond our jungle. I knew Sojóma and Calouise's presence and authority had been widely acknowledged and even followed far beyond our community.

But I hadn't won the war to simply bow out and have no part in the rebuilding of our name. I had planned to be there, at Calouise's side, to manage the aftermath. But now he was gone, and I was alone.

He wouldn't have wanted me to turn away from it. He would have wished me to step up, to fulfill my greater responsibility to the tigers, to follow through and do my rightful duty.

And that meant ascending to take the place of the fallen rajah.

All at once, a new weight was added to the unnameable mass that already brought me down. Somehow, I had to find some kind of strength in order to endure. I just didn't know what it would be yet.

The day of the Calouise's funeral was one of the hardest days I'd ever undergo. The scenery was much of the same as Sojóma's: Glory lilies, forget-me-nots, and blood-red roses. His body was delicately covered in large leaves, the lively green shielding the sight of death. I sat at the base of the rock outcrop, watching the rest of our community go through the motions of the ceremony, placing their flowers, taking a bow, finding a place to sit. For a band of cats that had won the war of the century, we were an incredibly morose group. This was the price of our success: the lives we'd lost.

Our community was noticeably smaller. Fewer spotted and striped forms were present, the meadow space appearing so much more empty than before. We hadn't lost everyone, or even that many, but somehow, it felt like no one was there at all.

Nashur began the proceedings, and I tried to prepare myself for what was to come.

"We are not here to celebrate the great triumph we achieved a couple of weeks ago. No, we are gathered to mourn the losses we suffered in order to gain such a victory. Our rajah, Calouise, did not die in vain. He fought hard with dignity, taken down by a horde of our enemies. Very few cats in the world could have beaten Calouise in one-on-one combat. He was fiercely strong and dedicated to the cause of reestablishing all that tigers were destined to be. Calm and patient, he led us with compassion and pure authority. His mighty presence demanded an audience and commanded respect. As you were in life, so shall you be in death: mighty and dignified."

It was my turn to say something, but every idea that had swam in my head for the last few days seemed wildly inappropriate for what we were taking part in. The faces of the crowd swam before me, their many patterns and mournful expressions lost in a collage of faded color. "Calouise was the cat I placed all of my trust in. It was because of him that I was able to become the commander I was. He ruled with grace, and he loved us dearly—more than he ever let show. It is his great love that I, and hopefully the rest of you, will remember him by. He was no ordinary tiger, but of the greatest esteem." I attempted to swallow, but my throat tightened on me as I stared unseeingly over the crowd. "We have lost another rajah, but we will not go ungoverned. It is the wishes of the dignitaries that I, Mix and Commander, shall be named your Rani. I shall rule in Calouise's stead, but I do not dare attempt to replace all that he was. I never could."

Nashur and Trapir's eyes were on me—I sensed their gazes. Both of them had warned me of downplaying my ability to rule. The community needed an example of confidence from their leader rather than an image of cowardice or timidity. I was going to have to lie to them just as I was lying to myself.

"My goal is help us prosper again, to encourage breeding and expansion of our domain, to establish other communities across India to further increase our chances of survival and growth. Under my rule, tigers shall prosper once again." I could see their postures straighten, their eyes more attentive, their interests snagged. I caught sight of

Somila's nod and Shrey's approving smile. They all seemed to believe in me.

If only I believed in myself.

If only he were there to help.

The following month did not get any easier. The weight I'd felt before the ceremony did not abate. The grief perhaps lessened some, but there was not a day that went by that I didn't feel his absence.

A few weeks after the final good bye, I was called to bless three new cubs on the outskirts of the community. It required a great amount of willpower to not break down in the process of pressing my nose to their tiny heads, to say the words to bless their lives and happiness.

It was the most painful reminder of Calouise I had managed to encounter since his death. His constant talk of finding what made him happy—his eventual admittance of his love—it was all too much and brought back the heavy grief all over again.

The dignitaries still pestered me about my choice of sleeping space, despite my insistence that I was not moving.

"The fortress *is* the place of the rajah—or rani. It is where everyone expects you to be," Nashur argued again, for the millionth time.

We were standing outside of my waterfall, the cool water splashing from the impact and covering us in a fine mist that caused our fur to shimmer in the light. The beauty of the spot was one of the many reasons I refused to sleep in the stone throne room.

Nashur was another.

"I will spend time there when I am needed, but I won't sleep there," I growled. "I told you I am not Calouise, nor am I Sojóma. My place is here." I stamped my paw, hoping this would be the final time we had to discuss it, or I would be taking drastic measures to make her understand and leave me alone. In all honesty, the grasses behind the waterfall were my comfort. It had been Calouise's favorite spot, and it was the one place I could go and be alone and think of him without feeling like I was going to implode with pain.

On a day when no one needed me, I made an effort to seek out Somila. I remembered how I avoided her when Sojóma had died, and I didn't want to repeat the offense this time around. But it had proved to be difficult in between the crushing will of sadness and all the responsibilities I had to maintain as Rani. I still hadn't figured out how Calouise had managed to get everything done and still spend as much time with me as he had. Perhaps Nashur had been correct, and Calouise had shirked some of his duties simply to be around me. Given the circumstances, I didn't care. I would've had him give up all his responsibilities in order to spend as much time together as we could have shared.

Somila waited near the beach, her belly and legs sunk in the shallow end of the river, the cool water rushing around her, undisturbed by her presence. The days were hot as we neared the beginning of autumn. I plunged into the water and fell beside her, my own body causing quite a splashing disturbance as it settled. The chill of the water numbed my legs, relieving my pent up tension for the first time in months.

Her eyes roved over my face, her expression soft, the familiar look of sympathy forming there.

"How are you doing?" she finally asked.

I stared at the water, watching the way it swirled around my hips and tail, a small obstacle in its neverending path. "I don't know," I replied. This was completely true.

"I don't blame you," she said. "You have a lot to deal with. How are you coping since the loss of Cal?"

She hadn't wasted a moment. "I thought it would get easier with time."

"Has it not?"

I watched a leaf float toward us, unsure how to answer. "It has... and it hasn't. Some days I'll be simply sad. Other days, something will trigger my grief as if he's just died again."

I tried to stomach the sympathy she had for me. If nothing else, it was getting easier to ignore the sympathies from everyone around me, even those who did not know how close Calouise and I had been.

"He was an amazing cat," she said.

I almost laughed. "Yes, Shrey was wrong about him after all."

She actually managed a small chuckle. "Did he love you then? Were you two able to be each other's?"

It was too difficult to speak, so I simply gave her an affirmative nod.

"And he didn't move on? He wanted only you?"

I wanted to just nod again, but that wouldn't have been explanation enough for what had happened. "We were together the night before ... before the battle. He told me how he felt, and the next morning, he stood by my side. I don't know how to say it. He was mine, fully. He wasn't interested in anyone else." I thought back to Sarga's attempt to seduce him and the way he had stood up for me against Dekovin. We had been each other's for a long while before he had died. If only we could have admitted it sooner.

"That's so rare," she said.

"But worth it," I replied.

"Even with all the pain? Losing him seems to have really hurt you."

"Despite the pain, it was all worth it." I had never spoken truer words. She was looking at me curiously, and I knew she could never understand how our love had worked. She was still too tiger. But that was a part of why I loved her.

We sat in silence for a little while longer, listening to the sounds of the jungle. I had missed them terribly during our brief journey to Gir. The sounds of the water, the squirrels, birds, monkeys, frogs—they were sounds of home.

"There's something else," I choked out, unable to keep it to myself anymore. I was too alone to handle it by myself—I needed a friend.

"What is it?" she asked.

I took a deep breath. There was no easier way to say it—I just had to get it out. "I'm carrying his cubs."

~6 MONTHS LATER~

WALL OF SMOKE

One of them was chewing on my ear. In the last few weeks, I'd attempted to teach them that all that incessant chewing on my ear was going to land them in trouble, meaning they would have to spend time with Nashur instead of uncle Trapir. We had spent at least an hour going over the gentle way to nibble and gently gnaw, practicing on Somila.

They were kinder to Somila than they were to me. Not that I blamed them: any opportunity to chew on a mother's ear could not be surpassed, whether verbally or literally. Between the furballs and my subjects, I was surprised I had any ears remaining.

But it was too early for them to be bothering me just yet. Daylight had barely broken.

"Did you learn nothing from our lesson last week?" I grumbled without opening my eyes. Whoever was resting on my neck and head gave pause. "What did I teach you about chewing on other cats' ears?"

It was Neysa—I could tell by the way she clambered off my back, her front claws digging into the sides of my head as she jumped onto the stone floor. "Sorry, momma," she said in her purest voice.

I opened my eyes to see her little yellow ones staring back at me, her nose maybe an inch from mine. I moved to press our noses together. It was hard to be irritated by a face as innocent as hers.

"You're awake!" came a loud voice from behind me. A moment later, something sharp jabbed into my back as another one of my children pounced on me. "Finally!"

I could feel him wobble along my spine as he attempted to walk toward my shoulders and head. "Easy, Calyn. Watch your claws."

I felt him collapse right on top of my shoulders, his small tail twisting around to whack me in the eye.

"Why are you all so full of energy this early?" I begged.

"You promised to take us hunting today," Neysa replied. I could tell that it required all of her energy not to rise from her lying position and run around in pure excitement.

I had been putting it off for several weeks, terrified to take them too far from the Sanctuary area or throne room, not willing to let them out of my sight without knowing someone else was keeping their eye on them.

"Where's Amirah?" I suddenly asked. I would have jumped to my feet, but Calyn was still perched on my back.

"Sleeping," Calyn replied from above me, causing my ear to twitch.

I released the breath that I hadn't realized I was holding. "That's what the two of you should be doing," I said.

"We want to go hunting," Calyn said, sliding down from my shoulders and padding around to face me, shoving his sister aside. Neysa pushed herself to her feet and crouched to pounce on her brother. In only a few seconds, they were rolling around, nipping at each other, kicking at each other, wrestling across the stone floor. With their commotion, whatever birds had been in the vicinity took flight. Since my neck was free, I twisted around to glance at my sleeping cub several feet behind me, her splayed-out form appearing so relaxed and carefree. I watched her breathing, her flank rising and falling in slow, even intervals that assured me of her well-being.

Becoming a mother had made me more hypervigilant than I could have thought possible. I had always secretly judged the overprotective mothers that appeared to coddle their young, but now I understood. My children weren't allowed out of sight of an adult, and never permitted to be near the river without my presence. I wouldn't lose any of my babies to a hungry crocodile.

Neysa let out a tiny roar of pain, Calyn's sharp fangs clamped down on her ear.

"Neysa, you are a tiger—we do not let anyone overpower us, not even our brother."

She gave the smallest of growls and turned to attack Calyn with her paws wide open.

"The same applies to you, Calyn."

He looked at me, his small eyes mostly black, his expression curious. Between the three of them, he appeared the most like his father. Even his imbalanced pattern of stripes at the top of his head looked the closest to his father's out of any other cat I'd ever seen. He'd inherited his father's curiosity and interest in observation as well. I had to keep an especially careful eye on him.

Nashur entered through the stone archway, a yawn stretching her face, her fangs flashing momentarily in the morning light.

"They're awake early," she commented, prowling over to us.

I sat up, and stretched, exposing my claws, attempting to get my blood flowing. "They think they're going hunting today," I whispered.

She sat beside me and eyed them as they tumbled across the floor, running into their slumbering sister. "I think it's time for them to do so."

Nashur was always so opinionated. I'd learned to understand by spending more time with her than I would have liked that everything she said was supposed to be considered a form of advice or council. But whenever she started advising me on how to raise my cubs, I grew irritated.

"They'll go hunting when *I* think they're ready. The world is a dangerous place."

"And sheltering them from it does not prepare them for how to handle those dangers."

I glared at her. I was not as effective at shutting her down when she went too far as Calouise had been able to do. It was days like these that I missed him the most.

And I wished he was there to help me teach our cubs how to hunt. Of course, it was natural for the mother to be in charge of raising her cubs, but I was not a purely natural tiger. Calouise hadn't been either. If he were alive, we would have been something different—united, in love, a family.

I shook myself from that train of thought. He wasn't alive, so I had to do this on my own. And I wasn't about to let Nashur worm her way into whatever role Calouise would have had.

"What am I needed for today?" I asked, orienting her back onto a topic she was qualified for.

"The dignitaries wish to meet with you today about some issues they've heard about from various cats and messengers."

I stood up and shook out my fur. "Let's start right away so the rest of my day is free."

She swiftly got up and padded out of the fortress to find the other dignitaries, and I walked over to where Amirah was waking up after being bowled over by her siblings. Of the three, she was the smallest, as well as the most reserved. I never had any problems with her chewing on my ear at the break of dawn.

"Are we hunting today, momma?" she asked between yawns.

"Would you like that?" I asked, nudging her to her feet.

"Yes," she said simply. She'd inherited *that* from her father.

Suddenly, Calyn skidded into our midst, his claws scraping on the stone, causing me to cringe as my fur stood on end. "Yeah, I want to kill a boar."

I wanted to laugh—he was ambitious for his size—but I wished to instill in them the importance of not killing simply for the sake of it. I had the opportunity, and the responsibility, to raise a new generation of tigers that could command and be worthy of respect and reverence.

"Neysa, come over here. I want to speak with all of you."

She bounded over and plopped on top of Amirah, her eyes fixed on me, ready for whatever I had to say. "If you want to learn to hunt, I need you to understand what hunting means. It is not a sport. We are tigers, not killers. We are cats, not monsters. Hunting is a tool we use simply to survive—only to eat. Tigers are one of the ruling species of the world, and good rulers are wise and kind and don't kill other animals just for fun." I wanted to be stern, but loving. It was so difficult to balance them, so hard to parent.

I had adopted an entirely new level of forgiveness for the way my parents had raised me. They weren't off the hook for their lack of involvement as I got older, but I now understood how difficult it must have been to learn to put someone before themselves, to have the responsibility to raise a child to be a good, decent being.

It was an even bigger responsibility than ruling the cats of the animal world.

"Do you understand?" I asked them.

Their eyes were still brightly fixed on me, excitement glowing from their innocent expressions. "Yes, we do," Neysa replied, the other two nodding in agreement.

I gave a small lick to the top of each of their heads. "Go run along with Somila. Mother's going to finish working for today, and then we'll go hunting."

They jumped up in elation and scampered off. I watched them disappear around the doorway with apprehension. It didn't get any easier to watch them leave my presence.

I made my way up to the blocky stone throne and tried to sit comfortably while still appearing majestic. In my head, I imagined myself looking as calm and collected and impressive as Sojóma had, but I knew it was a comical idea. I could never pull off an appearance of complete power and majesty.

It had taken me quite a lot of time to move myself permanently into the fortress. After I had given birth to my three cubs, I'd remained in the secluded cave for another month or so until I realized we couldn't all stay there comfortably as they continued to grow. As much as it was home, eventually, we'd made the transition. The cubs had been all for it, but sometimes, when the reminders threatened to overwhelm me for the day, I went back to the space and simply laid there, as if the falling water were shedding the tears for me.

The dignitaries entered one by one: Trapir, Nashur, Saltir, and Shrey. After losing Cyan to the war, one of my first duties as Rani had been to appoint a new cat as head advisor to the leopards. As much as I still felt that this position was utterly useless, I couldn't think of anyone better suited for the job than Shrey. Truth be told, there weren't very many other leopards I trusted, or even knew that well, to take on the job. Shrey had turned out to be surprisingly good and beneficial, finding uses for his position in ways that had never crossed Cyan's mind. Thanks to Shrey, another leopard community had formed a couple hundred miles east of us.

The four of them sat before me, alert and attentive. Even after a months of ruling, it was still strange to have them all look up to me as an authority figure.

"What news?" I asked, stifling a yawn.

"According to a few of our scouts, humans have been spotted near our perimeter on several occasions in the last few days," Saltir began.

"Do you know why?" I questioned.

"It's difficult to understand them when they talk too fast and their sounds are drowned as they travel through the trees."

"We need to keep a close eye on this lest it become a greater issue."

Saltir gave a slight bow. He'd managed to learn to be more respectful and obedient in the last year, finally having to accept that I held a position of authority. However, leading us to our victory had seemed to change a great deal of opinions about me. I was no longer a trouble-maker, but a liberator and leader. It had been a strange but welcome transition.

"What else do you all have for me?" I asked.

"The leopard we allowed to join our community two days ago has been transitioning well. She seems to be struggling with adjusting to sleeping in such close quarters with other leopards and tigers," Shrey reported.

"Well, please make sure, personally, that she feels welcome and has all the tools and space we can allow her in order to ease her shift from nomad to community member."

"I will do so," he replied diplomatically. I often wondered if I had sounded that strange to Calouise whenever I had talked to him formally.

I looked to Trapir. I had transformed his position slightly. Rather than simply a cat in charge of training and fighting, I'd added the responsibility of dealing with fights that broke out through the community. He was supposed to handle them as Sojóma would have wanted, with wisdom and direct authority. Fighting was only tolerated with the understanding that it could not be eradicated completely. As long as no one was severely injured, a simple stern warning was to be administered by Trapir. Having him be in charge of this left me open to handle other matters and spend time with my cubs. I only got involved if the fights had gone too far and legitimate punishment was needed.

"Do you have anything new for us?" I asked him.

"Not today," he replied simply. That was the best kind of answer.

"If there's nothing left to discuss, then you may all be dismissed. I have plans to take the little ones hunting this afternoon," I said, stepping down from the throne.

"That should be fun," Shrey commented.

"She's delayed it long enough," Nashur added.

I shot her a scornful glance. "I've had my reasons. But, yes, today will finally be the day. I think I'll simply show them how to stalk their prey for now. They're not big enough to kill anything yet."

"Sounds fair," Trapir said.

I exited through the archway and glanced up at the trees. Through the canopy, I could make out the grey cloud cover, an overcast blanket that held the humidity in the trees. It had been a much hotter summer than last year, monsoon season particularly shorter than what I had experienced before. I was grateful for the lesser rains since I had to keep track of three adventurous children who were entirely too curious about rain and puddles and the river itself.

I wound my way along the stone wall to the meadow I had spent so many days in before I had lost him. Now, it was where I had Somila look after my cubs whenever I had official Rani business to attend to.

She was crouched there, her eyes locked with Amirah's, both of them looking as if they were ready to pounce on each other. Neysa and Calyn were chasing each other, darting in and out of the long, withering grasses that had grown back after we had no longer needed the training arenas.

"Did they behave?" I asked, jumping down from the wall, my paws thudding against the soft dirt of the forest floor.

"They were just as feisty as I expect any litter to be," Somila replied, turning to look at me. Amirah pounced on her head the moment she looked away. I couldn't help but laugh. They were only baby cats after all. I remembered how my tabby cat had been when she was a rambunctious kitten. My children were just larger versions.

"Are you three ready to go? I need you to be on your best behavior if we are going to go do this," I said.

Calyn and Neysa scampered over, their pupils slivers in the bright light of day.

"You're doing it today?" Somila asked me, sitting up straight as Amirah slid off of her head.

"Yes, I promised them I would," I replied with a sigh. Hunting was a huge milestone for them.

They were already growing up so fast.

"I just worry about them. They're still so young," she commented.

"I know. I've already delayed long enough. Nashur assures me it's well past the time cubs would normally start learning to hunt."

Somila rolled her eyes. "Nashur has never had any cubs. She can't presume to know."

I secretly agreed, but I had already promised them. I wouldn't be a mother who couldn't keep her commitments.

"Say good bye to Somila, my cubbies, so we can go hunt."

They nuzzled and nipped at her toes before she wandered off.

All three of them sat as patiently as they were able, their tails swishing from side to side, anticipation clearly in their expressions.

"Before we go, I need to go over a few rules: first, you have to be super quiet. Silence is the most important in hunting so your prey isn't aware you're coming. Second, you have to move slowly so they can't sense you stalking them, either. Hunting is all about patience. Can you do that for me?"

All three of their heads bobbed up and down.

Some part of me knew that this was going to be a fruitless endeavor.

I stood up and headed into the trees and out of the meadow. "Keep close," I called to them. They ran up right behind my legs and tail.

I stepped carefully through the trees, making sure not to crush any dry leaves or snap any twigs. The little ones behind me were not so keen on avoiding these give aways, but there was only so much I could teach on the first day.

After a few hundred feet, something sharp dug into my tail.

"Calyn, you can't attack my tail when you're supposed to be focusing on hunting. You need to be quiet and listen for anything around that you might be able to catch."

"Sorry momma," came his small voice from behind me.

We continued forward, prowling slowly between the brush. In only a few minutes, I heard several sounds of squirrels, snakes, boars, and even a stag. But each of these creatures fled as soon as they heard the unmistakeable sounds of my children relatively crashing through the the trees.

We weren't going to be able to catch anything today.

A few hundred yards later, rather than running from us, many creatures were scurrying towards and around us, heading in the opposite direction. The peculiarity of it made me pause. A few moments later, I smelled the smoke, and then I knew we had to run. Any kind of fire in the forest would be out of control in seconds.

I grabbed the closest cub to me in my mouth, lifting whoever it was by the scruff, and began to run. I pounded through the trees, glancing side to side, the smell of smoke unbearably strong. The little bit of greenery I could perceive was already beginning to be consumed in the white and grey billowing clouds that equaled doom. I made to turn right, but was met with bright flames greedily devouring the undergrowth. In my panic, I paused, making sure the other two were near me. Both of them were standing beside my back legs, their little eyes wide with fear.

"Follow me and stay close!" I attempted to yell through the fur in my mouth.

I ran away from the fire, the sound of its crackles taunting me everywhere I turned. If I didn't hurry, we would be trapped, and we would burn. Ahead was a small space where all I could see was an ashy cloud, but there was no orange, red, or yellow. It was the only chance, the fire dancing on either side of us, its hungry tendrils nipping at my tail. With a grunt, I charged forward, bounding through the clearest, safest path I could find. I refused to stop, even though the air was noticeably cleaner. I wouldn't be safe until I reached the stone fortress where fire could not enter or reach me and my loved ones.

After a few hundred feet, I spotted other cats running beside me, all of us heading for safety, wherever that apparently nonexistent place resided. Whichever cub was between my jaws was growing heavy, but I couldn't stop. Not until we had reached a place with the illusion of safety.

The wall manifested from out of the smoky air, and I leapt to the top of it in a single bound. I set my baby down, realizing it was Amirah. "Run! Run to the fortress and do not leave it. Find Somila or Shrey or Trapir. Do not leave their side!" I yelled as I nudged her forward. She gave me one terrified look before scampering along the stone.

I looked below me to see Calyn pawing furiously at the stone wall, his small but sharp claws scraping down along the rough wall. I jumped down, grabbed him, and leapt back on top simply to set him down and send him running after his sister. I looked back at the ground, expecting to see Neysa, but she was not there.

From the top of the wall, I gazed out over the path we had taken, noticing the way the smoke billowed like an unstoppable force of nature, except it wasn't natural. The fire had not come from natural forces. No, I'd heard the voices of the men.

I leapt from wall and began sprinting back in the direction of the flames, searching frantically for Neysa. She had been *right* behind me.

The deeper in the smoke I ran, the harder it was to breathe. My vision was overcome as was my hearing, the sound of crackling flames and crashing branches and falling trees disrupting any chance I had of hearing her cry.

"Neysa!" I screeched, my throat filling with ash. "Neysa!"

I was in the thick of it now, the heat seeming to sear my lungs, bushes collapsing into heaps of glowing embers all around me.

And then I saw her.

She was also collapsed in a sooty heap just below a fallen log that hadn't quite managed to crush her.

But she was unmoving.

I shoved my head and shoulder against the fallen tree, forcing it to shift just slightly so I could pull her out. Carefully, I used my paw to drag her out, her limp body much too heavy. Just before I picked her up, I heard them.

At least four copper-toned men were traipsing through the ravaged, smoldering remains of the jungle, torches clutched in their hands, speaking loudly over the billows and crackles. They had not spotted me.

I could have killed at least two of them before they would have ever noticed me.

I waited too long, unsure if that was the choice I really wanted to make. They approached, kicking at bushes, helping the fire in its destruction. That was until one of them saw me. Our eyes met, brown to yellow, fierce face to fierce face, both of us unmoving.

I could kill him, one swift bite to the soft flesh of his throat. Vengeance for the ruining of my home, for the potential death of my child. Their acts were vile, born of vile creatures.

Humans.

They were the ultimate enemy. And they needed eliminating.

I crouched slightly, baring my fangs, glaring, growling from somewhere deep within my chest. His eyes widened slightly, and he tensed, holding his torch like a potential weapon.

But I couldn't do it. Whatever rational thought remained was strong enough to silence the pure anger and hatred that were storming within me. I couldn't kill the human. Not without becoming the monster I refused to be.

And as much I hated the idea, perhaps holding back and sparing his life would send a message of peace to the humans.

But I wouldn't leave him without some kind of scare and warning. He couldn't escape without any kind of repercussion.

I shot him one threatening snarl—frightening him enough to make him jump—before picking up lifeless Neysa between my teeth and turning my back on everything we had just lost, disappearing through the wall of smoke.

RETURN

She dangled limply from my jaws as I ran along the stone wall, heading for the fortress. At the arched doorway, I was blocked from getting in, a mass of stripes and spots obscuring my view and my way. I shouldered and shoved them out of my path, careful not to harm Neysa, forcing my way through in the direction of the throne.

Eventually, I made it to a spot where I could see Amirah and Calyn lying under the sheltering arms of Somila, just beside the stone throne. I struggled toward them until, at last, I stood beside them, still finding it hard to breathe, the air clogged with smoke.

"What happened? Are you okay? Is Neysa alright?" Somila frantically asked.

I set her still lifeless, little body on the floor and met Somila's wide, dilated gaze.

"The humans are attacking the jungle with fire. Probably to clear for land. Or drive us away. I don't know." I took a deep, steadying breath. It didn't help.

"What about Neysa?" Somila repeated quietly.

She hadn't moved since I'd found her under the tree. "I'm not sure. I found her stuck under a burning log."

We both stared at her small, blackened body. I was afraid to watch her belly, afraid of what I wouldn't see.

Images of death were beginning to assault me. The lifeless forms of Sojóma, cubs, the slain on the battefield, Calouise.

Calouise.

My difficulty with swallowing suddenly increased. Something large was lodged there—the extent of my grief and fear.

Calyn and Amirah were sniffing and nosing at Neysa. Amirah licked at her head, but nothing happened. Nothing changed. Nothing moved.

"Momma?" Calyn said in a quiet voice, looking at me, his expression drooping in sadness and fear.

I couldn't bear it.

I turned away from them all and shoved through the crowd, a roar of pain threatening to escape. I managed to make it out of the doorway and to the top of the wall, but my course was stayed. Standing there, all I could see was the black smoke and ravaging red that continued to spread before my eyes. No matter where I turned, everything was burning, both within me and around me. The fire had managed to enter my body and scared away all other feelings.

All that remained was agony.

All that had once been pure had been burned. Even my own child.

The roar that erupted from my dry, aching throat was lost in the crackles and billows and cries of the surrounding jungle.

It was then that something else arose within me—an emotion I hadn't experienced for a year, not since Zoriach had killed members of my family, lighting a different kind of fire inside me.

Revenge.

Through the smoke, I could just barely detect the faint scent of humans—soap and sweat. I'd stopped myself from killing the man earlier, but now, the pain was too great to attempt rational thought. Blindly, I leapt from the top of the wall and began pounding through brush that was untouched by fire, their scent my only guide.

I tracked it in the direction of the Sanctuary, losing it among the mixture of smoke and scents of tigers. The fire still blazed just a few hundred yards south of my location. The humans had to be near the fire they'd brought, spreading it, feeding it, coaxing it forward on its path of destruction. For a moment, I paused, considering whether or not it was worth moving in that direction. Fire had already claimed my Neysa. Wisdom would be turning back before it found me, too. But the fire within urged me forward, whispering reminders of my pain, trying to push me to release my anguish in a bloody, vengeful encounter.

Despite the pain, I was about to turn back when the wind shifted and the scent of a human caught my attention again, the strongest reminder yet. Filled with burning grief and searing anger, I prowled forward, following the scent. I knew it was human, but it was newer—almost cleaner and sweeter. Either way, it was enough. It would lead me where my dangerous passions desired.

The scent grew stronger every ten feet or so until it was almost burning my nose. I was not near the raging fire, but rather closer to where the fire had started at the edge of the trees. But there were no humans anywhere around me.

And then I saw it.

A small corner of dirty, dusty blue denim poking up out of the ground.

The remnants of my old, torn blue jeans buried in the dirt beneath me.

I had been tracking my own scent.

My human scent from years ago. The shock and fear that suddenly burst within me sent shivers down my spine. I hadn't thought of my human life for a long time, completely absorbed in my wild lifestyle, falling in love, fighting a war, raising cubs. But remembering my other self and realizing I had been tracking my human scent for the sake of revenge was enough to turn my veins cold. I felt such great hatred for the humans, but I'd forgotten what I once was. And I hated myself for being human, hated myself for not remembering, and hated myself for wanting to kill humans in the first place. The amount of self-loathing I felt was unnerving, but it brought about awareness that was needed to help me cool down and think. I couldn't kill the humans—not when I was once one. Not without becoming the monster I refused to be. Not without deepening the wound between tigers and humans. I would be better than that, no matter my pain.

All of it—the scent, the shock, the fear and hatred—they were enough to bring back the once familiar threads and tingles of electricity for the first time in over a year. The electricity that had started everything. I recalled the fear I'd felt while I had dealt with the first transformations, trying to understand what was happening, trying to wrap my head around what I had become. Now I had embraced my tiger nature to the point of forgetting my origin, attempting to wrap my head around what I had become once again.

I would not become a man eater.

I was not weak.

I knew something had to be done, but I couldn't do anything more as a tiger. Not when it came to the human world. And I couldn't sit idly anymore. Not when the humans were a threat to my children. They'd claimed one. They wouldn't get another.

It was this potential of losing any more of those I loved that was now my greatest fear and motivation.

Standing there, in the dusk, in the relative silence, I felt an aloneness I was not familiar with. It was like a weight settling upon my body, an awareness that something was different and things were changing. If I really wanted to try to save my family, I couldn't remain a tiger in the wild jungle any longer. And my unique ability to be both human and tiger was a sudden advantage. The only way to reason with humans without violence was to return to civilization as a human—if I could still refer to the human world as civilized. From my experience, my tiger community managed a more civilized living situation than any other place I had ever lived. My former college life least of all.

The fear of returning was suddenly very pervasive, engulfing my pain and anger. It was more fear than I'd felt when coming to India and the jungle. I was surprised to feel this much fear at the idea of returning to the human world. It wasn't as if that world was unknown to me—it was where I had grown up. Staring about my surroundings, at the remaining green and dusty dirt, I knew this place was my home. I had fought so long to become fully integrated here, to feel like I belonged, and now that I was, now that I had children and a greater family, I was going to leave it behind. It wasn't that I was scared of the human world.

I was scared of losing all that was precious to me.

But I wouldn't let fear stop me. If nothing else, I would return— there was no doubt about that. The jungle, India, was now my home. It always would be.

If I was returning to the human world, it was going to have to be handled carefully. My children would most likely have to learn what I was—unless I could find a way to avoid it. They'd have to still trust me, follow me, listen to me. Taking them with me, I was going to have to find a way to smuggle them into the United States. It had not been my intent to return to my homeland by committing a felony, but things were different now.

Things were changing.

And if I was going to go through with this, I had to transform. This was something I had not done in ages. The last time I had tried, it had been difficult after remaining a tiger for so long. I'd been a tiger even longer this time.

Until today, it had been a long time since I'd felt the tingling of electricity within me. I pulled at the faint currents with my will, attempting to reel them back in.

They seemed to stutter at first, reeling back along my legs, my paws turning into hands, while my nails remained claws. If I didn't reel it all back in, I was going to end up some kind of mutant hybrid. I pulled harder, my claws disappearing, my skin reappearing, my fur vanishing, my small, toned arms shivering in the sudden coolness of the night. I knew it was a weird sight: my large tiger body attached to human arms. But I stared at my hands as if I didn't understand their purpose. They were so small, so hairless, so utterly useless in terms of defense.

I didn't recognize them as my own.

It became more painful and difficult as my entire body and legs and head were forced to transform, shrinking, fur disappearing, my human hair growing longer and longer until it was at a length I was not used to dealing with, the tangled ends of my hair tickling my waist and elbows. However long ago I had come here, my hair had barely reached past my shoulders.

I shivered in the falling darkness and ash, without clothes and without any extra senses. The world so much darker than I was used to, and the jungle was so much quieter. I hadn't realized how ill-adapted humans were for the wild world. They were so weak, and yet, as I watched small, white pieces of ash drift in the air, I was amazed at the amount of damage they could cause.

I quickly released the stored currents and stifled a yell of pain as I morphed back to my tiger form, falling to all fours, feeling warm and safe and powerful. At least I knew that I could still manage to turn human. That was going to be essential to getting back.

Even as a tiger, the air was fairly silent around me, the usual noises of the jungle silenced or driven away by the fire.

Feeling as if rocks clung to my bones rather than muscle, I walked slowly back toward the fortress. It was going to be difficult to tell everyone my plan to leave. It was going to be even more impossible for them to understand.

But they weren't going to be able to stop me.

Hours later, I lay by Amirah and Calyn on the cool stone beside the throne, many others resting below us. The sky was obscured, but the sun had gone down and the fire had died.

As had many others.

Both Somila and Shrey were lying near us, their quiet breathing alerting me to their presence. All I tried to focus on was the breathing of my two sleeping cubs. They were not taking the loss of their sister well, but better than I was. They were able to sleep.

I had thought witnessing death on the scale of war had been enough to numb me to its effects. But there was nothing like losing a child. Not even the death of Calouise compared to the loss of Neysa. I didn't believe there could be worse pain than losing my mate, but some evil force had sought to prove me wrong.

We hadn't lost all of the jungle, merely a wide section on the southeast side of our territory. The Sanctuary was still intact, but no one felt comfortable enough to stay there, especially since the fire had only recently been extinguished.

"Mix? You awake?"

It was Somila.

I considered ignoring her, since she couldn't see my face or my eyes, but I knew she deserved better. "Yeah. There's no sleeping for me."

I listened as she shifted her weight and crawled over to lay beside me, her claws lightly scraping along the stone's surface. I was still in too much pain to even cringe at the sound.

"What are you thinking about?" she asked.

I sighed. "What to do next."

"What do you mean?" she whispered, glancing at the sleeping young ones.

"I mean the humans just took a piece of our jungle. They can't go on without consequences. Something has to be done. The more jungle we lose to the humans, the fewer of us there will be."

"So what do you plan to do? Prowl right into their village and reason with them?"

I knew she was being sarcastic, but at this point, she wasn't far off.

"Perhaps. If I could."

"But you can't."

My secret had to remain, but I knew she would not let me leave without some kind of proper explanation. Once again, the lies had to come to save me from being found out.

"Something has to be done," I said at last.

"There's nothing we can do," she replied, almost desperately, as if she could convince me. "You've made it clear to us that antagonizing the humans only makes matters worse for us. We aren't monsters. You've always made that a priority."

"I still believe that's true. And maybe that means I have to leave for awhile."

"What?!" Her suddenly loud voice echoed off the stone and bounced back to my ears. Several of the cats below stirred, as did Calyn.

I glared at her.

"You can't leave us. You're our rani. We just lost some of our home and our family. You'd leave us alone to deal with that?"

I could tell she was on the verge of outrage.

"If that means I can save us? Yes, to all of it. I don't plan to be gone forever." Somehow, this was feeling very familiar. I seemed to have said something similar to Sara months and months ago—was it years now?

"Where would you go? What can you actually do? You're a *tiger*," she said, stressing the last word, as if I was unaware.

"I'm not sure…," I replied completely aware of the fact that my ability to be both human and tiger was incredibly useful, besides what it had already accomplished for me. "But I can't do anything sitting around here."

Somila searched my face, her yellow eyes glowing in the darkness. At last, she seemed to understand that I couldn't be stopped. "Are you going to take the little ones?"

I glanced at them, small and safe and resting. Amirah twitched slightly, her nose wrinkling, some dream causing distress. "I don't think I can leave them behind," I said quietly, turning to face her again. "Where I'm going may be dangerous, but they need their mother. And I need them. Besides, as of today, even our own jungle isn't safe anymore."

She seemed to understand, even if she didn't completely agree. "Who's going to rule while you're gone?"

I couldn't deny that she was being much more practical about this than I was, but at the same time, I knew this had to happen. I had the unique ability to make change—it was my duty to do so. No one else could speak for the tigers the way that I could. No one else had my experience. No one else could quite understand the pain we were dealt and forced to handle. If I didn't try to save the tigers, our reign was going to be much shorter than we anticipated.

"The four dignitaries and you should be able to manage keeping things running while I'm away," I replied.

"For how long?" Somila asked.

I shook my head. "Maybe a few months. Perhaps a year? If I take the little ones, we can't be gone for very long. They'll need to learn to hunt and live in the wild before they get too old."

"What kind of change do you expect to make in a year?" She sounded skeptical.

She was thinking about this way more than I was. "I don't know. I'll have to get the humans' attention somehow. Let them know we are here, we exist, and we need help."

She sighed heavily. "When do you think you'll leave?"

I stared over my sleeping community, feeling another layer of sadness settle upon me. "Probably tomorrow or the day after." It was going to be difficult to leave, but the thought of Neysa swam in my head, and I knew this had to happen. I wouldn't be able to live with myself if I didn't at least try something.

"One fire, and everything changes," she commented.

I stood up, unable to sleep, with no more desire to talk about this. "Fire changes everything." Slowly, I picked my way around the slumbering forms of the community, careful not to disturb them. Outside of the fortress, the air was full of ash. I walked westward, into the dark forest where the fire hadn't managed to touch. For a night in the jungle, it was eerily quiet.

After a while, I knew I was relatively alone, several hundred yards from the community's presence, the normal sounds of the forest only slightly returning. Somehow, I had to figure out how I and my two tiger cubs were going to get back to the United States. Air travel was an impossibility. To even think of attempting to smuggle illegal endangered species through the airport and customs was a ludicrous joke. My only other option was by boat. As I thought about it, there was a slim possibility of persuading a cargo ship captain to transport us overseas. That led to the problem of getting money. For all I knew, my bank account back home had most likely been drained and shut down from inactivity.

I remembered the small roll of cash I'd stored in the backpack I had hidden when I first arrived. The same backpack two tigers had torn apart. But they hadn't destroyed the cash. It was still out there, most likely buried by my ripped and shredded jeans. There was at least $300.

That would have to do. It was my only chance.

All that was left was breaking the news to Amirah and Calyn. They weren't going to be happy about leaving the jungle. They probably weren't going to understand. But I wasn't leaving them behind. I couldn't.

I walked back in the direction of the stone fortress, preparing myself for what was to come. This decision was a bigger deal than coming to India. It was scarier and even more dangerous than deciding to live with a band of wild cats. It was horribly ironic.

But unbelievably true.

The next morning, I took Amirah and Calyn for a walk. We steered clear of the section of the forest that had been ravaged by fire. I did not have to warn them—they would be terrified of fire for as long as they lived.

Calousie's and my meadow remained untouched by fire. We stopped there, alone and secluded and surrounded by the still dancing ash in the air. The world was so dull, the green even less vibrant than usual, blanketed in a layer of white and grey. Our footsteps were muffled, and when we hopped from the wall to the ground, a puffy cloud engulfed us momentarily, settling on our heads and in the fur on our backs.

"Momma, the jungle is sick," Amirah commented, shaking the ash from her fur.

"Yes, it is, my cubbie," I replied quietly. I took a deep breath, closing my eyes for a second, afraid to see their reactions. "And that's why we have to leave."

"What?" Calyn said, his small face twisted in anger and confusion. "We can't leave. This is our home."

"I know it is," I told him, bending low, laying down to face them at their level.

"You told us it's not safe outside the jungle," Amirah, always the obedient one, said.

"And that is true. But it's also not safe in the jungle while the jungle is sick."

"But the fire is gone," Calyn said.

"The fire was caused by humans. Humans are the cause of the sickness, my cubbies. Not all humans are bad, but there are some humans that will destroy the forest for the land, kill us tigers for our fur, kill our friends for other selfish reasons. We must always be on guard when around humans."

"Are we going to be around humans?" Amirah asked.

"Sometimes, yes," I answered truthfully. I teetered on revealing to them my dark secret. But looking into their wide, frightened eyes, I couldn't do it. Not right now, at least. Perhaps never. If I could hide what I once was from them, I would for as long as possible. "We are leaving tonight, after the darkness has come. We can hide and travel in the dark—it is the safest way. But, the most important thing for both of you to do is to listen to me. When I say to do something or not to do something, you must obey or horrible things could happen."

They were too frightened to even nod, but I knew they understood. They shrank into each other.

"You two must always stick together. There will be times when I must leave you alone. You must stay together and stay hidden when that happens, until I return and tell you it's safe. Do you understand?"

"Yes, momma," Calyn whispered while Amirah nodded.

I sighed. We only had a few hours left.

"Do we have to go? What about Somila? Can she come?" Calyn asked, daring to ask in his small voice.

My heart sank. I felt like I was tearing them away from their family. In a way, I was. Somila was their family. My family. For a moment, I considered leaving them behind, leaving them to be watched over by Somila and the other dignitaries, in a familiar place with cats who love them.

But then Amirah rubbed her head against my shoulder and Calyn nuzzled against my front paw, waiting for my answer.

"You can't stay here, without me. We are family. We stay together. You don't want to be without me, do you?"

"Of course not, momma," Amirah said, curling up against me. "We are just going to miss everyone."

"I will, too. But we'll come back. I promise."

If I never was able to keep another promise, this one I would die trying to fulfill.

We would return.

Saving All That Remains

The boat ride was not easy. Nor was it fast.

The cubs had learned a lot during our short trip across India. Our travel to the sea was done mostly at night, under the cover of darkness, out of the sight of humans and their weak eyesight. Since most of our trip was not through the forest or jungle, the two of them learned to effectively hunt smaller creatures. Amirah became an expert at hunting squirrels, and Calyn still clung to his delusion that he could hunt boar and deer on his own.

I'd made them hide in bushes just outside the trade town on the shore while I went away to transform, borrow clothing, and attempt to persuade the captain to allow me passage with two young tiger cubs. It took us a while to communicate in his broken English, and he grew very scared when he realized I meant two *actual* tiger cubs. I don't know if he was afraid of the tigers or getting caught or a combination of the two. But when I discreetly offered him $200, plus a necessary $50 tip, he reluctantly agreed to find them and myself a secluded place to ride.

It was two crates and a cot. However, I remained grateful. It was convincing the cubs that the crates were safe and they had to remain in them for a couple of weeks that was the difficult part. I also had to convince them that the human sleeping beside them was one they could trust and that momma had to sleep elsewhere in a bigger crate they stored in another part of the ship.

Every few days, I appeared to them in the night as my normal self, our noses touching through the wooden holes of their crates, our whiskers tickling each other. They complained to me about the food, the uncomfortable quarters, their inability to stretch and wrestle and hunt and play. It broke my heart to hear their whimpers and quiet cries of discomfort. I always kissed them goodnight, knowing I would see them in a few moments as the hooded human who looked after them, but they wouldn't see their mother for a day or two or three.

It was an extremely difficult trip, least of all for feeling seasick during a summer storm.

We arrived in Miami about a month later, all of us entirely ready to step back onto solid, dry land. We were lucky we arrived in the night. The men were able to smuggle the crates onto the shore under the cover of darkness, and I paid the captain another $50 for his help and graciousness.

Still a hooded human, I broke open the crates and coaxed my children out, beckoning to them with small, furless hands, petting them gently as they stretched themselves out, extending their claws, rolling out their tongues. I patted my thigh as I walked away, signaling to them to follow. I was impressed with how they still trusted me, finally free on new land. Then again, all they knew was that they were alone without their mother on foreign land, surrounded by humans with only one possible human they had been told they could trust. They really didn't have any other choice.

We hid in the shadows, the cubs practicing their stealth movements, as we headed in the direction of whatever tamed-wilderness area we could find. They had to hunt, spend time with their mother, and have time to run around before being packed away in order to be shipped off one more time.

I felt awful that this was their lives right now, but it would have been worse apart. At least we were together—at least I could keep my eyes on them and keep them safe, even if they felt alone. And I wouldn't have been able to accomplish anything without them—I would have been too distracted and worried.

The three of us eventually found a forested section, the air moist and full of the hum of bugs in the early, early morning. My two cubs had remained at my heels the whole way, their tails low, their pupils very wide and dark. I was so proud of them for being quiet and obedient, even to a relative stranger.

I crouched low, and they watched me carefully. It was hard to communicate with them when I couldn't understand anything they were trying to say to me. I placed both hands on the soft, wet earth and patted the spot twice—stay put. They both nodded to me, understanding. I ran off, dashing between scattered trees, trying to run far enough away to transform and still return to them in a timely manner.

I stripped my clothes and stuffed them in the small bag I had slung over my shoulder. I quickly tucked the bag away in a bush and released the currents, fur sprouting, limbs lengthening, my senses returning. I fell to all fours in a matter of seconds and breathed in the humid air, shaking out my fur, feeling the muscles that I missed every day. I swiftly marked the tree next to the bush that concealed my bag with my subtle 'M' shape that I'd created back when Saltir had instructed me to do so in order to meet with the spies and messengers.

With the rising sun, I sped back to where my cubs were waiting, inexplicably terrified that they wouldn't be there when I returned.

But they were. Both of them sat huddled together, staring around with curious expressions. They looked up when they heard me coming, happy smiles taking over their faces, both of them running towards me. We came together, and I hugged both of them to my chest. Despite having spent all of my time with them since we had left India, I hadn't felt like we had been together until now—now that I could hold them and talk with them and feel their love reciprocated.

"Are you two alright? Was the human girl good to you?" I asked them.

"Yes, we're fine. She was helpful, but we missed you," Amirah replied.

"Of course you did. And I, you," I said, pressing my nose to hers. "Now you two play and hunt and do whatever you need to release energy. Because just before it gets dark again, we have to catch a ride on a train."

"A train?" Calyn asked, yawning.

"A fast-moving machine that carries boxes and humans. We have to sneak onto one with lots of boxes."

"For how long do have to stay on the train?" he asked, his brows furrowing.

"A week, at most," I told him. "It's not as bad as the boat."

"Yeah, the boat was horrible," Amirah said, pouncing on some drifting leaves.

"I agree, the boat was not very much fun. But we made it."

"What are we doing here?" she asked.

"Trying to make our jungle home safer," I said. "That way we can return."

"What if we can't make it safer?" Calyn asked, pausing in his hunt of a large, red-eyed beetle.

"I promised you we would return. If I can't make it safer for us, we will still find a way home. It is our *home*, after all. We belong there."

They seemed satisfied enough to return to playing around. I was grateful they felt comfortable enough to do so. I remained on high alert, my ears shifting every few seconds to any disturbance and potential harm. I felt fairly confident no one would come marching into a forest near Miami with a loaded rifle intended for killing tigers. We were safer here than other places. But if we were found, it would be a chase. I didn't feel like attacking humans or running for my life, so we had to remain hidden.

We had managed to stay safe as dusk was falling upon us. The cubs had eaten, wrestled, chased, and hunted to their hearts content. The local birds had learned a new kind of terror, taking flight whenever Amirah or Calyn gave their little roars, never having encountered a tiger before.

Once the sun had vanished behind the hills and only its rays remained, we carefully made our way across town. Miami didn't sleep like the little villages outside our jungle. People and cabs and buses still ran wildly around the streets. We stayed close to the shadows and dark alleyways, slinking between buildings and growling at homeless beggars when they were in our path. They had no strength to stop us and no authority to report to in time—we would be long gone before anyone could believe them, let alone catch up to us.

The train station was in central Miami, halfway between the forest area we had hidden in and the ocean we had arrived from. On our way there, we were forced to cross a couple of main roads. I debated whether or not it was smarter to lead them through the streets in my human form, attempting to shield them from traffic and onlookers and authorities. But I couldn't protect them from anything as a human, with no claws, fangs, or threatening roars at my disposal. The headlights in the descending darkness blinded us, and I knew from experience that headlights at night tended to blind other drivers. As dangerous as it was, we sprinted across the street as cars were coming. I put myself between the closest car and my children, making sure I would be hit first if it came to that.

Considering we made it to the train station without being chased or caught, my plan was a success. Or at least part of it. We avoided the main station building, were lights and cameras and people blazed. I knew there would be security cameras in the main yard, too, but far fewer. At least I hoped that was true.

We stayed out of where the flood lights shined.

"Amirah, Calyn—stay here, hidden under this disconnected car. I'm gonna find us a place to ride," I whispered to them.

They bunkered down, heads low, their glowing yellow eyes following me as I walked away.

I quickly padded between the tracks, searching for a train with freight cars. In a far corner of the car yard, I spotted two young hooligans preparing to spray paint one of the cars. I saw them way before they saw me, my dominant eyesight giving me the advantage. One of them had pushed open a door on the car and he stood inside, reaching high to paint a blank space of the car near the top. The blue paint splattered against the rusty metal, the messy, quick spurts of paint somehow combining into an artful curved line. But I didn't have time to watch his process—I was on a mission to secure our passage.

They still hadn't seen me, their weak human eyes no match for mine. I growled in the darkness, baring my teeth. They looked around and simultaneously jumped. The one in the car fell out, his paint can loudly rolling away over the rocks. I snarled, taking a threatening step forward.

"Dude, that's a tiger," one of them whispered to the other, slowly backing away.

"We're in Miami. There's no tigers in Miami," the other responded, his wide eyes not leaving my face.

I took another step forward.

"Maybe it escaped the zoo."

"We have to call animal control," the first one said, pulling out a cell phone.

The other kid knocked the phone from his hand. "Not while we're *here*, you moron."

His friend nodded and cautiously bent down to pick up his phone. "We have to make a run for it," he whispered, as if my hearing was not that of a cat's.

I rumbled from deep in my throat and leapt at them. They stumbled and fell as they screamed and ran in opposite directions. I almost released a laugh. I couldn't resist the opportunity to mess with vandalistic teenagers—not when I could appear as a monster in the night.

I shook myself. I wasn't a monster. I had never planned to actually attack them.

But they didn't know that.

I couldn't allow myself to do that again.

Letting the matter go, I jumped up into the open car and looked around. It was a standard cargo boxcar, relatively empty, recently unloaded, the strong smell of hay lingering in the air. This car was still connected to the train, meaning it would have to take off not too long from now. The cars in front of the empty one still held giant fallen trees, stacks of plywood, and remaining cars full of hay and straw. This was not its final destination.

I made my way back to my still hidden cubs.

"There's a car for us over here. Follow me. Stay close," I told them. We wound our way between the tracks and stationary cars until we came upon the one I'd found earlier. I helped them up, pushing their little bodies up onto the metal floors, their small, sharp claws clicking against the metal.

"Retract your claws, you two. We have to be quiet," I whispered. Glancing around me one last time, I jumped up into the car with them.

"It smells weird in here," Calyn complained.

"It's better than the wooden crate, isn't it?" I said sternly.

He didn't reply.

We curled into the dark corner and waited. They fell asleep after an hour. I remained awake, still waiting for when the doors would slide closed and the train would lurch forward.

As they slept, I took time to consider where we would go. On the boat, I had only been consumed with getting to the United States in one piece and then finding a way to travel further without exposing ourselves. Our final stop hadn't really occurred to me except with a small part of my unconscious assuming we would return to Oregon. I knew people there. I had friends and family there, even if I had been gone for almost two years. Surely they figured me to be dead, but perhaps if I showed up on their doorsteps, they would find it in their hearts to accept me as alive and well, much against their expectations.

I didn't know how they would react if I showed up with two tiger cubs.

For the briefest moment, I considered going back to my own apartment—safe, secluded, alone. I could house the cubs with minimum suspicion. But then I remembered that I had most likely been evicted for over a year, my rent unpaid, my body missing, my death probably publicized. The only person I might be able to trust would be Sara. However, I still was unsure of how she would react. She'd obviously be upset with me for not communicating with her after all this time being alive.

The question was *how* upset she would be.

I shook my head. I'd worry about that later. I had a week-long train ride to figure out what to do and make a decision. Sara would be a last resort. Even my own mother would more than likely be more receptive to my sudden reappearance—she would understand my wish to travel with zero communication. She'd probably even accept the tiger cubs as a strange souvenir. Or she would think I was completely crazy. But thinking me crazy was better than being uncontrollably angry with me as Sara could be.

I wouldn't blame her if she was. Either of them.

But Oregon was familiar to me. I could return there and be in a place where I knew of opportunities to try and make change. If nothing else, it was a starting point.

Suddenly, I heard voices. I shielded my two cubs behind me, pressing them and myself into the dark corner as two men in dirty working clothes walked nearby. One of them quickly glanced in our cart, his eyes barely sweeping from one end to other, passing right over us before he shut the door with a loud, echoing clang of metal on metal. Amirah started awake.

"Momma, whats—"

"Shhh," I whispered. "We're about to start moving." I licked the top of her head. "We're safe, for now."

She snuggled against my flank, burying her head in my fur. Calyn was curled up against my thigh, his head resting on his small but bulky paws.

I let out a deep breath, feeling the slightest amount of tension unravel from my muscles. We would be okay for at least a little while. They wouldn't check this car for at least a couple more stops. Not until they needed to start trading cars for full ones again. We would have to switch at that time anyway to find the train heading west.

I laid my head upon my own front paws, staring into the dark, empty car, listening to the sound of the wheels beneath us as they began to roll along the tracks, squeaking and rattling before reaching a higher, more consistent speed. It felt strange to be where I was, lying with my children in a train car, having just smuggled two tiger cubs into the United States via cargo ship. Even more strange than moving to India and living in the wild jungle. Stranger still than leading tigers and leopards to war against the lions.

There was no turning back now. Not yet. I had to try, or I'd never forgive myself.

I allowed my eyes to close once the train was moving at its travel speed, the car gentling rocking me to sleep, the rattling metal almost like the sound of nocturnal birds of the jungle many miles away.

The three of us arrived in Portland five days later. It only took three trains and numerous stops, but we survived. They unhitched our car from the train while we were still in it, just before we had planned to jump out. I huddled the two of them in the corner, hoping they'd leave the car alone long enough for us to escape before they began cleaning it out and loading it up again.

After a half an hour or so, we were relatively alone, the men unhooking other cars, preparing the next train for its departure.

"Stay here. I'll be back in a few minutes. I have to find a safe way out of here," I said to them.

Amirah's yellow eyes became blacker as she looked at me. "What if they find us?"

"They shouldn't. Not if you stay here, in the shadows, and stay quiet. I won't be gone long."

I touched both of their noses with mine before I turned to the metal door and squeezed through the small opening out onto the tracks. They sky was just beginning to lighten, the sky a pale pink and blue with the rising sun. The air was warm for Portland, the end of summer apparent by the premature turn of the leaves on the trees. Green speckled with gold and red, some burgundy ones already littering the train yard. I avoided stepping on those ones, stealthily sliding underneath and between cars until I came to the edge of the train station.

I could smell the water of the nearby river and hear the cars on the streets nearby. I could even see a bridge not far away overhead, a train passing over it as I watched.

I needed clothes. I hadn't been able to grab my bag before leaving Miami, and I had to have a way to communicate with humans and get the three of us through the city without getting caught.

It was too early for any stores or shops to be open, but we were at the train station—a land of forgotten and unwanted luggage. I padded over to the dumpster behind the station building, careful to skirt out of sight of any security cameras now that it was daylight. Sure enough, two suitcases were on top. With one surreptitious glance, I leapt into the dumpster and hunched down. Both of them had coded locks. I opened my powerful jaws and wedged one of my fangs into the crack at the seam. It popped open enough for me to stick my claws in there as well and in a few short moments, the whole suitcase sprung open.

I retracted enough electricity from my paws to allow my human hands to come forth. Then I rifled quickly through the clothes, looking for something that would remotely fit. Two men's suits weren't going to make the cut, but at the bottom, I found a faded pair of straight leg jeans and an old Trail Blazers t-shirt, the red and white pinwheel dominating the front of the shirt. I pulled them both out and examined their sizes:

medium shirt and 32 inch waist jeans. I wasn't quite that large, but there happened to be a belt in the suitcase, as well.

It was going to have to do.

I reeled the rest of the currents back in and pulled the clothes on as fast as I could. The jeans were a bit long, the leg opening acting as a pair of socks rather than stopping at my ankles. I rolled them up and searched for a pair of socks. They were a bit big as well, but I didn't have time to worry about it. The shoes were uselessly too large.

I jumped out of the dumpster and quietly ran on the balls of my feet back in the direction of the train yard. My feet had not quite toughened up as much as the pads on my tiger paws had, but they were a lot less sensitive than they had been two years ago. The little rocks and bits of twig under my feet didn't hurt enough to make me stop.

To get them through the city, I was going to have to transport them as a human. I would have to transform again to inform them to trust the girl human who was about to help them. At least now I had clothes to change into when I reverted back to human. I'd have to hide them under the car before I faced my children as my normal tiger self.

I paused two tracks away from the car my cubs were in, checking to see if the coast was clear. If no one was around, I could simply transform now and hide the clothes where I was several cars away, a safer, more secluded area to deal with the transformations back and forth.

I didn't get the chance to hide my clothes or transform.

Two men were standing by the car that had my children, one of them on the phone, talking very fast, the other holding the door shut, his sweaty face full of fear as he watched the other man speak.

A few seconds later, I heard the sirens.

Two cop cars and a suburban pulled up, blue and red lights flashing. They were followed not too long after by a white van with "Oregon Department of Fish and Wildlife" stamped across the doors. I crouched behind one of the boxcars and watched as they all rushed into the train yard, the wildlife men holding nets and what looked like tranquilizers.

Blood coursed through my veins, my heart pounding loudly in my chest, thudding in my ears, my mouth extremely dry. I clutched at my shirt, watching them with fear. Feeling the faint tingles of electricity—a reminder that I could transform and jump out at them as my true and terrible self.

But a voice of reason held me back. They'd catch me. Or worse, threaten the safety of my cubs. I remained hidden, scared of what was going to happen next.

The cops took over the situation, pushing the train workers aside. The men with the nets and scary looking guns walked up, poised to attack whatever was on the other side of the metal door.

The officer pulled open the door, stepping back as he did, his own face full of fear. I saw them—both of my children, their faces terrified, their eyes so large, like glassy, black marbles shining brightly in the morning light. When the men with nets reached for them, they cried out, their little roars echoing through the yard. Their cries sent shards of ice through my heart and a wall of water immediately blurred my vision. The tears spilled before I could stop them. I wasn't used to dealing with tears. I wiped them away angrily and stood up straight. They'd already netted Amirah. She was so small, unable to fight them off.

Calyn was biting at the net and the mens' gloved hands, his claws scraping against the metal floor of the car as they dragged him out with the net over his head.

"Careful with them. They're only babies," the wildlife man with the tranquilizer called.

"Should we put them out?" the other asked, struggling to keep Calyn from escaping.

"Not yet. Not unless we have to," the other replied.

I heard Amirah's strangled cry of fear—her cry for me.

I couldn't stand idly by anymore. I rushed out from behind the car, my socked feet pounding against the pavement as I ran toward them. "STOP!" I screeched. "You must stop!"

Two of the officers ran up to me, grabbing my arms as I struggled toward my children.

"You're trespassing!" one of them shouted to me, holding my arms behind my back.

"NO! Stop! You can't take them! You can't hurt them!" I yelled, tears cascading down the sides of the face, snot starting to pour from my nostrils. I could feel it running into my mouth, but I didn't care.

"Do they belong to *you*?" the officer asked, yanking my arms further behind me, supposedly causing pain that I could not feel.

I stared at my captured children, my tiger cubs, and felt my heart shatter within me. I couldn't claim them without going to prison. If I claimed them, I'd never see them again.

"No, they're not mine," I whispered, the lie a bitter poison on my tongue. "But you can't hurt them. They're endangered as a species. You have to protect them!"

"Trust me, miss, they'll be in a safe place. They're only cubs and without a mother. The safest place for them is a reserve or a zoo," the tranquilizer man said to me patiently.

I wanted to scream at him some more, but there was nothing else I could say. Except: "Where will they go? Tigers are precious animals to me. Where will I be able to see them?"

Another wildlife man walked past me and the cops, carrying two metal cages. He set them down beside the man with the nets. The two of them managed to get my cubs into the cages, but not without a fight.

I was proud of them for not giving up.

The man with the nets walked over to me as his associates carried the cages back toward their van.

He eyed me up and down, from the old Blazers shirt and the baggy jeans to the now holey socks.

"Look, miss, these are dangerous wild animals. Tigers are not creatures to be taken lightly. They aren't native here—I'm not sure where they came from. I'm sure there'll be an investigation. Most likely, someone smuggled them in. However, we are determined to treat them humanely and find them good homes. Most likely, they'll end up at the Portland Zoo or the Winston Wildlife Safari." He paused and shared a look with the officer still holding me. "I would be more concerned with yourself, right now, than these tigers. They'll be fine."

He walked around and away from us, heading back in the direction of his van.

I looked at the officer holding me. "Well, will you let me go now, or what? I didn't do anything wrong."

"You were trespassing on this property," he replied sternly.

"I was dumpster diving for clothes. I meant no harm."

He eyed me. "We have a few questions to ask you before anything else happens."

"Then go ahead, and ask them. But I'm telling you, I had nothing to do with the tiger cubs. I just happened to be here when this happened."

"Then why didn't you just run when we were all distracted by the cubs, huh?"

"Why would I have stayed if I was the one who smuggled them in?" I asked, looking him straight in the eye. We stared at each other, stubborn face to stubborn face. A blue bird flew overhead, his tail feathers flashing in the sun.

"Why do you care about the tigers so much?" he asked, more curious than angry.

He had loosened his grip on my hands, so I pulled them free without much struggle. I turned to face him, my hands balled into fists, tears still pooling in the corners of my eyes

"Because I've loved tigers since I was child," I said. "And they're in danger of dying off. Nothing that majestic deserves to be butchered. And I'll be damned if I can't make a difference in saving all that remains of them."

He raised his brows, surprised by my answer.

"Any more questions, sir?" I asked, prepared to answer whatever he wanted from me. Anything to get free and find my Amirah and Calyn.

"No, I don't have anything more right now. But can I get a name and number to contact you if I do need more information later?"

I considered him for a moment. If Jade was dead, then I couldn't tell him my human name. "Mix," I replied. "My name is Mix. And you can find me at this number here." I used his pen to write down my mother's phone number. If I had any luck left, she'd be traveling when he called.

"You have a nice day, Mix. And stay away from private properties. This is your warning," he advised, tipping his hat to me.

Some force from above had smiled down upon me for this small, infinitesimal moment. Perhaps it was Sojóma or Calouise.

The wildlife van had already disappeared, but a news van had arrived. They were interviewing another one of the police officers. I teetered between camera bombing the officer's interview to get the world—or greater Portland area's—attention about tigers or choosing to do all in my power to find my children.

The choice was not really a decision at all. The cop and the incident that had happened here would be enough press for now. At least tigers were the topic of news.

For now, I had to get a hold of some money and a telephone.

There was a big difference between Winston and Portland, but I wasn't going to let distance stop me from getting to Amirah and Calyn. I prayed that whatever odds I had left, they would all be in the favor of the Portland Zoo. It was only about four miles from where I was at. I'd call the Department of Fish and Wildlife every hour if I had to in order to find out where the cubs—my children—had been taken.

I'd never give up.

With nothing else to do, I spent a few days making spare phone-change by allowing the electricity to transform my hearing just enough to play guessing games with passer-bys of what was coming around the blind corner. They never stood a chance against me. I was a determined mother who was not afraid to use every trick up my sleeve to get back to my children. After a few days of repeatedly calling the Oregon Department of Fish and Wildlife, they finally revealed to me that the tiger cubs were being held in quarantine. According to the people at ODFW, it was policy to observe and isolate them for a few weeks until they were sure the cubs had no problems or diseases that would negatively impact other animals should they be transferred to a zoo or safari.

This was disheartening news. Panhandling on the streets of Portland for a few days had not been that difficult after living in the jungle. But hunting in the city was not quite the same as hunting in the wild, and my lack of fur and night vision was a great detriment in the night time of the human world. I was ill-equipped to live on the streets for several weeks without being a tiger. My options were slim, but I felt one of my only choices was to visit my mother's home.

I set out for her building around late evening, when the sun was beginning to sink and the clouds had begun to glow red. She lived in an expensive studio apartment in the pearl district on the northwest side of town. I had never understood why she spent so much money on a home she hardly ever stayed in, but when she had no husband or children to support, she really had nothing else to do with her money when her life was her work.

My life had become my family--both my friends and community back home and my stolen and frightened children--and they needed me desperately. But I could not return home without my cubs, which meant I would have to swallow my pride and accept my predicament.

The pearl district was only a ten minute walk from my current street corner location. I navigated the streets as fast as I could in my socked feet and found myself in the dimly lit hallway just outside her door. I had no idea if she was actually home, and I was terrified of her reaction should she open the door to her nowhere-to-be-found daughter.

I was already at the doorstep--what was a confrontation with my mother compared to defeating Zoriach?

With a deep breath, I raised my closed fist and rapped on her door.

Twice.

Three times.

No reply or hurried footsteps. Nothing but silence.

Years ago, when I had visited more often, my mother had kept her hidden key under the loosely nailed doorsill. She had put it there when I was in high school so I could always get in, even when she was absent on one of her journalism trips. As far as I knew, I was the only other person who knew about it.

I pulled it from its rusty spot and inserted it into the lock. It clicked as I turned it, and the door opened up into my mother's dark, lonely, and empty living space. I flipped on the light and shut the door with a slight echo. Her house was spotlessly clean with the exception of some skewed papers on her dining table. I walked over to them and stared down only to be met with my own reflection. Or what appeared to be my reflection.

I snatched at it to find myself staring at a rather outdated picture of me. I scanned the rest of the newspaper page to discover that I was under the obituary section. I attempted to read the column, but it was too painful. I could already see the water smears--evidence of the emotional turmoil my mother must be going through. It was a strange out of body experience to think of yourself dead to the world. That everyone thought me deceased even though I was standing right there. Quite alive.

But dead inside.

I threw the paper back onto the table. I had bigger problems to worry about. My human friends and family would be alright. They'd grieve. They'd learn to accept the loss, much like I had. Something would give them strength again. I had come to understand this better than anyone.

I flopped onto her couch with the lights still on and attempted to find reprieve from my fears in sleep, but with little success. My eyes swam from the blazing lights overhead. There was no way I could sleep with the lights brightly aglow. With a grunt, I got up and slammed my hand down on the switch and sank back into the couch cushions as if I was comfortably curled up in my favorite waterfall spot back home.

A few weeks later, still wearing the Blazer t-shirt and baggy jeans, I stood in line at the Portland Zoo admission counter, staring down at the worn tennis shoes I'd pulled from some box buried in the back of my mother's closet. I'd continued to call the department of wildlife every other day for the last two weeks until someone had grown tired of me and agreed to tell me that the cubs were finally being released to the Portland zoo after being cleared from quarantine. It had been a moment of pure hope. I had been so terrified that they would be shipped hours or even days away. But they were in my hometown.

And now I was so close.

I paid for my ticket and hurried forward, grabbing a map as I went.. Another line of admissions employees waited just down the zoo lane, ready to check my ticket and stamp my hand. A shiny green elephant blazed on the back of my hand as I quickly rushed through the crowd, studying the map carefully, searching for the tiger exhibit.

It was on the west side of the zoo, near the leopards and lorikeets. I shoved my way between people and children, resisting the fear and trying to hide the uncontrollable shaking that was racking my entire body. I knew they were there—I was just entirely terrified of what I would see. How would they look? Would they be okay? Unharmed? Or, Godforbid, happy?

People were crowded around the tiger enclosure, camera phones pointed, flashes disappearing in the daylight. I pushed my way between everyone, fighting for a front row spot.

As I wedged myself between a burly man and a toothpick woman, I saw them. Amirah and Calyn huddled together beside a tiny tree, their wide eyes staring at the hoard of humans in confusion and fear. It was only their second day at the zoo, as I had been informed.

The tears returned as I stared at them, feeling a helplessness and hopelessness that weighed heavily in every fiber of every muscle. I sank to my knees, my fingers scraping down the sides of the glass. I was surrounded by smiles and laughs and coos and awes from the crowd. None of them understood my pain—their children were relatively safe beside them. But mine were alone and lost, far away from their home.

They were distressed and afraid without their mother—I could see it in their little, whiskered faces. And it was heartbreaking that I could not get to them.

How would I get them out?

That was the real question. I loved them too much to leave them locked up in a zoo any longer than necessary. I now understood everything Shrey had been talking about when it came to zoos. They were display cases for humans—cages for the sake of humans' pleasure. They would have been much better off in a reserve or safari. At least they would have had the illusion of freedom. However, perhaps placing them in a zoo was good for me. They would hate it so much, all they'd want would be to leave, to be rescued by their mother. And whatever I figured out, they would be rescued, we would escape together, and we would return home. I would not go back on my word.

I would save them. I'd save my cubs and take us home, back to the jungle of India, back where we belonged. We would be a family again— I'd promised that.

I balled my hands into fists and pressed my nose to the glass. I was the only one watching the two baby tiger cubs filled with great determination and a deep sadness. Not only because they were trapped.

But because they were my children.

And they didn't even know I was there.

I would attempt whatever it took to break them out, even if it meant transforming right where I was.

I glared through the glass, trapped by all the sweaty bodies pressing in from every angle. The electricity was sparking, tingling tendrils reaching out from my burning heart.

I closed my eyes, trying to hold them back, battling every impulse and thought that wanted to let the currents loose.

I sucked in a deep breath, preparing for whatever came next, knowing that somehow, whatever happened, it would result in saving all that remained of my family.

Acknowledgements

There are so many people who have been instrumental to the development, creation, and production of this book:

Dr. Katherine Schmidt, my advisor, content editor, teacher, and good friend without whom my book would be a great travesty.

Dr. Gavin Keulks, a great sponsor to my writing and education, without which I would not have produced such a project.

Daniel Thom, my very enthusiastic content editor who was greatly skilled in catching plot holes and influential to the revision process.

Emily Walley, my accomplished copy editor who caught more than I ever dreamed possible, allowing for a more smooth, polished, and perfected text.

Amanda Clarke, for her love of my story and characters and her divine inspirational suggestions and encouragement in the deepest moments of writer's block.

The Western Oregon Writing Center crew, my dear coworkers and friends who have been essential to my development as a writer and person.

Every teacher and close friend that has encouraged me throughout my growing journey as a writer—they are a part of who I am today.

My parents and siblings, the source of my success and determination in this world.

And always my fans, who bring the characters and stories to life in a way I could never manage.

Last but not least, my two beautiful cats—Ember and Ashes—whose many wiles and fancies were moments of inspiration and love that helped fuel my creative fires.